Thane: Idlebury Series Book 2

Magic
&
Mayhem

JM Hughson

Idlebury Books

Thane: Idlebury Series Book 2
Magic & Mayhem
Copyright © 2018 JM Hughson
ISBN 13: 978-0-9991338-3-5 (Paperback)

This is a work of fiction. Names, characters, places, and incidents either are the product of the author's imagination or are used fictitiously, and any resemblance to any actual persons, living or dead, events, or locales is entirely coincidental.

Cover Art: SelfPubBookCovers.com/RLSather
Editing/Proofreading/Oops Detection/Formatting: The staff of Victoryediting.com
Printed in the United States of America

For Cody, my doggedly loyal friend.

Contents

Introduction

"He is dead. He is dead. My precious baby boy is dead," Queen Filanthropi screamed as she held her aching head.

She'd been dizzy and in a tizzy all morning. But this behavior was not new. It had started nearly five years earlier, following the almost simultaneous return of her three children—two of whom she'd believed to have died at birth. Her eldest daughter, Gwendolyn, who had been placed for adoption at birth with loving parents in Dimension X on planet Earth, had returned to Idlebury and claimed the title of Gwendolyn the Great, Savior of Idlebury, Protector of the Universe. Thane, who was thought to have been stillborn but in fact lived, had been stolen and raised for the first five years of his life by the queen's servant, Morgana. And Prudence, also thought to have been stillborn, had been stolen by another servant until the woman nearly went mad from the stress of hiding her devious deed. To save her sanity and soul, she'd returned the infant to Queen Filanthropi and King Heroian.

Since then, Queen Filanthropi had suffered periods of nervousness that at times were so physically and emotionally overwhelming she thought she would die.

The queen consulted several doctors regarding her

debilitating situation, but none provided a reassuring diagnosis. One told her she suffered from a classic case of hysteria, gave her a slew of pills to calm her down, and insisted she get a grip and snap out of it. Another declared she had Sudden Mother Syndrome due to the return of her three children after years of childlessness. Yet another told her she suffered from a severe case of worthlessness after she and King Heroian granted the Idleburians their freedom and declared Idlebury no longer idle. One doctor had had the audacity to claim there was absolutely nothing wrong with her. But one doctor knew the truth; Queen Filanthropi was desperately in love.

It was not your everyday, run-of-the-mill kind of infatuated love that makes schoolgirls swoon. Nor was it the kind of love experienced by those who've found their soul mate. Nor was it the kind of love one has for a parent or a dear friend. No, this wasn't like that at all. This love was the deepest anyone could imagine because it was the love of a mother for her children. And as every mother knows, with love comes worry.

Queen Filanthropi worried about her eldest child, Gwendolyn, because as Gwendolyn the Great, Savior of Idlebury, Protector of the Universe, the child faced unimaginable challenges and life-threatening situations from which no one, not even the Great Wizard, could protect her. And she worried about her youngest child, Prudence, because although she was still an innocent five-year-old, at times her thoughts and behaviors appeared sinister, leaving her parents to fear she would grow up to be evil. Then there was her middle child and only son, Thane, who with curly black hair, piercing blue eyes, and skin the color of creamy caramel was believed to be the most beautiful child in the universe. He was now ten years old and quite a handful. In fact, he was nearly as bad as he was beautiful. But if truth be told, Queen Filanthropi only pretended to be strict regarding her son's behavior because deep down inside she was a softie and loved Thane unconditionally. Even more, she viewed him as mischievous, inventive, and adventurous—not bad.

But lately Thane's behavior gave his mother great cause for concern because he was becoming more careless and courageous with each day. And as everyone knows, carelessness and courageousness is a dangerous and possibly deadly combination. Worse, he had learned about his special powers and appeared unable to refrain from using them. But the millennia-old treaty among Hexidonia in Dimension II and the many other kingdoms of the universe's thirteen dimensions that clearly stated only Hexidonians could use magic worried Queen Filanthropi the most. And if magic was used anywhere in the universe by anyone of any age for any reason, the offender, no matter how young, could be tortured or killed by a wand from the queen of Hexidonia's infamous Wicked Wand Collection.

But despite that law, King Abracadabra and Queen Opunzayzme of Hexidonia turned a blind eye to several well-known non-Hexidonians who not only used magic but also misused magic, including Wilameena, the universally disliked enchantress.

So when Queen Filanthropi woke up screaming that her baby boy was dead, her mind went to the possible horrors that might have befallen Thane. Her heart raced and her breathing became labored.

To calm her nerves, she relaxed into the comfort of her fluffy pillows, which were perfectly positioned on her luxurious bed in her otherwise sparse bedchamber. As her nerves settled and her thoughts slowed, she wondered if her anxiety was nothing more than the overactive imagination for which she was well known.

Hoping to escape into her dreams, Queen Filanthropi closed her eyes and muttered, "Yes, my Thane has the gift to make magic… and mayhem."

CHAPTER ONE
THANE'S DASTARDLY DEED

Prince Thane, with his elbows resting on the windowsill and his face cupped by his hands, peered out the large window of his dreary quarters. The morning sun shrouded him, providing warmth and giving him an angelic look—a look he didn't deserve, particularly after the previous night's escapade and the evil, envious thoughts he harbored about his sister Gwendolyn the Great, Savior of Idlebury, Protector of the Universe.

Next to him, nervously slinking back and forth on the windowsill and mumbling to himself was a curious-looking worm wearing large red-framed eyeglasses. With his tiny hand he waved a solid-gold magic wand that was no larger than a sewing needle. "What goes on in that hard head of yours? If you're punished for your late-night adventure, you could suffer calamitous consequences."

With each word the worm uttered, he smacked Thane with his wand. "Ridiculous."—smack—"Outlandish."—smack— "Moronic."—smack—"Ludicrous."—smack—"Absurd."— smack—"Preposterous."—smack—"Silly."—smack—"Dim- witted."—smack—"Outrageous."—smack— "Unbelievable."—smack—"Stupid." Smack, smack, smack.

But Thane didn't hear the worm or feel the whacks of the tiny creature's wand, for he was lost in exhilarating memories of the clever yet dangerous stunt he'd pulled off the night before in Chocolatonia and Deadonia. He smiled as he thought about how he'd one-upped his big sister, Gwen. He envisioned people everywhere enjoying breakfast while reading the morning paper's version of his antics. He laughed to himself when he pictured Gwen nearly blowing her top after she found out what he'd done, because his adventure was more exciting than anything she'd done lately. But Thane was especially thrilled at the thought that every creature throughout the universe would now know he was better and smarter than his universally admired sister.

Yes, Thane was proud of himself for pulling off his stunt, but he couldn't take credit for the idea because he'd discovered the instructions, complete with a complex magic spell, in a book penned by an obscure wizard. But where he'd found the book was most mysterious. It had been hidden in a metal box under a floorboard in his mother's bedchamber. He hadn't gone looking for it; he couldn't because he hadn't known it existed. Finding the book was a total accident; a lucky accident, so he thought.

This is how it happened.

One day when Thane was playing hide-and-seek with his little sister, Prudence, he hid in his mother's bedchamber. As he ran into the room, looking for the perfect hiding place, he stumbled on the edge of a raised floorboard and tumbled to the floor. When he gathered his bearings, he noticed a light glowing under the board. And as any ten-year-old boy worth his salt would do, he immediately investigated. When he raised the board, the light got brighter. He noticed the light emanated from inside a small battered metal box.

Without hesitation, he picked it up and examined it. "Wow. I bet there's something amazing in this box." As he carefully raised the lid, he noticed light seeped from beneath the cover of one of the largest books he'd ever seen. *How does something so big fit in such a small box?* he wondered. Carefully he picked up the glowing book. Light oozed from the edges of the heavy leather cover, revealing raised gold lettering and an intricate pyrographic image of a horse. Thane whispered the title of the book. "*A Magic Maniac's Many Ways to Make Mischief* by Feefifofum Fiddledeedee Fiddledeedum."

He ran his hand over the cover. Eyes wide with wonder and hands shaking from excitement, he cautiously opened the book. A brilliant light nearly blinded him. As his eyes adjusted, he discovered the light shone from the wand of an odd little creature that appeared to be engaged in a mysterious dance but in fact was practicing magic spells. Startled by Thane's huge eyes peering at him, the creature stopped. For a moment the two beings, one a worm and the other a boy, shared a silent stare. Spooked yet intrigued by what he saw, Thane slammed the book shut and then put the empty box back in its hiding place. With the book securely tucked under his left arm, he whipped off his right shoe and used it to hammer the board back in place. With his shoe in one hand and the book in the other, he ran to his room to explore his wondrous find, completely forgetting about Prudence and their game of hide-and-seek.

Safely back in his quarters, Thane jumped on his bed, placed the book in the gap between his crossed legs, took a deep breath, and then opened it. Bright light obscured his vision. He couldn't see anything, particularly not anything that looked like a worm brandishing a wand, leading him to wonder if his mind had played tricks on him. Slowly the light dimmed, and sure enough, he had seen a worm with a wand, for there it was staring back at him.

"Are you Feefifofum Fiddledeedee Fiddledeedum?" Thane asked.

"No. Are you?" the worm asked.

"No."

"Good. And don't say that name again," the worm said. "It could be dangerous."

"Why?"

"Can't tell you. Don't know you. Don't trust you."

Thane furrowed his brow and stared at the worm. "Oh" was all he said.

Despite the trite beginning to the conversation, Thane and the worm, who went by the name Blabberdish, spent hours talking about the details of the most fascinating book the boy had ever read. Thane was thrilled when, after much begging and bribing, the worm agreed to teach him every trick in the book, so to speak.

Just before dinner, with the castle veiled in darkness, Thane sneaked back to his mother's bedchamber, pulled up the board, and put the book and his new friend to rest in the protective metal box. He stomped the board into place, then he skipped with delight all the way to the dining room table where he was greeted by a raised eyebrow from his mother and a growl from his angry little sister. But he didn't care; nothing could spoil his mood.

As Thane and Blabberdish's friendship grew, Prudence became a huge nuisance. She followed her brother everywhere, pestering him about why he always locked himself in his room and refused to play with her. Once, when she banged on her brother's bedroom door for the umpteenth time and cried for him to come out and play, Thane used a newly learned spell and turned her into a bug in hopes someone would step on her or give her a good swat. No one did. And after several hours, she turned back into herself.

Needless to say, Thane worried nosy Prudence would find out about Blabberdish and the magic book. So he came up with the brilliant idea of disguising himself with a fake mustache and a wide-brimmed hat and scoping out the hallway like a spy before entering or exiting his mother's bedchamber. Oddly, Thane didn't care about his mother catching him. After all, he believed he was way too clever to get caught by her or any other adult for that matter. And on the off-chance he did get caught, he knew he could use his special talent—the ability to talk his way out of any situation. Yes, Thane believed he was smarter and cleverer than anyone, especially his parents.

He was in for a surprise.

Chapter Two
A Mother's Denial

Queen Filanthropi was engaged in her favorite escape-from-the-real-world activity—sleeping. She loved to sleep, not because she was lazy but because she loved to dream. Her dreams were vivid, fanciful, entertaining, imaginative, freeing, revealing, and enjoyable—everything her life wasn't. So on this morning, she put her worries to bed and enjoyed extra time in dreamland. She imagined her children as healthy, happy, popular, clever, smart, and successful—everything she wasn't when she was a child.

But her dreams came to an abrupt end when a rat-a-tat-tat on her chamber door startled her awake. In an instant her mind returned to worries of her children.

Queen Filanthropi shot up in bed and clutched her blanket to her chest. "What do you want? What's happened to my children?"

"'Tis me, Yer Majesty," Morgana, the queen's favorite servant, replied, speaking through an opening between the door and its frame. "I have yer breakfast and today's *Universal Scandals* magazine."

"Oh, Morgana, I'm happy to hear a friendly voice." The

queen released her hold on her blanket, propped herself against her bed's headboard, and folded her still-shaking hands to steady them. "Please do come in."

Morgana opened the door, carefully balancing a tray that held the queen's breakfast, trying not to drop the early edition of the *Universal Scandals* magazine she'd tucked under her arm. One look at the queen startled the servant. "Yer Majesty, I must say ya look as if ya seen a ghost."

"No. No ghosts. Just the worries of a mother."

Morgana looked down. "No worries 'bout Thane, I hope, ma'am," she said as she placed the tray and magazine on a table next to the queen's bed.

"I am afraid I worry about all my children equally." The queen shared a concerned look with her servant. "I am sure you understand as I know you still care about Thane."

"Yes, ma'am. I worry 'bout him too." Morgana smiled and took a deep, relaxing breath. "But not taday. I checked on him meself just a few minutes ago, and he's sleepin' like a baby, he is."

The *Universal Scandals* magazine jumped off the table, flew over to Morgana, rolled up, and whacked itself against the back of her head. "Of course he's sleeping like a baby. He's exhausted after his long night swooping across the universe and wreaking havoc in Chocolatonia and Deadonia."

"He *what*?" the queen screeched as she grabbed for possession of the magazine but missed.

The *Universal Scandals* magazine shook open and revealed its cover story to the queen. The headline read SPECIAL REPORT: LITTLE PRINCE THANE IN BIG TROUBLE. To the queen's horror, there was a live-action picture of Thane sprinkling fairy dust over King Morrebidd and Queen DeMysora of Deadonia as they lay in their bed.

The queen fought back tears at the thought that Thane had misused his powers and gotten himself into irreparable trouble. But part of her wasn't surprised, because as Thane had grown in height, so had his insatiable curiosity and intolerable impudence. It was the latter that worried her most.

"No, it cannot be. Is that fairy dust?" the queen whispered.

The image of the fairy dust raised her hopes as she remembered prophecies about a child who had magical powers and who one day would unite the dimensions and ignite universal peace and prosperity. As foretold, fairy dust was the sign of the child destined for this glory.

"Of course it's fairy dust. Chocolate fairy dust to be exact," the *Universal Scandals* magazine replied as it jumped in front of the queen and flipped open its pages.

A hologram of a reporter appeared before the queen and Morgana. The reporter spewed the story of Thane's late-night adventure, complete with footage of the child soaring through the dimensions. Queen Filanthropi and Morgana grew paler with every word and image.

"Several trillion reliable sources throughout the universe have confirmed that last night Prince Thane, the ten-year-old son of King Heroian and Queen Filanthropi of Idlebury in Dimension XIII, was observed traversing through the dimensions unescorted and apparently on a mission to cause unimaginable mayhem. Although some reported they had no idea what the young prince was up to, reports flooded in to this publication that the child had inflicted magic curses and charms on commoners and royalty alike. It is believed the prince misused magic powers for which he could be severely punished and quite possibly killed.

"King Kokoa of Chocolatonia has confirmed the young prince made a late-night trip to his kingdom in Dimension VI and raided his

personal supply of coveted sweets. Evidently Prince Thane achieved this feat by disguising himself as a cocoa bean and hitching a ride on the Interdimensional Cargo Train. Further, King Kokoa declared, 'Prince Thane of Idlebury is without a doubt the doer of the most dastardly deed to occur in my kingdom since the great bonbon heist nearly a thousand years ago.'

"King Morrebidd and Queen DeMysora of Deadonia in Dimension IX have also confirmed reports that on his way back to Idlebury from his nighttime adventure, Prince Thane stopped in the kingdom of the dead, woke the king and queen, and had the nerve to tell them they might be more cheerful if they had a bit of chocolate. The child then sprinkled the royal couple with chocolate fairy dust and disappeared.

"Many sources were queried as to how a child so young could travel freely among the dimensions. Several thousand sources reported Prince Thane was heard reciting a forbidden ancient nonsensical chant known to few yet feared by many, which allowed him easy entrance into all the dimensions. It is believed the phrase the child chanted was 'Last night at ten o'clock this morning, an empty wagon full of people ran over a dead horse and killed it.'

"Hexidonia's Council of Horrendous Behaviors and Horrible Deeds has been notified as to the prince's possible misbehavior. The council is expected to question the child sometime today regarding the serious accusations. It is not clear as to whether or not the king and queen of Idlebury are aware of their son's reprehensible nighttime adventures, but King Abracadabra of Hexidonia in Dimension II has vowed to get personally involved in hopes of avoiding a universal scandal and possible punishment of a child so young. Needless to say, the prince is in deep, deep doo-doo."

The images dissipated as the *Universal Scandals* magazine rolled itself into a tube that transformed into an arrow. It pointed itself at Queen Filanthropi and said, "So there."

Queen Filanthropi sprang out of bed, knocking over her breakfast tray. Food and drink crashed to the floor. As Morgana hurried to clean up the mess, the queen yelled, "Get out. Both of you… get out now!"

Morgana grabbed the *Universal Scandals* magazine and charged out of the queen's bedchamber.

Queen Filanthropi cried softly as she paced. The thought of magic powers in the hands of one so young sickened her. And for good reason, for when she was the princess of Seedonia and not much older than Thane, she'd also discovered her powers. Mostly she used them to conjure candy, change school grades, or clean up her dress when she had disobeyed her parents and played outside in her good clothes. But one time when she was nearly past the age of innocence, she did something unspeakable that almost cost her father his kingdom and her, her life.

Thoughts of the possible horrors that might have befallen her only son caused adrenaline to race through her veins, giving her energy to barge out of her chambers, race down the cavernous hall, and stop short in front of Thane's door. She wheezed as she tried to catch her breath and recapture her composure. The matter needed to be addressed immediately, but she didn't want to be accusatory until she heard Thane's side of the story.

"Surely he has a good explanation," she mumbled. "Just because the story was in *Universal Scandals* magazine does not make it true. There has to be another child who has powers. Yes, that is it. It was *not* my Thane, it was another boy—a very bad, depraved boy who deserves to be whacked with a wicked wand."

But she only deluded herself in an attempt to deny what she knew in her heart to be true—Thane was the bad boy, and he was in serious danger.

Queen Filanthropi took a deep breath and reached for the doorknob. As she exhaled, someone standing next to her startled her.

"Oof," the queen said, clearly annoyed at being interrupted. "May I help you?"

"Your Majesty," the queen's master head servant said as he bowed his head in respect. "I hope I am not being presumptuous, but I must tell you to go lightly on the boy. He is still innocent. To scare him with punishment or death will only make matters worse."

"Thank you, Oof. Your concern is duly noted. Nonetheless, I must address the matter with my son immediately. I wish King Heroian were here to talk to Prince Thane, but the king is attending to business in another kingdom. It seems he is always away when he is needed most."

Oof nodded in agreement and disappeared.

Queen Filanthropi was about to barge into Thane's room when the unmistakable thunder of the king's horses and carriages approaching Idlebury Castle stopped her. With renewed hope, she ran toward the stairs to greet the king, relieved her husband had not failed her, not this time.

CHAPTER THREE
KING HEROIAN'S
UNFORTUNATE FAILURES

Thane continued to stare out his bedroom window, and Blabberdish continued to admonish him for his bad deeds. But the sound of footsteps that stopped at Thane's bedroom door jolted them back to reality. Thane and Blabberdish jumped into Thane's bed and took shelter under the blanket.

The clippety-clop of horses' hooves on the castle's drawbridge alerted Thane to the arrival of the king and his entourage and caused the person at his door to hurry away and rush down the stairs.

Thane listened intently. *"Oh no.* Father's home."

"You're dead meat," Blabberdish whispered back. "And you deserve it."

Thane gulped.

<hr />

King Heroian raced on horseback across Idlebury Castle's drawbridge, leaving his entourage and carriages in the dust. With rage-fueled energy, the king rode his horse hard and fast. As the duo approached the castle, the king screamed, *"Open the doors. Open the doors now!"*

Fortunately, the doorman heard the king's desperate request in time. At full speed, the king and his horse charged through the open castle doors. The servants and chambermaids dashed for cover. But Oof appeared unfazed as he stood in a corner, nonchalantly talking to Syvil Gossep, *Universal Scandals* magazine's famed reporter and Idlebury's official correspondent.

The king ignored his staff as he dismounted and stormed up the long winding staircase. His sword banged against the rails, creating a racket. At the top of the stairs, still dressed in her nightgown, Queen Filanthropi stood in anxious anticipation of her husband's arrival. As King Heroian neared, she reached out for him, but with complete disregard for his queen, he pushed past her and then rushed down the dark narrow hall.

King Heroian's anger, which was out of character for the normally gentle man, unnerved Queen Filanthropi. With concern for her son, she followed her husband. When the king reached the door of Prince Thane's quarters, he took a deep breath and glanced at what he clutched in his hand. Queen Filanthropi immediately recognized a copy of *Universal Scandals* magazine. She waited for the king to comment. Instead, he barged into Thane's room.

"Where is the book?" the king said through clenched teeth as he shook the sleeping child.

Thane faced his father, opened his eyes, and yawned. "What book?"

"Do not play games with me, young man. There is only one way you could have done what you did last night," the king said as he shook the *Universal Scandals* magazine at his son. "You used magic. Magic, I say."

Thane propped himself up on his elbows and looked his

father square in the eye. "What book, Father?"

King Heroian glared at Thane. "I will not tolerate your insolence." Without further comment, he stormed out of the child's quarters.

Lost in rage, the king knocked into Queen Filanthropi, who had been waiting patiently outside the door. Without an apology, he rushed down the corridor toward his chambers. "Stay with Thane, Filanthropi. Do not let him out of your sight."

Queen Filanthropi scowled and shook her head. "What has gotten into him?" she said as she entered the prince's room to address her son's nightly activities.

When King Heroian reached the door of the queen's bedchamber, he checked the corridor to make sure he was alone. Not a soul was in sight, so he entered the queen's room. Once inside, he leaned against the door and took a deep breath. "I pray *A Magic Maniac's Many Ways to Make Mischief* is where I hid it when I was a teen." He scanned the floor. The floorboard under which he'd place the book was easy to pick out.

King Heroian lifted the board. The battered metal box he'd stolen from a servant in order to conceal his prized book was still there. He knelt on the floor and grabbed the box. He ran his hand over the top, momentarily mentally and emotionally transported back in time to when, as the prince of Idlebury, the room had been his. He carefully opened the box. Much to his relief, the book was safe and sound. He gently lifted it and stroked its cover.

"Oh how I have missed you. Oh how I have needed you," King Heroian whispered. He started to lift the cover but stopped. "No. I cannot. I will not be tempted by magic."

After he quickly returned the book to the box and put it back in its hiding place, he gently pounded the floorboard back in place. Before he closed the door to Queen Filanthropi's bedchamber, he glanced back. "How Filanthropi or a servant has not found the book under that obviously worn floorboard is beyond me," he mumbled. "It's a magnet for a curious ten-year-old boy. I must hide it elsewhere before Thane finds it."

King Heroian entered his son's room, joined the queen, and in a commanding voice said, "He is innocent. He has done nothing wrong."

"But what about the pictures?" the queen said. "They prove he did that of which he is accused. He used magic."

"Trickery. Mere trickery. The prince has done nothing wrong. I cannot waste any more time. I must get on with my royal duties." King Heroian quickly left the room.

Queen Filanthropi brushed Thane's hair off his forehead and gently kissed him. "Do not use your special powers, my son. You are treading into mysterious territory. It could spell disaster for you."

Thane rolled over and smirked. "Yes, Mother."

Queen Filanthropi tucked a blanket around her son and gently kissed him on the back of his head. As she left the room, she closed the door quietly so as not to disturb her sleeping child. The old metal latch clicked loudly into place, informing Thane the coast was clear.

Thane bolted up in bed. "Whoa! Close call."

"You can say that again." Blabberdish snickered. "But in all seriousness, I've got to get back in the book where I belong. If my parents find out I'm gone, I'll be punished."

"But you can't go. We need to plan our next adventure."

"Fat chance. I've got to go."

"Wait. How does my father know about the book?" Thane asked.

"Well…" Blabberdish hesitated. "He knows… he knows because… he knows because he… he… he's read it. Yes! Besides, everyone knows about it."

"So my father's read it too?" Thane's eyes widened with awe. "Is he a wizard?"

"Yes, he's read it. No, he's not a wizard."

"What about my mother? Does she know the book is hidden in her room?"

"Umm… not really."

"How could she not know? You can't miss it."

"Obviously your mother's observation skills are lacking." Blabberdish scratched his head. "All I know is many creatures, including my family and me, have lived in the book for generations, and your father is the only person who's ever opened it… with the exception of that skinny man—" Blabberdish's eyes bugged out.

"So my father has powers too?" Thane asked, not picking up on the bookworm's sudden silence.

"No, he doesn't have the talent for magic. He tried many magic tricks from dozens of other books, but he failed miserably. In fact, he was the only boy in his school who couldn't perform magic. So he decided to—" Blabberdish cleared his throat as if to stall for time, then he continued. "The book was different from anything your father had ever seen. Different spells, charms, curses, and hexes. He knew they could work, but they didn't work for him. Your father became frightfully frustrated and finally forfeited to his failures. He's known to those who live in the book as 'the royal with the wimpy wand.'"

"So why do the spells work for me?"

"Because you have the gift of magic, that's why."

"My mother has powers. I know she does. Where did she learn them?"

"She didn't learn her powers. They were a gift; a gift she misused, and it got her into serious trouble."

"What kind of trouble?"

"Another time. I don't want to give you any ideas. And right now I need to get back home… back to the book."

"I'll go with you."

"No. Stay here. I can slip under the floorboard and back into the book, and no one will know. Besides, if your father comes back and you're not here, you'll be in a heap of trouble."

Thane furrowed his brow. "But what about our next adventure?"

"Can't make any promises right now. Let me make sure everything is okay in my world, and then I'll be back in yours soon. Ta."

Thane watched Blabberdish make his way to the door. "Wait. Why did my father hide the book? Why didn't he share it?"

Blabberdish nervously cleared his throat again. "Don't know. I guess he wanted the power of the book all to himself." He quickly squeezed under the door, continued down the hall, shimmied under the door to Queen Filanthropi's bedchamber, pushed himself under the floorboard, and slithered back into the metal box and into the book.

Meanwhile, Thane lay on his bed and thought about what Blabberdish had said. "It doesn't make sense. Why would Father want to keep the book a secret when he knows everyone in the entire universe already knows about it? And why hasn't anyone stolen it?"

Chapter Four
Family Secrets Revealed

With Blabberdish safely home in the book, Thane decided to practice a little magic on his own. He didn't tell his bookworm friend, but he had skipped way ahead in *A Magic Maniac's Many Ways to Make Mischief*. As he waved a wand he'd found in a secret drawer in his mother's dressing table, which he carefully returned each night, he couldn't help but feel proud of his ability to succeed where his father, the king, had failed.

"I can't believe I'm better than my father," Thane said as he twirled across the room, wand raised high. "Wait until Gwendolyn the Great finds out how great I am. I'm going to rule the world. I'll make sure of it."

As Thane continued to whirl around the room, waving his wand, he noticed fairy dust swirled around him. He remembered when a tornado of fairy dust lifted him to the hut where Wilameena, the enchantress, had morphed into his father, King Heroian of Idlebury, in an attempt to convince a roomful of Idleburians to protest against his mother, Queen Filanthropi, and stop Gwen's investiture as princess of Idlebury.

Thane plopped on his bed. "Hmm. I wonder if fairy dust can

still take me anywhere I want." He jumped up and shouted, "Why not?"

In the center of the room, his head lowered so his chin touched his chest, he said, "I want to go to my sister."

Thane glowed as if he were a human lamp. Fairy dust engulfed him. Seconds later, he appeared in Prudence's room.

Prudence, who played quietly with her dolls, looked up at her big brother and smiled. "Goody. You want to play?"

How revolting? Thane thought. *I'd wear a tutu and dance in front of my friends before I'd play with your stupid dolls.* In as nice a manner as he could muster so as not to hurt Prudence's feelings and incite one of her tantrums, he said, "Sorry, but I can't. I have something important to do. I'm sure you understand."

But of course she didn't. So she begged Thane to play with her. When her begging turned to desperate screaming, he did the only thing he could—he ignored her and left. Prudence's cries echoed throughout the cavernous hall as Thane made his way back to the tranquility of his room. He arrived at his quarters none too soon and slammed the door behind him.

"I've got to be more specific with my requests," he muttered, for he hadn't wanted to go to Prudence's room. He wanted to go to his big sister, Gwen, in Idleburg, Pennsylvania, Dimension X, planet Earth, where she lived with her adoptive parents Arston and Evaline Fanny when she wasn't on a mission to save the universe.

So once again he stood in the center of his room and lowered his head. "I want to go to my *big* sister, Gwendolyn the Great, Savior of Idlebury, Protector of the Universe in Idleburg, Pennsylvania, Dimension X, planet Earth."

Nothing happened.

He repeated his request. Still nothing happened.

He rephrased his request. "Take me to Gwendolyn the Great, Savior of Idlebury, Protector of the Universe in Idleburg, Pennsylvania, Dimension X, planet Earth."

He opened his eyes only to find he still stood in the middle of his room.

He stormed across the room. "Take me to Gwendolyn the Great, Savior of Idlebury, Protector of the Universe."

A matronly, middle-aged woman appeared before the child. "You're wasting your time."

"Wow, Wilameena. You appeared like magic."

The haggard old enchantress sneered at Thane. "Appearances aren't everything. Your problem is you think magic is a big deal; you think it makes you special. Well, let me tell you, young man, it's no big deal and it doesn't make *you* special at all."

"I *am* special," Thane said. "And my powers are special; so powerful that Mother warned me not to use them."

Wilameena chuckled. "Powers, you say? Now that's a different story. Powers aren't magic. Magic is for those who like to fool people, those who like to play tricks on others. Magic is for the powerless. But real powers are for those who are destined for greatness. Understanding the fine line between magic and powers is the real trick."

"Why did Mother tell me not to use my powers?"

"Because you're too young to understand the power of your powers. Just as your mother was when she got herself in trouble and barely avoided a hundred whacks with a wicked wand. She hasn't used her powers since, even when it would have been to her advantage to do so."

"I knew Mother had the gift."

24

"You can call it a gift, but remember, powers in the wrong hands do more harm than good."

"What did Mother do?"

Wilameena winced. "I'm not sure I should tell you."

"I want to know."

"Well, since you're practically begging me to reveal the details of your mother's outrageous, unforgivable, despicable act... I'll tell you... But it will have to be our little secret."

Thane plopped on his bed and smiled at the enchantress. "Okay. What did she do?"

"Well, if you must know, she turned a classmate whom she detested into a chicken. That in and of itself was not so horrible, but what happened next was. The terrified girl, or I should say, chicken, ran away, was captured by an unscrupulous person who sold her to another person who took her to Butcherdonia where she was scheduled to be slaughtered, stuffed, broiled, and basted, then served to King Prymribb and Queen Barbieque for dinner. Fortunately, the chicken girl snatched an intergalactic signal device from one of the chicken-coop workers. And since in human form she was no birdbrain, she pecked out a message to Princess Filanthropi and a few friends, reporting her whereabouts and begging the princess to remove the magic spell before she was an entrée on the king and queen's dinner menu."

Thane sneered. "I don't believe you."

"You're the one who wanted to know about your mother's wickedness, so shut up and listen."

Thane grunted and lay on his bed. "Okay, go ahead."

"For nearly two weeks, the girl's parents lamented over their missing child. They met several times with police and missing-persons organizations, none of which had any idea what your mother had done. They spent days filling out pages of reports. They talked to anyone and everyone, handed out fliers, and made countless phone calls, hoping for positive information. All the girl's parents knew was their lovely daughter had gone missing. And they longed for her to return home safely."

Wilameena paused, watching Thane cup his ears in an attempt to not hear her story. She grabbed his arms and pulled his hands away from his head. "Listen. This is a story you, of all people, need to hear. You're already in serious trouble. You need to know what's in store for you."

Thane took a deep breath. "Okay."

"Well, the Intergalactic Department of Lost, Missing, or Deliberately Gone Astray Persons sent out a team of officers to question those who were the last to see the child, namely *your* mother and her classmates. But your conniving mother had bribed her classmates into silence with the promise of candy and cookies for life if they kept her secret. And if they didn't, she threatened to turn them into chickens or pigs or cows and send them to Butcherdonia to suffer their fate. Nonetheless, several classmates who couldn't live with their guilty consciences turned in your dear mother just before overwhelming guilt caused her to confess. *Universal Scandals* magazine was the first to obtain and run the story.

"Fortunately, on the day of the chicken girl's scheduled execution, the king and queen of Butcherdonia, who were avid readers of *Universal Scandals* magazine, read the story about the incident and immediately halted all chicken slaughters.

"Queen Barbieque, horrified at the thought the girl might already have met her death or worse, that she and King Prymribb had already eaten the child, took to her bed and refused to eat at all. Several more days passed before your mother's spell wore off and the chicken transformed back into the girl, at which point she was returned to the kingdom of Seedonia and into the arms of her anxious yet grateful parents.

"King Prymribb and Queen Barbieque celebrated the child's survival by hosting a feast for all of Butcherdonia, giving the chickens a stay of execution, of course.

"But the happy ending was not the end of the situation. Your mother's act was so egregious that her father, your grandfather, King Harvestor of Seedonia, was called before Hexidonia's Council of Horrendous Behaviors and Horrible Deeds and publicly admonished for his daughter's misuse of powers. Before he was allowed to leave the kingdom of magic, he was forced to promise the council that his daughter, your mother, would never use her powers again. He was required to sign a document declaring if your mother ever engaged her powers, she would be unmercifully tried before the council, and if it was deemed just, she would be forced to choose a wand from Hexidonia's universally infamous Wicked Wand Collection. Without the supervision of a wizard, the wand would be let loose and allowed to inflict punishment as it saw fit—up to and including death. To further impress upon King Harvestor the breadth of punishment the wands could inflict on his precious princess, he was reminded of the time he misused his powers as a boy not much older than you and endured one hundred lashings with a particularly wicked wand that left scars he would bear for the rest of his life."

Thane stared at the enchantress and stuck his hands in his pockets to hide the fact he was shaking from fear. "Grandfather was whacked with a wicked wand?"

"Yes. And remember, it's our little secret."

"Why?"

"Your mother is ignorant as to her father's misdeeds and punishment. In fact, she believes she's the only person in her family who has such powers. Every time she was with child, she prayed she wouldn't pass the horribly dangerous powers on to her children. Obviously her prayers went unanswered. And if you repeat one word of what I've told you, you'll cause great embarrassment to your entire family."

"How come you know what my mother did?"

"That's my secret," Wilameena said.

"And what about you, Wilameena?"

"What about me?"

"If you can appear and disappear like magic, you must have powers too."

"Powers? I have no powers. But I'm quite *good* at magic." Wilameena winked at Thane, leaned in close to him, and said, "Know what I mean?"

"Yeah, you play tricks on people."

"Only if they let me," Wilameena said as she transformed into Gwen.

Thane smirked. "I'm *not* impressed. But I might be if you can bring the real Gwen here."

"Good try, my boy," Wilameena said as she morphed into herself. "When you're skilled enough, you can go to her. Since you're obviously lacking in skill, you'll have to wait for her to come to you."

"What do you mean I'm lacking—"

"No more questions," Wilameena snapped. "Be careful with your powers. Do not confuse them with magic." As she let out a crazed laugh and evaporated into thin air, she said, "You've been warned."

CHAPTER FIVE
THE SOUL SEEKER'S WARNING

T hane thought about what Wilameena had said. "I wonder
how she avoided a whacking with a wicked wand. She's
either lying or someone's protecting her," he mumbled. "I don't
believe her, particularly the part about my lack of magic skills.
After all, her reputation is less than admirable."

Wilameena's words made Thane more determined than ever
to perfect his magic tricks and become the greatest magician
who ever lived. And now was the perfect time to start. He lifted
the mattress and retrieved a notebook in which he'd scribbled
hundreds of charms and spells. He knelt by the bed, put the
notebook on the mattress, and opened it. Much to his horror,
the pages were blank.

"My notes. They're gone." Thane furiously flipped through
the pages, hoping the words would magically reappear. "Who
took them?" He went down a list of possible suspects.
"Prudence? No. Blabberdish? Never. Wilameena?"

A blast of cold air followed by an acrid smell made Thane
gag, stopping him in the midst of compiling his list of possible
note thieves. He coughed, hoping he could prevent himself
from throwing up. The smell was familiar, but he couldn't
place it. Still kneeling by his bed, he scanned the room for the

source of the horrid odor. His bed shook, the window rattled, his desk chair crashed backward on the floor. Coldness permeated the room. The window frosted as if it were the dead of winter. Thane nervously searched the room, but the vapor of his warm breath hitting the frigid air fogged his vision. Through the mist, he saw a dark figure in the corner. His heart pounded as a being stepped out of the darkness and into the light. There was no mistaking the creature. It was nearly ten feet tall and totally covered in a black cape, its face obscured by a hood.

Thane ran to the caped man. "I'm so happy to see you," he said with excitement, remembering when the Soul Seeker had taken him so his young, innocent soul could revitalize the many weary souls the Soul Seeker harbored, including that of his father, King Heroian. It was an experience Thane would never forget.

"The feeling is *not* mutual," the Soul Seeker said in an angry, booming, raspy voice.

"What do you mean?"

"King Abracadabra of Hexidonia is on his way here. It is never a positive thing when he leaves his kingdom."

"King Abracadabra? Coming here? Why?"

"He is on his way to meet with your mother and father about your misuse of magic last night. You may be in grave danger."

"But I was only having a little fun."

"What you call fun, King Abracadabra calls a crime," the Soul Seeker said. "You, your father, and your mother will pay for your childish error in judgment. And you should hope he does not bring his wife, Queen Opunzayzme."

"Why?"

"Queen Opunzayzme is the keeper of the Wicked Wand

Collection. She is the only wizard who can control the wicked wands. So if she accompanies the king, I predict wicked wands will be used. I suggest you own up to what you have done and promise you will never pull such a stunt again."

"Help me," Thane pleaded.

"It is out of my hands. I have no control over matters of magic. You are on your own."

Thane nervously ran his hands through his hair. "But you're one of the most powerful beings in the universe. Everyone's afraid of you. Surely you could frighten King Abracadabra and Queen Opunzayzme just enough so they'd leave me and my parents alone."

"No, I cannot. Only one being in the universe can save you."

"Who?"

"It is for me to know and for you to find out." The Soul Seeker wrapped his cape tightly around his body and disappeared.

Thane was now alone in his room, too scared to cry, too scared to breathe. A knock on his door startled him.

"Who is it?" Thane said, choking back fear.

"Oof, Your Royal Highness. May I come in?"

"Okay," Thane replied sheepishly, worried as to Oof's use of his formal title.

When Oof entered Thane's quarters, the boy realized how scary his mother's master servant appeared. He was tall, lanky, and nearly colorless with the exception of his bulging blue eyes. His bald head shone under the light, and his sharp nose cast a shadow over his full, cracked lips. His hands were pale, his fingers knobby. As always, he was impeccably dressed. His manner was what most people would call haughty. *He must be at least two hundred years old*, Thane thought. Little did Thane know, Oof was much older than he looked.

Oof handed the prince formal clothes. "You are to dress for your interrogation by King Abracadabra and Queen Opunzayzme. They are expected to arrive shortly."

"Thank you, Oof."

Without uttering another word, Oof left the room. Once outside the door, he mumbled, "May God be with you, my child."

Thane sat on his bed, still holding his clothes. "Queen Opunzayzme?" he muttered, remembering the Soul Seeker's warning. "*Oh no!* I'm going to get whacked with a wicked wand."

He also remembered the Soul Seeker said there was one person in the universe who could save him. *But who?* he wondered.

Thane paced his room. "Obviously it's not my parents. Could it be Morgana? No, she doesn't have powers. Could it be Matilda, Beastonia's great dragon queen? No, that doesn't seem right. King Kokoa? No, that's preposterous considering my adventure in Chocolatonia last night. Wilameena? Couldn't be. She already warned me. Then who?"

Thane racked his brain but couldn't think of anyone who could help him. The fact was, he was only ten years old, and like most ten-year-olds, he simply didn't have many friends or foes. He remembered what Wilameena said: "When you're skilled enough you can go to her. Since you're obviously lacking in skill, you'll have to wait for her to come to you."

Thane thought hard. "*Gwen!* Of course. She has to help me. She's my sister. I'll go to Gwen. But how?" Thane paced some more, lost in thought. "I know," he said with excitement. "If I were older, I'd naturally be more skilled. So I'll just make myself older, then I'll transport myself to Dimension X and get Gwen." Thane giggled with delight, proud of what he believed to be a brilliant solution. "I'll prove that mean Wilameena wrong."

Thane examined himself in an ornate mirror adorned with carvings of dragons, cauldrons, stars, and undecipherable words. Many a night he'd stared into the mirror, imagining it had powers of its own—powers that could take him on adventures in other dimensions. As he stared at himself in the mirror, he felt sleepy. Something was happening. His head dropped to his chest.

"I want to be older," he whispered. He slowly raised his head and looked in the mirror. When he saw Oof staring back at him, he screeched, *"Not that old!"* Soon he felt sleepy again, and his head fell back to his chest. "I want to be older but not as old as Oof." When he looked into the mirror this time, an incredibly handsome young man with curly black hair and crystal-clear blue eyes stared back at him. The young man's face was expressionless, but his eyes conveyed sadness. "Wow. Is that me all grown up? I hope so because I'm really good-looking."

The man in the mirror opened his shirt, turned his back toward Thane, and let his shirt slide down his arms to reveal a horribly scarred back.

"Grandfather?" Thane said.

"Save yourself," the man in the mirror said. "And remember, you cannot be older than the age of innocence, or your search for Gwendolyn could end in disaster."

"What's the age of innocence?"

"That is for me to know and for you to find out."

The image of the man dissipated, leaving Thane looking at

himself. "That's for me to know and for you to find out," Thane said, mimicking the man.

Thane tried to remember the age of innocence. He knew Gwen had been ten when she became Gwendolyn the Great, Savior of Idlebury, Protector of the Universe. "How old is Gwen? Is she still innocent? Can I be older than ten and still be innocent?"

Sleepiness overcame him again. His head fell to his chest, and he muttered, "I will not use magic. I promise to behave. Take me to Gwendolyn so I can be saved."

A tornado of fairy dust engulfed Thane. A few seconds later, he appeared in the Fannys' kitchen. Gwen sat at the kitchen table eating breakfast. Her father, Arston, sat next to her, and her mother, Evaline, had her nose buried in the latest edition of *Universal Scandals* magazine. Thane was relieved to see the Earth edition didn't carry the story of his adventure to Chocolatonia and Deadonia, at least not yet. But he was most surprised to see he hadn't aged at all. He remembered time varied from dimension to dimension. So much so that Gwen was still ten years old.

"Thane? Is that you?" Gwen asked.

"Yes, it's me."

"You look nearly as old as me."

"That's because I am. Time isn't the same in Dimension X. You age much more slowly. I'm nearly eleven now. Enough with the idle chitchat. I'm here to take you back to Idlebury. You must return at once. Everything's out of control. Some of the people have fallen back into their bad habits. Father has disappeared again, and Mother is distraught. And Prudence has become a total brat."

"Why do I have to go back?"

"Because you're the Savior of Idlebury, remember? Let's go." Thane grabbed Gwen's hand, and they both disappeared in a cloud of glimmering fairy dust.

Chapter Six
Hexidonia's Threat

I t was early afternoon when the sky over Idlebury darkened. No stars, only pitch-blackness. In most cases, the appearance of the night at any time of day would have enticed the famously lazy Idleburians to retreat to their homes for a much-cherished nap. But due to the king of Idlebury's pronouncement declaring Idlebury no longer idle and granting his people their freedom at the royal assembly nearly five Dimension XIII years ago, most Idleburians were busy at work with the continued transformation of their kingdom from its dirty, disgusting drabness to stunning, spectacular splendor.

So as the sky darkened, they dropped what they were doing and rushed toward Idlebury Castle. They felt their way through the dark, arms outstretched as they bumped into each other like zombies in the night. No one uttered a word as all gazed into the blackness.

As the Idleburians strained to focus their eyes in pitch-blackness, a fireworks display blazed across the sky. Everyone shielded their eyes against the sudden dazzle of light. Soon their eyes adjusted, and young and old alike were mesmerized by the twinkling, sparkling explosives in shapes of wands, wizards, magic hats, snakes, smoking cauldrons, bottles of magic potions that bubbled and burst, flashes of multicolored lightning, laughing skulls, letters that spelled curses, and of course, a black cat that transformed into a dragon. Everyone oohed and aahed at a spectacle beyond their imaginations. The Idleburians were spellbound.

But the thrill of the magnificent fireworks show was short-lived, and the Idleburians were once again left in total darkness. Soon a deafening squawk caused everyone to protect their ears as an illuminated image of a massive bird took shape before them. With each flap of the huge bird's powerful wings, the darkness gave way to bright sunlight. Soon the bird fizzled into a cloud of smoke.

Many Idleburians, thinking the delightful fireworks display had ended, headed back to the work at hand. Smoke from the fireworks hung in the air, curtaining their view of Idlebury Castle. But a gust of wind cleared the smoky air and turned the Idleburians' delight to despair, for before them stood King Abracadabra and Queen Opunzayzme of Hexidonia, who were known to leave their kingdom only in the direst of circumstances. Hence their presence was met with curiosity and fear.

King Abracadabra, decked out in his finest wizard garb—a beautifully embroidered robe and magnificent wizard's hat—struck a menacing pose as he thrust his etched, bejeweled solid-gold sword out toward the crowd as if to threaten harm to anyone who attempted to approach him. The etching on the sword was believed to spell a potent curse in a language no one in the universe, not even King Abracadabra, understood. The king's long white beard and hair and his bony fingers adorned with rings completed the stereotypical image of a masterful, wise wizard.

Queen Opunzayzme, dressed in a stunning white gown

bejeweled with thousands of glistening diamonds and spectacular pearls, was the picture of couture perfection. Her envied long, silky black hair delicately flowed down the honey-toned skin of her back. In her right hand, she held a large key. On her middle finger, an immense crystal ring flashed rainbows of light. The ring, famed and feared throughout the dimensions, foretold the fate of all who came before Hexidonia's Council of Horrendous Behaviors and Horrible Deeds for judgment as to the misuse of magic. But the key opened the cabinet that sheltered the Wicked Wand Collection. And as the keeper of the key, Queen Opunzayzme was the only person in the universe with the power to unleash unimaginable pain on those found guilty of performing magic outside Hexidonia. And if a non-Hexidonian was the accused, the punishment could be devastating—even deadly.

The crowd waited with bated breath for King Abracadabra and Queen Opunzayzme to speak. When the silence became unbearable, a brave Idleburian spoke up.

"Well, bless me old and weary eyes, it's da king and queen of Hexidonia. What are they doin' here?" Fergus, a particularly old Idleburian, exclaimed.

"Somethin's very wrong. Very wrong, I say," whispered a middle-aged woman next to Fergus.

"Someone in Idlebury's been usin' magic. And dat always comes ta no good," stated a man loudly enough for the entire crowd to hear. "I hope it's not da queen again."

"Worse dan dat, it's our lovely Prince Thane. He's been out and about at night, he has. And he's been usin' magic. It's all right here," a woman said, waving a copy of *Universal Scandals*.

"That is correct," King Abracadabra yelled. "And Prince Thane must be punished immediately." He turned his back on the crowd and mounted a ghastly, ghostly horse on which he raced toward Idlebury Castle.

Queen Opunzayzme defiantly waved the key to the Wicked Wand Collection at the crowd and then floated after her husband. She gently landed behind King Abracadabra, joining him on the ghostly horse. Once on Idlebury Castle's drawbridge, the horse disappeared, leaving the royal couple to walk the rest of the way to the castle door.

King Abracadabra and Queen Opunzayzme stood before the massive yet unimpressive door, waiting for it to open in their honor. But it remained shut. King Abracadabra clearly was not amused. "This is highly insulting," he said to Queen Opunzayzme. "I am the most powerful ruler of the most important kingdom in the universe. I expect nothing short of a royal welcome."

When it was obvious no welcome was forthcoming, he pulled his jewel-encrusted gold sword from its sheath and used its pommel to pound on the castle door. The door remained tightly shut. The king of Hexidonia looked at his queen with a disapproving glare as he pounded the door once again.

<hr />

The meaning of the fireworks display was not lost on King Heroian and Queen Filanthropi. Obviously it was a prelude to the arrival of the king and queen of Hexidonia. So as the first firework lit the dark sky over Idlebury Castle, King Heroian and Queen Filanthropi took refuge in the queen's chambers for a private discussion about their imminent meeting with the king and queen of Hexidonia and their concern about their son.

Queen Filanthropi, weak with worry, sought comfort in a cushiony chair while King Heroian paced the room as he glanced over and over at the worn floorboard, then back to his wife.

Lost in emotional pain the likes of which she'd never before experienced, the queen quietly wept. Visions of the punishment Thane might endure coupled with the king's silence, his pacing, and his darting eyes increased her anxiety. She took deep breaths in an attempt not to faint.

"We must stand our ground," King Heroian emphatically stated with renewed vigor, breaking the silence. "Thane did not do anything wrong. He did not use magic." The king paused as he stood on the floorboard that sheltered the magic book. With the conviction and anger of a father desperate to protect his child, he said, "I do not care what that silly magazine claims he did. My son will not be punished for something he did not do. Even if he did do it, he is just a child, for God's sake."

"I agree, my dear. Thane is just a boy. He is totally innocent. It had to be another bad boy. Possibly that spoiled-rotten nasty little Prince Tooky or Tushy of Derrieria. Not our Thane."

"Touché," King Heroian said.

"I am glad you agree, dear."

"No. The boy's name is Touché. Prince Touché. Not Tooky or Tushy. It is Prince Touché of North Cleverbury," the king grumbled.

"Whatever. He is a royal pain in the butt, so Tooky or Tushy would be more appropriate. Do you not agree, dear?"

"Have you ever seen him use powers?"

"Who? Tooky? Tushy?"

"*No! Thane,*" the king screamed.

"No, I have not," the queen lied.

"Good. And what about fairy dust?"

"What about fairy dust?"

"Have you seen it on or around Thane?"

"No… never." The queen lied again.

"Well, what about you?" the king asked. "Have you used your powers of late?"

"Oh, Heroian, you know I have not used them since I was a girl," the queen replied, this time telling the truth.

"Under what circumstance would you use your powers?"

"None." Queen Filanthropi averted eye contact with her husband for fear he would see the doubt in her eyes. "Not ever. Never."

"I hope you can fight your motherly urge to rescue Thane. I fear what would happen to you if you ever used your powers… again."

A loud knock on the castle door abruptly ended King Heroian and Queen Filanthropi's conversation.

"King Abracadabra and Queen Opunzayzme have arrived, no doubt," King Heroian said. As he moved toward the door, he motioned for Queen Filanthropi to follow him.

"Just a moment, dear," Queen Filanthropi said as she scrutinized her appearance in a huge mirror. It was a well-known fact that those who had not learned to control their emotions were most likely to fall victim to magic curses, charms, spells, and hexes—all of which King Abracadabra and Queen Opunzayzme were famous for. So with her handkerchief, she gently wiped her tearstained face. From a secret pocket in her gown, she removed a small bag in which she kept her emergency sundries. She opened her tortoiseshell compact and powdered her face. She carefully removed her crown from its perch atop her head, retrieved a hairbrush, and brushed her hair. She applied a generous coat of red lipstick and smacked her lips to ensure even coverage. When she was through primping, she put her grooming items back in her pocket, smoothed her gown, and gently replaced and adjusted her crown. One last glance in the mirror confirmed she had erased all evidence of her emotional breakdown.

Queen Filanthropi joined King Heroian at the door and said, "I am ready."

To the queen's surprise, her husband didn't appear the least bit annoyed about the delay. In fact, he lovingly embraced her. For the first time in years, she knew she wouldn't face a challenge alone. This time she and her husband would face things together, united in the love for their son.

King Heroian tapped on the door, alerting the guard to open it in preparation for their departure. Before they exited the queen's bedchamber, King Heroian squeezed his wife's hand, instilling confidence that together they were ready to face King Abracadabra and Queen Opunzayzme.

Oof appeared out of nowhere, startling the king and queen. "Your Majesty," he said to King Heroian and Queen Filanthropi as he respectfully bowed. "King Abracadabra and Queen Opunzayzme have arrived. They are awaiting your arrival in the great hall."

"The great hall?" King Heroian exclaimed.

"Yes, sir, I thought it best," Oof replied.

"Of course... my dear man." With a tilt of his head and a nearly undetectable smile, he indicated he understood Oof's intentions.

"Why are we not to meet with King Abracadabra and Queen Opunzayzme in our visiting chambers?" Queen Filanthropi queried. "It is only proper."

"My dear wife, Oof is a genius. The great hall, which shares its back wall with the Wall of Truth and the side wall with the Wall of Passages, is protected from the use of magic. Therefore, while in the great hall, King Abracadabra and Queen Opunzayzme are…" The king snickered. "Well, they are rendered harmless."

"How so?" the queen asked.

"Well, magic is trickery. Trickery is a form of lying. Therefore, magic is not truth. So the power of the Wall of Truth overpowers magic. The Wall of Passages houses all human virtues such as love, compassion, gratitude, forgiveness, respect, honesty, et cetera, et cetera, and… of course, truth. And—"

"Since one of the most powerful human virtues is truth, the Wall of Passages voids any display of magic. Oh, Heroian. No wonder you failed miserably when you were a boy and practiced magic in the great hall," Queen Filanthropi said with delight.

"Yes… indeed," the king said and then hesitated as if remembering his youthful failure as a magician. A moment later, he rubbed his hands together. "But today the power is in our hands, so to speak." King Heroian reached out as if to pat Oof on the shoulder and said, "Good job, my man."

But Oof had already departed.

"Oof has miraculously appeared and disappeared at will as long as I can remember," Queen Filanthropi whispered. "I have heard rumors about that mysterious man all my life, yet I know so little about him. I must find out who he truly is."

"What?" King Heroian asked.

"Nothing, my dear, just wondering how Oof knew magic is useless in the great hall."

"You do not know?"

"I have my suspicions. There is something puzzling about him, do you not agree?"

"Yes, *puzzling* is the word," King Heroian replied.

"Let us hope the king and queen of Hexidonia do not figure out too soon that they and their magic are powerless."

"Come. We must go. King Abracadabra and Queen Opunzayzme await our company."

King Heroian and Queen Filanthropi did not speak as they approached the great hall. When they were a few steps from the room, the door opened and the herald announced their arrival.

Chapter Seven
King Abracadabra's
Loss of Power

"King Heroian and Queen Filanthropi of Idlebury," the herald said as he bowed, then exited the room.

King Abracadabra and Queen Opunzayzme, who were engaged in whispered conversation with their backs to the door of the great hall, turned to greet King Heroian and Queen Filanthropi. The kings bowed and the queens curtsied as all four royals respectfully welcomed each other, yet no words were exchanged.

After a few awkward moments of silence, Queen Opunzayzme broke the tension. "So, Filanthropi, we meet again under eerily familiar unfortunate circumstances," she said. "It would appear you passed on the stupid gene to Thane. Like mother, like son."

Queen Filanthropi's retort was thwarted by King Heroian. "Do not get off on the wrong foot, my dear," he whispered as he grabbed his wife by the arm and quickly escorted her to a table that had been set up for the occasion in the far corner of the room.

Queen Filanthropi jerked away from her husband. "I would

not dream of it," she mumbled.

King Abracadabra and Queen Opunzayzme sat with their backs to the wall. King Heroian and Queen Filanthropi sat facing the other royal couple. As a servant poured tea and served biscuits, Queen Filanthropi wondered why Oof had jammed the table in a corner, forcing her and King Heroian to face the wall and nearly holding King Abracadabra and Queen Opunzayzme captive. She noticed the looks of displeasure from the king and queen of Hexidonia and knew their mood only served to make matters worse. She would discuss this blatant breach of protocol with Oof later.

"How was your trip to Idlebury?" Queen Filanthropi politely asked Queen Opunzayzme, hoping to ease the obvious tension.

"Fine," Queen Opunzayzme abruptly replied.

"The fireworks display was marvelous. We and our people thoroughly enjoyed it," the queen of Idlebury added as she offered another biscuit to the queen of Hexidonia, who refused the offer with a quick wave of her hand.

"Would you like a biscuit, dear?" Queen Filanthropi asked, startled to see her husband impolitely staring at Queen Opunzayzme.

But King Heroian wasn't staring at the queen of Hexidonia. Something else had diverted his attention to the wall behind her. His vexing stare caused the queen to glance at what, other than her, was so captivating. Seeing nothing, she turned her attention to the others at the table.

However, Queen Filanthropi saw something—a vague outline on the wall, the sight of which teased her memory. She glanced at her husband and noticed he was lost in thought. She wondered if he was lost in memories he'd shared with her of his childhood. She remembered him telling her about an incident that occurred when he was the twelve-year-old prince of Idlebury. He was happily practicing magic charms and curses in the great hall—his favorite place to hide from his parents, who disapproved of his interest in magic and his shelter from the embarrassment of others who might witness his miserable attempts at tricks, hexes, and curses. But when his parents, King Inaeblurr and Queen Pirmizzible, walked into the great hall to have a private conversation, his fun was interrupted.

Afraid of being scolded if caught practicing magic, young Heroian scurried to find a hiding place, but the best he could do was smash himself against the wall, hoping to go unnoticed. Much to his surprise, the wall swallowed him. Within seconds, a force tossed him to the floor of a small room on the other side. He was about to scream for help when he noticed something most intriguing. From behind the wall, he could hear his parents' conversation loud and clear. For years, the room remained his little secret. Queen Filanthropi wondered if anyone was hiding behind the wall now.

As Queen Filanthropi struggled to engage in idle chitchat with her guests, she questioned what had overcome her husband. *Why is he staring at Queen Opunzayzme? Did she put a spell on him?* King Heroian's apparent rudeness embarrassed her. To bring him back into the conversation, Queen Filanthropi cleared her throat, gently tugged on his sleeve, and said, "The fireworks display was brilliant, my dear. Do you not agree?"

"Oh… yes… It was… spectacular," King Heroian replied, trancelike as he continued to stare at the wall.

Queen Filanthropi wondered if the king and queen of Hexidonia would disappear if they accidentally leaned against the wall, half hoping they would.

"Enough," King Abracadabra brusquely said as he attempted to stand, but he only achieved leaning across the table, barely able to steady himself. "It is obvious you are avoiding conversation as to why we are here. In fact, there is no conversation to be had." King Abracadabra tried but failed to push the table away and free himself. "Bring the boy to me, and I will confirm he is guilty of the crime as to the use of magic by a non-Hexidonian."

"Yes, of course," King Heroian replied as he stood, pressing his body against the table in an attempt to keep King Abracadabra and Queen Opunzayzme in their places. "But before we do, Filanthropi and I want to know exactly on what grounds you accuse our son of said crime."

With great effort, King Abracadabra reached inside his robe and withdrew a tattered *Universal Scandals* magazine. "I do believe this is proof enough," he said, waving the magazine at King Heroian as Queen Opunzayzme stood in a show of support for her husband. "After all, you have a direct quote from none other than King Kokoa of Chocolatonia, declaring your son's act to be the—" Struggling to maintain his balance, the king of Hexidonia leaned on the table for support as he flipped through the magazine to find the quote. "Here it is... 'Prince Thane of Idlebury is without a doubt the doer of the most dastardly deed to occur in my kingdom since the great bonbon heist more than one thousand years ago.'"

At the mention of the great bonbon heist, Queen Opunzayzme gasped and collapsed in her chair.

Queen Filanthropi stifled a giggle, knowing Queen Opunzayzme had emotionally and mentally checked out of the conversation, silently reliving the trauma of surviving for weeks without her addiction—King Kokoa's beloved chocolates.

Queen Opunzayzme's eyes rolled back and her eyelids fluttered as she struggled to remain conscious. Despite the close proximity of her body to the wall and the table, Queen Filanthropi feared the queen of Hexidonia would faint and crumble to the floor.

Queen Opunzayzme's hand shook as she dipped in the pocket of her dress. She withdrew a large key and placed it on the table and then continued to search her pocket. When she touched her daily supply of Chocolatonia's universally loved bonbons, she sighed and perked up, regaining full consciousness.

King Abracadabra shook the *Universal Scandals* magazine at King Heroian.

To avoid a smack in the face, King Heroian stepped back. "Why would you believe the prattle written in that magazine?" he asked.

"Three things, my dear man," King Abracadabra said. "One, this kind of behavior appears to run in Prince Thane's family." He glared at Queen Filanthropi. "Two, the article is written by Syvil Gossep, who, if I remember correctly, and I always do, wrote the book you so enthusiastically endorsed about Idlebury titled *Idlebury: The True Story of the Kingdom of Hope* or some such nonsense. Am I correct?"

King Heroian angrily stared into King Abracadabra's charcoal eyes. "Yes. Go on. What is the third thing?"

"Third, and by far the worst evidence, is trillions of beings throughout the universe heard the prince or, more correctly" — King Abracadabra pointed his finger at Thane's parents — "your son, Thane, repeat a forbidden phrase. In fact, it was hoped the phrase had been forgotten, never to be uttered by a living being again. Never. Ever. It is the most dangerous charm any Hexidonian, let alone a non-Hexidonian, could recite."

"Of what phrase do you speak?" Queen Filanthropi asked.

"I cannot repeat it," King Abracadabra announced. "Did you not read today's *Universal Scandals* magazine?"

"No. I did not have time as we are busy here in Idlebury," Queen Filanthropi replied. "We do not have magic charms to expedite our daily chores. Ergo, I do not know exactly what you are accusing a ten-year-old boy of doing. Besides, I would think since you claim to be the most powerful wizard in the universe, you could repeat the phrase without harm to yourself or others. Hmm... I guess you are not as powerful as you would like others to believe."

King Abracadabra's face turned blood red, the veins in his neck bulged, he wrung his hands and clenched his teeth, leaving no doubt he was explosively angry.

In a show of support, Queen Opunzayzme stood next to her husband.

"Do not challenge me, Filanthropi," the king of Hexidonia said. "You are not a person of power."

"You may be right. I am not a person of power outside Idlebury. But have you considered I may be a person with powers?"

"Filanthropi, enough," King Heroian said.

Queen Filanthropi winked at her husband and said, "I do believe he owes us a demonstration of his magical talents. After all, Abracadabra has accused our son, who according to the rules of the universe is still of the age of innocence, of a serious crime that may be punishable by death. I do not take that lightly. Do you, my dear?"

"Of course not," King Heroian replied. "It is of the utmost importance to me—"

A loud noise behind the wall where the royal couples had

been seated startled everyone. King Abracadabra aggressively pointed his sword at the wall in preparation to annihilate anyone or anything that emerged, but no one and nothing did.

"As I was saying," Queen Filanthropi continued, "if you are truly all powerful, then a silly little chant should do you no harm."

King Abracadabra pulled Queen Opunzayzme closer to him and whispered in her ear, "Shall we show these fools what our magic can do?"

Queen Opunzayzme smirked and glared at King Heroian and Queen Filanthropi. "Yes. I believe a little magic lesson will leave quite an impression," she whispered and then kissed her ring for luck.

"It is agreed," King Abracadabra said. "I will entertain your request. But just let me say this"—the king of Hexidonia sneered—"be careful what you wish for."

King Heroian and Queen Filanthropi huddled as they squelched laughter and feigned fear. Queen Filanthropi forced her hands to tremble as she placed them over her mouth. King Heroian spoke in a deliberately shaky voice. "U-un-d-der-st-stood. Do proceed."

The king of Hexidonia pushed away from the table just enough so he and his wife could squeeze between it and the wall. Once in the center of the room, the aged king closed his eyes, lowered his head, and meditated. For a few seconds nothing happened. Soon light shone on him, making him look angelic. As he levitated, diamond dust twinkled and swirled around him.

Queen Filanthropi squeezed King Heroian's hand, concerned at what appeared to be the king of Hexidonia's ability to perform magic in the great hall.

King Abracadabra opened his eyes, and in a booming voice he said, "Last night at ten o'clock this morning, an empty wagon full of people ran over a dead horse and killed it."

The walls of the great hall shook. Everyone gasped in anticipation of annihilation by falling bricks and mortar. Nothing happened.

Queen Filanthropi barely stifled a giggle when she heard the king of Hexidonia recite a silly phrase she remembered from her childhood. Obviously she'd forgotten the *Universal Scandals* magazine had read the same phrase to her earlier. She was puzzled by the confused looks on the faces of the king and queen of Hexidonia when the phrase didn't elicit the expected results. *Certainly this can't be what they think is the most powerful magic phrase in the universe*, she thought.

Queen Filanthropi glanced at King Heroian, who appeared shocked. She knew he'd only scanned the *Universal Scandals* article. And from the look on his face, it was obvious he hadn't read the part about the phrase Thane was purported to have spoken. But upon hearing King Abracadabra repeat the phrase Thane was accused of reciting in order to gain access to the kingdoms in the various dimensions, there was only one conclusion—Thane was not innocent of the crime, and worse, he'd read *A Magic Maniac's Many Ways to Make Mischief*.

Queen Filanthropi did her level best to hide her concern regarding Thane's guilt. But the look in her husband's eyes confirmed what she felt in her heart—unless there was a miracle, Thane was doomed to severe punishment by one of Queen Opunzayzme's wicked wands.

King Abracadabra, still intent on proving Prince Thane was indeed a bad boy who deserved to be punished, once again closed his eyes, levitated as light shone on him, and repeated the magic phrase. "Last night at ten o'clock this morning, an empty wagon full of people ran over a dead horse and killed it."

The king of Hexidonia stumbled and then landed hard on the floor. As he rose, he grumbled to himself, obviously disappointed that once again he'd failed.

"Try eleven o'clock in the morning, dear," Queen Opunzayzme said. "I believe eleven o'clock is correct."

King Abracadabra closed his eyes, levitated, and under the umbrella of light, recited the magic phrase with the change suggested by his queen. "Last night at *eleven* o'clock this morning, an empty wagon full of people ran over a dead horse and killed it." This time the phrase produced a most surprising result. It created a forceful wind that threw the old king through the window of the great hall onto freshly clipped bushes outside. Queen Opunzayzme ran to the window to check on her husband's condition as Queen Filanthropi stifled laughter and King Heroian remained in shocked silence.

King Abracadabra crawled through the window and back into the great hall. Without uttering a word about his toss out the window, he screamed the original magic spell once more. This time nothing happened at all.

"If the magic phrase has no power when spoken by a powerful wizard," Queen Filanthropi said to the king and queen of Hexidonia, "I cannot for the life of me see how an innocent child could have caused any ill effect by repeating it. That is if he did, in fact, repeat the phrase."

"Come, Opunzayzme," King Abracadabra said. "Maybe the phrase has lost its charm after all. I guess there was no crime committed by Prince Thane."

Queen Opunzayzme nodded her agreement before she and King Abracadabra departed. The king of Hexidonia barely bowed to King Heroian and Queen Filanthropi as he exited.

But the queen of Hexidonia took a moment to issue a warning. "You can wipe those smiles off your faces, because if your son steps out of line one more time, I will choose the wickedest of the wicked wands from my collection and let it loose to do its will to him." She pointed her finger at the royal duo and continued. "Do you understand me, Heroian and Filanthropi?"

King Heroian nodded and then glared at the queen of Hexidonia.

But Queen Filanthropi didn't utter a word because the appearance of age spots on Queen Opunzayzme's knobby hand mesmerized her. In an attempt to hide her amusement, she turned away. That's when she saw Oof emerge from the wall where the two royal couples had been seated. He removed something from the table, and in an instant he was gone, only to reappear on the other side of the door to the great hall where he greeted King Abracadabra and Queen Opunzayzme and escorted them out of Idlebury Castle.

Queen Filanthropi noticed King Heroian appeared to be lost in thought, leading her to believe he had not seen Oof in the room. "I must find out who that man is," she muttered.

"What, my dear?" King Heroian asked.

"Nothing. Just talking to myself."

As the king and queen of Idlebury headed for their respective quarters, Queen Filanthropi glanced over the banister and saw Oof and Syvil Gossep of *Universal Scandals* magazine engaged in serious conversation. Ms. Gossep, whom the queen had entrusted with free access to the castle, her people, and her family, busily jotted notes in a leather-bound notebook. There was something about Oof's and Ms. Gossep's intimate posture that gave the queen pause. She wondered if her trust in Ms. Gossep was a mistake. But her main concern was about Oof.

"I have known him all my life, yet I do not know him. Who is he?" Secretly she wondered if the rumors about him were true.

———◈◈◈———

Morgana greeted Queen Filanthropi as she arrived at her bedchamber door. A guard bowed as he opened the door. Morgana took a step back in reverence to the queen, allowing the queen to enter the sparsely decorated room first.

With her servant's help, the queen began to undress. "Morgana, have you heard the phrase Thane supposedly repeated last night?"

"What phrase, ma'am?"

"You know, that silly old phrase: last night at ten o'clock a dead horse ran over some people. Or some such nonsense."

"Can't say I know dat one, ma'am. Never heard it before just now," Morgana said.

"You did not hear when the *Universal Scandals* magazine said it this morning?"

"No disrespect, ma'am, but I don't pay no nevermind ta dat magazine."

"So I guess you do not know who wrote the phrase?"

"No, ma'am, I don't. Just assumed it's been around forever. Dat's all."

"Hmm. Well, if you have never heard it before, why would you assume it has been around forever?"

Morgana stared at the queen but didn't answer.

"Oh, never mind. I guess I will have to ask the king."

"Why would he know, ma'am?"

"I seem to remember the king and I recited the phrase when

55

we were children. It used to give us quite a giggle. So I figure he might know."

"Maybe he does, ma'am, 'cause I can't tell ya."

But Queen Filanthropi knew the author was Feefifofum Fiddledeedee Fiddledeedum. And she knew perfectly well who that was.

CHAPTER EIGHT
PRUDENCE'S STROKE OF LUCK

S tars zoomed by Thane and Gwen as they hurtled through the universe at lightning speed, catching only glimpses of the thirteen dimensions and their kingdoms. The sight of Beastonia in Dimension I made Gwen long for her friend Mistofisee, a young dragon at only a little more than two hundred years of age. His devout friendship had given her successful entrance into the Wall of Passages, allowing her to prove she deserved the titles Gwendolyn the Great, Savior of Idlebury, Protector of the Universe.

"That's strange," Gwen said as she and Thane approached Dimension XIII. "I appear to be getting bigger and older by the second. I think I've aged nearly five years."

"Probably. Time is faster here. You're catching up."

"I guess. But do you know what's stranger?"

"What?"

"The dimension is pulsating. And the kingdoms are blinking in and out. Someone doesn't want us to return to Idlebury."

"So do something about it. You're the Savior of Idlebury."

"That doesn't mean I can do anything I want."

"Then what good are your titles? What good are you?"

"Never mind," Gwen said, refusing to explain herself to her bratty brother. "By the way, what was the magic phrase you used to get through the other dimensions?"

"Why?"

"Because it might come in handy right now."

"I'm not allowed to use it anymore. I might get whacked with a wicked wand if I do."

"I'll whack you if you don't use it. Hurry. We're about to be thrown out of Dimension XIII. We could be lost in space."

"Okay, but if I get in trouble, I'll tell Mother and Father and the king and queen of Hexidonia it was your idea."

"Why would you do that?"

"Well… they wouldn't mess with Gwendolyn the Great, now would they?"

"Just say it," Gwen pleaded.

Thane took a deep breath and said, "Last night at ten o'clock this morning, an empty wagon full of people ran over a dead horse and killed it."

A loud thud followed Gwen's and Thane's landing at the edge of the Slothful Forest just outside Idlebury.

"Ouch. My elbow," Thane complained.

Gwen ignored him as she admired her more mature body. She noticed her clothes had grown in proportion to her new height and weight. "Wow. It's a good thing my clothes grew with me. Otherwise I'd be busting out all over. How old do you think I look?"

"At least five years older than I do," Thane replied, still rubbing his aching elbow.

"So I look fifteen?"

"I don't know. My elbow hurts."

"Shh. Listen."

Thane listened intently, but he didn't hear anything.

But Gwen heard someone whisper, "Get *A Magic Maniac's Many Ways to Make Mischief*. Now." Gwen immediately recognized the voice as that of the same woman who had instructed her on how to enter the Wall of Passages. She knew this person, being, spirit, whoever or whatever it was, needed to be taken seriously. "Come on. We have to find the magic book."

"What magic book?" Thane said. "I don't have a magic book. Did I mention a magic book? How could I when I don't have one?"

"Come to think of it, you didn't mention it. But you doth protest too much, so obviously you know about it."

Gwen broke away from Thane and ran toward Idlebury Castle. Thane charged after her, but she ran so fast that in no time she was way ahead of him. So he ran for all he was worth until he caught up with her. Together they ran up the drawbridge and stopped at the castle door, gasping for air. Gwen pushed the door until it opened just enough for her and Thane to squeeze through. They darted to the long, winding staircase and sprinted up two stairs at a time. When they reached the second floor, they raced down the hall to Thane's quarters, elbowing each other as they fought their way to be the first to reach it.

Simultaneously Thane and Gwen reached the door. Panting, they fought over the doorknob. Gwen won. She turned the knob and flung the door open.

As they stumbled into the room, Gwen pointed at Thane's bed. "There it is."

Thane couldn't believe his eyes. *Why is the book on my bed?* he wondered. *I returned it to the box.* "Blabberdish," he exclaimed as he pushed Gwen aside and rushed to the bed. He grabbed for the book, but it rose and moved just enough so that he missed it. Gwen reached for it. Again the book moved, and she, too, missed it. Thane nabbed it a second before Gwen. They both jumped on the bed and furiously fought for possession of the book.

Gwen pulled the book with all her might. "Give it to me."

Thane yanked the book toward himself. "No, it's mine."

"I said, give it to me. So let go."

Prudence appeared at the doorway, her eyes bright with excitement. "I want to play too."

Gwen and Thane looked at her, but neither relinquished their hold on the book.

"No. Go away, Prudence. Go back to your room," Thane said as Gwen took advantage of the moment and gave the book a tug, but to no avail.

"Gwen, you play with me?"

"Go to your room," Thane yelled again, keeping his focus on the book.

"I want to play too," Prudence whined as she walked into the room.

"Okay," Gwen said. "Go get your dolls. Then bring them back here and I'll play with you."

As Prudence clapped her hands and skipped out of the room on a quest to get her dolls, Gwen and Thane continued their fight for the book. A ripping sound stopped their mad struggle.

"Look what you did," Gwen said, staring at the now coverless book. "You ripped off the cover."

Thane dropped the book's cover on the bed. "Me? You were

the one who wouldn't let go."

The cover rose and reattached itself to the book. Suddenly it shriveled to a marble-sized wad of leather and paper. Aghast, Gwen and Thane watched as the little marble of a book burned a hole through the blanket, sheets, and mattress. When they leaned over to inspect the hole, a force neither was powerful enough to resist sucked them into a world no one knew existed.

Gwen and Thane screamed as they slid deeper and deeper down the dark hole. They came to a sudden stop and found themselves suspended in midair. In the distance, a speck of light twinkled. As it grew larger, the room became brighter. Encased in a glowing beam of light, a young woman appeared. She was tall with raven-black hair and penetrating golden eyes.

"Prudence?" Thane whispered.

"Yes, it's me, dear brother. Did you think your rejection of me wouldn't come back to haunt you?"

"I didn't reject you. I just didn't want to play with you."

Prudence sneered at Thane and then pulled Gwen toward her until they were face-to-face. "And you, dear sister Gwendolyn. Did you expect me to worship you just because I'm a lowly princess and you're Gwendolyn the Great… Savior of Idlebury… Protector of the Universe?"

"Nope."

Prudence grunted and pushed Gwen upward, causing her to spin like a top.

Gwen flapped her arms furiously, trying to slow down. "No matter how old you look, you're still only five."

"Despite what you think, I'm not five years old, dear sister." Prudence walked over to Gwen and Thane and examined them as they floated around her. With a wave of her hand, she tossed them farther down the hole. A few seconds later, they plopped on a dirt floor. Prudence floated down the hole and gently landed in front of them. She stared at her older sister and brother, looking as if she were hypnotized. Prudence shook, and like a building that can no longer sustain its weight, she crumbled into thousands of pieces.

"Fooled you," Blabberdish exclaimed.

"That was mean," Thane said as he stood and wiped his dirty hands on his pants.

"Mean? It was brilliant," the worm replied. "You were scared, weren't you?"

"Enough," Gwen said. "Who are you and what are we doing down here?"

"My name is Blabberdish. I'm Thane's friend."

"And how does one befriend a worm?" Gwen asked as she dusted off the grimy dirt from her clothes and hair.

"A bookworm, if you don't mind," Blabberdish said. "And the answer to your questions is quite simple."

"Yes?" Gwen said.

Blabberdish shuffled his feet and clasped his hands behind him. "Well... it depends on what type of book the bookworm lives in."

"He's from Dimension XIV." Thane interrupted him. "His father is the king of Bugdonia."

Gwen glared at Thane. "Bugdonia? Do you think I'm stupid? There's no such kingdom as Bugdonia." She turned her glare on Blabberdish and said, "So tell me who you are and why we're here?"

"I'm a bookworm. I live in the book known as *A Magic Maniac's Many Ways to Make Mischief* written by none other than Feefifofum Fiddledeedee Fiddledeedum, otherwise known as—"

"Shut up!" Thane screamed, frightening the small creature so much he fell over.

As Blabberdish struggled to rise, Gwen said, "Otherwise known as?"

"Yeah. Otherwise known as?" Thane asked, giving his full attention to his friend.

"If I hadn't been so rudely interrupted, I would have said... Hmm, I would have said... Well, I would have said—"

"King Heroian," Gwen blurted out.

Thane's jaw dropped. "What? Father wrote the most powerful magic book in the universe?"

Blabberdish lowered his head and rocked back and forth. "That wasn't what I was going to say," he mumbled.

"Everyone knows King Heroian is the author, with the exception of your mother... I mean our mother," Gwen said.

"How could she not know?" Thane asked.

"In case you haven't noticed, Queen Filanthropi is not the brightest bulb in the family."

"Oh." Thane looked down, his face flushed.

Gwen huffed. "She barely knows what goes on in Idlebury, let alone the universe. And someone wants it that way. Someone has scared everyone in the universe into keeping their mouths shut so Queen Filanthropi doesn't find out about the book. Lots of people want the book for their own evil purposes, and one of them is King Abracadabra."

"Why would the king of Hexidonia want a magic book?" Thane asked. "Doesn't he already know every trick in the book?"

"Oh, very funny. Very funny indeed," Blabberdish said, then snorted with laughter. "But King Abracadabra doesn't know every trick in the book."

"He just pretends to be powerful and all-knowing," Gwen said. "It's a ruse. It's the biggest magic trick of all. He's a magician, not a wizard."

"That's what Wilameena said," Thane said.

"*What?*" Blabberdish yelled. "Did you say Wilameena?"

"Yes. Wilameena. You know, the old enchantress whom everybody hates," Thane responded.

"Oh, her. Of course." Blabberdish lowered his head. "I hate her too."

Thane looked up, lost in thought. "But what about the stories of the Great Wizard? If he's not King Abracadabra, who is it?"

"That's what we need to find out," Gwen replied.

Blabberdish clapped his hands and looked up at Thane. "Then let's not waste another minute."

Gwen shook her head and put her hand up. "Whoa. You guys are *not* going with me on this quest. This is a job for Gwendolyn the Great, Savior of Idlebury, Protector of the Universe."

"Oh brother," Blabberdish said. "You don't know magic, and Thane is pathetic at best. You need me."

Thane furrowed his brow. "Hey, I'm good at magic."

"No. You will not use magic unless you want to suffer the wrath of King Abracadabra and Queen Opunzayzme," Gwen said. "There's a reason they want to keep all the tricks of the trade to themselves. It's their way of controlling people. That in and of itself is proof they're not wizards. After all, a true wizard never uses powers for purposes of control."

Blabberdish rolled his eyes. "Well, I'm not a wizard, I'm a worm. So I'll use magic if and when I deem it necessary."

"Ditto," Thane replied.

Gwen took a deep breath and shook her head in disgust. She knew she'd lost the argument and would have to use all her resources to keep Thane and Blabberdish from causing harm to themselves, the dimensions, and the universe. "A ten-year-old and a bookworm. Where's Mistofisee when I need him?" she muttered.

"Yes, but I'm an intelligent and talented bookworm," Blabberdish boasted as he waved his wand and transported the trio back to Thane's quarters.

Thane immediately rushed out of his room and down the hall to his mother's bedchamber. "I have to check on something," he yelled.

Gwen wasn't sure where Thane was going, but she had an idea. She started to follow him but thought better of it. As she sat on Thane's bed to contemplate her next move, the magic book magically appeared, fully intact. She could hardly believe her luck. But as she reached for the book, a bolt of lightning zapped it and it disappeared.

Blabberdish lowered his wand. "You're no match for me, Gwendolyn the not so great."

Gwen raised her foot, fighting the urge to squash Blabberdish. "Don't be so sure, you brazen, slimy little bookworm."

Gwen watched Blabberdish squeeze under the door. After a few minutes, she exited Thane's room and slammed the door behind her.

Immediately Prudence emerged from under the bed, clutching her dolls. "Gwen, wait. You said you'd play." She rushed to the door and yanked it open. When she looked down the hall, it was empty. "No one wants to play with me. I'm going to tell Mommy."

Prudence was about to bolt out of the room to tattle on Thane and Gwen when a book lying on Thane's desk grabbed her attention. Clutching her dollies, she waddled to the desk and tried to lift the book. "Wow. It's heavy." She reached with both arms, letting her precious dolls fall to the floor. She tugged the old book, but it wouldn't budge. The stubbornness of the book clearly angered Prudence. She wanted it. And if you asked anyone who knew the child, they'd tell you she had a talent for getting what she wanted.

"You're mine," Prudence said as she focused hard on the book. Without breaking her piercing stare, she waved her hands over it and said, "Do not deny me, for you are mine. Do not defy me, for I am divine."

The book flew off the desk and crashed to the floor, opening to page 655. An illustration of a handsome prince came to life. "Thane?"

With her stubby little fingers, Prudence flipped back through the pages until she landed on page 327. A picture of a little girl who sat cross-legged on the floor as she peered at a large book delighted her. The picture came to life. "*Me!*" she squealed.

She flipped to another page on which a live-action image showed her running down a long corridor. The image froze and turned back into an illustration. Prudence turned to the next page. Again, an illustration of a little girl carrying a large book came to life. The little girl struggled with the big book as she tried to open a door.

Prudence turned to the next page, revealing an image of her sitting on her bed, reading the book. Her image came to life and said, "Take the book to your room and hide it. *Now!*" She tried to close the book, but it resisted. Its pages fluttered forward and backward until they stopped on page 402.

King Abracadabra's face appeared. "Give me the book, you brat."

"No, it's mine."

"I'll get that book if I have to kill you."

"No, I said it's mine."

The book slammed shut. Prudence tried to lift it, but it was too heavy. So she pushed it under Thane's bed, bolted out of the room, ran to her quarters where she retrieved her doll carriage, and then raced back to Thane's room. She sprawled on the floor, reached under Thane's bed and pulled with all her might until she dragged the book out. She tried to pick it up but couldn't. She pulled and pulled, but the book wouldn't budge.

Prudence stared at the book, her body rigid, her eyes fixed as if an evil spirit possessed her. "Up," she said. The book rose to her command. "In there," she demanded, pointing to her doll carriage. The book gently landed in the carriage. Prudence picked up her dolls, placed them on top of the book, covered them with a doll blanket, and then rolled the carriage out of Thane's room. She checked the hall. When she saw no one hanging about, she happily set off for her room.

"What do you have in the carriage?" a man said, blocking the child's way.

Prudence looked up and saw Oof towering over her. She held his gaze and said, "Dollies."

Oof lifted the blanket. At the sight of Prudence's dolls, he dropped it. Without a word, he walked away.

Prudence ran the rest of the way to her quarters. Once inside, she dumped the carriage's contents. The book shimmied across the floor, taking refuge under the child's bed.

"Stay," Prudence said.

She left her room and headed for her mother's bedchamber. "I'm going to tell Mommy. I'm going to tell Mommy," she sang as she skipped down the long hall.

Perched on her tiptoes, she tried but failed to turn the doorknob of her mother's bedchamber. As she struggled to open the door, a skinny, pale hand reached down and locked it. Prudence looked to see who had thwarted her attempt to get in her mother's room, but no one was there. She yelled, "Mommy, Mommy. I have to tell you what Thane and Gwen did."

"Don't you dare tell your mother about Thane, Gwen, or the book," a discarnate woman said. "If you do, I'll kill your dollies."

"No!" Prudence screamed as she scampered down the hall. Safely in her room, she picked up her dolls and jumped on her bed. "I won't tell Mommy. I promise."

"Good. Keep it that way," the disembodied woman said.

Chapter Nine
Mistofisee's Worst Nightmare Comes True

In Beastonia, Dimension I, Mistofisee had grown big and bored. He missed Gwen and often reminisced about their past adventures and friendship. As he relaxed on the grass outside Canny Castle, he thought he heard Gwen say, "Where's Mistofisee when I need him?" His heart skipped a beat. He swung his massive head, looking for her, but she was nowhere in sight.

Mistofisee laughed as he remembered the day he'd met Gwen in Personadonia where Queen Masklyn raised him after his mother, Queen Matilda, fell into Dragon's Sleep and couldn't care for him. He remembered Aislinn and Kendall, Gwen's other selves whom she picked up in Personadonia and with whom she had merged before she entered the Wall of Passages. He missed them too and felt sad he would never see them again.

The young dragon wondered what Gwen was like now. He knew time was different in her dimension, but he couldn't remember if it was slower or faster. So there was no telling just how old she was. "Would I recognize her if I saw her?" he mumbled. "I've changed a lot, but maybe she hasn't changed at all. Would she still want to be my friend?"

"My, my, you've gotten huge," a woman said. "You're going to be bigger than your mother pretty soon."

Mistofisee looked around. His heart raced with excitement at the thought Gwen had returned. To his disappointment, a plump, middle-aged woman stood before him.

"Oh, it's just you." Mistofisee scoffed as he stood. "What do you want this time?"

Wilameena shook her finger at the adolescent dragon. "Don't get snippy with me. You're still no match for your father, King Anima, and you'll never be as clever or as powerful as your mother, Queen Matilda. You're doomed to failure, and you're still so young. Pathetic."

"I'm not a failure. I saved Gwen."

"Ha! Gwen saved herself. Besides, that's in the past. Thane is your next challenge."

"Thane? He's only ten years old. How much help could he need?"

The old enchantress leaned toward Mistofisee, and in a loud whisper she said, "He found *the* book. Worse, he's read it and used it."

Mistofisee pulled away from the enchantress. "What book?"

"The book," Wilameena nearly screamed. "The book every creature in the universe would love to get their grimy little hands, paws, or claws on."

"Oh. What book is that?"

Wilameena curled her lips into a snarl and said, "I think you know what book I'm talking about. If you don't, I'm not going to tell you."

"I don't think you know about any book." Mistofisee pushed his snout at Wilameena. "You're just trying to get information out of me. Well, I'm not that stupid." He blew a puff of smoke, confident he'd beaten the old enchantress at her own game.

Wilameena waved the smoke from her eyes. "I believe you are as dumb and naïve as you pretend."

"Well, if I'm as dumb and naïve as I pretend, then I wouldn't be pretending, now would I?"

"Don't play with me. You either know about the book or you don't."

Mistofisee slumped in defeat. "What book?"

"Oh please. Stop this pitiful banter. You either want to help Thane or you don't."

Mistofisee stared at Wilameena. *Is she telling the truth?* he wondered. But if her reputation was correct, she was more than likely being deceptive. Nonetheless, he decided to play along. "Okay, I'll help him, but how?"

"Find the book and give it to Oof," Wilameena said as she vanished.

"What book?" Mistofisee yelled at the diminishing figure of the enchantress. No reply was forthcoming. "Now what have I done? I've promised to save Thane by finding a book, but I have no idea which book."

Mistofisee meandered back inside the castle and up to his room. Lost in thought, he didn't notice his mother, Queen Matilda, the largest creature in the universe, watching him. As he looked out over the kingdom of Beastonia, he muttered, "I'm an idiot. I really am dumb and naïve."

"Don't ever talk to yourself like that," Queen Matilda said. "Negative self-talk is verbal abuse. If someone else said to you what you just said to yourself, you'd tell them off."

Mistofisee shuffled his feet. "But someone did say I was dumb and naïve."

"Who would have the nerve to say such a mean thing about you?"

"Wilameena."

"Wilameena?" Queen Matilda roared. "Whom did she say it to?"

"To me, Mother." Mistofisee wiped his tears with his enormous clawed paws. "She was just here."

"Wilameena was in Beastonia?" Queen Matilda lowered her head. "What did that conniving, miserable excuse for a human want?"

"She wants me to save Prince Thane of Idlebury."

"Why?"

"Because he's found some book and he could be in a lot of trouble."

The dragon queen glared at her son. "What book?"

"That's what I wanted to know. She said it was a book everyone in the universe wants to get their hands, paws, or claws on."

The dragon queen looked away. "What else did she say about the book?"

"Nothing, other than Thane found it and used it. Whatever that means."

The dragon queen jerked her massive head so she was eye to eye with her son. "He what?"

"He found it and used it," Mistofisee said as he took a step back in fear his mother might blow fire at him. "Those were her exact words, Mother."

Queen Matilda pushed her son aside, lumbered to the

window, and spewed a flame that shrouded her kingdom. "Where did he find it?"

"I don't know. I don't know what book she's talking about."

The queen of Beastonia squinted at her son. "You don't know about the most famous, envied, sought-after book in the universe?"

"No."

The dragon queen suspiciously eyed Mistofisee. "You really don't know about the book?"

"No, Mother."

"I guess now is the time for that mother-to-son talk I've put off for far too long."

"Okay." Mistofisee made himself comfortable in his mother's chair. "I'm all ears."

Queen Matilda paced. "My father was so nervous to tell me about the book that he continuously burped fire. Nearly burned down the castle." Matilda smiled and then frowned. "I don't know how to tell you. Maybe you're better off not knowing."

"Tell me, Mother," Mistofisee begged. "I want to know. I need to know."

The queen of Beastonia sat in a chair next to her son and placed her hand on his knee. Her voice quavered as she began to tell Mistofisee about the most famous and feared book of magic. "When I was just a little dragon, my father held me in his arms, hugged me tightly, and whispered in my ear, 'Last night at ten o'clock this morning, an empty wagon full of people ran over a dead horse and killed it.'"

Mistofisee chuckled.

"You may laugh, but those are the most dangerous words in the universe."

"Oh, Mother, they're too silly to be dangerous."

"I giggled at the silly phrase too. And my father reprimanded me and said serious trouble would befall me if I ever repeated it. He made me vow to never let those powerful words cross my lips."

"You just did, Mother. And nothing happened."

"Nonetheless, those words unlock the magic to what is believed to be the most powerful book in the universe. And it is said whoever possesses the book, no matter how massive or minuscule, will reign supreme over all beings in the universe for all eternity."

"Wow!"

"My father also told me to never go looking for the book because anything that could make one being invincible and all powerful over others must be avoided at all costs. But more importantly, he made me promise not to tell anyone what I knew."

"So I guess you told all your friends?"

"Well... yes. He didn't tell me not to tell anyone about the book, he only told me not to tell anyone the phrase. So I immediately told my girlfriends, Lambrita and Prissipantalonas, who told their friends, who told their friends, and so on and so on until all of Beastonia, Land of the Innocents, and all beings throughout the universe knew about the book and were no longer innocent as to the possibility of complete power over all living things. So I guess you could say I'm responsible for everyone in every kingdom in every dimension knowing about the most dangerous book in the universe. I shudder to think that all the creatures in the universe have become so complacent that no one is worried the book could fall into the possession of the wrong being and be used to control all others? And according to a *Universal Scandals* magazine survey, most creatures in the universe don't bother to search for the book because they don't believe it's real. But it is real, and it appears it's fallen in the hands of Prince Thane, a spoiled, immature boy."

"Moth...er. What book?" Mistofisee asked.

"*A Magic Maniac's Many Ways to Make Mischief* by Feefifofum Fiddledeedee Fiddledeedum." Queen Matilda covered her mouth, because saying the title of the book followed by the name of its author was forbidden.

"Never heard of it," Mistofisee said.

"Well, now you have," a woman said. "And pray tell, Matilda. Where did you get that tidbit of information? Lots of beings know about the book, but no one knows its title or author. At least no one who would be stupid enough to admit to it. So, Mistofisee, it seems your mother let the cat out of the bag, now doesn't it?"

"Shut up, Wilameena," Queen Matilda said. "No one invited you here. So scram."

"*Wait,*" someone yelled.

A humped figure appeared in the doorway, waving what looked like a magazine.

"What brings you calling, Crabbina?" Wilameena asked.

The old creature sneered at Wilameena. "I think *Universal Scandals* magazine let the cat out of the bag first," she said as she handed the magazine to Queen Matilda.

The dragon queen graciously accepted the tightly rolled magazine from Crabbina, the eldest of the revered Sullywobbles—a family of creatures that had served and protected Beastonia since its inception. And during the kingdom's long history, Crabbina herself had singlehandedly saved it many times from total disaster, including the two hundred years Queen Matilda suffered from Dragon's Sleep during her exile in Idlebury.

Clutching the magazine with her huge talons, Queen Matilda carefully unrolled it. The *Universal Scandals* magazine screamed, "*Little Prince Thane in Big Trouble!*" The dragon queen did her best to ignore the magazine's histrionics as she held it up to her large yellow right eye and read the article. When she'd finished reading, she rolled up the magazine, handed it back to Crabbina, and walked out of the room. "Come, Mistofisee, it's time for you to find out what really goes on in the universe."

"I'm not so sure I want to." Mistofisee reluctantly followed his mother down to the courtyard. "Where's Gwen when I need her?"

Wilameena morphed into a miniature version of herself with wings, flew over to Mistofisee, and floated in front of him. "Gwen? What good is she? She can't protect you from the power of the book. She's useless. She's worthless," the enchantress spat out. "She's a loser who hangs out with losers like you." Wilameena buzzed around Mistofisee's head like an annoying gnat. She landed on the young dragon's snout and yelled, "Birds of a feather flock together."

Mistofisee swatted at the enchantress, but she vanished before the full force of his claw impacted her. "I hate that woman."

"Hate is a very hateful word. She's to be pitied, son, not hated," Queen Matilda said as she took to the sky.

"I still hate her," Mistofisee yelled as he flew after his mother.

As he soared over Beastonia, Mistofisee felt free and happy like he'd never felt before. Yet that feeling was tinged with the fear that something wonderful and terrible was happening at the same time. "Where are we going, Mother?"

"To find the book."

"Didn't Grandfather tell you not to?" Mistofisee asked. But his mother didn't answer. He took his mother's silence as a sign to shut up. So he decided to enjoy the journey no matter where it took him.

After a few minutes, Mistofisee glided behind his mother with the greatest of ease. In the distance, multicolored lights appeared. Something about the lights calmed his fears and compelled him to join them. The orbs twinkled in red, white, blue, green, yellow, and purple as they swept under, over, and through him. Their playfulness delighted the young dragon.

Queen Matilda, who was quite a distance ahead, heard what sounded like children giggling. As she continued to glide, she turned to see from whom or what the laughter originated. When she saw Mistofisee surrounded by fairy orbs, obviously enjoying their company, her heart pounded. Blood rushed to her massive muscles, instantly preparing her for battle against the harmless-looking twinkles of light.

As clearly as if she were beside him, Mistofisee heard Queen Masklyn of Personadonia say, "Don't go toward the lights." The words triggered a vivid memory of the queen telling him and a group of children one of the most frightening stories he'd ever heard—*The Myth of the Sparkling Fairy Orbs*—an age-old story of fun-loving twinkling orbs with the ability to delight their victims before they cunningly devoured them. According to legend, these fairies of light had power over every creature in the universe—even the largest, most powerful being of all, the first great dragon king of Beastonia.

"Mother. Help me," Mistofisee pleaded.

Queen Matilda darted toward her son as she spewed fire at the orbs. They squealed with delight. The high-pitched noise caused excruciating pain to radiate through her brain. She clutched her ears in a futile attempt to muffle the sound. She blew fire at the fairies again. Their excited squeals intensified, rising to a torturous level. She flung her head back and forth as if to toss off the menacing orbs. She covered her ears with her claws, but nothing helped. Queen Matilda went limp.

Mistofisee tried to yell to her, but his throat choked from fear. He fought to free himself from the fairy orbs. It was no use. He was doomed to bear witness as his mother spiraled back into Beastonia and slammed into the ground, creating a cloud of dirt and debris that rose into the sky like that of a nuclear blast.

Dusty tears streamed down Mistofisee's face and dripped off his snout. He remembered how his mother's tears had brought his father back to life. He hoped his tears would do the same for her. Using his telescopic vision, he watched his tears fall, but he wouldn't know if they fell on his mother or not, for the fairy orbs transported him out of Dimension I. In a blip of time, he found himself in Dimension III and the realm of Illumindonia where he would experience a reality beyond his wildest imagination.

CHAPTER TEN
QUEEN OPUNZAYZME'S MOST UNFLATTERING VIEW

B ack in Dimension II, Hexidonia was abuzz with the news of Prince Thane's misuse of magic. Syvil Gossep, *Universal Scandals* magazine's most popular reporter, wrote a captivating account—complete with damaging quotes from reliable sources—of King Abracadabra's and Queen Opunzayzme's every move during their visit in Idlebury, including the king's failed attempts to prove Prince Thane's guilt.

Awaiting the arrival of the king and queen of Hexidonia, reporters and camera crews from *Universal Scandals Tonight*, as well as other news and entertainment shows, broadcasted nonstop from the square outside Hexidonia's Cauldron Castle, making this event nearly as newsworthy as Gwen's investiture at the royal assembly in Idlebury.

Universal Scandals Tonight stole the spotlight when it aired a story detailing the heated exchange between the king and queen of Hexidonia and the king and queen of Idlebury. The segment closed with a photo of King Abracadabra shaking a copy of the *Universal Scandals* magazine at King Heroian as the reporter said, "For all the scoop and photos, get your copy of the latest edition of *Universal Scandals* magazine before it sells out."

Needless to say, the magazine flew off store shelves at record speed, causing riots in many areas throughout the universe.

Reporters, desperate to land an exclusive story, clambered to interview anyone willing to talk. One reporter interviewed a ten-month-old baby who burped and accidentally caused the reporter's mic to disappear, briefly halting the broadcast.

By noon, thousands of Hexidonians, decked out in their finest wizard garb, gathered in the square. Hours crawled by as they waited anxiously for a stream of smoke to billow from the peak of Cauldron Castle, signaling King Abracadabra and Queen Opunzayzme's imminent arrival.

Bored children entertained themselves by performing a favorite magic trick—turning each other into animals. In no time, there were fewer children and many more dogs, cats, pigs, cows, and a variety of exotic creatures.

One particularly ingenious girl turned her baby brother into a cupcake complete with creamy vanilla frosting and multicolored jimmies. Just when she was about to take a bite of her luscious creation, her mother flicked her wand and turned the cupcake back into the infant, much to the girl's disappointment.

Bored adults conjured food and drink, and before long, the worried crowd became quite festive. Conversations focused on the hope that Prince Thane would be punished with a wicked wand, for that type of punishment of a non-Hexidonian always called for a three-day celebration.

Finally a wisp of smoke rose from the castle, silencing the crowd as the animals changed back into children and the food and drink magically disappeared. The Hexidonians looked to the skies, desperate for the first glimpse of their king and queen.

Mike Muckraker, *Universal Scandals Tonight's* famous or infamous reporter, depending on one's personal opinion, pushed and shoved his way to the perfect spot as his news crew as well as reporters from other publications and news shows scurried after him.

The reporter from *Galaxy Fashion* magazine stopped to interview a particularly well-dressed wizard. But when she had the audacity to fondle the fine fabric of his fabulous robe, he stormed off in a huff.

Fulla Bulship from *Star Gazer* magazine, who, without conducting research, believed herself to be the most illustrious reporter in the universe, instantly started to spin a tall tale about what was happening before anything had happened.

A reporter for *AM Universe*, a popular morning show in Dimension III, thrust his mic at his assistant, stated arrogantly that due to his union status his shift was over, and demanded the assistant alert the reporter for *PM Universe* to take over.

Inside a large tent, the entire cast of the *Universe Today* morning show joked with each other about the many times they'd attempted to boost the show's ratings by allowing the king and queen of Hexidonia to transform them into strange creatures in front of a live audience. Pictures of those transformations popped up on a massive screen behind them.

Finally smoke from the castle turned into a black mass. The Hexidonians backed away and raised their wands in defense. Mike Muckraker raised his arm high over his head, mimicking the bravery of a military general holding back his troops and inspiring the news crews to hold their ground as the cloudy mass grew larger and larger, shuttering the sun and turning the blue sky black. The tips of the Hexidonians' wands glowed, casting an eerie light on the event.

From the smoke, an image of a flying beast emerged. When it landed in the middle of the crowd, the Hexidonians and the many news crews rushed for cover. As Mike Muckraker skedaddled for shelter, he yelled at his cameraperson to capture the great beast on video. The terrified cameraperson bravely stood before the beast, struggling to still his shaking hands and knees, desperate to get a focused image.

"It's Queen Matilda of Beastonia," a woman yelled. "What's she doing here?"

"She's not allowed here. Her kind was banned from Hexidonia thousands of years ago," an elderly man in a droopy wizard's hat said.

"Yet here she stands," another Hexidonian said.

The beast spewed fire on the crowd of Hexidonians, who defended themselves by pointing their wands at the dragon queen and chanting, *"Begone. Begone. For we have won. For we are wizards and you are scum."*

Instantly the great beast turned into a frumpy, middle-aged woman.

"Wilameena, you scoundrel," a large man said, wielding his wand at the enchantress. "Go away or I'll change you into something cute and cuddly. That ought to drive you nuts."

"I'm not here to play games with you. I'm here to warn you."

"Warn us about what?" the man asked.

"About the book."

The crowd fell silent. Not a single wizard knew how to respond to the enchantress's statement; not that they didn't know about the book, for everyone in the universe knew, but because they had been told to never mention it for fear of retribution from their own king and queen. After all, they believed only King Abracadabra and Queen Opunzayzme could handle the book without harm. At least that's what the king and queen had professed to their people.

"Hear me out," the enchantress said in a voice tinged with desperation. "I said I'm here to warn you about the book. It's been discovered. And it's in the possession of one who is way too young to understand its power."

"Why should we believe you? You're one of the most repugnant creatures in the universe," a woman said as she looked to the crowd for support.

"Yeah, repugnant. That's what you are," said a young man who clutched a small child as if to protect it from the vile enchantress.

"What you think of me isn't important. What's important is that you do not… I repeat… *Do not* allow King Abracadabra or Queen Opunzayzme to get their grubby hands on the book. Their intentions for wanting it are less than honorable."

"Like I said, why should we believe you? Ye of so little honor," the woman said.

"You probably want the book for yourself," a young man said.

Wilameena was about to defend her reputation when a clap of thunder and the sound of horses' hooves caused her and the crowd to look skyward. Out of the still-smoky sky, a chariot carrying King Abracadabra and Queen Opunzayzme careened toward the crowd.

"You have been warned." The enchantress's words echoed over the crowd as she disappeared.

The *Universal Scandals Tonight* cameraperson, who bravely captured every moment, rushed to the chariot as it landed in the center of the crowd where Wilameena, disguised as Queen Matilda, had stood. When it was obvious a big story was about to break, Mike Muckraker and the other news crews emerged from hiding.

King Abracadabra exited the chariot, but he didn't address his people. The Hexidonians booed, obviously insulted by their king's behavior. In response, the king of Hexidonia huffed at them and mumbled to himself. Then, as if something had totally unnerved him, he broke into a full run. His long robe billowed behind him, revealing his skinny legs covered to the calves by threadbare tattletale-gray socks. Needless to say, attempts by the reporters to get a statement about Prince Thane's future were unsuccessful.

Queen Opunzayzme remained in the chariot, triggering speculation as to her delayed appearance. One reporter commented, "In my opinion, the queen is too ashamed to greet her people. Could this be due to the failure of her and King Abracadabra to prove a child guilty of using magic?"

But that was far from the truth. For truth be told, Queen Opunzayzme had a whopping secret. Everyone agreed she looked gorgeous for a woman past childbearing years, let alone a woman more than a millennium old, making her youthfulness the talk of the universe. Behind her back, many referred to her as well-preserved. When asked how she maintained her flawlessly smooth skin, glossy black hair, and beautiful figure, she chalked it up to good genes and healthy living. But it was a lie. In fact, Queen Opunzayzme's eternal youth was due to her two addictions: King Kokoa's bonbons and one other—age-defying magic spells she performed on herself every day. They were personal, secret spells, and she planned on keeping them that way. However, while she'd been in Idlebury, her secret antiaging charms failed. And much to her horror, she had aged nearly one thousand years. For her people to see her for who she truly was would be too much for her to bear. So Queen Opunzayzme remained holed up, alone in the chariot as she pondered her predicament. "Why were our magic powers useless in Idlebury?" she mumbled. "Did this affect the effectiveness of my youthful charms? I'll get to the bottom of this if it's the last thing I do."

A few minutes later, the queen's head servant arrived carrying a case that protected the queen's favorite wand and her book of secret antiaging spells. The servant knocked on the chariot door to alert the queen as to her presence. A bony, wrinkled, knobby-fingered hand the color of a plucked chicken and covered with age spots emerged through the window and grabbed the case.

What happened next held the Hexidonians, the new crews, and the paparazzi spellbound. The chariot swayed back and forth. Bolts of lightning burst from inside. The queen's screams pierced the air. Everyone covered their ears to prevent shattered eardrums.

The servant held back a few Hexidonians who rushed the chariot in an attempt to rescue their queen. "Under the strictest order of the king, I am to allow no one near the queen," the servant said with utter authority as she pulled her wand from inside her smock and waved it at the crowd, creating a force field to keep the Hexidonians, press, and paparazzi at bay.

After nearly fifteen minutes of what sounded like a torturous experience, the chariot went still and silent. A few seconds later, the door opened and Queen Opunzayzme emerged, smiling and waving to a cheering crowd and looking like her old youthful self. With help from her servant, she daintily disembarked. She was about to address her people when the servant not so gently escorted her to the castle, silencing and disappointing the Hexidonians who were eager for information about their king and queen's trip to Idlebury.

Motioning for his camera crew to follow him as he tailed Queen Opunzayzme, Mike Muckraker from the *Universal Scandals Tonight* show noticed something odd about the queen's appearance. Although the queen looked like her ever-young self from the front, the rear view was a different story. Her hunched back, skinny legs, pale sagging skin, and sparse white hair gave away her true age. Worse, her clothes were ragged, offering a most unflattering view of her derriere. Mike Muckraker smiled to himself, happy he'd stumbled upon what could be the scandal of the millennium.

But there was something even more damaging to the queen. Unbeknownst to Queen Opunzayzme, a cameraperson from the *Galaxy Fashion Spotlight* show—a subsidiary of *Galaxy Fashion* magazine, the universally renowned fashion publication in which Queen Opunzayzme appeared frequently for her eternal youthfulness and beauty—had been filming through the chariot window before the servant created the force field that cloaked the chariot in secrecy.

As fortune would have it, the force field trapped the cameraperson, allowing him to record every detail of the queen's transformation. He rushed over to Stella Grabber, the award-winning reporter for the *Galaxy Fashion Spotlight* show, and showed her the video of what had transpired in the chariot.

Ms. Grabber patted the cameraperson on the back. "Roll film," she demanded. When the cameraperson signaled for her to start her broadcast, she grinned and said, "Lesser shows and publications would like you to believe today's big news story is about Prince Thane wagging his little wand and chanting some old curse. Well, I've got sizzling news for you. Queen Opunzayzme is harboring a secret that women… and men… would kill or die for. It's a scandal of universal proportions. Film at eleven. Cut."

Mike Muckraker, who had overheard the reporter from the *Galaxy Fashion Spotlight*, rushed over and grabbed the camera from the camera operator. "I saw it first. This is my story," he yelled as he tugged but failed to dislodge the camera from the cameraperson's grasp.

"Your story? If it was stale and boring, then it would definitely be your story," Stella Grabber replied, poking fun at the famously obnoxious Mike Muckraker. "But this is the most intriguing... the most revealing... the hottest... the most scandalous story of the millennium. And it's exclusively mine."

"It's mine," Mike Muckraker whined. "And if you don't give me the footage, I'll rake you over the coals. I'll do a tell-all exposé about our relationship and your crazy behaviors. Then you'll see who the biggest star in the universe is."

"Oh please. You aren't the biggest anything." Stella Grabber giggled and then paused. "Oh, excuse me; I do believe I'm wrong. You are in fact the biggest... hmm... the biggest something in the universe." She tapped her lip, pretending to search her memory for what it could be. "Oh yes. You're the biggest *jerk* in the universe, and I have the footage and photos to prove it."

Mike Muckraker's face turned red. "Come," he demanded of his news crew as he stomped off. "I've got a story that will ruin her."

But his crew shrugged off his attempt to soothe his wounded ego because, as usual, he had nothing on Stella Grabber.

⟶◈◈◈⟵

Queen Opunzayzme proudly floated into Cauldron Castle, totally unaware of her incomplete transformation, including the exposure of her wrinkled, droopy derriere. Once inside, she gently landed in front of a gargantuan mirror and examined herself. "I look perfectly perfect," she said and then greeted her staff with a smile and a nod. In return, her staff curtsied and bowed. But as the queen floated toward the grand staircase en route to her chambers, the servant who carried her wand case and who floated behind her gasped, stopping the queen in midair.

"What, pray tell, is the problem?"

"In all due respect, Your Majesty, now is not the time to discuss the matter. We can discuss it when we get to your chambers."

"I will not allow you or any other servant to keep something from me. So what is it?"

"If you insist, ma'am, your... Well, your... your buttocks are showing."

"My what?"

"Your buttocks, ma'am."

"That is ridiculous." Queen Opunzayzme glared at the servant. "If one's buttocks were showing, one would definitely notice. Now wouldn't one?"

"Yes, ma'am. I suppose one would."

"Well then. Onward and upward." The queen continued to float up the stairs, exposing her shriveled buttocks to the horror and amusement of the castle staff.

The servant could barely contain her laughter as the queen and she ascended the stairs.

"Stop sniveling, Magilica. It is most unbecoming of a grown woman," Queen Opunzayzme said.

"Yes, ma'am." Magilica snickered. "I'm sorry, ma'am."

When Queen Opunzayzme and Magilica arrived at the queen's chamber, a guard opened the door for the queen as a male servant holding a gold tray approached her. On the tray was a black envelope. The queen snatched it without a polite word to the servant, who remained in place as he patiently waited for the queen to excuse him. Instead, she brushed past him and entered her room.

Queen Opunzayzme's face flushed and her hands shook, for the envelope she held bore a gold wax seal pressed with the king of Deadonia's emblem—a skull and crossbones. She held the envelope to her chest and, gasping for breath, stumbled to a chair positioned in front of a window.

"Magilica, please leave me."

"But ma'am, we have that little issue to discuss."

"We have nothing to discuss. Now leave."

"Yes, Your Majesty." Magilica curtsied and exited the queen's chambers, after which she and the guard shared a hearty laugh regarding the queen's appearance.

But Queen Opunzayzme didn't hear them, for she was completely captivated by a letter from an old love, a love she publicly denied and privately yearned for, a love more powerful and potent than what she shared with King Abracadabra. Tears streamed down her cheeks as she savored every word written by the one man she loved with her heart and soul.

> *My Dearest Opunzayzme:*
>
> *It is with great longing and a heavy heart that I write to you. I hope you know my undying love for you has withstood the ravages of time. And although we both know we are not intended to share our lives, my heart, yes, my coal-black heart longs for you. The love that unites others has divided us. And although I offer no excuses for the hell I put you through during the conflicts between*

our kingdoms and dimensions, I implore you to forgive my past hurtful deeds and words so we can unite for the welfare of the universe. So I'll get to the point.

As you know, Prince Thane of Idlebury has used, or possibly misused, magic. That in and of itself is of little importance to most of the universe, but I fully understand it is of paramount importance to you, King Abracadabra, and the people of Hexidonia. But what concerns me most is the young prince's knowledge of the ancient saying written eons ago by an author who shall remain nameless. If you remember, King Heroian was the last person to utter the horrible phrase and live. The fact that Thane is still alive is quite mysterious indeed.

Anyway, thanks to the Universal Scandals magazine report of Prince Thane's nocturnal activities, the entire universe is aware that the most treasured book of magic has been discovered and more than likely is in the possession of this mischievous child. Thankfully, due to the fact that most beings are dim-witted and lazy (present company excepted, of course), I believe few to none have figured out the ramifications of this. But as we both know, it's only a matter of time before the dimmest of the dim-witted figures out that great power is theirs for the taking, and when they do, creatures everywhere, whether they harbor good or bad intentions, will fight to the death to gain possession of the book. This is perfectly understandable as ownership of the book ensures powers beyond the wildest imagination. What terrifies me is that at this moment, the power of the universe is in the hands of a ten-year-old boy.

You may be asking yourself why I'm detailing facts of which you're already painfully aware. Well, here's the *answer. It is my love for you that compels me to make this pledge. When I gain possession of the book from Prince Thane, that snotty-nosed, arrogant, ne'er-do-well who has everyone fooled by his remarkable good looks, I promise to share its glorious power with you and only you. But to do so, I need your complete and utter confidence and loyalty.*

If you are willing to embark on this magnificent adventure with me, meet me at the edge of the Slothful Forest, on the outskirts of the kingdom of Idlebury, Dimension XIII, on Saturday next at the stroke of midnight. I believe my superior sly intelligence coupled with your incredible magic abilities will enable us to gain possession of A Magic Maniac's Many Ways to Make Mischief.

Hope to see you there.

Your most dedicated lover,

Morrebidd, king of Deadonia, the kingdom of the dead.

PS: I hope you'll have your little problem solved by then.

Queen Opunzayzme read King Morrebidd's letter three times, ignoring the PS for she didn't know of what little problem he wrote. But she read the part about how he pledged to share the power of the universe with her and only her at least a dozen times.

"He loves me. He wants to share unlimited power with me." She squealed as she swirled across her chamber, clutching the letter to her chest.

As she celebrated her upcoming alliance with King Morrebidd and plotted how she'd get out of Hexidonia for their liaison in the Slothful Forest, she passed a full-length mirror.

The mirror coughed in an attempt to get her attention. But

the queen was consumed with excitement—an emotion she had not felt for hundreds of years.

"Ahem," the mirror announced, trying to garner the queen's attention. "Hellooo," it said, this time loud enough to bring the queen out of her fantasy world.

"What?" Queen Opunzayzme snapped at the mirror. "What could you possibly want?"

"Well, if you'll turn around and look at your backside, I think you'll thank me."

"Thank you? Whatever for?" The queen turned her back to the mirror and twisted her neck to check out her rear. When she saw her shriveled buttocks, sagging arms, hunched back, and nearly bald head, she fainted.

"You'll thank me later," the mirror said.

CHAPTER ELEVEN
WILAMEENA'S DECEPTION

G wen stood in the cavernous hallway, leaning against Thane's door as she tried to catch her breath and recover her courage. She felt betrayed by Blabberdish's antics in Thane's room, leaving her in a state of anger and confusion. *What am I supposed to do now*, she wondered.

From the corner of her eye, she saw Thane crack open the huge door to Queen Filanthropi's bedchamber and squeeze in. She was about to follow him when she saw what looked like a flattened worm on the floor next to her right foot.

"Blabberdish?" Gwen stooped to get a closer look. "Did I step on you? Oh no," she said as she examined the squashed worm. She lifted the lifeless worm ever so gently. Closer inspection revealed it wasn't a worm at all but a bit of an old shoelace. "Blabberdish, you beast. You deliberately left this here. I know you did, you good-for-nothing, slimy, spineless worm."

On her way to Queen Filanthropi's chambers, Gwen saw Blabberdish slink under the queen's bedchamber door. A chill ran down her spine. Goose bumps covered her arms. Instinct told her the worm was up to no good. Adrenaline pulsed through her veins, allowing her to race down the hallway at top speed in hopes she'd reach Thane before Blabberdish harmed him. But she was too late. Under the control of Blabberdish, Thane, limp and obviously unconscious, floated near the ceiling.

Wand in one hand and struggling to hold an oversized notebook in the other, the bookworm chanted a harrowing curse. "The Great Wizard speaks to me. His every command is my will. He's given me power. He's given me strength. He's demanded it's you I must kill. Die, die, shrivel, and dry. Take your last breath and rise to the sky. No questions to ask. No answers to give. For you must die so the Great Wizard can live."

Gwen took a flying leap at Blabberdish. But she was no match for the bookworm's quick reflexes as he flashed his wand behind him and instantaneously foiled her approach. Frozen in place, she was powerless to help her brother.

Blabberdish recited the curse over and over as Thane remained unconscious and airborne. A flash of light created a warm yellow glow that blanketed Thane. Sparkles captured by the light engulfed the boy.

"Fairy dust," Gwen said as her anguish turned to joy, knowing the fairy dust would protect Thane from Blabberdish's spell.

As the effect of Blabberdish's magic curse weakened, he chanted louder and faster. As he did, Thane flickered in and out of existence. The yellow light that shielded the boy began to pulsate. It flashed faster and faster, spewing fairy dust. The sparkling dust covered Blabberdish and dissolved him like salt on a common garden slug. His tiny gold wand fell to the floor and rolled under the queen's bed. Despite excruciating pain, the bookworm refused to relinquish his power. He continued his chant until his voice became so squeaky his words were indecipherable, rendering both the worm and his curse powerless. His shriveled body jerked as his life bubbled to an end. Silence filled the room, only to be broken by the thud of Thane crashing to the floor.

Gwen rushed over to him. "Are you okay?"

Thane tried to sit up. "I'm fine, but Blabberdish isn't."

"Well, he got what he deserved," Gwen sniped.

"No, he didn't."

"How can you say that? He just tried to kill you."

"He's my best friend. I know him." Thane pointed at the shriveled carcass of the creature that had tried to kill him. "And that wasn't Blabberdish."

"Are you sure?"

"Yeah. When we were sucked into the hole and Prudence appeared and then changed into Blabberdish, I knew something was wrong."

"Why?"

"He wasn't wearing his glasses. He's as blind as a bat. He always wears his glasses. So someone was pretending to be him."

"But who would do such a thing?" Gwen asked. "Who would want to kill you?"

"Wilameena," Gwen and Thane blurted out in unison.

"Something's happened to Blabberdish, and Wilameena has his wand." Thane rose and dashed to the door. "Come on, we have to find him."

Gwen charged after him.

When the coast was clear, the withered remains of the creature stirred. It wiggled and writhed in pain. Soon it was motionless as if defeated by death. A few minutes later, it stirred again as its body began to grow. It got larger and larger as it morphed into a tall, handsome young man with a head of beautiful blond hair. He was dressed in an ornate robe, distinguishing him as none other than the Great Wizard.

The Great Wizard fell to his knees and scrambled over to Queen Filanthropi's bed. He lifted the bedspread and peered underneath. Flat on his belly, he swept his arms under the bed in search of Blabberdish's tiny wand. He found nothing but lint, a pearl button, and a rather large key. He pocketed the key and shimmed under the bed to the side of the bed closest to the window. Light streaming in illuminated the room. Then he saw it. Stuck in the gap between two floorboards, the tiny gold wand shimmered. He reached for it, but it evaded capture. He was about to chant it out of its hiding place when the door to Queen Filanthropi's bedchamber squeaked open. The Great Wizard snapped his fingers, said, "Invisible awareness," and hid in a dark corner.

He watched Morgana enter the queen's chamber and scan the room as if to make sure she was alone. She went to the queen's dressing table, opened a drawer, reached deep inside, turned a latch, and looked in. "Be still me heart," she said as she clasped her hands over her chest. She closed the drawer and scurried out of the room.

Maintaining his invisibility, the Great Wizard was about to venture out when he saw Blabberdish slither under a raised floorboard and disappear. A few seconds later, Blabberdish reappeared, busily looking for something and muttering aloud, "Oh no. My wand's gone. I'm in a heap of trouble. In the wrong hands, it could do oodles of harm. Father will kill me if I've lost it."

Blabberdish slunk around the queen's bedchamber until something shiny caught his eye. "Oh... there it is." He slithered under the bed and retrieved his wand. He peeked out from under the bed to make sure the coast was clear. When he saw he was alone, he ventured back to the floorboard under which the magic book was hidden. Just as he started to slip under the floorboard, something or someone snatched him.

"Give me the wand," the Great Wizard said in a powerful whisper.

Blabberdish tried to hide the wand behind him. "No. It's mine."

"Visible awareness," the Great Wizard said, regaining visibility. He grabbed the tiny wand and tried to yank it out of Blabberdish's hand. But the bookworm was extraordinarily strong and determined not to forfeit his wand.

Eventually Blabberdish proved to be no match for the Great Wizard, who flung the worm by his wand until the tiny creature lost his grip and was hurled out the window.

"That ought to teach you." The Great Wizard held the wand, which was no bigger than a sewing needle. He squinted with his left eye as if he were looking through a telescope and examined it. Without taking his eye off the wand, the Great Wizard reached in his robe pocket and removed an intricately decorated velvet pouch, befitting someone of tremendous status. He clenched the wand between his front teeth, opened the pouch, carefully removed the wand from between his teeth, admired it again, kissed it, and dropped it in the soft, plush pouch. He secured the pouch with a firm tug on its satin cord and placed it in a secret pocket inside his robe.

The Great Wizard knelt next to the floorboard under which Blabberdish had retreated and then emerged. He carefully lifted it, revealing a battered metal box. With eyes wide with wonder and his heart pounding with excitement, he lifted the box from its hiding place. He held it for a moment and ran his hand over the worn latch. He took a deep breath and opened it. It was empty.

"Who would hide an empty box? This has to be it. This has to be where the magic book is kept." He turned the box upside down and shook it furiously. Filled with rage, he shook and shook as if expecting to dislodge a book that wasn't there.

Weakened by anger, the Great Wizard flashed in and out, momentarily transforming into his true self—Wilameena. Unable to maintain the energy needed to continue her deception, the image of the Great Wizard and the old enchantress flickered in and out like two ghosts engaged in a wrestling match. Wilameena tried desperately to keep up her false image. She failed.

"Lies. Myths. Rubbish. Rumors. There's no magic book," Wilameena griped as she transformed into herself. She threw the metal box to the floor and stormed to the door of the queen's bedchamber. She reached for the doorknob and hesitated. "What's wrong with me? I'm losing my magic powers. This is the second time in only a few days I've been unable to maintain my disguise and perform my usual tricks. This can't be."

Wilameena rested with her back against the door. The enchantress reached into her dress pocket, wrapped her stubby, nail-bitten fingers around the soft velvet pouch, and sighed with relief. "At least I managed to get the stupid worm's wand," she mumbled. "Maybe I haven't lost it after all." She morphed into Morgana and slowly opened the door before stepping into the hallway.

"Oh, there you are, Morgana," Oof said, appearing out of nowhere. "Queen Filanthropi requests your presence in the dining room. May I suggest you skedaddle?"

The servant woman gave Oof a blank stare and, without

uttering a word, walked toward the staircase. Her knees shook. Her palms perspired. "Oof, my one and only love," she whispered. "As much as I wish I could declare my affections for you, I'm happy you do not know it was me and not Morgana you spoke to." She giggled. "The Soul Seeker knows not what he has done. He created a monster when he gave me the power to change myself into anyone and anything I want."

Oof watched as the woman who looked like Morgana disappeared down the stairs. When she was out of earshot, he shook his head and mumbled, "Oh Wilameena, your games are so obvious. Will you never stop?"

The old man instantly appeared in the queen's bedchamber. He saw the empty metal box on the floor. He examined it and then gently laid it in its hiding place under the floorboard. With the heel of his spit-shined shoe, he stomped on the floorboard until the nail was flush with the board. He began to exit the room when he jerked back and walked over to the queen's bed. He looked around as if to check the room for spies before he removed two handkerchiefs from the breast pocket of his jacket and placed them on the floor, side by side, exactly six inches apart. He raised his pant legs and flipped the tails of his jacket as he gently placed his knees on the handkerchiefs. He lifted the side of the bedspread and peered under the queen's bed. He saw only dust and a pearl button. The key he'd hidden there was gone.

The usually stoic man grimaced and grunted his displeasure. Then Oof did something that would have shocked anyone who knew him. With total disregard for his clothes, he sprawled flat on his stomach, pushed himself under the bed, and swept the area as if he were making a snow angel.

Coughing from dust inhalation, Oof sat on the floor with his back against the bed frame, and panted. "Damn you,

Wilameena," he muttered. "You took the key. I only hope you do not know what it is for."

After he caught his breath, he picked up the two handkerchiefs, meticulously folded them, placed them in his breast pocket, and left the queen's bedchamber as if nothing had happened, obviously unaware of the dust that clung to his usually impeccable clothes.

With his head held high in his typical haughty manner, he walked back to his quarters. On his way down the corridor, he noticed Prudence's door was ajar. He glanced at the opening and saw the child looking at him. He pretended not to notice and went on his way.

When Oof had passed, Prudence slipped out of her room and skipped down the hall to her mother's chambers for some much-needed attention. But a beautiful velvet pouch pushed up against the wall just outside her mother's bedchamber caught her eye. She grabbed it and ran back to her quarters to investigate her find.

Safely inside her room, Prudence examined the pouch and said, "Pretty. Mine." As she rubbed it against her cheek, the pouch glowed, immersing her in soft light. "Ooh," Prudence exclaimed. "What's inside?" She pulled the cord and peeked in the bag. When she reached in the velvet bag, something that felt like a needle pricked her finger. Before she could scream for help, she disappeared. The pouch fell to the floor.

Chapter Twelve
Oof's Redemption

O of was nearly down the long rickety staircase when a voice startled him.

"Ahem."

Oof stopped but didn't look up or around. It was certainly not within his character to let anyone see him in any state other than complete control.

"Ahem. Over here," someone said.

Oof took a deep breath, then exhaled as if annoyed at the interruption. He looked up at a massive old mirror that had hung on the wall for a thousand years. Its ornate wooden frame was worn and partially eaten by woodworms. Its glass, which had obviously been shattered and sloppily reassembled, was only partially reflective due to black patches from a millennium of wear.

"Yes?" Oof said, avoiding eye contact with the mirror. "I assume you have an extraordinarily good reason for impeding my progress."

"Impeding your progress?" the mirror responded. "You're lucky I decided to talk to you after what you did to me."

"As I recall, you slid off the wall and tumbled down the

stairs in a rare attempt at usefulness."

"Slid off the wall with a little help from you," the mirror chided. "That cracked me up," it said and then giggled.

"That was long ago. I was a young man and you… Well, dare I say you were a beautiful piece of art?" Oof quickly examined the mirror. "But I see the years have not treated you well."

"Nor have they been particularly gentle to you."

Oof clenched his teeth, fearing that for the first time in nearly a thousand years, he was about to lose his cool. "What is it you want?"

"I have a message for you from your father."

"There is nothing he can say that would be of any interest to me," Oof grumbled, once again refusing to look into the mirror.

"Oh, but I think there is. But first you must let go of your ridiculous childhood grudge against him and look at me."

Oof began to descend the stairs again. "No, never."

"So you are an arrogant, coldhearted, good-for-nothing fool," a man said. "It is no wonder a woman never loved you."

Blood rushed to Oof's face, turning his usually pale skin scarlet. He rapidly turned toward the mirror, his eyes full of rage, and said, "How dare you—"

"I see I have your undivided attention." A handsome young man with wavy brown hair, dressed in the finest wizard's garb, peered at Oof. He spoke from behind an ornate desk in a room that would be the envy of the greatest of wizards—cauldrons of potions bubbled and steamed; a miniature ogreish creature tested wands, tossing the faulty ones into a multicolored fire; without the aid of a writer, a quill wrote on the parchment pages of a massive book; and shelves of meticulously maintained magic books lined the walls—but on one shelf, a gold vault with an intricate tumble lock sat between the books.

Etched on the face of the vault were the words A MAGIC MANIAC'S MANY WAYS TO MAKE MISCHIEF—GONE MISSING.

"Father," Oof muttered, momentarily regaining his composure and looking at the man with childlike awe before his typical, arrogant sneer returned. "What has prompted the pleasure of your company after so many years?"

"You still have not forgiven me for my *minor* indiscretion?" Oof's father asked.

"No. Although it seems silly now, it was extremely embarrassing to me at the time," Oof said, averting his eyes.

"You were a child."

"I was in love." Oof glowered at his father. "And you ridiculed my affections. It is because of you that I never loved anyone."

"If that is what you need to believe."

"You hurt me deeply... You never apologized."

"You were twelve years old." Oof's father waved his hand in a dismissive manner. "How serious could your love have been?"

Oof glared at his father. "Deeper than you will ever know."

"I am sorry. I did not know someone so young could love so deeply."

"They can. I did. But your apology, if that is what it is, is too late. As you can see, I am a very old man. What woman would want me now?"

"If you had stayed in the family business, you would have eternal youth. But being bullheaded like your mother... Well, you can see where that has taken you."

"Do not ridicule my mother!" Oof yelled. "She understood and loved me."

"As I did her…" In a soft, caring voice, Oof's father added, "…and you."

Tears welled in Oof's eyes. "I did not know you loved me."

"I did. I do. Probably as deeply as you love your brother… and Wilameena."

At the mention of Wilameena, tears streamed down Oof's cheeks. With his dusty handkerchief, he dried his tears. "She has become an old busybody."

"Nonetheless, she deserves to be loved…" Oof's father's eyes expressed the many feelings he'd been unable to express for years. "…as do you."

Oof blew his nose in his handkerchief. "She would never want me."

"I think she would if she knew you still loved her."

Oof choked back tears. "I have always wondered, but I am afraid to find out she does not harbor affections for me anymore. It is the Soul Seeker she loves."

"Not true. It is nothing more than sibling rivalry. What are you going to do about it?"

"What can I do?"

"I think you know. I think you have always known. You let your anger at me stop you from achieving your greatness. But that is not what I need to discuss. I know who wrote *A Magic Maniac's Many Ways to Make Mischief*—the greatest magic book ever written. But remember, it is full of magic tricks, charms, spells, and incantations, none of which have any real power. The power of the book is in the belief it is powerful. Nonetheless, it must be kept out of the hands of King Abracadabra and Queen Opunzayzme. And by all means, do not let King Morrebidd even glance at it. You prove who you are, and the universe will be at your command. If you let the book fall into the wrong hands, the universe is doomed."

"But I cannot do it alone. I carry a heavy burden."

"Tap the power and energy of Gwendolyn, Mistofisee, Thane, and Blabberdish. They are your allies. Put them to good use. And my son, keep a close eye on Prudence. She is quite inquisitive and possibly dangerous." Oof's father's image began to flicker and ripple. "My time is up. I am truly sorry for hurting you. Remember, my son, I love you. It is time for you to love yourself so you can love others. That is the only way you can do what needs to be done in order to better the lives of all who reside in this great universe." One last flash and Oof's father was gone.

Oof sat on the stairs and wept. It had been hundreds of years since emotions had overcome him. The conversation he'd just had with his father raced through his head. He knew his life had changed. He felt it to his core. Soon his thoughts returned to the job before him. He had to find the book, and he had to find it before anyone else did.

The image of Prudence watching him through the opening of her bedroom door haunted Oof. So he changed his mind about going downstairs. He wiped his tearstained face with his handkerchief, dusted off his clothes, and ascended the stairs on his way to Prudence's room. The door was still ajar. He pushed it open only to find Prudence was gone. He spotted a velvet pouch on the floor. He looked inside. What he saw sent shivers down his spine—a mini wand, unmistakably covered in blood.

"She would not. She could not. She did not. Her soul is in danger, and she is only a baby."

Chapter Thirteen
The Reappearing Notebook

Voices from downstairs deterred Gwen and Thane from sneaking out of Idlebury Castle via the staircase. So they decided to take refuge in Thane's room to plot their next move. As they skidded to a stop in front of Thane's bedroom door, Gwen saw the top of Oof's bald head bobbing as he slowly descended the stairs.

"There's Oof. Hurry. Open the door or he'll see us," Gwen demanded.

Thane tugged on the door. "I can't."

"Move!" Gwen shoved Thane aside and pushed on the door. It was stuck. She took a deep breath, closed her eyes, and said, "I wish I may. I wish I might. I wish this door was not closed tight." She pushed on the door again, and the twosome stumbled inside.

Thane rolled his eyes. "Awesome. That was *sooo* cool."

Gwen smirked at Thane's sarcasm. "If you're such a pain in the butt now, what will you be like in a few more years?" she said. Gwen was about to lock the door when she heard Oof talking. She peered out the door. Oof was alone on the stairs, but he looked up at the old mirror and appeared engaged in conversation with someone.

"Does that mirror talk?" Gwen asked as she watched Thane search his room for something.

"What mirror?"

"The one that hangs over the staircase," Gwen said as she continued to monitor Oof's behavior.

"Yeah, I think it does. I saw the Soul Seeker talking to it once."

"The Soul Seeker? What was he doing here?"

"He's here a lot." Thane rummaged in his desk, obviously more interested in his search than in conversation with his older sister.

"You sure?"

"Yeah. I see him all the time."

"Has anyone else seen him?"

"I *don't* know. I think Prudence has seen him. One day I heard her running to her room crying and yelling, 'Bad man, scary man.' She told Mother there was a big monster in her room."

"That's typical kid stuff. I doubt if she's seen him."

Thane shrugged and continued to search his room for some unknown object as Gwen went back to studying Oof.

"I don't believe it," Gwen said. "I think Oof is crying."

"Let me see." Thane pushed Gwen away from the door and peeked through the opening. "Wow. He *is* crying."

"I guess he's human after all."

"I think he's scary, but Mother likes him." Thane relinquished the door to Gwen.

"Shh… he's coming this way. Now he's headed to Prudence's room."

Thane bolted out of his room and started down the hall. "Let's go see what he's up to."

"Thane, no!" Gwen yelled as softly as possible. But she was too late, for Thane had miraculously leaped through the air and silently landed at Prudence's door. "How did he do that?" she whispered and then shut the door so Oof wouldn't see her.

Thane watched Oof pick up a velvet pouch from the floor and study it. Then he heard the old man say, "She would not. She could not. She did not. Her soul is in danger, and she is only a baby."

Much to Thane's surprise, Oof, in possession of the velvet pouch, disappeared into thin air. No fairy dust, no bolt of lightning, no whoosh. He was simply there one second and gone the next.

Thane took another leap, flew down the hallway, and like a ghost, passed through the closed door to his quarters. In his excitement to tell Gwen what he'd seen and heard, he failed to notice he'd achieved one of the most difficult magic tricks of all—momentary dematerialization. But his room was empty; Gwen was gone. Thane ran to the window and saw Gwen running into the Slothful Forest.

Angry that Gwen had left him behind, Thane immediately started to plot his revenge. "Who does she think she is? I'll show her who the most powerful person in the family is," he said as he headed for the door. But something on his bed caught his eye and stopped him in his tracks. It was his notebook. Mysteriously it had reappeared. Thane picked it up and flipped through the pages. "I hope it's all here," he muttered as he quickly turned to the middle of the notebook. But everything wasn't there. Someone had torn out page twenty-five. But who and why? *Who other than Blabberdish knows about the power of the curse I copied from* A Magic Maniac's Many Ways to Make

Mischief? he wondered. "Blabberdish has some explaining to do."

With his notebook in hand, Thane jumped out his bedroom window and floated to a gentle landing in the courtyard, a feat that surprised him. But Thane was too young and naïve to realize he wasn't controlling the magic, it was controlling him, and that was a dangerous sign.

Despite the number of Idleburians idling about, no one noticed Thane—no one with the exception of Blabberdish, who was still woozy and wobbly from being flung out the queen's bedchamber window coupled with a not-so-gentle landing on the stone path.

"Thane!" Blabberdish yelled.

Thane heard his friend's voice but didn't see him. "Blabberdish? Where are you?"

"If you'd look down, I do believe you'll see me standing in front of your left foot."

Thane picked up his friend and balanced him in the palm of his hand. "I have so much to tell you. Wilameena, disguised as the Great Wizard, tried to kill me. But fairy dust saved me."

"Good for you, my dear boy."

"By the way, where have you been?"

"Well, it's a long story, but since you asked… I was in your mother's bedchamber. I squeezed under the floorboard, as I have zillions of times, to retrieve my wand, but it wasn't in the box. I was scared silly I'd lost it. Much to my relief, I saw it under your mother's bed. I scurried after it and happily fetched it. But on my way back to the box, a big, strong man tried to steal my wand."

"So?"

"So he looked like a wizard. You know, a long robe, rings on every finger—"

"Wizard? What sort of wizard?"

"I don't know. Just your typical wizard," Blabberdish said. "Anyway, I held on for dear life—"

"Was he old?" Thane asked.

"No. In fact, he was rather young and nice-looking. Now if you'd *please* let me finish my story."

Thane tilted his head. "Go on."

"Thank you. As I was going to say, the wizard shook me so hard I lost my grip and was tossed out the window. Next thing I knew, I was in another dimension, surrounded by glowing, giggling, twinkling, twittering balls of light. But that's not the worst of it. I looked over and saw a huge, and I mean huge, green claw. Attached to the claw was an enormous dragon. Fortunately for me, he was quite friendly. He calls himself Mistofisee."

"Mistofisee?" Thane exclaimed. "He's the prince of Beastonia."

"Whatever. What was most odd was he was crying, and as his tears fell from his massive snout, they popped the twinkling lights. One by one, pop, pop, pop."

"What's so weird about that?"

"The lights loved it. They squealed with de...light. Excuse the pun." Blabberdish laughed uncontrollably at his own joke.

"Okay, so the lights love being destroyed?" Thane said impatiently.

"Exactly. But here's Mistofisee's misfortune. His tears are toxic to every living creature, with the possible exception of his mother, who, by the way, was killed by the lovely little lights when they caused her to fall to her death. When she smashed into the ground, she created a mushroom cloud that snuffed out all light for millions of miles into the universe."

Thane groaned as Blabberdish's story became silly and unbelievable. "Yeah. Sure. No one and nothing can harm the queen of Beastonia. She's the largest creature in the entire universe. Besides, don't you think if all light in the universe was snuffed out, it would be dark and dusty right now?"

The words were barely out of Thane's mouth when a dust cloud engulfed Idlebury. Immediately the frightened Idleburians scurried to their homes, coughing and covering their mouths, noses, and eyes.

"Told ya," Blabberdish said.

With one hand over his mouth and nose and the other clutching Blabberdish, Thane ran into the Slothful Forest for two reasons. One, for protection from the falling dust, and two, because with the news of the queen of Beastonia's death and the questionable safety of Mistofisee, he knew finding Gwen was a priority.

"Hey, there's more." Blabberdish's voice trailed off, muffled from Thane's closed fist. "Where are you taking me?"

Chapter Fourteen
Thane Tells a Whopper

The thick foliage of the Slothful Forest provided blessed relief from the dust storm. But because the dust obscured the sunlight, the forest was darker and eerier than usual. Nonetheless, Thane trudged onward.

"Egads. This place stinks," Thane said, pinching his nose with one hand and opening the other so Blabberdish could regain his freedom.

"I've smelled worse," Blabberdish said, rubbing his nose and eyes.

"You've smelled worse?"

"Well, sort of… I got stuck in a really bad book titled *The Search for Intelligent Life in Dumbdonia: Where Ignorance is Bliss and Bliss is Ignorance.* The storyline was so dumb no one bothered to read it. In fact, no one ever opened it. So if you think it stank when it was published, imagine how bad it smelled after not being opened for a thousand years. A bookworm's worst nightmare." Blabberdish jumped on Thane's shoulder. "So what are we doing here?"

"We're looking for Gwen. We need some light. Do you have your wand?"

"I told you the wizard took it. Where's yours?"

"Don't know. It wasn't in its hiding place. I looked everywhere for it, but couldn't—" Thane stopped and looked around. "Did you hear that?"

"Hear what?"

A shadowy figure clad in a black cape with its face concealed by an oversized hood appeared before them. The weight of its enormous body cracked twigs and crunched dried leaves that littered the floor of the Slothful Forest. As the being emerged into the hazy forest, he remained silent.

"Do you see that?" Blabberdish whispered.

"I'm *not* blind." Thane approached the being. "It's the Soul Seeker. Nothing to be afraid of."

The Soul Seeker raised his hand, warning Thane to stand still. "Stop. Do not come closer. You are not out of danger. King Abracadabra is pursuing you as we speak. Queen Opunzayzme and King Morrebidd are plotting to confiscate the magic book you have hidden. If you do not do as I say, they will succeed in hunting you down and killing you to get their hands on the coveted book."

"I don't have it."

"What do you mean, you do not have it?" The Soul Seeker grabbed Thane by the collar. "Have you lost it? That could be calamitous."

"I don't know… Someone… someone took it."

"Who would be idiotic enough to take the book?"

"Wilameena. She has it. I swear."

"I should have known." The Soul Seeker released his grip on Thane. "The most powerful magic book is in the hands of a total idiot. You are in dire danger." The Soul Seeker looked at a large bush behind him as if something or someone had rustled its branches. When he saw no one, he snapped his attention back to Thane and yelled, "Return to Idlebury Castle at once. And do *not* follow Gwendolyn. She is on a mission. She must succeed. If you interfere, she will fail, you will be dead, and the universe will be thrown into chaos."

Thane didn't move or utter a word.

"Get out of here. *Now!*" the Soul Seeker screamed as he took to the sky, the dusty air clouding his ascent.

"What does interfere mean?" Thane asked Blabberdish.

Blabberdish jumped from Thane's shoulder and landed in his hand, shaking from his first encounter with the Soul Seeker. "It… it means… to get in the way."

"I won't get in Gwen's way. Let's go."

"No. The Soul Seeker clearly told you to go back to Idlebury Castle at once."

"He was just trying to scare me."

"Worked for me," Blabberdish said as he jumped out of Thane's hand and onto the filthy, disgusting forest floor.

"Sissy," Thane said and then walked farther into the Slothful Forest on a quest to find his sister.

Blabberdish shook his head and followed Thane. Suddenly a bird swooped down, nabbed him, and flew off. "Help! Help!" he yelled as he wiggled, attempting to escape the bird's death grip.

When Thane noticed that his friend was in a serious predicament, he instinctively reached for his wand, but it wasn't there. "I don't have my wand," he yelled. "I can't help you. Use your magic, you nincompoop."

"Oh, that's just brilliant. Wish I had thought of it myself," Blabberdish yelled back. "I don't know what spell to use."

"Think of something. Anything."

Blabberdish chanted the only incantation he could remember. "Blabber, dabble, snabble, and snoo. Crittle, brittle, prittle, and droo. Wally, winkle, stinkle, and croo. Mumbo, jumbo, crumbo, and zoo."

It worked. The bird flew off, seemingly unaware Blabberdish had slipped from its grasp.

Thane watched Blabberdish plummet to the smelly, mucky ground. "Oh no, he's a goner," he said as he raced to his friend's aid. He placed the bookworm in the palm of his hand and gently stroked him. "Blabberdish? Are you okay?"

"I'm okay," Blabberdish said, gasping and coughing.

"Where did you learn that charm?"

"It's in the book on page 255. It's the charm that gets you into Beastonia's secret society. I'm surprised you don't know it since you've jumped way ahead in our lessons."

"No, I haven't."

"You can't fool me. I saw your notebook."

"So *you're* the one who stole page twenty-five."

Blabberdish looked down and shuffled his feet. "I'm insulted you would accuse me of such disloyalty." The worm pointed his finger at Thane. "Last I saw it, it was on your bed. What's on page twenty-five that's so important?"

Thane stared at Blabberdish as a horrible thought raced through his head—*Wilameena took my notebook. That means she has the log of my personal magic chants. Now I am in big trouble.* "Never mind. Let's go find Gwen."

"But the Soul Seeker said—"

"I don't care what he said. No one is going to take the magic book from me. It's rightfully mine."

"But you told the Soul Seeker Wilameena took it, so it would appear someone has already stolen it from you."

"I didn't want him to get it. It's under the floorboard in my mother's bedchamber inside the metal box, like always."

Blabberdish shook his head. "No… it's… not. I was just there. The box is empty."

"*What?* My future and the future of the universe are in that book. Let's find Gwen. She needs to know the book is missing, that Wilameena has page twenty-five of my notebook, the queen of Beastonia is dead, and Mistofisee is in danger." Thane took off, leaving Blabberdish to fend for himself.

Blabberdish sighed as he watched Thane disappear into the Slothful Forest. "Trouble, here we come… again."

CHAPTER FIFTEEN
THE SECRET LIAISON

A large bush rustled as Wilameena emerged. She'd hidden in the bush most of the day and had witnessed the spectacle with the Soul Seeker, Thane, and Blabberdish. When she heard Thane blame her for stealing *A Magic Maniac's Many Ways to Make Mischief* as well as a page from his notebook, it wounded her pride. In fact, she was so upset she took a nap to recover her senses.

"That stupid kid," the enchantress mumbled as she fought her way out of the gigantic bush. "He won't get away with it. No one tells lies about me and lives. I may be a lot of things, but a thief I'm not. A liar? Maybe. A cheat? Maybe. But not a thief. No indeedy." Then she remembered stealing Blabberdish's wand. "Well, maybe a thief, but it was such a small thing."

Wilameena brushed off and straightened her frumpy dress, ran a hand through her tangled hair, and trudged on through the Slothful Forest, not quite sure of where she was headed. Normally she would have made herself disappear and reappear wherever she wanted, but she was too emotionally drained and physically weak to perform magic. So she walked.

"Why is it so dark?" she muttered as she searched her pockets for her ancient yet reliable timepiece. "Ah, there you are." She checked the time. "After midnight?" The enchantress shook the watch and held it to her ear to make sure it was still ticking. "It must be broken. It can't be that late. I must have been exhausted to sleep so long." Wilameena yawned. "I'd better get moving."

Up ahead, she saw what appeared to be a clearing. "Good, I think I'm almost back to Idlebury. I'll hide out in Idlebury Castle until morning. Or better yet, maybe I'll scare the bejesus out of that little brat of a prince." She laughed to herself, feeling a slight surge of energy at the thought of frightening Thane.

Wilameena reached the edge of the Slothful Forest, relieved to see Idlebury Castle in the near distance. She was about to race into Idlebury when she saw two people standing under a large tree, snuggling and looking at the castle as if it were the most romantic backdrop. They appeared to be lovers, caressing and kissing. When the two released their embrace, there was no mistaking who they were.

"Well, I'll be damned," Wilameena whispered. "It's King Morrebidd and… No, it can't be. My eyes are deceiving me. Is it Queen Opunzayzme? Surely King Abracadabra would know if his beloved wife had gone missing in the middle of the night."

The enchantress slipped behind a large fallen tree to hide from the two most unlikely lovers. "Unbelievable. What in the world are those two up to?" she whispered as she peered over the log. She watched the couple and contemplated the possible reasons for King Morrebidd and Queen Opunzayzme's liaison. "Thane," she exclaimed, shocked at the loudness of her voice.

King Morrebidd jerked his head toward the enchantress's hiding place. His ghastly face glowed in the dark as he scanned the area with eyes honed to penetrate pitch-blackness. Queen Opunzayzme, who didn't divert her admiring stare from the only man she truly loved, appeared oblivious.

"Yikes. He heard me." Wilameena quickly withdrew behind the dead tree.

Soon King Morrebidd turned his attention to Queen Opunzayzme. He wrapped his arm around her shoulder and gently guided her to sit at his side under the massive tree. The queen of Hexidonia gently rested her head on the broad, bony shoulder of the king of the dead and cuddled with her long-lost lover.

Wilameena was beside herself with disgust. But mostly she feared the lovers would remain the whole night and deter her from taking revenge on Thane. As she continued to watch them, disgust turned to jealousy as memories of the man she'd loved and lost haunted her. *If it's only a little lovefest, why did they choose Idlebury?* she wondered.

"The book," she blurted out. "The rumors are true. The most powerful magic book in the universe is hidden in Idlebury Castle."

"Who said that?" King Morrebidd and Queen Opunzayzme said in unison. Hand in hand, the king of Deadonia and the queen of Hexidonia floated to where the enchantress had hidden. When the queen of Hexidonia landed in front of the giant log, she whipped out her wand, which expelled a burst of light and annihilated it, leaving the Soul Seeker standing before them.

King Morrebidd stared at the Soul Seeker but remained mum. Queen Opunzayzme's eyes darted between two of the most powerful beings in the universe. Without a word, the Soul Seeker vanished.

"Come." King Morrebidd grasped Queen Opunzayzme's arm. "We must go at once. Our plan will have to wait."

The queen of Hexidonia jerked free of King Morrebidd. "You are afraid of the Soul Seeker?"

"That was *not* the Soul Seeker."

"So why did you not destroy it?"

"I can't say."

"Why are you so secretive?"

King Morrebidd stared at Queen Opunzayzme but didn't answer her question.

"Obviously you are chickening out on me," the queen of Hexidonia continued. "You promised we would find the magic book and share its glorious power. I am disheartened to say I cannot trust you."

"Trust is not the issue."

"I believe it is."

"So be it. I'll get the book myself." King Morrebidd took to the sky and soared into the night.

Queen Opunzayzme chased after the king of Deadonia. "You will do nothing of the sort," she howled. "I will get my hands on that book even if I have to kill you."

King Morrebidd roared with laughter. "Oh, Opunzayzme, you remembered how much I love a good fight."

While the two old lovers were preoccupied with their chase, the Soul Seeker landed on Idlebury Castle's drawbridge. He looked around to ensure no one was watching.

"That worked," Wilameena said as she transformed from the Soul Seeker into herself. She giggled as she recalled the number of times, disguised as the Soul Seeker, she'd fooled even the most astute observer. But what she didn't realize was that tonight she had not fooled King Morrebidd.

The enchantress reached for the latch on the enormous

double doors that protected Idlebury Castle's entrance but withdrew her hand and then pondered her next move. *Is anyone still awake? There must be a guard on the other side. But if he's as lazy as most of the other Idleburians, he's more than likely asleep. Nonetheless, I must be as inconspicuous as possible. But how?*

As she searched her memory for the most effective means by which to fool the guard, she scrunched her face into what looked like a snarl, making herself most unattractive. A moment later, she grinned and snorted as she remembered a trick she'd seen King Abracadabra perform to make himself nearly invisible. She rubbed her hands together with delight. "Yes, this could work." Next she took a deep breath and then exhaled, blowing the air out of her body. Soon she was as thin as a sheet of paper, thus allowing her to slip through the narrow space between the castle doors. A gust of wind lifted her and gently laid her on the cold stone floor. As expected, a lone guard was propped against the wall, steadying himself with his sword and gently snoring. When the enchantress was satisfied she was the only person in the castle who was awake, she transformed into herself.

Perched on her toes so as not to make a sound, she moved toward the stairs. She was about to climb the old winding staircase, but loud voices and cries from the next floor up stopped her. A door creaked open. Panicked, Wilameena scurried and hid underneath the stairs. To her surprise, she wasn't alone.

CHAPTER SIXTEEN
A MOTHER'S TORMENT

King Heroian left Idlebury immediately after King Abracadabra and Queen Opunzayzme's visit, leaving Queen Filanthropi alone with her wild imagination and unbearable anxiety. Worried sick about Thane, she holed up for hours in the cellar, crying uncontrollably. Despite her emotional turmoil, for the benefit of her people and her children, she pulled herself together, fully intending to carry on with the evening's royal duties. As she sat alone at the dinner table, she couldn't help but worry as to why her children were absent. She was about to call for Morgana when the servant woman appeared with tears streaming down her face, her body shaking.

"For heaven's sake, woman, what's the matter," the queen asked. "I have had enough bad news for one day. Pull yourself together."

"I can't, Yer Majesty. Thane and Prudence are missing."

"Missing? How can they go missing?"

"I've looked everywhere fer 'em. They're gone."

Queen Filanthropi went completely mad. She yelled and screamed at anyone and everyone. She threw plates, bowls, cups, and cutlery as the staff ran for cover.

Morgana tried to comfort the queen, only to be pushed away. As the queen bolted from the table, food, dishes, goblets, and candlesticks crashed to the floor, for in her rage, the tablecloth had caught in her clothing. The dining room staff didn't intervene as they witnessed the queen's temper tantrum. She paced the dining room and screamed. "If King Abracadabra and Queen Opunzayzme have my Thane, I... I... I will kill them." Despite her threatening outburst, in her heart, she knew they wouldn't hurt her son. Maybe let a wicked wand scare him a bit about his alleged use of magic, but not hurt him. *But what about Prudence? She is practically a baby. Who would have taken her? Why would they take her? Is she hurt? Is she scared?*

"Why has no one found Prudence? For God's sake, she is only a baby. How far could she have gotten on those two... short... little... adorable legs?" the queen screamed and then broke down in tears.

Morgana rushed to console the queen, but once again, her efforts were rejected.

"If I read about Thane's and Prudence's disappearance and whereabouts in *Universal Scandals* magazine, heads are going to roll." Queen Filanthropi pushed Morgana aside, causing the woman to stumble to the floor. "And where is King Heroian when I need him?"

"I don't know, ma'am," Morgana said from her position on the floor. "A sentry has been sent ta alert da king as ta his need ta return home."

"Tell the sentry to hurry up," Queen Filanthropi yelled, unaware of the servant woman's fleeting look of hurt that changed into a controlled stare.

Queen Filanthropi impatiently pushed past Morgana, muttering something about having to do everything herself.

She stormed out of the dining room, up the stairs, and down the cavernous hall to her bedchamber.

She flung open the door, rushed to the window, and yelled at the top of her lungs, "Heroian, get your derriere back here. *Now!*"

The queen of Idlebury fell to her knees. Looking like a lonely, hurt child, she rested her chin on the windowsill and looked up at the night sky. "Why is Heroian never here when I need him most? Thane and Prudence are his children too."

"Ma'am, it's late. Ya need ta sleep," Morgana, who'd had the courage to follow the queen to her chamber, said. "Thane's me son too," she whispered.

Breaking protocol, Morgana placed a comforting hand on the queen's shoulder. "I'll wake ya as soon as I hear anythin'."

Morgana waited for Queen Filanthropi's response, but the self-absorbed queen ignored her servant's supportive gesture. So Morgana sighed and walked toward the door of the queen's bedchamber.

But Queen Filanthropi wasn't finished with her. "My dear woman, do not patronize me. My children are lost out there… in the universe… and you expect me to sleep. You of all people, Morgana, should understand my desperation to find them."

"Yes, ma'am. I'm sorry, ma'am. I just thought—"

The queen's diabolical glare scared Morgana silent. The servant bowed and backed away from Queen Filanthropi. When she reached the queen's bedchamber door, she hesitated. "Yer Majesty, I—"

"*Get out!*" Queen Filanthropi screamed.

Morgana bowed and hastily exited the queen's room. "I love him too, I do," she said. Weeping uncontrollably, she scurried back to her quarters.

Queen Filanthropi sat on her bed and gently wept, feeling angry with herself for scolding Morgana. "She's always been such a faithful servant. I know she meant well."

"Exactly, Your Majesty," Oof said as he bowed in reverence to the queen, having materialized out of nowhere.

"Oof, where did you come from? How did you—"

"Not to worry, ma'am. There is no time to wonder about me. I am here to tell you something rather shocking." The aged master servant waited for the queen's approval before continuing.

Queen Filanthropi sighed and furrowed her brow, obviously growing impatient with Oof's flair for drama. "Go on, man."

"Yes, ma'am. Thank you, ma'am." Oof paused and stared at the queen.

Queen Filanthropi's eyes widened as she grew increasingly annoyed. "I said go on, so go on."

"Very well then. I think it is of the utmost importance you are made aware of Gwendolyn's presence in Idlebury today."

"Gwendolyn? Why was she here?"

"Although I am not one for tattling or prattling, I must in all good conscience inform you that Thane traveled to Dimension X, planet Earth, and retrieved her."

"He *what?*" Queen Filanthropi sprang from the bed and paced her bedchamber. "How did he get there?"

"I am afraid he used magic, ma'am."

Dread spread across the queen's face. Her legs weakened. Her stomach tossed and turned. Her mouth became so dry her lips stuck to her front teeth. When she spoke, she sounded as if she were loopy on alcohol. "Who is teaching magic to that child? It could get him killed."

125

"He is teaching himself, ma'am."

"Fiddledeedee. I do not understand a lot of things, but how can one teach magic to oneself?"

When the queen said Fiddledeedee, Oof momentarily shuddered and then smirked, clasped his hands behind his back, and continued in his usual haughty manner. "One does not teach oneself. One usually has a teacher."

"I thought his teacher taught him reading, writing, and arithmetic. You know, those sorts of subjects."

"Yes, ma'am. That is true. But this is a different type of teacher, one who has magical powers himself."

"Who might that be?"

"His name is Blabberdish, ma'am."

"Blabberdish?" The queen averted her eyes. "What kind of name is that?"

"It is a most fitting name for a… for a… bookworm."

"A what?" Queen Filanthropi collapsed in a chair. "My children are missing… in danger… maybe even dead, and you, my most valued master servant, want me to believe a bookworm is teaching Thane magic?"

"Exactly."

The queen moved close to Oof, wondering why the man seemed to enjoy mentally torturing her. "Go on then."

Oof didn't respond to the queen's demand to continue the conversation, for something about the floor distracted him. He stared at one particular floorboard and gently rubbed it with the sole of his right shoe. Then he glided around the room, apparently obsessed with examining each and every floorboard before returning to the first one. He bent down to give it a closer look. Sure enough, the nails he had pounded flat earlier were gone.

126

Queen Filanthropi interrupted Oof's floorboard study. "Ahem."

Oof didn't respond.

"Ahem!"

Oof remained absorbed with his search of the floorboards.

"What are you doing?" the queen yelled. "I demand you stop it at once."

Oof raised his hand, signaling for the queen to be quiet.

"How dare you hush me? I am the queen of Idlebury. You are merely my servant. Now rise and tell me about this Blabberdish."

Oof, now on his hands and knees, ran his hands over the floorboard. He tried to lift it with his fingers but stopped and examined his hands as if to ensure he hadn't ruined his perfectly manicured fingernails. He reached in his inside jacket pocket and removed a small switchblade. He pressed a button on the handle, releasing a small silver blade. He ran the tip under the floorboard and raised it. When he saw the metal box, he sighed, closed the knife, returned it to the inside pocket of his jacket, then pounded the floorboard back in place with his hands. As he rose to his full height, he found himself face-to-face with an angry, glaring Queen Filanthropi.

"Get out!"

"Yes, ma'am. At once, ma'am." Oof bowed and exited the queen's bedchamber.

The door slammed shut, indicating the guard either had left his post or was asleep. That's when the queen heard something disturbing—Oof quietly chuckling as he headed down the corridor.

Queen Filanthropi was so angry she nearly ran after the old servant, perfectly intending to wring his neck. But instead, she slumped to the floor on hands and knees and lifted the floorboard Oof had just returned to its position. Intrigued by the battered old box, she gently lifted it and carried it to her bed. With childlike wonder, she sat cross-legged on the bed, released the box's delicate latch, and peered inside.

It was empty.

She rubbed her hands inside and outside the box. She turned it upside down and shook it.

There was nothing.

It was just an old metal box.

Disgusted, she tossed it to the foot of her bed. Utterly exhausted, she fell asleep. Within moments, the queen was deep in a dream. She muttered incoherently as she tossed and turned, knocking the box to the floor. It bounced and clattered. Nonetheless, the emotionally tormented queen didn't wake up.

<hr>

The door to Queen Filanthropi's bedchamber slowly opened as Wilameena and King Abracadabra, both of whom had been hiding under the staircase, entered. Upon seeing the metal box that was reported to house the coveted magic book, the enchantress and the king of Hexidonia dived for it. They tumbled to the floor, each trying to push the other away as they fought to gain possession of the box. But it evaded capture and, of its own volition, moved under the queen's bed.

Wilameena inhaled deeply.

Immediately King Abracadabra did the same. When he was completely flat, he slid under the bed and reached for the box before Wilameena was able to beat him at his game.

Shortly, Wilameena slid under the bed and rested on top of King Abracadabra. She fought for the box but lost, allowing the king of Hexidonia to snatch it before he flew out the window and disappeared into the night sky.

"Curses. I hate that old wrinkled wizard," Wilameena said, forgetting that if she spoke, she would instantly return to full size. "Ouch, ouch," she yelped as her head banged on the underside of the queen's bed. She tried to scoot out on her belly, but her matronly figure gave her no wiggle room to free herself. So she grabbed the leg of the night table, hoping to pull herself out from under the bed. But she only managed to pull it closer, making a loud screech that woke the queen, who instantly investigated the noise.

Queen Filanthropi rolled over on her stomach, hung her head over the side of the bed, and peeked underneath. "Oh, it is only you, Wilameena," the bleary-eyed queen said before relaxing on her pillows and returning to a deep sleep.

Wilameena's relief at the queen's lack of interest in her was dashed when a pair of highly polished men's shoes appeared, the toes of which nearly touched her nose. She knew they belonged to Oof.

Her heart pounded.

She panted.

She wanted to call out to him.

She wanted to talk to him, but so many years had passed and she wasn't sure if he cared about her anymore. If only she could touch him one more time. She reached out for his shoe but rapidly withdrew her trembling hand.

In a state of complete stillness, she watched as Oof walked over to the dislocated floorboard. He pressed it into place and then left the room.

Wilameena sighed. A few seconds later, she managed to drag herself from under the queen's bed. She rose in the air and glided to the door so as not to wake the sleeping queen.

As she gently landed at the door, she heard a man say, "I love you, Wilameena. Always have. Always will."

"Be still my heart," she whispered. "He does love me." The enchantress yanked open the door, but no one was there, not even the guard. "I must be hallucinating," she muttered.

As Wilameena departed Queen Filanthropi's bedchamber, she remembered spotting Oof entering King's Heroian's bedchamber with what looked like the velvet pouch that held Blabberdish's wand. So she changed course and headed to the king's bedchamber. "I wonder if Oof hid that stupid bookworm's wand in the king's room. I want it back. And I want it now."

The Soul Seeker watched Wilameena enter King Heroian's bedchamber. Tears welled in his eyes. "I still love you, Wilameena. But I do not love your deceitful ways. I cannot forgive you for stealing *A Magic Maniac's Many Ways to Make Mischief*. I will not speak to you. Not today. Not tomorrow. Maybe not ever."

Chapter Seventeen
Blabberdish's Dreadful Concern

G wen stopped at the edge of the Slothful Forest and looked over her shoulder. No Thane. No Blabberdish. "Good," she mumbled, happy she'd managed to escape from them yet nervous to be alone. She longed for Mistofisee but had no idea how to find him. So she plugged on and entered the sickening forest.

Although it was late morning, the Slothful Forest was darker and more disgusting than Gwen remembered. Sunlight fought its way through the forest's normally musty, murky air, made worse by the dust from the dragon queen's death crash, of which Gwen was unaware. Her eyes watered, and she found it hard to breathe. Gasping for breath and fearing she would pass out, she stopped and leaned against a tree for support.

The tree rustled its leaves. "You do not have a moment to spare."

"Oh great, a talking tree," Gwen said.

"So you heard what I said?"

"Yes. But if I can't breathe, I can't go on."

"Thane and his friend are following you. It is imperative you find the Great Wizard. Ergo, taking a break is not in your or the universe's best interests."

"But I don't know where to go. I don't have a clue as to the whereabouts of the Great Wizard. I don't even know if the Great Wizard is real."

"The Great Wizard is very real. But your preconceived notion of the Great Wizard's identity is misguided. Remember that and you will do well."

The tree disappeared, and Gwen fell to the ground. She got up and dusted herself off, revolted at the condition of the Slothful Forest. "Disgusting. How can anything live in this—"

Voices and the sound of squeaky wagon wheels bouncing along a cobblestone path stopped Gwen amid complaint. She scanned the area but didn't see anyone. Nonetheless, the voices and squeaking got louder. Within seconds she felt the presence of a crowd of people, yet she couldn't see it. The voices increased in intensity. The squeaking became so shrill she cupped her ears for fear her eardrums would pop. The heaviness of the foul air caused a crushing pressure in her chest. She tried to move but felt weighted down as if a force had invaded her very being. She looked for someone or something to materialize. No one and nothing did. As quickly as it all started, it stopped.

In an attempt to calm her nerves, Gwen took a deep breath, inhaling the Slothful Forest's notoriously putrid air. She gagged, coughed, and nearly vomited from the horrible stench.

Off in the distance, Gwen spotted something white silently yet rapidly approaching. Her body tensed in anticipation. She listened intently as the sound of a horse racing through the forest made her heart pound, fearing the invisible people in the invisible wagon had returned to harm her. When she recognized the approaching being, a soothing calm rushed over her. She slumped to the ground, exhausted.

The horse skidded to a stop where Gwen sat. With his nose, he gently nudged her. She didn't respond. He snorted and nudged her again. Too tired to rise to her feet, Gwen reached up and patted the horse.

"Lightening, I'm happy to see you," she said, her voice hoarse.

Lightening nickered and snorted his approval.

The presence of Queen Filanthropi's steed, which had aided Gwen on her path to becoming Gwendolyn the Great, Savior of Idlebury, Protector of the Universe, provided her with renewed strength.

"I see you have grown," Lightening said. "It's odd to see you are nearly an adult."

"You have no idea how odd it is for me to have grown so fast."

"No time for chitchat." Lightening snorted and stomped his feet. "Hurry. Get on."

Gwen tried to engage her weakened muscles. "I can't," she whined. "Besides, what's" — she coughed — "the rush?"

"You don't know?"

"Don't know what?"

"The most feared chant in the universe has been spoken again. And this time its forces have been unleashed."

"Was that what just happened to me?" Gwen asked. "Was it the forces of the chant?"

"What do you mean?"

"I heard voices and a loud squeaking sound. It was horrible."

"Oh no. You heard the empty wagon full of people. I certainly hope I'm not the dead horse it runs over and kills."

"How could you be? You're not dead."

"Just kidding. That old curse can't kill me."

"Why?"

"I'll explain later." Lightening stomped his foot, alerting Gwen as to the urgency to leave. "Chop-chop. Let's go."

Gwen used her last ounce of strength to climb on Lightening, who was kind enough to kneel on his front legs to ease her way. Once she was safely and securely atop the horse, the twosome charged through the Slothful Forest. The air blowing in Gwen's face refreshed her, increasing her strength, but the stench still made her stomach churn.

After a few minutes, Gwen and Lightening happened upon a beam of light well known for its ability to quickly transport people or creatures anywhere throughout the dimensions and the many kingdoms.

The beam vibrated and hummed.

Lightening sniffed it.

It vibrated faster and hummed louder.

Lightening appeared hypnotized.

Gwen remained silent.

Soon the beam dissipated and Lightening stumbled backward, nearly knocking Gwen off his back. "It's not time," he whispered as if exhausted.

"Not time for what?"

"Can't say. We must wait for Thane and someone named Blabberdish."

"*No!*" Gwen jumped off Lightening and looked him straight in the eye. "I will not embark on a journey to save the universe with those two idiots. Thane is a child. And Blabberdish is a stupid bookworm."

Lightening's eyes twinkled with delight. "A bookworm? Blabberdish is a bookworm? Does he wear red eyeglasses?"

Gwen groaned and nodded.

"Excellent." Lightening raised his head skyward as if to give thanks to a higher source. "Everything is falling into place."

"What do you mean?"

"Blabberdish is not, as you would say, a stupid bookworm."

"I see you haven't met him."

"No. But I've heard amazing things about him. It's believed he has the greatest magic abilities," Lightening said in a voice that conveyed complete awe. "Some say he's been taught by the Great Wizard himself."

Gwen was furious. A horse, albeit a horse she greatly respected, was telling her what to do, and he appeared awestruck with Blabberdish, of all creatures. "But I was told to go alone to find the Great Wizard."

Lightening snorted. "I hate to break it to you, but no one finds the Great Wizard. The Great Wizard finds you."

"What do you mean?"

"What do you mean, what do I mean? I mean just what I said. You cannot find the Great Wizard. The Great Wizard finds you when he is good and ready. In fact, no one has ever met the Great Wizard."

Gwen let out a gasp of disgust. "Then how do you know he's real?"

"It's a little matter of faith, my dear. I believe the Great Wizard exists."

"Well, I'm not so sure." Gwen shook her head disapprovingly. "I need proof, but I'm willing to suspend judgment for now."

"Excellent. You're gaining patience. Impressive."

Gwen squinted at Lightening, not sure if he'd complimented or ridiculed her. Soon her thoughts went back to Thane and Blabberdish. She hoped she wouldn't have to deal with them, but her gut told her she would. *Nothing's ever easy. Why is everyone always getting in my way?* she wondered. "So now what?"

"We wait." Lightening stepped into a surprisingly clean area of the Slothful Forest. "This is suspicious."

"Why?"

Lightening sniffed the ground. With a dirt-covered snout, he said, "Other than the fact someone tried to erase an imprint of what looks like a large key, this spot is virtually spotless."

"So?"

"So who went to the effort to clean it and why?"

"Oof? He's a clean freak."

"Oof… yes… of course… who else? Hmm… has to be… thought so… Nah, probably not… that's preposterous—"

"What are you going on about?"

"Well, I probably shouldn't tell you, but since you're Gwendolyn the Great and all, I guess you need to know."

"So tell me."

"Well… there's a rumor circulating throughout the universe regarding Oof's true identity." Lightening hesitated. "Well, for quite some time… Well, some people think Oof is… No. The rumor is ridiculous. I am not going to repeat it."

"What? I want to know. I need to know."

"No, you do not. End of discussion."

Gwen was about to protest being shut down by Queen Filanthropi's steed when a rustling noise caught her and

Lightening's attention.

"Shh! Did you hear that?" the steed whispered as he swung his head back and forth, looking for who might be lurking.

"Yes. And I think I know who and what it is." Gwen put her hands on her hips. "Thane, come out from behind the bush and bring your little friend with you."

Thane bounded from the bush, his face aglow with mischief. "How did you know it was me?"

"I know you well, little brother. And wipe that dumb look off your face. It's most unbecoming."

"Prince Thane, it's with great pleasure that we meet again," Lightening said with the respect due someone of great importance as he knelt before the boy. "It's been a few years. I see you have grown into a fine young man."

Gwen glared at Lightening. Her furrowed brow displayed her displeasure with the horse's subservient behavior— behavior that gave her the willies. *This isn't like Lightening. He doesn't kowtow to anybody. What's so special about Thane? Is it because he's so beautiful? Big whoop. Looks will only get you so far.*

Lightening motioned toward the small creature standing in the palm of Thane's hand. "I suppose this is Mr. Blabberdish."

Blabberdish jumped off Thane's hand and landed smack in the middle of Lightening's nose, making the horse look at him with crossed eyes. "Well, I'll be a monkey's uncle. Is that you, Lightening?"

"Yes, 'tis I. It is a great honor to meet you, Mr. Blabberdish."

"Just call me Blabberdish. Ya doesn't have to call me mister."

Lightening whinnied at the old Beastonian joke as he rose. "If you insist, but it's difficult to speak informally with one so admired."

"What's up with those two?" Gwen whispered to Thane.

"Beats me."

"As far as I'm concerned, Blabberdish is nothing more than an annoying pest."

"Well, I like him even though I don't think his magic talents are all that special."

Still perched on Lightening's nose, Blabberdish said, "Thank you. I appreciate your admiration. By the way, how's Crabbina, the greatest of the Sullywobbles, protectors of Beastonia? I heard she was ailing."

"Ailing? Crabbina has been ailing for five hundred years. I'm sure she'll survive another five hundred." A tear sparkled in Lightening's eye. "At least I hope so."

"Me as well. I miss her greatly. It's as if it were just yesterday she and—"

"All right already," Gwen said. "It's time for the Mutual Admiration Society to get back to the task at hand."

"Well, aren't you uppity," Blabberdish said to Gwen. "But I have to admit you're right. After all, Thane's in serious trouble and the magic book is missing, which means my family is in danger... along with the rest of the universe, of course. Don't get me wrong, I am concerned about the universe."

"What do you mean I'm in serious trouble? You agreed to go with me on my adventures."

"Yes, but I had to," the bookworm replied. "I didn't have a choice."

"Why didn't you have a choice?" Gwen asked.

"Because of my special assignment. I'm—"

"Too much information, Mr. Blabber... I mean Blabberdish," Lightening said, interrupting.

"I'm sorry. I do go on at times." Blabberdish squirmed down Lightening's nose and hopped onto Thane's shirt. "So what are we to do now?"

"That's what I was wondering," Gwen said. "Thane brought me to Idlebury, and now it appears I'm caught up in his mess. Like I didn't have enough to do saving and protecting the universe."

"A mess?" Thane whined.

"You can call it that if you wish. But I think I have a bit of information that might interest you," Blabberdish said.

"What?" Gwen asked.

"Well, in case you haven't noticed, the air in the universe is a bit heavy with dust."

"I noticed. So?"

"Why would be a more appropriate question."

"Okay, why?"

"Because…" Blabberdish hesitated. "It pains me to report this, but… but the dust is caused by the death of Queen Matilda of Beastonia."

"Queen Matilda's dead?" Tears streamed off Lightening's snout as he flogged himself with his massive tail and wailed, "No. Not our beloved Queen Matilda."

"What about Mistofisee, her son?" Gwen asked.

"Oh, lovely chap," Blabberdish said. "I met him on my journey through the dimensions. He was held captive by tiny, twinkly fairy orbs of light that took delight in being killed by his tears. So it goes without saying, our conversation was short… but sweet."

"So Mistofisee is okay?" Gwen asked.

"I wouldn't say that. I can only say he's still alive. Thane, remember I told you there was more to the story of the orbs?"

Thane nodded.

"Well, here it is. When the fairy orbs pop, they don't die. Their energy scatters, making it easy for them to invade the body of the person or being who popped them. When the orbs' energy reaches a threshold, the person or being explodes into billions of other fairy orbs. So you could say Mistofisee has become their host in the worst meaning of the word."

"Oh no," Gwen said. "Not Mistofisee too."

"Oh, there's one other little thing I believe you should know," Blabberdish said.

"What?"

"The book of magic—"

"Ahem," Lightening interjected, stopping Blabberdish from blabbering too much.

"Excuse me. But she already knows about the book." Blabberdish winked at Lightening. "But she doesn't know it's… Well, there's a little matter of it missing."

Gwen took a deep breath. "Wait just a minute. As I recall," she said to Blabberdish with the sternness of the strictest school teacher, "you were the last one to have the book. When I reached for it in Thane's room, you zapped it out of my hands. So what did you do with it, you slimy little worm?"

"How dare you disrespect the famed Blabberdish?" Lightening snorted.

"Hold your horses, Lightening. There's more to this than meets the eye. For starters, the most powerful book of magic is missing. And whoever finds it will have complete dominion over all creatures great and small throughout the entire universe, and your most-admired Mr. Blabberdish was the last to have it. I think that's just a little suspicious, don't you?"

"Well, I didn't exactly have it," Blabberdish said in his own defense. "I didn't want you to get your hands on it because I didn't know if I could trust you. So I whipped out my wand and sent it back to its hiding place."

"Obviously that didn't work." Gwen sneered. "I guess you're not such a good wizard, are you, Blabberdish? The entire universe could be destroyed because of you." Gwen looked at Lightening. "And as for you, Lightening, I'm shocked you pander to this stupid creature. He's an idiotic amateur. Any decent wizard would have ensured the safety of something so powerful and deadly. Now, once again, I have to clean up everyone else's mess."

Lightening, Blabberdish, and Thane were speechless.

"Well, it looks like I have a universe to save," Gwen said. "And as for you, Thane, I suggest you lock yourself in your room, refrain from using magic, and stop fraternizing with your dumbo of a friend. I can only handle one disaster at a time. I would hate to return and find you've been whipped to death with one of Queen Opunzayzme's wicked wands."

Gwen stormed away with the utmost conviction of someone who was in complete charge of herself. In reality, she didn't know where she was going or how to get there. A hum followed by a vibrating beam of light appeared before her. Without hesitation, she walked into the beam and was gone.

"Well, I don't know where she's going, but I hope she makes it okay," Lightening said.

Thane sighed. "Me too."

Blabberdish leaped on Lightening's ear and whispered, "My biggest concern is Thane. He isn't ready for greatness. And if he isn't ready soon, the most powerful book of magic could fall into the wrong hands, making Gwen powerless to save the many beings in the many dimensions from possibly the most disastrous, deadly, and dreadful events ever perpetrated in the history of the universe."

CHAPTER EIGHTEEN
A MOTHER WILL DO
WHAT A MOTHER MUST

The latest edition of *Universal Scandals* magazine gasped for breath as it slunk toward Idlebury Castle. Despite the heavy, dirty air caused by Queen Matilda's untimely demise, the periodical meandered down the drawbridge toward the towering front doors. But today it lacked its usual enthusiasm, for today the news it brought to Idlebury and Queen Filanthropi was the direst it had reported for many years.

The *Universal Scandals* magazine's final approach was exhausting, and just as it reached the front doors, it collapsed. Almost immediately a layer of dirt covered it. If only a gust of wind would blow off the dirt, it could wiggle its way under the doors. But two days went by, and not a breeze blew and not a soul opened the castle doors.

On day three, the doors creaked open a bit. The *Universal Scandals* magazine used its last ounce of strength to wiggle in an attempt to catch the person's attention. Instead, the doors shut.

The magazine wheezed. "No. Don't go."

Soon the door reopened. Someone wearing a black shiny shoe stepped on the magazine and snuffed out its last breath. It lost consciousness. When it awoke, it was lying on the corner of a long, battered wooden table in the kitchen of Idlebury Castle.

"How appropriate. Dis rag of a magazine is covered in dirt," Lazona, one of the kitchen staff, said. She read the headline, then slammed the *Universal Scandals* magazine on the table. "It never comes bearin' good news. Not a good idea ta let da queen read it, I say."

The cook stirred a large pot of piping-hot porridge. "Ya can't hide it from her. She finds out anyway. Besides, she's got dat Syvil Gossep woman snooping around, diggin' up dirt on her kingdom, her people, even her own family."

The arrival of Morgana silenced the chatty kitchen staff. "Where's da queen's breakfast? The poor woman is starving."

"So are we, but ain't no one makin' no kind of breakfast for us," a servant mumbled, inciting chuckles from the others.

"From the looks of ya, Albeata, skippin' a few meals might do ya some good." Morgana picked up the *Universal Scandals* magazine and blew off the dust. "Well, well. I haven't seen ya around here fer a few days."

The *Universal Scandals* magazine managed a weak reply. "If you had just looked outside the front door, you would have seen me lying there, suffocating from the dusty air." The magazine coughed. "But nooo, no one bothered to wonder where I was."

"It's been a little busy round here, it has." Morgana dusted off the remaining soot from the magazine and revealed its startling headline. "*No.* When did dis happen? Why wasn't da queen informed?"

Morgana glared at the kitchen staff as they nervously busied themselves with the final touches on the queen's breakfast. "How long have ya known?" she yelled.

Albeata dried her shaking hands on her apron. "Just now. I swear. Like it said, it's been outside covered in dust for three days."

"Well, I guess I'll have ta break da news ta da queen meself." Morgana slammed the *Universal Scandals* magazine on the tray that held the queen's meal. As she angrily snatched the tray, orange juice sloshed from its glass and soaked the magazine.

"Hey, take it easy," the magazine said. "I know I've come bearing bad news, but I need a little tender loving care. I'm sad too, you know."

Morgana charged up the stairs that led from the kitchen to the main hall where she noticed Oof sitting in the corner, reading what looked like a *Universal Scandals* magazine. "I thought we got only one copy of ya."

"I wouldn't know. As you can see, I've been out of circulation."

"If dat old buzzard knows what's happened and didn't tell da queen, his head is gonna roll, it is," Morgana complained as she huffed and puffed up the winding staircase to the second floor. At the top of the stairs, she paused to catch her breath and get her bearings. "How do I break such sad news ta da queen?"

"Let me do it," the *Universal Scandals* magazine said. "It's my job to break bad news, not yours."

"I suppose yer right."

With renewed energy, Morgana nearly strutted down the hall. "With da way da queen has been actin' lately, I'm glad I don't have ta break da bad news about da death of her dear friend, Queen Matilda of Beastonia."

At the door of the queen's bedchamber, Morgana paused and took a deep breath. She knocked and waited for Queen Filanthropi to give her permission to enter. There was no reply. She knocked again. No reply. She knocked with more earnest. Silence was all she heard. So she did the next best thing; she resorted to yelling. "Yer Majesty. If ya don't answer, I'll break down dis door, I will." Her threat was met with more silence.

So Morgana laid the tray on the floor and then made a full-throttle run for the door. An injured shoulder was her only accomplishment. She decided to give it a second try. But rather than ramming the door with her shoulder, she gave it a mighty kick. It didn't budge. As she massaged her throbbing big toe, she looked for the guard. "Where's dat damn guard?"

"A better question would be 'where's the queen?'" the magazine said.

"Stop it. I won't be reprimanded by a stupid magazine."

"*Stupid?* You called me stupid? Well, I'll—"

The presence of a shadowy figure silenced the magazine and the servant. Morgana looked around for the person who'd cast the menacing darkness. She saw no one. And the windowless hall, poorly lit by only four candles, wasn't about to give up its secret. The shadow slid under the queen's chamber door unnoticed. The queen's head servant was about to run for help when she noticed a bright light, seeping from under the door. She carefully turned the handle. The door opened easily. A blinding light flooded the servant woman. With a loud hiss, the light retreated under the queen's bed, leaving the glow of smoldering logs in the fireplace as the room's only source of light. As Morgana's eyes adjusted to the dimly lit room, she saw Queen Filanthropi fast asleep in her bed, comfortably cradled by pillows. The servant rushed to the queen's side and gently shook her.

The queen roused, opened her eyes, and groggily asked, "Morgana, my dear. What are you doing here in heaven?"

"Heaven? Dis ain't no heaven." Then Morgana did the unimaginable. She slapped the queen and said, "Snap out of it."

Now fully awake, the queen grabbed Morgana and pulled the woman toward her until the two were face-to-face. "Morgana, what *are you* doing here in heaven?"

"I'm not in heaven."

"That's right, you moron, because you're in hell," the queen said, her voice eerie as her face turned blue while her skin melted off her skull and her usually beautiful eyes turned into bulging black saucers.

Morgana jumped back from the horrific being. "King Morrebidd, dat was unkind of ya ta scare me in such a way."

"Was it now? Well here's something that should scare you to death. I'm not King Morrebidd."

"Ya are. I know ya are."

"I see he's kept me a secret."

"Whaddya mean?"

"Oh, now I've got your attention."

"Who are ya?"

"My dear woman, if I told you who I was, I'd have to kill you. But I will tell you this…" The being raised a bony arm, grabbed the terrified servant woman, and yanked her closer. "King Morrebidd and Queen Opunzayzme are plotting against the universe. The two of them had a little rendezvous right here in Idlebury. And don't think King Abracadabra didn't notice Queen Opunzayzme's absence in Hexidonia. In fact, he followed her here. He even paid a little visit to this very room. He thinks he outsmarted them and found what they wanted, but he didn't. When he discovers the metal box he stole is empty, he'll have no choice but to go after Prince Thane. And when he catches him... Well, let's just say the boy will be tortured and beaten within an inch of his life."

"Why are ya tellin' dis ta me?"

"I think you have a bit of your heart invested in the boy, now don't you?"

Morgana gulped.

"Does he still call you mother?"

Revulsion gave Morgana the strength she needed to pull away from the being. It roared with laughter.

"What have ya done with da queen?"

"I'm right here, Morgana." Queen Filanthropi sat up in bed. "Are you all right? You look like death warmed over."

"I'm fine, Yer Majesty." Morgana scanned the room for the being who had just occupied the same place in which the queen now rested. "I'm just happy ta see dat yer okay."

"Why wouldn't I be?"

"No reason, ma'am."

Queen Filanthropi propped her pillows and sat straighter. "Hand me my breakfast tray."

"Yes, ma'am. Of course, ma'am." Morgana rushed to the door, opened it, and picked up the tray from the floor where she'd left it.

"What's the news today?" Queen Filanthropi asked. "It had best be good for a change."

Before the words were out of the queen's mouth, the *Universal Scandals* magazine jumped in front of the queen and unfolded to reveal its headline, dumping dirt on the queen's breakfast. "Matilda, Queen of Beastonia, Is Dead!" it blurted out.

Queen Filanthropi didn't hear the details of her friend's death, for she had fainted straight away.

"Get out of here. Ya good-fer-nothin' piece of trash. How dare ya blurt such news without regard fer da queen's feelin's."

"I was just doing my job."

Morgana grabbed the publication and tossed it in the fireplace. As she watched it burst into flames and burn to ashes, the words said by the hideous being she'd mistaken for King Morrebidd about Thane's possible punishment and death raced through her head. No words had ever stung so badly. As she marched out of the room, she muttered, "Ashes ta ashes and dust ta dust, a mother will do what a mother must."

Embers from the fire sparked, revealing a dark figure lurking in the corner. An ember floated across the room and landed on the still-unconscious queen. For a moment she transformed into Wilameena. The enchantress smiled. "Ha! I scared that stupid servant half to death." She quickly scanned the room and then vanished, leaving the real Queen Filanthropi still unconscious.

A few seconds later, the queen awoke. "Matilda is dead, and my children are in danger. It's all too much to bear." Deeply in despair, Queen Filanthropi gazed out the window at the kingdom of Idlebury. A few minutes later, she went to her dressing table and picked up the gown Morgana had laid over the chair for her. She hugged it to her chest for a moment, completely lost in thought. She quietly dressed and checked herself in the mirror before she headed for her bedchamber door. As she reached for the doorknob, she hesitated and glanced at her dressing table.

"No, no, I must not. It is too dangerous, possibly deadly." Nonetheless, she opened a drawer and reached inside. Her eyes widened and her hand trembled when she felt the latch to the secret drawer. "No. I must not."

Breathing heavily, the queen pulled the latch and unlocked the drawer. She removed an item, tucked it down the side of her gown, and said, "Ashes to ashes and dust to dust, a mother will do what a mother must."

Queen Filanthropi slipped out of the castle and ran down the drawbridge, holding a handkerchief over her mouth and nose with one hand and lifting the front of her gown with the other. In her hurry, the back of her gown dragged in the dust, creating a path and several swirls where she'd stopped to glance back at Idlebury Castle.

As the queen of Idlebury disappeared into the murky distance, another person emerged from the castle. The woman noticed the cleared path of dust that continued down the drawbridge. When she peered into the distance, she saw the hazy image of Queen Filanthropi as the queen dashed toward the Slothful Forest.

"Queen Filanthropi, wait," the woman yelled. "Wait fer me."

Queen Filanthropi increased her pace as she headed to the edge of Idlebury. An instant before she disappeared into the Slothful Forest, the queen took one last look at her kingdom. She saw someone racing toward her. "No. Morgana. Go back. Do not follow me," she yelled.

"I'm comin' with ya," Morgana yelled as she closed in on the queen.

"I command you to go back. This is something I must do alone."

"Ashes ta ashes and dust ta dust, a mother will do what a mother must."

"What?" the queen of Idlebury said. "You are right. I must find my children. I must save them at all costs. What kind of mother would I be to leave them at the mercy of evil?"

Tears streamed down Morgana's cheeks. "Ashes ta ashes and dust ta dust, a *mother* will do what a *mother* must."

"What has come over you?"

"I'm his mother too. I love him too."

"I know you do. But I cannot put you in harm's way. I and I alone must save Thane."

"No. I must help ya. Only a mother's love can save him. So if somethin' happens to ya, I can save him. Those who'd do him harm know not my heart, but they know yours."

"You are willing to sacrifice yourself for Thane?"

"Yes, ma'am, I am."

"Then you are as much his mother as I." Queen Filanthropi held out her hand to her servant.

Hand in hand, the two women, who were of different worlds but of one heart, entered the Slothful Forest.

⋙◈◈◈⋘

Back at Idlebury Castle, Oof stood in a third-story window, peering over the drawbridge as he watched the queen and Morgana fade into the distance. Framed by the light of the fireplace, he cast a wicked image. Barely visible next to him, Syvil Gossep jotted notes on her trusty memo pad. A charred copy of *Universal Scandals* magazine stood on the window ledge. Its headline read REVENGE!

Chapter Nineteen
Queen Matilda's Awakening

After her death spiral, Queen Matilda didn't move a muscle for days. But when she cracked open her eyes for the first time, she saw Wilameena materialize next to her. The dragon queen watched Wilameena scout the area, disappear, reappear, and then bend down and poke her. But the great beast didn't stir.

"I guess she's dead." Wilameena leaned in closer and peered into the dragon queen's massive nostrils.

Still the dragon queen didn't move.

Wilameena stared at the supposedly dead dragon, transformed into Queen Filanthropi, the dragon queen's treasured childhood friend, and said, "Matilda, it's me, Filanthropi. Please open your eyes so I know you're alive."

Queen Matilda remained dead still.

With great effort, Wilameena changed into Gwen, but she didn't have the energy needed to hold the image of the powerful child, so she flickered in and out until she transformed back into her pathetic self.

"Wake up, lazybones," Wilameena said as she smacked Queen Matilda on the snout.

But the dragon didn't respond.

"Hmm. I know what worthless, lazy, vile, good-for-nothing dumb creature will revive you." With some effort, the enchantress transformed into Mistofisee. "Momma, Momma, wake up. I need you, Momma. I'm being chased by little bright lights. I'm scared, Momma," Wilameena whined, perfectly mimicking Mistofisee.

The great beast stirred.

"Momma, you're alive."

Queen Matilda lifted her massive head and snorted mucus-soaked dirt on Mistofisee. "Give it up, Wilameena. I know it's you," the great beast said in an unexpectedly powerful voice.

Wilameena wiped dirty dragon snot off her face, hair, and clothes. "That's disgusting, Matilda."

"I think *you're* disgusting," Queen Matilda said.

"I'm only trying to help."

"Yeah. Sure."

"Well, while you lie around doing nothing, your son is being annihilated by freaky little lights. Might I remind you of their power of destruction?"

Queen Matilda raised her enormous body from its dirty grave, creating another massive dust cloud. As Wilameena gasped and wheezed, the queen of Beastonia rose on her weakened legs. With a blast of hot dragon breath, she blew the despicable enchantress high into the sky.

The dragon queen blew another fireball at Wilameena, spread her massive wings, took flight, and yelled, "Ashes to ashes and dust to dust, a mother will do what a mother must." As she soared past Wilameena, the force of her wings flung the enchantress to the ground. Queen Matilda stopped in midair. "Take that, you imbecile. And don't ever ridicule my son, not ever, *never*." With that, the queen of Beastonia flew off.

Wilameena slumped to the ground. "Why can't she see I'm just trying to help?" she whined. She tried to muster a few tears but quickly gave up. "Now what?" she said. She was about to leave when someone startled her.

"Wilameena," the Soul Seeker said. "I cannot tolerate your behavior any longer. I have given you powers you obviously put to poor use. I have forgiven your indiscretions to no avail. I have allowed you to make mistakes, hoping you would see the evil of your ways. I see I was wrong. So as of this moment, I strip you of all powers. You are nothing more than a mere mortal. Good luck."

"Wait! Don't do this to me. I promise I'll never act irresponsibly again. I was only trying to help."

"Help? You must be insane, ignorant, or both," the Soul Seeker roared. "You are an utter menace. You are a universal pain in the posterior. Begone. I know what you have done."

"What have I done?"

"Oh please, Wilameena. I know you stole what every being in the universe wants."

"If you're talking about the ugly rumors that I stole the most powerful magic book in the universe, you're wrong."

"I am never wrong," the Soul Seeker said. "I saw you with my own eyes."

Wilameena took a step toward the Soul Seeker, then posed with her hands on her hips and one leg extended forward as if to challenge him. "As I recall, you weren't there. It was that brat, Thane, who told you the book had gone missing. It was Thane who lied about my taking it."

"How would you know I wasn't there if you weren't there?"

Wilameena relaxed and stepped back. "Okay, I know you

know I was under Queen Filanthropi's bed with King Abracadabra. He stole the metal box. He's the culprit who stole the magic book."

"What makes you think I would have knowledge of this information?"

"Because you were there. You came into the queen's room while I was hiding under her bed. You were lurking in the corner when Oof came in the room."

"You are mistaken." The Soul Seeker turned away from the enchantress and then quickly faced her. "No. I stand corrected, you are right. I was in the room. I saw Oof stand by Queen Filanthropi's bedside. I saw him hammer a floorboard in place. But for what purpose, I do not know."

"If that's what you want to believe."

"It is not a belief; it is a fact," the Soul Seeker said. "I also heard what Oof said after he left the queen's bedchamber."

For a few seconds, silence lingered between the two beings.

"I have nothing more to say," the Soul Seeker said as he swirled his cape and vanished.

"So he heard Oof declare his love for me." Wilameena smirked. "Doth jealousy rear its ugly head?" The enchantress chuckled to herself. "I have complete control over two of the most powerful beings in the universe, both of whom love me. But only Oof is *my* true love." She morphed into Thane and smiled when she discovered she still had her powers. "Now I'm going to get that box from Abracadabra if it kills me."

As Queen Matilda glided through the dimensions on her way to save Mistofisee from the orbs, the gusts created by the force of her wings pushed the dust from her crash into the far reaches of space, restoring sunlight to all the kingdoms in every dimension. Kings, queens, and residents alike rushed to windows or ran outside to witness and celebrate the return of the sun.

Although Queen Matilda knew time was of the essence if she was to save her son, she slowed her pace and took in the startling beauty of the many kingdoms in the various dimensions. The great dragon queen spied on everyone as they resumed the activities put on hold since the dark days following her near-death experience.

In Dimension VI, King Kokoa of Chocolatonia savored one of his delectable chocolates as a new batch of the universally famous candies rolled off the assembly line, ready to be wrapped in their signature brown-and-gold paper. And King Merlo and Queen Shardonei of Sommelierdonia clinked crystal wineglasses as they celebrated the sumptuous wines that would tickle the taste buds of connoisseurs everywhere.

In Dimension VII, the dragon queen saw Queen Garbini of Dresstoria inspecting bolts of fanciful fabric. As expected, the queen was decked out in a breathtaking gown. The queen of Beastonia grew envious knowing she would never have the luxury of wearing beautiful clothes. She visualized how she would look dressed to the nines. The ridiculousness of it brought a smile to her face. Soon she spotted Queen Imelda of Cobblerstonia, cloistered in a humongous closet in the midst of her massive shoe collection and gently caressing several pairs of glorious shoes. *No matter how beautiful the shoes, they'd look horrible on feet as big as mine*, the dragon queen thought.

As Queen Matilda flew into Dimension IX and closed in on Deadonia, the kingdom of the dead, she focused her telescopic vision on what appeared to be a woman. What she saw was more than disturbing because the woman was Queen DeMysora and she was weeping as she stood at a freshly dug grave. Queen Matilda focused on the headstone. To her horror, it read Thane, Prince of Idlebury.

Fearing King Abracadabra and Queen Opunzayzme had made good on their threat to kill the young prince, she charged toward Hexidonia in Dimension II, completely forgetting about rescuing Mistofisee.

As she entered the kingdom of magic, the sky lit up with fireworks, flashing lights, sparkling dust, images of wizards, bubbling cauldrons, and dragons. But the great dragon queen was not impressed. "It's nothing more than a smoke screen. They think they can hide the fact they're only tricksters with no real powers. But I do give them credit for putting up a good front."

Queen Matilda swooped in and saw King Abracadabra arguing with Thane. For a moment she was relieved to see the boy was alive. When the young prince changed into Wilameena, the dragon queen raged. "I knew it. That wretched enchantress is always at the center of every problem in the universe."

King Abracadabra and Wilameena struggled with what looked like a box. The old king hexed Wilameena, instantly shrinking her to the size of a newborn baby.

In a screechy, high-pitched voice, the enchantress screamed at the king of Hexidonia, "Give me that box, you decrepit old man."

King Abracadabra mocked her as he flew off in possession of the box.

Seconds later, Wilameena transformed into the queen of Beastonia and raced after King Abracadabra. The real Queen Matilda charged after Wilameena. As she tailed the old enchantress, she saw a child bounce through the dimension.

"Thane?" she whispered so as not to alert the enchantress. The dragon queen was torn. Should she rescue Thane or catch the old enchantress? "I'll deal with him later," she muttered as she soared after Wilameena.

As Queen Matilda chased the enchantress, she saw the woman flicker in and out of existence, as if her power had diminished. "So the old biddy isn't as powerful as she wants everyone to believe. Or is it I'm too much woman for her," Queen Matilda muttered and laughed. But her intent to capture Wilameena was thwarted by the sight of King Abracadabra, who had stopped up ahead as if to allow the enchantress to catch up with him. Suspicious as to the king of Hexidonia's intentions, Queen Matilda backed off. But Wilameena, still disguised as Queen Matilda, continued on.

"King Abracadabra," a child yelled. "Wait. I have something to show you."

The dragon saw Thane bounce his way toward the king of Hexidonia. Moments later, she saw Wilameena transform into Queen Filanthropi and watch from a distance.

"What do you want?" King Abracadabra snapped at Thane.

"It's not what I want. I believe it is what you want that matters."

"Do not be impudent, boy. I'm not impressed with your antics."

"I know, but I am."

The king of Hexidonia's eyes widened as he lifted his eyebrows and pursed his lips, obviously displeased with Thane's cheekiness.

"I know about the book," Thane blurted out.

"Really?"

"Yes."

"Everyone knows about the book, you ignoramus. Tell me something I don't know."

"All right." Thane floated around King Abracadabra. "I know who wrote it."

"Who?"

"My father, King Heroian of Idlebury," Thane said pridefully.

"Ha! You are indeed an ignorant boy. Those of no social standing, such as you, think King Heroian is the book's author, but a select few, of which I'm one, know who really wrote the most magnificent and most powerful book in the universe." King Abracadabra looked eye to eye with the child. "Hmm... should I tell you who wrote it?" He jumped back as if he'd been stung by a vile insect. "No, I mustn't."

"Tell me. I want to know."

"Is it worth your pathetic little life?"

"What do you mean?"

"Well, if I told you, I'd have to *kill* you."

Thane shrugged. "Queen Opunzayzme is going to kill me anyway. Or at least one of her wicked wands will. So maybe you can beat her to the punch."

King Abracadabra raised his wand as if to strike the boy.

"Leave him alone," Queen Filanthropi interjected.

"Mother?"

"Lower your wand, Abracadabra."

"I will do nothing of the sort." King Abracadabra stepped toward Queen Filanthropi and held out his wand as if to cast a spell on her. "I do not take commands from the likes of you."

Thane stepped between the king of Hexidonia and his mother, the queen of Idlebury. "Don't you talk to my mother like that."

The queen pulled Thane close to her. "I'm not your mother," she said in a stern whisper. "You're in danger. Now go."

Thane jerked away. "If you're not my mother, then who are you?"

King Abracadabra rolled his eyes and lowered his wand. "My dear, dim-witted boy, you are addressing none other than the most conniving creature in the universe."

"Oh, it's you, Wilameena."

"I beg your pardon," Queen Filanthropi said as she changed into the frumpy enchantress. "I don't care what you think of me." She grabbed Thane by the hair and peered into his eyes like a crazed hypnotist. "Heed my warning, child. Go." She pushed the boy away, but he insolently ignored her, allowing the king of Hexidonia to make an impulsive decision he would soon regret.

Chapter Twenty
Familiarity Breeds Contempt

Queen Filanthropi and Morgana walked through the Slothful Forest in silence. If truth be told, neither woman knew how to converse outside the formalities of Idlebury Castle.

After nearly an hour, Morgana broke the torturous silence. "Yer Majesty, I'm wonderin' if—"

With a raised hand, Queen Filanthropi dismissively silenced the servant woman.

"What's up with her?" Morgana mumbled. "I thought we were bound by our common love fer Thane?"

After a few more minutes of silence, Queen Filanthropi stopped and sniffed the air like a predator in search of its prey. She whirled to the right—sniff, sniff. She whirled to the left—sniff, sniff. Then to the right—sniff. Then to the left—sniff.

Morgana rolled her eyes and then obediently followed Queen Filanthropi deeper into the Slothful Forest.

Nearly a half hour later, the two women arrived at the edge of the forest. Before them was a field. Queen Filanthropi put out her arm to block Morgana from proceeding. "You must stay here. No matter what happens to me, do not step into the field.

That is an order between queen and servant. Not a suggestion between friends. Do you understand me?"

Morgana nodded.

Queen Filanthropi's eyes darted back and forth as she scanned the forest for someone or something. She breathed heavily and trembled. When her right foot touched the ground of the Field of Wisdom, light illuminated the entire field. She slowly made her way to the center. The beam narrowed until its rays engulfed her. She fell to her knees.

Morgana watched as the queen, cloaked in silence, appeared to beg for mercy.

"I will not allow it," the queen said. "I beg your forgiveness for what I'm about to do."

An electronic hum rose from the field. In a reverberating voice, the Field of Wisdom said, "Once before I allowed you to witness your greatness so you would understand why your people needed to be freed. And now you want to defy me and ruin it all?"

"It is not defiance. It is because I must save my son."

"Yes, you must. But the way in which you plan to save him will not work."

"Why not?"

"I think you already know why. Now do not waste my time asking me for forgiveness. It is something I cannot give. I can only provide wisdom."

Still on her knees, Queen Filanthropi looked up at the beam. "Then show me your wisdom."

"My dear Filanthropi, I repeat, I already let you see yourself in all your glory. If you did not gain wisdom, well, I guess you are either stupid or stubborn. Either way, you are hopelessly doomed."

"I will not allow you to stop me." Queen Filanthropi checked to see if what she'd slipped down the side of her dress before she left Idlebury Castle was still there. "I will not allow anyone to stop me."

"I cannot stop you from doing anything. That is not within my power. But I can tell you this. If you carry out what is in your head, you will fail. But if you carry out what is in your heart, you will succeed. Now go. Remember my words."

The beam dissipated, leaving Queen Filanthropi slumped on the ground. After a few moments, she quickly walked back into the Slothful Forest. As she passed Morgana, she said, "Let's go."

"Where ta now?"

"To save Thane. To save our son."

Morgana smiled.

A few minutes later the queen of Idlebury and Morgana arrived at the beam known for its ability to transport anyone or anything anywhere in the universe. It vibrated and hummed as it beckoned the women to step into its light.

"Morgana, I know it is forbidden to travel via the beam, but—"

"Ashes ta ashes and dust ta dust. A mother will do what a mother must."

The queen smiled. "You first."

Without hesitation, Morgana stepped into the beam. Seconds later, she landed hard on the ground. Queen Filanthropi tumbled next to her.

Morgana stood, shook off her frock, and held out her hand to the queen. "Where are we?"

"I am not sure. Although I do believe we have arrived in Dimension II," Queen Filanthropi replied as she rose with a little help from Morgana.

"Is it Hedonia then?" Morgana asked.

"No, it is most definitely not Hedonia. Hedonia is in Dimension XII."

"Hexidonia?"

"No, certainly not. Correct dimension. Wrong kingdom. But this barren land does look familiar." Queen Filanthropi paused and studied the area. "For joy. We are in Imaginoria—Land of Pretend. Where make-believe is truth and truth is make-believe."

"Imaginoria? Where da king and his people believe dey are invisible?"

"Yes. That is why our presence here is most delicate. For they can see us but we cannot see them."

Morgana shook her head in disbelief. "Impossible."

"Au contraire. It is quite possible." Queen Filanthropi glanced around. "Well, it does not appear anyone is here to welcome us, so let me fill you in while we wait." The queen sat on the ground and motioned for her servant to join her. When both were comfortable, the queen launched into the story of Imaginoria's invisibility.

"The Imaginorians' invisibility is the fault of their king, Ovazealous the XXXII. You see, when the king was only three years of age, he had a propensity of pretending no one could see him. Legend says one day he looked in a full-length mirror and saw nothing. From that day forth, he believed himself to be invisible.

"The king and queen of Imaginoria, ever the most indulgent of parents, allowed their precious son to engage in his delusion. In fact, they thought it quite cute. But his nanny did not. And despite her insistence that the mirror had been flipped to the mirror-less backside, thus preventing Prince Ovazealous from seeing his reflection, the prince remained steadfast in his opinion. When he could no longer stand his nanny's attempts to change his reality, little Prince Ovazealous decided he could not see her or hear her anymore.

"The frustration of being ignored by the child was so unbearable she ran away to another kingdom in a far-off dimension. And because the prince never saw his nanny again, he believed she, too, was invisible, which only reaffirmed his faulty belief.

"Years flew by, and no one challenged Prince Ovazealous's perceptions. On his twenty-fifth birthday, he became king of Imaginoria. But still believing in his invisibility, he was not appropriately dressed for his coronation. Dare I say he was nearly unclothed? And although all of Imaginoria thought him insane, no one dared tell the new king they could see him.

"Over the years, King Ovazealous's belief in his invisibility led to repulsive situations in which the king paraded through his kingdom in various stages of undress. Worse, each year on his birthday he insisted on wearing only his birthday suit.

"All this apparent nonsense became a reality when King Ovazealous met with Prince Pozzitiv from the kingdom of Nostinkinthinkin in Dimension XII. Due to the prince of Nostinkinthinkin's failure in his State of the Dimensions classes, he was unaware as to King Ovazealous's belief that no one could see him. So upon meeting the king of Imaginoria, Prince Pozzitiv, ever the one for etiquette and propriety, graciously bowed before King Ovazealous. The king of Imaginoria welcomed the prince and informed him they were twenty-fifth cousins fifteen times removed on his mother's side. Elated to meet his long-lost family member, the prince of Nostinkinthinkin gave King Ovazealous a full-body hug.

"Naturally, King Ovazealous was horrified at the realization that in order for Prince Pozzitiv to hug him, he would have to be able to see him. Therefore, the hug from Prince Pozzitiv was a bad omen, a very bad omen indeed.

"King Ovazealous voiced this opinion to Prince Pozzitiv, who was apologetic and swore he could not see the king at all. He made up a plausible explanation that the reverberations from King Ovazealous's melodious voice indicated to him exactly where the king was standing. King Ovazealous accepted the prince's apology and explanation, after which he dined with Prince Pozzitiv, who did his best for the entire evening to pretend he could not see the king.

"A sumptuous meal, stimulating conversation, and a few glasses of wine helped King Ovazealous to relax. Once his guard was down, he told Prince Pozzitiv about the hardship he'd endured being invisible and how he wished his kingdom and its people were invisible too.

"Prince Pozzitiv, who despite the fact his senses were fully intact, began to believe the king was invisible and thought if the king was invisible, of course his people could be invisible as well. So he informed the king he was the victim of stinking thinking and convinced him he could achieve anything, including making his people and his kingdom invisible, if he just put his mind to it.

"Well, King Ovazealous was overcome with excitement at the possibility he could help his people achieve invisibility, so he begged Prince Pozzitiv to show him how. Prince Pozzitiv was happy to oblige, and well into the wee hours of the morning, he taught the king of Imaginoria several affirmations that if practiced nonstop for exactly four days, three hours, eleven minutes, and fifty-nine seconds would with certainty make the king's wish come true.

"As you can most likely guess, King Ovazealous lived up to

his name and spent the next four days, three hours, eleven minutes, and fifty-nine seconds reciting Prince Pozzitiv's affirmations. And they worked. Imaginoria and its people have been invisible for nearly three hundred years. Not because they are truly invisible, but because Prince Pozzitiv's affirmations were magic spells that made the real Imaginoria invisible to those who venture into the kingdom. And when you cannot see people or things for whom and what they truly are, you are free to project your fantasies on them. In other words, while in Imaginoria, what you imagine becomes your reality."

Morgana pointed to something in the distance. "But it's not invisible. I see it."

"Exactly. You see what you want to see."

"Well, I see toys, games, animals, candies, and cakes. I see lots of fun goin' on."

"I see what I want to see, and you see what you want to see. That is the magic of Imaginoria."

"So whaddya see?"

"Time to move on." Queen Filanthropi stood abruptly. Morgana sprung to her feet. "I do not know why we are here," the queen said. "But there must be a good reason, for the beam always sends one where one needs to go."

"I hope yer right."

Queen Filanthropi squinted at Morgana as if to admonish the servant for having the audacity to question her. "Positively. Absolutely. Do not doubt me, woman."

Morgana looked away. A few moments of uncomfortable silence passed.

"Well, it does not look like there is a welcoming party," Queen Filanthropi said. "Shall we proceed?"

"Ashes ta ashes and dust ta dust," Morgana said.

"A mother will do what a mother must," the women said in unison.

With that, queen and servant headed into the unknown reality of Imaginoria to discover why the beam had sent them to this kingdom.

Morgana bumped into someone.

"Watch it. You would think I was invisible or something," a man said and then snorted with laughter.

"Excuse me. I didn't see ya, I didn't."

"Well pardon me, sir. Are you not aware that you are in the presence of a queen?"

"Your Majesty, Queen Filanthropi no doubt. We have been expecting you. I apologize for any rudeness on my part, but I want you to know that although you cannot see me, I am respectfully bowing before Your Grace."

Queen Filanthropi furrowed her brow. "Expecting me?"

"Yes, ma'am. The beam informed us of your expected arrival nearly three days ago."

Queen Filanthropi and Morgana locked surprised stares.

"Please take me to your king, my dear man," Queen Filanthropi requested.

"Certainly. I will take your hand to guide you. No disrespect intended, ma'am."

"My pleasure." Queen Filanthropi extended her hand in the direction of the man whose voice had created an image of a dashing knight. But when she grasped the man's plump sweaty hand, she quickly withdrew hers and discreetly wiped it on her dress.

"And you are?"

"Oh, how silly of me. I have lost my manners and insulted the queen of Idlebury."

"No apologies necessary, just answer my question."

"I am Awernez, Duke of Reality."

"I would assume you are not the most popular person in Imaginoria," Queen Filanthropi said.

"Truer words were never spoken," the duke replied. "But every kingdom must have balance, so my purpose is noble if not welcome."

"Yes, indeed it is most noble."

"And who is the servant woman with whom you travel?"

"My name is Morgana. You can address me directly."

"I am so sorry, my dear woman. No offense intended. I was only acting according to the protocol of Idlebury."

"Well, I forgive ya then. I didn't know Idlebury had... whaddya call it? Protocol?"

"Every kingdom has rules of decorum. I was only respecting those proposed by your king and queen."

Morgana sneered at Queen Filanthropi.

In response to her servant's contemptuous reprimand, the queen tilted her head and squinted her eyes, reminding Morgana that she wasn't the queen's equal.

"Well, enough chitchat," the Duke of Reality said. "King Ovazealous awaits your arrival. He is most eager to see what your imagination conjures."

Queen Filanthropi felt a gentle touch on her elbow as the Duke of Reality guided her toward the palace of Imaginoria.

Morgana walked a respectable few steps behind Queen Filanthropi. When she saw the palace of Imaginoria flash into view, she whispered, "Egad. Imaginoria appears ta lack imagination. It's drab and dreary, it is."

Seconds later, she disappeared into nothingness.

Chapter Twenty-One
Queen Filanthropi's Reality Check

Q ueen Filanthropi and the invisible Duke of Reality casually walked toward Imaginoria's palace. The queen reveled in the scene her mind had created.

Before her was a gorgeous field of wildflowers. Children and animals romped and played. Giggles, squeals, barks, whinnies, and bleats filled the air. Adults, dressed in the most elegant clothes, strolled and chatted as they enjoyed a breathtakingly beautiful day. In the background, a stunning palace stood as an example of the most magnificent architecture the queen of Idlebury had ever seen. Despite the foreignness of its splendor, it was disturbingly familiar. It was Idlebury Castle—restored and transformed to its original magnificence. It was the vision of her kingdom and its people she'd held in her heart for so long. Instantly what had been joy turned to sorrow, for she knew Idlebury would never be this idyllic. Nonetheless, she couldn't shake the image.

"We are here, Your Majesty," the Duke of Reality said. "Please take one step up."

The double doors opened, revealing the interior of the spectacular palace. Queen Filanthropi's eyes darted back and forth as she tried to take in its gilded glamour. Gold chandeliers lit her passage. Gold doorknobs opened gold-trimmed doors to rooms decorated in splendor beyond her imagination. Flowers bursting with color and fragrance teased her senses.

"I do not want this to ever end," she whispered.

For the first time in her life, Queen Filanthropi felt like a carefree princess. She wanted to run through the halls, plop on the overstuffed chairs, and slide across floors so shiny they appeared to be made of glass. She wanted to dance and sing. But most of all, she wanted to live forever in this glorious paradise.

"Your Majesty," the Duke of Reality said, living up to his name as he interrupted Queen Filanthropi's fantasy. "King Ovazealous awaits your presence. I am not allowed to enter the palace, so I will leave you here. I assure you, you will have no trouble locating the king."

Queen Filanthropi nodded. "Come, Morgana. And please be on your best— Where is my servant?"

"She has been sent to Imaginoria's holding station at BORE."

"She is where?"

"She is at the holding station at the Bureau of Reality Elimination, otherwise known as BORE. It is where King Ovazealous holds those who have lost their imagination. Unfortunately, the woman was unable to maintain her imagination and saw Imaginoria for what it truly is."

"I demand you return her immediately."

"Not to worry, ma'am. I will watch over her. After all, as the Duke of Reality, I am the chief of BORE. Your servant will be treated like royalty and enjoy a sumptuous meal. Upon your departure from the kingdom of Imaginoria, she will be returned to you."

"Well—"

"I am afraid protesting this action is of no use," the Duke of Reality said. "King Ovazealous has declared that anyone without an imagination must be sequestered."

"As I was going to say, if you can guarantee my servant's well-being and return, I will be more than happy to hold audience with King Ovazealous."

"Yes, ma'am. Of course. Your servant will be returned to you safe and sound. I guarantee it. The king guarantees it."

"Then I shall proceed."

"As you wish," the Duke of Reality said as he bowed.

Queen Filanthropi was about to step over the threshold of Imaginoria Palace when the once-beautiful doors turned dingy and dowdy and slammed in her face. "I must not lose my imagination," she mumbled. "I could be exiled to BORE." So she focused on the doors, trying to transform them into something spectacular. Try as she might, nothing happened.

She replayed the images of the fantasy kingdom she'd conjured earlier. To her amazement, a painted image of her fantasy began to appear on the doors. Gold trim and solid-gold handles appeared. Overjoyed with her creation, she gazed at her stunning work of art. "I want to remember this forever," she whispered.

A conversation she'd had with Lightening, her trusted steed, about the power of thoughts raced through her head. "You create your own reality," she heard him say as if he were present. "Your life is the culmination of every thought you've ever had. Your thoughts dictate your actions. So if you think you can do something, you'll put the persons and things in place to make it happen. If you think you can't do something, you'll create the circumstances to ensure it doesn't. So be careful with your thoughts, for they create your past, present, and future."

"Be careful what you wish for," Queen Filanthropi said aloud. The doors opened, revealing a breathtakingly beautiful room. Her jaw dropped. Her eyes widened. She stepped inside. "This is the most beautiful room I have ever seen."

"Yes. And thank you for creating it. You do have a fantastic imagination."

Queen Filanthropi looked around the room but saw no one. She wondered who'd spoken, for if it had been King Ovazealous, she wanted to make sure she greeted him appropriately with the utmost respect.

"Welcome, Queen Filanthropi," King Ovazealous said as he gently touched her on the right shoulder to let her know he was there. "I have been awaiting your arrival. I was eager to see what you would imagine. I must say, you have honored me with a most wonderful creation."

"King Ovazealous, it is with great pleasure that I stand before you," Queen Filanthropi said as she graciously extended her hand.

"The pleasure is mine." The king of Imaginoria kissed Queen Filanthropi's hand. "Formalities are not necessary among friends. I have watched the transformation of the kingdom of Idlebury with great enthusiasm. Much has changed since the investiture of Princess Prudence and proclamation of Gwendolyn the Great, Savior of Idlebury, Protector of the Universe. I must say, it was a fabulously fun time. But since Queen Invisabell, who regretfully could not join us today, and I are invisible, I think our presence may have gone unnoticed."

"Of course you were noticed."

King Ovazealous gently guided Queen Filanthropi to the dining room. The queen of Idlebury gasped when she saw a massive table set with the finest china and crystal on which a bounty of food from the many kingdoms was beautifully presented in her honor. King Ovazealous motioned for her to sit, but of course she could not see him.

"Please be seated," the king of Imaginoria said. "There is much to discuss and much food and entertainment to be enjoyed."

Queen Filanthropi felt King Ovazealous guide her to a luxurious chair. She sat and waited for further guidance. An uncomfortable silence filled the room. While the queen of Idlebury waited for King Ovazealous to start the conversation, she got a knot in her stomach, for the king's invisibility made for an odd and possibly awkward situation. *How easy it would be to forget someone else was in the room. How easy it would be to make an embarrassing blunder,* she thought. So she smiled and looked at the chair next to her, hoping she was smiling at the king.

"Queen Filanthropi, how rude of me to not make my whereabouts known. I am, in fact, sitting at the head of the table and you are grinning at my cat."

"Forgive me, King Ovazealous. I—" The queen stopped, amazed by a carafe of wine making its way across the room in her direction.

"No need to apologize. If I had not been watching my staff and wondering why they had not attended to your needs, I would have noticed your discomfort. So the apologies are mine."

The carafe stopped to the right of Queen Filanthropi. "Your Majesty," an invisible young man said. "May I pour you a glass of wine?"

"Yes, that would be lovely," Queen Filanthropi responded, hoping a glass of wine would settle her nerves. She watched as the pitcher tilted and red liquid filled her crystal wineglass. The pitcher then moved to the king of Imaginoria, tilted, and filled the king's wineglass with water.

"To a wonderful meal," King Ovazealous said.

"Yes," Queen Filanthropi said as she raised her wineglass in honor of the king of Imaginoria's toast. "It promises to be a lovely time."

King Ovazealous took a sip of water. When he set his glass on the table, the water changed to wine. The king took another gulp and completely drained the glass. When he placed his glass back on the table, the pitcher tilted and filled it with water again, which immediately turned to wine. This went on and on, and before long, King Ovazealous was undeniably intoxicated.

Queen Filanthropi was not amused with the king's behavior. She found it rude and disrespectful. Worse, she knew it was now impossible to have an intelligent conversation with King Ovazealous, which dashed her hopes regarding his ability to help her find Thane and Prudence. But her disappointment soon turned to horror, for sitting in the king's chair was a person who was not a creation of her imagination at all but was, in fact, the king himself. It seemed the wine revealed his true nature, which would not surprise the people of Imaginoria but was disconcerting for Queen Filanthropi, because she was now aware the king was nothing more than an aged three-year-old brat—always had been, always would be.

As the queen's disappointment turned to anger, the gloriously decorated room disappeared and she found herself sitting on a hard bench at a dilapidated wooden table in a room best described as drab. She looked at King Ovazealous just as he smiled, burped, and passed out. His head made a loud thud on the ugly old table.

Queen Filanthropi wanted nothing more than to charge out of the room and out of the kingdom of Imaginoria. Instead, she smiled and decided she would make believe everything was perfect. "When in Imaginoria, do as the Imaginorians do."

She rang the bell for the servant. A few moments later, a man dressed in rags appeared. Although he was visible, Queen Filanthropi pretended she could not see him.

"I have had a marvelous time, but I must go. Please bring my servant, Morgana, to me. And when the king awakens, please tell him I thoroughly enjoyed his company."

"Yes, Your Majesty." The servant bowed and exited the room.

Moments later, the Duke of Reality returned with Morgana. He silently and swiftly escorted both women out of Imaginoria's palace to where the beam waited.

He bowed as he said, "I trust everything was to your liking."

"Most definitely." Queen Filanthropi tilted her head and arched her eyebrows. "Quite unexpected."

Immediately the queen of Idlebury and Morgana stepped into the beam.

CHAPTER TWENTY-TWO
GWEN'S ROYAL WELCOME

Nausea.
Confusion.

Dizziness.

Dread.

These were Gwen's companions on her unrelenting tour through the dimensions via the beam. The beam's hum and bright light became unbearable. And just when she thought the torture would cause her to pass out, the beam silenced and stalled. The realization that she was suspended mid-universe scared her.

Her teeth chattered.

Her heart raced.

Her knees knocked.

To instill calmness, she reminded herself she was Gwendolyn the Great, Savior of Idlebury, Protector of the Universe, but to no avail.

She wanted to cry.

She wanted to run.

She just wanted to go home.

She was about to scream when the beam sped up again. Soon she felt better. *Does the beam know I'm sick? Did it slow down to help me? Does it have feelings?* she wondered.

Suddenly she plopped to the ground. The beam glowed and hummed to the right of her. Queen Filanthropi and Morgana appeared inside the beam, and instantly they were gone.

"I'm somewhere, but where? Why were Queen Filanthropi and Morgana here?" Gwen muttered as she got up and brushed off her clothes. "Come to think of it, why didn't they notice me?"

"Hard to say," someone said, the eerie voice unrecognizable as male or female.

Gwen looked around in search of who or what had spoken. No one was there. But what she did see was disturbing, because in the distance an ugly, dilapidated building cast an eerie shadow on the dead bushes and bare trees. The grass was gray, and the flowers appeared black.

"This place is ugly. It is utterly lacking in imagination. It reminds me of Idlebury before I saved it."

"No, my dear. It would appear you're the one lacking in imagination," the same person said.

"Who are you?" Gwen looked for who lurked behind her. "Where are you?"

"Use your imagination. Who do you think I am?"

A monstrous being with huge black eyes, the snout of a wild boar, and a body made up of a mishmash of animals appeared before Gwen. Blood dripped from its gleaming white fangs. The droplets splashed to the ground, momentarily providing color to the otherwise dreary scene before the parched soil consumed them.

"So you're afraid of me, are you?" the being roared.

"I'm not afraid of anyone... or anything, for that matter," Gwen said. Her lips quivered and her hands shook. "You're just trying to scare me."

"Scare you?" The creature howled, splattering blood on Gwen. "Why would I scare you? What could possibly be my purpose?"

"I don't—"

"Don't tell me you don't know, you conniving, spoiled, arrogant little girl," the creature screeched.

Gwen slumped, took a deep breath, and laughed. She laughed so hard she stumbled to the ground. When she looked at the creature, she laughed even harder.

"Why do you take delight in ridiculing me?" the being asked, its voice whiny and childlike.

"I'm not ridiculing you," Gwen said. "It's just that your ridicule of me is hysterical."

"Why?"

"Because I believe you just described yourself."

The creature dissipated.

"Yikes. I hope I didn't offend him, her, or it."

"Him? That was a woman," a bodiless man said. "And believe me, no one and nothing can offend her."

Gwen giggled. "That was one ugly woman."

"In more ways than you can imagine."

"Like Wilameena?"

"You said it, not me. Now come. We must go. Time is wasting."

Gwen looked for the person who had spoken. "No. I won't go anywhere with someone I can't see. So show yourself."

The words were barely out of her mouth when a large, moist,

meaty hand grabbed her by the arm.

"Let go of me."

"I will do nothing of the kind," the invisible man said. "I have every inclination to ban you to BORE, but... well... because of who you are, I fear retribution."

"What's BORE?"

"The Bureau of Reality Elimination." The man inhaled and released a groaning exhale.

"What does that mean?" Gwen asked.

"It is where we send those who lack imagination... those who live in reality."

"What? Where am I?"

"Do you know nothing?" the man snapped. "You are in Imaginoria—where make-believe is truth and truth is make-believe."

"I've heard of this place. This is where the king believes he's invisible."

"As do his people."

"Actually, I believe the king and his people are invisible not because they are but because the king put a spell on the universe, making all creatures believe he and his people are invisible."

"No more," the man yelled. "We must go. I believe you have something to tell King Ovazealous."

"I do?" Gwen said as the invisible man yanked her in the direction of the bland building.

Gwen let the invisible man drag her along for a few silent minutes. But Gwen being Gwen, she couldn't maintain silence too long. "Is that horrible building Imaginoria's castle?"

"No. It is a palace. There's a difference, you know."

"A palace is usually more grand," Gwen said. Instantly the drab, dreary structure wobbled as the ground on which it stood shook. Twinkling orbs surrounded it and transformed it into the most glorious gilded palace Gwen could imagine. "Wow, that's gorgeous."

"I see your imagination is now firmly intact," the man said.

"My imagination did that?"

"Yes, it most certainly did. You mention it in the third person as if it is not a part of you."

"Oh, I didn't realize—" Gwen jerked her hand away from the invisible man. "Who are you and where are you taking me?"

"My name is Awernez. I am the Duke of Reality. I am taking you to King Ovazealous."

Gwen wanted to ask more questions but decided it was best to be quiet. Within seconds, the Duke of Reality escorted her to the palace of Imaginoria.

"This is where I leave you. As the Duke of Reality, the imaginative creations of Imaginoria's guests are not for me to see. So I bid you a fond adieu."

The gold double doors opened to reveal the activities of invisible servants who rushed about as they fussed over the final touches for what Gwen assumed to be a royal event.

Feather dusters busily cleaned magnificent paintings and furniture.

Brooms swept beautiful mosaic floors.

Candlesticks floated and gently landed in place on a marble mantel.

Stacks of towels and sheets glided up the intricately carved staircase to the many luxurious guest rooms.

Beautifully groomed dogs of many breeds enjoyed belly rubs and treats provided by unseen hands.

Trays of delectable food accompanied by no one floated into a glorious dining room where they gently landed on a massive table over which hung an enormous, richly decorated chandelier.

The musical sound of an orchestra warming up added to the regal atmosphere.

Fresh-cut flowers cradled in magnificent vases adorned every nook and cranny. Their luscious scent filled the air.

Gwen was spellbound, for she had created a scene beautiful beyond her wildest dreams.

"Welcome," a woman said as she gently laid a hand on Gwen's shoulder. "We were expecting you but not so soon after your mother's departure."

"My mother was here?" Gwen squinted suspiciously, wondering why her mother, Evaline Fanny, would visit Imaginoria.

"Yes, Queen Filanthropi and her servant left barely moments before your arrival. I apologize for our lack of readiness, but until you arrived, we had no idea what vision of us you would manifest."

"Queen Filanthropi is not—"

"What, my dear?"

"Oh, nothing. It's not important," Gwen said, realizing how tedious it was to explain the difference between her biological mother, Queen Filanthropi, and her real mother, Evaline Fanny.

As Gwen and the woman approached the dining room, a red carpet unfurled across the floor, stopping at Gwen's feet. She jumped out of the way. "Excuse me. Who is the red carpet for?"

"It is for you, my dear," the woman said. "It is our way of welcoming you, Gwendolyn the Great, Savior of Idlebury, Protector of the Universe."

"Me?" Gwen was astonished. She felt special and elegant, just like the princess she had wished to be. She imagined herself in a beautiful purple gown decorated with diamonds and pearls. And as she did, it appeared on her person, complete with matching shoes and a tiara.

"King Ovazealous awaits your presence," the woman said. "I certainly hope he is feeling better. It seems your mother, the queen of Idlebury, imagined him as a spoiled-rotten, drunken brat, causing him to engage in the worst possible behavior and partake of too much wine."

The woman positioned Gwen on the red carpet and gave her a gentle push forward. Gwen floated down the carpet toward the dining room. The massive ornate doors opened as horns hoisted in the air by invisible trumpeters sounded her arrival.

Chapter Twenty-Three
A Secret Pact Exposed

"**G**wendolyn the Great, Savior of Idlebury, Protector of the Universe," the herald announced.

Gwen cautiously entered the room. She noticed seating for at least a hundred people at the longest table she'd ever seen. Because the chairs were pulled away, she assumed the guests were standing in her honor. At the head of the table, a chair that looked like a throne was pushed in, close to the table. *That must be King Ovazealous's chair. Is he sitting, or has he not yet arrived?* she wondered. Gwen felt awkward as she stood before what could be a roomful of invisible people. *What if the chairs are pulled away from the table to fool me and no one is there? What if the king is seated and having a good laugh at my expense? What is the proper thing to do?*

Much to Gwen's relief, someone took her by the arm and escorted her across the room. Applause broke out, making it apparent that many Imaginorians packed the room. As she and her escort approached the dining table, the chair at the head of the table moved back, indicating King Ovazealous had risen.

Gwen felt a hand on her wrist.

"I shall take it from here," the king said. The invisible king assisted Gwen to the chair next to him. "Please sit, Your— I am not sure how to address one so noble."

"Gwendolyn is fine, Your Majesty," Gwen said as she curtsied.

"Welcome, Gwendolyn. Again, please have a seat."

"Thank you."

Gwen took a moment to take in the splendor of the room. She admired an elegant, richly decorated chandelier hung over the center of the long table. *A little gaudy. Sparkling crystals would be prettier.* The chandelier immediately changed to what she'd imagined. The light from hundreds of candles shone on the multifaceted crystals, causing mini-rainbows to dance across the walls. Gwen was awestruck with the power of her imagination.

"Let the festivities begin," King Ovazealous declared.

A great shuffling sound accompanied the movement of the chairs as many Imaginorians settled in at the table. Soon carafes of wine drifted into the room and filled the many goblets on the tables.

"Do you partake of wine?" King Ovazealous asked Gwen.

"I'm a little young, Your Majesty. My mother and father would be angry if I did."

"What would you prefer instead?"

"Chocolate milk would be marvelous."

"So be it," the king of Imaginoria said.

Instantly Gwen's wine became chocolate milk. "How did you do that?"

"I did not do a thing. You did. Not unlike your mother's talent for turning water into wine," the king said and then laughed.

Gwen smiled and sipped her chocolate milk, noticing how unusually delicious it tasted. She took another sip, completely absorbed by the creaminess of the luscious drink. She was about to ask the king why Queen Filanthropi had paid him a visit, but trays of food carried by invisible servers diverted her attention. She watched in awe as food floated off a tray and settled on her plate. "I can't believe you prepared all my favorite dishes. How did you know what I like?"

"This is your creation, my dear, not mine," King Ovazealous said. "I must say I'm thoroughly enjoying it. You have a spectacular imagination and a great sense of elegance."

Gwen ate as she made small talk with several Imaginorians seated closest to her. The fact that she felt comfortable conversing with invisible people amazed her. Seated next to her was a boy about her age. She imagined he was incredibly handsome. She tried to picture the details of his face, hoping he would materialize, but he didn't.

There was music and dancing. Gwen was the belle of the ball as she danced with at least a dozen men and boys. When she danced with the boy who had sat next to her at the table, she noticed he was unusually tall for a twelve-year-old. She instantly fell in love.

As love often does, it took over Gwen's better judgment and caused her to lose her imagination, giving her a momentary glimpse of the real Imaginoria. To her horror, the boy she'd fallen madly in love with was, in reality, a homely, decrepit old man. Filled with disgust, she looked toward King Ovazealous. What she saw was not more palatable. The king, who sat at the head of a now obviously worn, marred table around which a hundred homely and ill-dressed people were gathered, appeared to be naked. *Thank goodness he's sitting and not standing.*

Quickly everything returned to the glorious vision Gwen had created. She looked around, wondering if anyone had noticed she'd lost her imagination and revealed Imaginoria for what it truly was. But because she could no longer see them, she had no idea if they'd noticed or not. "I hope the Duke of Reality doesn't send me to BORE," she muttered.

Gwen watched as the Imaginorians continued with the festivities. She was about to ask King Ovazealous a question when the party was interrupted by a tray carrying what looked like a magazine. The tray made its way across the large room and stopped next to King Ovazealous.

An invisible man said, "Your Majesty, the latest edition of *Universal Scandals* magazine has arrived, bearing some extraordinary news, of which I am certain—"

The king snatched the magazine off the tray. "Just give me the magazine. I will determine if the news is extraordinary or not."

Gwen, scared as to what the news might be, stared at the magazine as the king silently read the headline.

"Argh!" The king sighed as he opened the magazine to read the article. With the magazine's headline now facing everyone at the table, a collective gasp was heard. Gwen silently read the headline. PRINCE THANE KIDNAPPED BY KING ABRACADABRA. PRINCE FEARED DEAD! She nearly fainted.

"I must go." Gwen rose quickly, knocking over her chair. "I mean no disrespect, but I really must go."

"No." King Ovazealous grabbed Gwen's wrist. "Sit. There is something we need to discuss."

Someone righted Gwen's chair, and she obeyed the king's order.

"As for the rest of you, go. This is not your concern."

Loud chatter and chairs screeching as the Imaginorians pushed back from the table created a ruckus. A few minutes later, the room was dead quiet.

"My dear child," King Ovazealous said in a fatherly manner. "The news about your brother must be most upsetting. I perfectly understand your need to rescue him. But—"

"It's not Thane I'm worried about. Believe it or not, he can take care of himself. And I don't believe King Abracadabra will harm him. He may be a fool, but he's not stupid."

King Ovazealous remained silent as Gwen appeared to struggle with her thoughts. After a few minutes, Gwen broke the silence. "Your Majesty, may I ask you a favor?"

"Certainly," King Ovazealous said.

Gwen leaned in toward the king. "Will you help me find the book?"

"What book?"

"*A Magic Maniac's Many Ways to Make Mischief.*"

King Ovazealous cleared his throat. "Never heard of it."

"Sure you have," Gwen said, unknowingly looking directly into the king's eyes.

"Are you questioning me?"

"I'm questioning whether you're telling the truth or not."

"And why would you do that?"

"Well, I kind of put two and two together. You know the phrase 'Last night at ten o'clock this morning, an empty wagon full of people ran over a dead horse and killed it'?"

"You are either very brave or very stupid to repeat that phrase."

"Maybe, but I don't believe it has any power," Gwen said. "In fact, I think the phrase is a clue as to the identity of the three

187

people who have conspired to gain possession of the book."

"Who do you think is behind something so ridiculous?"

"King Abracadabra, King Morrebidd, and… you."

King Ovazealous gulped audibly. "Me? Pray tell why?"

Gwen thought she heard fear in the invisible king's voice, so she paused a moment and then continued. "Clue number one: last night at ten o'clock this morning. There is only one person in the universe who can shift time, and that's King Abracadabra of Hexidonia.

"Clue number two: an empty wagon full of people. Well, an empty wagon can only be full of people if the people are invisible. And everyone knows only the people of Imaginoria are invisible. That appears to implicate you."

"Clue number three: ran over a dead horse and killed it. Obviously, in order to kill a dead horse, the horse in question would have to be among the living dead. That implicates none other than King Morrebidd of Deadonia, ruler of the kingdom of the dead."

"What do you want from me?"

Gwen felt the king's breath on her cheek. She nearly recoiled in fear, but she remembered that although she couldn't see him, he could see her. So she pretended not to notice the king had invaded her space. "I want you to get the book and give it to me. And I want your promise Thane will not be harmed."

"I cannot promise Thane will not be harmed," King Ovazealous said. "His safety is not in my hands."

"Okay," Gwen said, fearing the king of Imaginoria had no real power.

"And I cannot promise to give you the book either." The king's chair scraped the floor, indicating he'd pushed away from the table.

"Why?"

"Because right now no one knows the whereabouts of the book. No one... not even the Great Wizard."

"I don't believe you," Gwen said, not realizing she was looking directly into the king's eyes again. "And I don't believe there's a Great Wizard."

King Ovazealous leaned toward Gwen, nearly touching her nose to nose. He blasted her face with his warm breath as he said, "That, my dear child, is most unfortunate."

CHAPTER TWENTY-FOUR
KILLING WILAMEENA

Q ueen Matilda continued her mad search for her son, Mistofisee. She hunted for the orbs, fearing she would find them, fearing she would not. As she soared through Dimension II and into the kingdom of Imaginoria, a beam of light distracted her, revealing Gwen's arrival in the kingdom of make-believe and the simultaneous departure of Queen Filanthropi and Morgana. *Why is Gwen here? And why was Filanthropi here with her servant?*

As the beam whisked away the two women, Queen Matilda thought she heard Queen Filanthropi say, "Ashes to ashes and dust to dust. A mother will do what a mother must."

The dragon queen yelled, "Yes, yes." She wanted to chase after them and tell them she shared their sentiments. She wanted their help to find her son, and she wanted to help them find Thane. But overwhelming helplessness and fear made her question if she was still the most powerful creature in the universe. Despite her self-doubt, her desperation to do what must be done recharged her energy; she was ready for a fight.

The queen of Beastonia curiously watched Gwen. She wondered how the girl had become so mature and why she appeared to be talking to herself. She saw Gwen walk toward the dilapidated building the Imaginorians called their palace with her arm outstretched as if she were holding something. She thought Gwen looked silly, and she almost laughed, but twinkling orbs distracted her, instantly turning her amusement to rage.

As Gwen walked into the palace of Imaginoria, the queen of Beastonia attacked the orbs. They squealed, giggled, and flashed as they swirled around the great beast's head. The dragon queen opened her huge mouth, captured the orbs, tightly clamped her mouth, and soared out of Imaginoria toward Dimension III to the kingdom of Illumindonia where she knew she would find another mother—one she had every intention of killing.

The beam carrying Queen Filanthropi and Morgana hummed and glowed in midair. Queen Matilda charged after it. Seconds before she would have crashed into it, it absorbed her. She was now face-to-face with the queen of Idlebury and her servant. The look in Queen Filanthropi's eyes expressed her delight to see her old friend alive and well.

In response, Queen Matilda grinned, revealing the squealing, flashing orbs. No words were exchanged because no words were needed for what the three mothers knew they were about to do.

Pitch-blackness surrounded them. Seconds later, a light flashed in the distance. There was no mistaking it; it was the mother of the orbs. As she neared, she changed colors with every flash.

Does she see us? Does she sense danger? Matilda wondered. *Will she fight back? Will she kill us before we kill her?* The dragon queen fought to escape the beam, but it held her captive as it continued to close in on the giant orb.

The mother orb raced toward the beam. She skirted its

exterior. Agitated, she pulsated faster as she continued her attempt to penetrate the beam. But she couldn't. The beam was too powerful.

Queen Matilda grinned. The light from the orbs she held in her mouth glowed through her fangs. The orbs squealed and cried. In a frantic attempt to save her children, the mother orb smashed into the beam, but she bounced off. The queen of Beastonia fought to free herself from the beam's force. She wanted to face the mother of the orbs and let the vibrating, pulsating blob of light know her pain. But most of all, she wanted her son, Mistofisee, returned to her.

Something approached so far in the distance its form was indiscernible. Queen Matilda thought she heard Mistofisee calling for her. She stopped struggling and listened. She activated her microscopic vision to capture a view of what approached.

"Mistofisee," she groaned through clenched teeth, keeping the orbs securely jailed in her mouth.

"Mother. Mother. Help me."

Mistofisee's cries sent the dragon queen into a frenzy, but the beam held fast. Even the largest and strongest creature in the universe couldn't escape its hold. The mother orb swirled around the beam, blinding the two women and dragon with flashing multicolored lights.

Mistofisee rapidly approached. His wings flapped uncontrollably as he came to a full stop alongside the mother orb. Oddly, she ignored him. The beam weakened just enough for Queen Matilda to reach out and pull her son to safety. Seconds later, the beam transported the foursome to the kingdom of Beastonia in Dimension I.

The beam dropped Queen Matilda, Queen Filanthropi, Mistofisee, and Morgana on Canny Castle's drawbridge.

Queen Matilda, aware she still carried the orbs in her mouth, wondered what to do with them. But she didn't have to think too long, for the mother orb had followed the beam and now encircled the dragon queen. The mother orb screeched. Queen Matilda, Mistofisee, Queen Filanthropi, and Morgana cupped their ears in an attempt to stop the excruciating pain.

"Give her the orbs," Mistofisee begged. "Mother, please. Give them to her. They can't harm me."

Queen Matilda saw desperation in her son's eyes. So she opened her mouth a crack and allowed the orbs to escape. The horrible screeching stopped. The mother orb ceased circling Queen Matilda. She pulsated in front of the dragon queen as if to thank her for releasing her children, and then she and her offspring flew skyward and disappeared. Queen Matilda grabbed Mistofisee and hugged him tightly as if to never let him go.

"Stop," Mistofisee demanded.

The queen of Beastonia planted a wet kiss on top of her son's head. "I will never let you out of my sight again."

"Gross," Mistofisee whined as he tried to break free of his mother's grasp.

Queen Matilda giggled with joy as she continued to kiss and hug her son. "Why did you say the orbs couldn't harm you?"

"Because... because... I'm not..." Mistofisee dissipated. Within seconds, he rematerialized as the enchantress.

"Wilameena, how could you?" Queen Filanthropi said. "If Mistofisee dies, you will be held accountable."

Queen Matilda was at a loss for words. Anger surged through her. She impulsively spewed a stream of fire, incinerating the enchantress.

When the flames died down and the smoke cleared, it was

apparent Wilameena was nothing more than a pile of smoldering ash.

Morgana stared at what remained of the enchantress.

Queen Filanthropi fought back tears.

Queen Matilda appeared emotionless. But she knew she had done something horribly regrettable.

No one knew what to do or say.

Knowing dragon tears had the power to restore life, Queen Matilda stared at the pile of ash that only moments ago had been the enchantress as she tried to squeeze out a tear. But no matter how hard she tried, she couldn't muster sorrow for Wilameena. Queen Matilda tried thinking of sad moments in her past. Nothing. She bit her lip. Still nothing. She simply couldn't make herself cry for the annoying enchantress. Desperate, she turned to Queen Filanthropi and Morgana.

"Do not cast a look at me," the queen of Idlebury said. "I am not sorry the old hag is dead."

"Me neither," Morgana said with conviction.

"So why do you have tears in your eyes, Filanthropi?" Queen Matilda asked.

"Well, they are not what they seem."

"Exactly what do you think they seem?"

"Well, I would suspect you would think they are tears of sorrow."

"Obviously," the dragon queen replied. "So what are they?"

Queen Filanthropi cleared her throat in an attempt to stall for time.

"Filanthropi, what do they mean?" Queen Matilda nearly yelled.

"Well... before I tell you, I want you to know I am mortified

194

about what I am about to say."

"Just say it."

"Okay. Well, they are… they are tears…" Queen Filanthropi hesitated, then in rapid-fire she said, "They are tears of joy. There, I have said it."

Queen Matilda strummed the talons of her right back paw. After some thought, she smiled. "Let's let sleeping dogs lie, so to speak."

The two women and the dragon looked at each other and broke out in laughter. They laughed so hard Queen Filanthropi and Morgana hung on each other for support. Tears rolled down Queen Matilda's face. A single tear dripped off her snout.

The great dragon roared, *"Nooo!"* But she was powerless to stop it, and it splashed on the enchantress's remains.

Queen Filanthropi scrunched her face, obviously thinking about something. "Matilda, I believe one of your tears brought your dear husband, Anima, back from the dead. Did it not?"

"Yep," Queen Matilda said.

Queen Filanthropi, Morgana, and Queen Matilda studied the ashes, waiting for the unwanted resurrection of the enchantress.

"It's just sittin' on top of da ashes," Morgana said. "Maybe we can soak it up before da ashes absorb it."

"You are brilliant." Queen Filanthropi removed a handkerchief from her pocket and handed it to her servant. "Here, you do it."

Morgana scowled. "Thanks."

The servant woman studied the queen's handkerchief and folded it eight times for maximum absorbency.

"Hurry up," Queen Matilda said.

"I'm hurryin'." Morgana knelt before the pile of ashes. "Dis is a delicate procedure. I don't wanna mess it up." She reached out and tentatively touched the tear with the handkerchief, but nothing happened. She made a second attempt to capture the tear. Still nothing happened.

Queen Filanthropi snatched the handkerchief from Morgana. "Give it to me. Just how hard can it be?"

The queen of Idlebury lifted her gown and knelt. She shifted her weight so she could lean in to Wilameena's ashes. But her right knee rested on a pebble, producing just enough pain to throw her off-balance. As she attempted to not fall into the ashes, she accidently dropped the handkerchief. "Darn stone," Queen Filanthropi said as she brushed off her knee. She grabbed the handkerchief, shook off the dirt, scrunched it, and leaned forward. She almost touched the tear when a speck of dirt beat her to it. A slurping sound preceded the disappearance of the tear into the gray ashes. "Oops," she said.

Morgana and Queen Matilda stared at the ashes in disappointed silence.

Queen Filanthropi joined the others.

"Looks like no harm's done," Morgana said.

The dragon queen took a deep breath. "I hope you're right."

"How long did it take for Anima to come back to life?" Queen Filanthropi asked.

"Don't know. I didn't hang around. Could have been seconds, minutes, hours, days—"

"Okay. Okay. I get it," Queen Filanthropi whined. "Now what?"

"Well, it appears dat even in death, Wilameena is in da way of us doin' what we need ta do," Morgana said.

"*Mistofisee*," Queen Matilda roared. "How could I forget

196

about my son?"

"*Thane.*" Queen Filanthropi said.

"Ashes to ashes and dust to dust, a mother will do what a mother must," the three mothers said in unison.

The dragon queen raised her wings and said, "Time to find our sons." As she took off, she snatched Queen Filanthropi and Morgana and then soared through the dimensions on a mission to find Mistofisee and Thane.

The pile of ashes stirred and Wilameena emerged. As she dusted off her frumpy dress, she watched Queen Matilda, Queen Filanthropi, and Morgana disappear from sight. "Why do they hate me? I was only trying to help."

Chapter Twenty-Five
The Fight of the Three Kings

Deep in the Slothful Forest, King Abracadabra and Thane engaged in a deadly fight, resulting in flashes of light, yelling, and pained grunting. Despite the darkness of the forest and King Abracadabra's blurred eyesight, he held his ground against Thane. But a few minutes into their fight, the old wizard realized he was no match for the young prince, making him regret kidnapping the child.

Although the king had astonishing powers, Thane had stamina. And if King Abracadabra admitted it, despite his youth, Thane was an incredibly talented wizard.

Nonetheless, the king of Hexidonia refused to give up. In fact, he doubled his efforts, yelling magic curses and thrusting his sword at his young nemesis. No matter what, the curses had no effect on the prince of Idlebury. But every curse, hex, and charm Thane hurled at King Abracadabra threw the old wizard to the ground, sapping his energy. What was more extraordinary, Thane was wandless, invoking power from the tips of his fingers—a feat not lost on the king of Hexidonia, who had often declared himself to be the greatest wizard who'd ever lived and who was now being made a fool of by a boy, albeit a boy destined for greatness.

"Hippity, dippity, yummy, and cruel. I am the one who will make you a fool," King Abracadabra yelled.

"What?" Thane gasped for breath. "You've got it all wrong. It's not hippity, dippity, yummy, and cruel. It's snippity, whimpity, yahoo, and drool. I am the great one and you are the fool."

Instantaneously King Abracadabra turned into a court jester. The king was not amused. Soon he turned back into himself, drew his sword, and lunged at Thane. The sword passed through the boy's body as if he were made of butter. Shocked at his impulsive act, the king withdrew his sword. He fully expected Thane to get up and admonish him. But the sight of blood oozing from the child's body dashed all hope that Thane was unharmed.

"What have I done?" King Abracadabra cried as he knelt to check Thane's wound. The king lovingly stroked the boy's hair. "You will be all right. I know you will. Just hang in there."

Thane turned blue.

"No. No," the king of Hexidonia cried. He took Thane's limp hand in his and sobbed. "Live, live, wake, and stay. Death leave you be, for today is not your day."

"You should brush up on your charms, my dear man."

"What?" King Abracadabra asked, too distraught to glance at who had addressed him.

"You rusty old wizard, look what you've done."

"I know not what I have done."

"Get up. Stop acting like a moron."

With tears streaming down his wrinkled cheeks and in a voice cracked from weariness, King Abracadabra said, "Morrebidd, do something. You are the king of the dead. Save him."

"Why should I save him?"

"Because he has the book."

"Give me another reason."

"He is only a boy. An innocent boy."

"Give me a good reason."

"He is destined for greatness."

"No. I said give me a good reason."

"I have done something horribly regrettable." King Abracadabra choked back a sob. "And I cannot live with myself if this child dies."

"Now you're talking." The king of the dead scooped Thane up in his bony arms. He studied the young prince, then abruptly handed him back to King Abracadabra. "I can't save him."

"Why not?"

"He's not dead yet."

"So keep him from dying," King Abracadabra pleaded.

"I'm the king of the dead, not the king of the dying."

"So save him anyway."

"No. You have to finish what you've started."

"What do you mean?"

"You have to kill him, you old fool."

King Abracadabra took a step toward King Morrebidd, his eyes blazing with anger. "I will do no such thing."

"It's your choice, but if you want him to live, you have to kill him first. Only then can I restore his life."

"And if I do not?"

"He will live, but he will not have a life."

"What are you saying?"

"I'm saying you did horrible damage to his body. So thanks to you, Abracadabra, although Thane will survive, he will not *live*."

"So he will always be unconscious, in a coma?"

"Something like that."

"But if he dies, then you can bring him back to life?"

"I see you weren't listening, Abracadabra. I said if *you* kill him, I can bring him back to life."

King Abracadabra stared at King Morrebidd. "I cannot. I will not. I think you are trying to trap me."

"Trap you?"

"Yes."

"Why would I do such a thing?"

"Because if I kill the prince of Idlebury, I will be scorned by every creature in the universe. I will be banished for eternity."

"And the problem is?"

"Do not get snide with me, Morrebidd." King Abracadabra looked away, trying to keep his burning anger in check. "If I am banished to who knows where, I will never gain possession of the book. And that means either you or Ovazealous may someday rule the universe."

"Ovazealous will never rule the universe. He's—"

An unseen force pushed the king of the dead. He stumbled into King Abracadabra and knocked Thane from the old man's grasp. Thane rose, his body shaped as if someone held him across their arms.

"I may not rule the universe," the voice of an unseen man said, "but I will not be party to the death of this child."

King Morrebidd grunted. "What are you doing here, Ovazealous?"

King Ovazealous, who had been friends with King Morrebidd and King Abracadabra for hundreds of years, obviously bore no shame when he materialized before them, clad in ragged clothes and holding Thane. "I came to warn you, but now is not the time. This child is dying. And I know who can save him." Ovazealous walked away, carrying Thane.

"I could save him if Abracadabra would kill him."

King Ovazealous looked over his shoulder. "You are crazy, Morrebidd."

"Who do you think can save the child?" King Morrebidd asked.

"The Great Wizard. That is who."

King Morrebidd and King Abracadabra laughed.

"Thane will be dead before you find the Great Wizard," the king of Deadonia said. "No one knows who he is."

"It is just like you to be so deceitful, Morrebidd. We all know who the Great Wizard is. And he will save him. Just wait and see." Instantly King Ovazealous and Thane disappeared.

"I don't trust him," King Morrebidd said.

"I do not trust Ovazealous either," King Abracadabra said as he stood.

"Not Ovazealous. I don't trust Thane."

"What do you mean? I stabbed him."

"Are you sure?"

"I think I am sure. But now that you mention it, the sword did seem to pass through his body a little too easily."

"Like he had no bones?"

"Yes, like he had no bones."

"We've been duped," King Morrebidd said.

"By whom? Who would be so stupid as to try to fool us?"

"Oh please, Abracadabra, anyone could fool you. Your wife has taken you for a fool for years. I for one know you've fallen for her schemes."

"Do not be so quick to judge me. I know Opunzayzme's heart yearns for you. Nonetheless, it is me to whom she is loyal."

"She'll be loyal to whomever gets their hands on *A Magic Maniac's Many Ways to*—" A branch snapped, interrupting the king of the dead. "Who's there?"

He was answered with silence.

"No one is there," King Abracadabra said. "You are stalling so we do not have to discuss my wife's true intentions."

"Believe what you want. But I must get back to Deadonia. It appears my *lovely* wife believed me when I told her I would return with the body of Prince Thane. She spent the greater part of the morning digging his grave. When I left, she was weeping beside it. I guess I should console the poor soul and tell her Thane lives. No thanks to you, of course."

"I never intended to kill him."

"Well lucky you, you didn't."

King Abracadabra sneered at King Morrebidd.

"Now, now, Abracadabra. Don't fret. I'm sure one of Opunzayzme's wicked wands can do the job. Don't you think?"

In anger, King Abracadabra aimed his sword at King Morrebidd and shouted, "Humongous ratoria."

King Morrebidd shook his head. "As I thought, you're a pathetic wizard." He raised his fleshless arm, pointed a finger at the aged king of Hexidonia, and as a bolt of light escaped his finger, he shouted, "*Humongous* ratoria."

King Abracadabra immediately transformed into a huge rat.

In shame, he scurried off.

King Morrebidd watched as the large rat took flight and disappeared. "Go home to your gullible people and your stupid hag of a wife," he yelled.

The king of Deadonia walked over to a bush. He ruffled its leaves and then leaned against a tree, nonchalantly picking at a fingernail. "Thane, I know it wasn't you who King Abracadabra stabbed. But oh, how I wish it were. And just so you know, when King Abracadabra finds out, run like your hair's on fire."

Moments later, King Morrebidd laughed, dematerialized into a cloud of ash, and disappeared into the universe.

Chapter Twenty-Six
Thane and Blabberdish's Reunion

T hane waited for several minutes before emerging from his hiding place behind the bush. Forgetting about the Slothful Forest's putrid air, he did something he immediately regretted—he took a deep breath. A few hacking coughs and gasps later, he regained his senses. "Blabberdish?"

No answer.

"Blabberdish, where are you? I know it was you pretending to be me."

No answer.

Thane was alone and scared in the dark, eerie forest with no one to protect him from the creatures of the night. When he saw Idlebury Castle in the distance, he took off running. He was hungry and exhausted. But right now nothing mattered more than getting home to the safety of his own bed. He ran so hard and fast that he tripped several times and soiled his clothes with stinky muck. But he didn't care; he just wanted to get home.

As Thane neared Idlebury Castle, the echo of footsteps behind him increased his fear, but he dared not look back. *If it was someone I know, they'd call my name*, he thought. As he raced down the drawbridge in full stride, he realized he was running, but whoever was behind him was taking slow, deliberate steps. Still, Thane refused to look behind him. He slid to a stop in front of the castle doors and pulled the knobs, but he was too weak to open the huge, heavy doors.

The footsteps grew louder and then stopped. Thane looked to see who was behind him, but no one was there. Magically the castle doors creaked opened just enough for Thane to slip inside. With his last bit of strength, he charged upstairs to his room. He slammed the door behind him and collapsed on his bed. As he gasped for breath, the door to his room opened a crack and then closed.

Thane shook as he recalled the harrowing exchange with King Abracadabra and King Morrebidd. "When King Abracadabra abducted me, I thought I was a goner. If it weren't for Blabberdish, I'd be dead," he mumbled.

"Righto, my friend," Blabberdish said, standing at the foot of Thane's bed. "If it weren't for me, you'd be dead."

"Blabberdish!" Thane exclaimed as he lifted the worm and held him in the palm of his hand. He was so happy to see his friend that he wanted to kiss him. But he fought the urge, knowing displays of affection weren't a guy thing.

"How did you know it was me?"

"At first I thought it was Wilameena up to her old tricks. But when you used the same tricks we've practiced, I knew it had to be you. I didn't know you could transform into a human."

"Piece of cake," Blabberdish said, bragging. "I don't do it often though. In fact, I haven't done it for nearly one hundred years because it's exhausting to transform my tiny self into a ginormous creature as large as a human."

"Well, I'm glad you're okay. I thought King Abracadabra

had killed you."

"Killed me?" Blabberdish jumped off Thane's hand and landed on the boy's chest. "He'd never harm me."

"Why not?"

"For starters, King Abracadabra holds me in high regard."

"But he didn't know I was you, he thought you were me."

"I don't believe he would kill you either, at least not deliberately."

"That's reassuring?" Thane rolled his eyes. "Where did King Ovazealous take you?"

"That wasn't King Ovazealous."

"Then who was it?"

Blabberdish took a deep breath. "You're not going to believe it, but it was none other than the most despicable person who gets into everyone's business and creates chaos wherever—"

"Wilameena?" Thane said with disbelief. "She wanted to save me?"

"I wouldn't go that far. Until she picked you up, I mean picked me up, she thought I was you. When she realized I wasn't you, she dropped me and raced after you. While I was falling from the sky, I saw you running up the drawbridge. That's when I noticed the most curious thing." Blabberdish stopped and stared at Thane, as if to contemplate the necessity of continuing.

"What? What was curious?"

"Well, if you must know, Oof was walking ever so slowly behind you, yet he kept up with you despite the fact you were running with all your might."

"It was Oof's footsteps I heard?"

"Yep. He opened the door for you. Didn't you see him?"

"No. I wonder why he followed me." Thane paused, lost in thought. "So what happened to Wilameena?"

"When she saw Oof, she hid behind a bush. I think I heard her crying."

Thane abruptly jumped off his bed, knocking Blabberdish to the floor. He leaned on his desk and looked out the window. "I wish Wilameena would butt out. She could have gotten you killed."

Blabberdish jumped on the windowsill. "I can't be killed by anyone or anything, let alone Wilameena and her pathetic tricks."

"Why can't you be killed?"

"Because I'm a worm." Blabberdish threw his hands up, clearly frustrated with Thane's lack of understanding as to worm rejuvenation. "If you cut me in half, I'll just grow into two of me. Even three of me if need be."

"That's a scary thought. One of you is enough. But what if you get squished?"

"Well, that's another story."

"So you can be killed," Thane said, frightened at the thought he could lose his best friend.

"Not really. If I get squished, it just takes me longer to regenerate, that's all."

Thane plopped in his chair and put his feet up on his desk. "Well, it's good to know I don't have to worry about you."

Blabberdish jumped on the toe of Thane's shoe and shook a tiny finger at the boy. "I wish I didn't have to worry about you. But I see that I do."

"What do you mean?"

"It was quite clear King Morrebidd wanted you dead. And I

for one don't believe he would have restored you to life if King Abracadabra had killed you."

"Whatever." Thane got up, knocking Blabberdish to the floor again. He went back to his bed, stretched out, and yawned. "I'll take a nap. Then we can continue our hunt for *A Magic Maniac's Many Ways to Make Mischief*."

The bookworm jumped on Thane's nose, and with his little hands, he smacked the boy on the forehead. "Oh no, you don't. We're going now. We don't have time for you to sleep. It's beyond belief that you, of all people, would want to suspend your search for something so important. And remember, my family is in the book. I have to find it, and you have to help me. *Now*." Blabberdish waited for a response from the young prince. When one wasn't forthcoming, the worm slapped Thane on the cheek. "*I said, now*."

"All right already." Thane went to a large mirror on the other side of the room. He studied himself and scrutinized his face. "I look terrible."

"Not as terrible as you'd look if you were dead," Blabberdish said, his tone serious.

Suddenly Thane was shoved through the mirror as if it were an invisible door to an invisible world. The next thing he knew, he was floating. Soon he began to fall, faster and faster. He tumbled onto a floor. The back of the mirror was in front of him. He noticed he was still in his room. But a closer look revealed that although it looked like his room, it was different. He tried to walk around the right side of the mirror, but a force field stopped him. When he tried to walk around the left side of the mirror, the force field stopped him again.

Thane had an idea. "Since I fell through the front of the mirror and ended up here, maybe if I go through the back of the mirror I'll be back in my room." Before he gave it a try, he took a look at the room. "It looks like my room. But there's something different. It looks more grown-up. It looks like a wizard's room." He spotted something that made his heart skip. *A Magic Maniac's Many Ways to Make Mischief* sat on a bookshelf along with many other books about magic.

Thane bolted for the book, but the force field threw him to the floor, knocking the wind out of him. He propped himself with his arms stretched out behind him, his knees bent, and his feet flat on the floor. As he tried to catch his breath, he saw Blabberdish shimmy across the floor, climb up the bookcase, and wiggle his way into the universe's most coveted magic book.

Someone entered the room. Thane's eyes nearly popped out of his head as he strained to see who it was. But all he saw were a pair of highly polished men's shoes. Thane tried to stand up but couldn't. The man reached through the force field, grabbed Thane, and threw him through the back of the mirror. Thane's world went black, followed by a sensation of racing uncontrollably through space. He couldn't see, hear, or feel anything.

Seconds later, a wave of peace overcame him. He saw a bright light and instinctively went toward it. As he got closer, he saw a person. The person held out his hand as if to tell Thane it was okay to go with him. Thane reached out, completely unafraid. Just before his and the man's fingers touched, he realized who it was. Thane snapped his hand back. The man reached for him again.

And although the man didn't speak, Thane heard him say, "Please set me free. I need you. The universe needs you."

Thane yelled, *"No."* To his surprise, he was thrown back through the mirror and into his real room. He landed hard on the floor and slid into his dresser. As he rubbed his knee, he glanced around his room. It looked the same, but he knew everything had changed because he had changed. But he had yet to discover just how much.

Chapter Twenty-Seven
The Great Wizard's Letter

G wen rolled her eyes, then banged her head on the table, momentarily forgetting any number of invisible Imaginorians could be watching the heated exchange between her and their king regarding the king's role in the search for *A Magic Maniac's Many Ways to Make Mischief*. Although Gwen loved a good argument, she'd grown frustrated debating an invisible person. Despite that, she maintained her fantasy image of a glamorous, regal Imaginoria. As Gwen and the king of Imaginoria continued their heated discussion, a tray floated toward the king.

Obviously Gwen couldn't see King Ovazealous glance at the tray as he continued the conversation. "It is utterly ridiculous that you continue to accuse me of colluding with the likes of King Abracadabra and King Morrebidd. And it is astounding that you do not believe in the Great Wizard."

"Then prove me wrong on both counts," Gwen said as the tray diverted her attention. When she saw the image of a horse stamped in wax on the envelope, her stomach churned because the same insignia graced the cover of *A Magic Maniac's Many Ways to Make Mischief*.

The envelope appeared to jump off the tray signifying King

Ovazealous had snatched it. For a moment the envelope remained suspended in midair before it flipped over as if the king wanted to look at the seal again. It flipped back and was still for a suspiciously long time.

Is he studying the handwriting? Does he recognize it? Gwen wondered.

The invisible king flung the envelope at Gwen. It hit her in the chest before it landed in her lap. "It is for you," he said.

Gwen picked up the envelope without saying a word or looking in the king's direction. Truth be told, she was angry at King Ovazealous's childish behavior. *A king throwing an envelope at a child. What a moron.* But she wasn't about to voice her disdain with King Ovazealous because she wasn't finished with him yet, not until she determined if he could be of use to her or not.

Gwen rubbed her finger over the wax seal, then turned over the envelope and studied the writing. Seeing her full title in beautiful calligraphy made her feel important. *Why did King Ovazealous hold it for so long? What was of such interest to him?*

King Ovazealous yanked the envelope from Gwen. "Just open it," he grumbled as he ripped it open, not so gently removed the letter from the destroyed envelope, and then flung the letter at Gwen. It landed on her plate.

Gwen graciously picked up the letter, hoping her restrained behavior would annoy the childish king. *Why is he so anxious for me to open the letter? Does he know who it's from? Does he know what news it will tell? Probably not. He's not that smart.* Finally Gwen opened the letter.

"Well, what does it say?" King Ovazealous asked impatiently.

Gwen held up the open letter to let King Ovazealous see its

contents. "Nothing. It's blank."

"The letter is not blank. It is merely invisible."

"I believe it would be correct to say the ink, if there is ink, is invisible. The letter, or more correctly the paper, is quite visible." Gwen shook the piece of paper at the invisible king.

"Who is stupid enough to send *you* an invisible message? I demand to know."

"The stupidity of it is yet to be determined." Gwen nonchalantly picked up her glass and took a sip of chocolate milk. Condensation on the glass caused a drop of water to splash on the letter. Much to her surprise, the droplet's contact with the paper revealed letters. Gwen grabbed her napkin, and forgetting etiquette, she plunged part of it into the pitcher of water. She gently rubbed the water over the paper, revealing its message.

Gwen read with silent interest.

My dearest Gwendolyn the Great, Savior of Idlebury, Protector of the Universe:

It has been brought to my attention you have made a serious allegation regarding my existence. Your belief that I do not exist does not make it true. After all, belief and reality are two different things. Personally, I do not care whether or not you believe in me, for I am fully alive no matter who believes or does not believe in my existence.

That said, I want you to know I and many others believe in your greatness. You did not become Gwendolyn the Great, Savior of Idlebury, Protector of the Universe by chance or birthright. You put forth great physical and intellectual effort, you trusted in the power of friendship, you overcame challenges to your moral convictions, and most of all, you trudged forward when you questioned your ability to succeed. Those traits are what I need most from you now.

Your brother, Prince Thane, is in serious danger. And although my deepest desire is for the survival of this precious child, I am in a quandary. Let me explain.

As you may know, Prince Thane is destined for greatness and will eventually overthrow me and be ordained as the Great Wizard. At that time, I will die. On the other hand, if Prince Thane dies before reaching his destiny, I will live until another person—one worthy of the title and responsibilities afforded the Great Wizard—is chosen. Unfortunately, that may never be. As I am already an ancient man, my energy and the fortitude necessary to perform my duties are rapidly waning. This increasingly threatens the well-being of all creatures in the many dimensions. Thus the future of the universe is dubious.

To ensure the survival of the universe, my death would be a much-welcomed relief. Unfortunately, Prince Thane is far from ready to become the Great Wizard. And I am far from able to perform my duties. Therefore, as the Protector of the Universe, it is imperative that you save your brother.

Hence, I wish to make you an offer. I know your powers are limited, so I am willing to temporarily grant you mine and bestow upon you the title of Great Wizard **Temporarius,** *thus ensuring your ability to save Prince Thane from the evils and dangers that may befall him before he gains the maturity and integrity necessary to deserve the title Great Wizard. Beyond that, I cannot guarantee the safety or survival of anyone else, including you.*

If you are willing and able to accept my offer, meet me at

Idlebury Castle in the great hall tomorrow night at the stroke of midnight. And remember, you must not whisper a word of this to anyone, especially not King Ovazealous.

With all my heart and soul, I remain respectfully yours,

The Great Wizard

Gwen folded the letter and stuffed it in her dress. Emotions fought the thoughts racing through her head. In an attempt to calm her nerves and slow her mind, she chugged her chocolate milk.

"Well?" King Ovazealous asked. "Who was it from? What did they say?"

"No one. Nothing." Gwen shot up from her chair with the stiffness of a robot. "I have to go. I've been called home to…"

"You've been called home to where?"

"I have to go home, that's all." Gwen curtsied. "Thank you for a lovely time. I hope we can do it again soon." Without waiting for King Ovazealous's response, she ran out of the room, raced through the palace, and then burst through the gilded entrance doors. She glanced at the palace grounds, not sure how to get out of Imaginoria.

An invisible hand grabbed Gwen by the arm and yanked her in the opposite direction from which she was looking.

"Hurry. You must leave," a man whom Gwen recognized as the Duke of Reality said. "The beam is angry. And that is never a good thing."

Gwen and the duke ran hand in hand across the lawn. "Why? What does it mean?"

"It means the Great Wizard has been awakened." Huffing and puffing like either someone very old or someone extremely out of shape, the Duke of Reality tugged Gwen toward the beam.

"Is that a good thing or a bad thing?"

"I do not know. No one knows."

"Why not?"

"Because no one knows who the Great Wizard is." The duke gasped for breath. "And no one has seen him for nearly a thousand years."

The duke thrust Gwen before the beam. Its light, no longer a warm yellow, flashed red as it struggled to hold its form. Gwen took one last look at Imaginoria's palace before the beam engulfed her and she was gone.

The Duke of Reality walked toward the palace, which was still visible as Gwen had imagined it. He stopped to admire its beauty. "What an incredible girl. She is gone, and yet her vision of Imaginoria is still holding. If what is foretold of her brother is true, then Thane surely will be a force to be reckoned with. And to think, no one of greatness has ever come from Idlebury, and now there are two. What is the universe coming to?"

Chapter Twenty-Eight
The Soul Seeker's Revelations

"*Stop,*" Queen Filanthropi yelled, nearly causing the dragon queen to lose control as she halted her flight.

Queen Matilda scanned the area. "What do you see?"

"Nothing. Absolutely nothing. That is the point."

"Say what?"

"You have no direction. You know not where you are going. It would appear to me your only hope is to stumble upon Mistofisee and Thane."

The dragon queen turned her huge head behind her and glared at Queen Filanthropi. "Do you have a better idea?"

In her typically snooty manner, Queen Filanthropi said, "Not exactly."

"I'm not surprised," the dragon queen said and then angrily snorted a plume of fire.

"Do not mock me, Matilda. We are in this together, and it is only together that we will find our sons."

"Here, here," Morgana said.

"So, Filanthropi, what do we do now?"

"We go to Idlebury."

"*Idlebury?* What makes you think we'll find our sons in Idlebury?"

"I do not think we will find them there, but we need to rest, refresh, and regroup. And right now I know of no better place to do just that."

"I do," Queen Matilda said.

"Where? Pray tell," the queen of Idlebury said.

"Hedonia."

"Hedonia? Where fun is serious business and where serious business is no fun? Do you think finding our sons is some kind of joke?"

"Of course not." Queen Matilda took off for Dimension II with such speed Queen Filanthropi and Morgana nearly slid off her back.

A chill ran through Queen Filanthropi. *Has Matilda gone mad?* she wondered. *No, it must be the instinct of the queen of the Innocents. I must trust she is right. She would never risk the life of her son on a silly whim.*

A ripple in the universe signaled the dragon queen's and her riders' passage into Dimension XII. Soon Anhedonia came into sight. The whining and crying of its citizens reverberated throughout the dimension.

"Wah wah wah wah wah wah wah," Queen Filanthropi said, poking fun at the whiny crybabies of Anhedonia. "Sometimes I think my people are more closely related to the Anhedonians than they know."

Later, Hedonia in Dimension II came into view. Sounds of music and laughter echoed in the distance. Matilda flew full speed ahead, only to be stopped by a force. The three mothers froze in space and time as they floated separately in a void. The universe went black and silent. Queen Matilda, Queen

Filanthropi, and Morgana could see and hear nothing but each other. They remained silent, cocooned in darkness and fear.

"Where are you going?" a man asked, his voice booming.

The three mothers didn't answer.

"I asked you where are you going?"

Queen Filanthropi addressed the being. "Get out of the way. You are hindering our progress."

"How dare you tell me what to do?" the man said. "Tell me where you are going, or I will toss you to the end of the universe."

"Well, Matilda, tell the man where we are going," Queen Filanthropi said. "After all, it was your idea."

Morgana nodded in agreement.

"We're going to Hedonia," Queen Matilda said.

"Why?" the man asked.

"Go ahead, Filanthropi," the dragon queen said. "Tell the man why we're going to Hedonia."

"To rest, refresh, and regroup."

"Why must you always speak in alliteration, Filanthropi?" the man asked.

"Who do you think you are to address me in such a manner?"

Stars, galaxies, and kingdoms appeared to the right and left of the threesome.

"It's backin' up, it is," Morgana said.

The creature took form before them.

"Oh him," the dragon queen complained. "What do you want with us?"

"I have something to show you." The Soul Seeker opened his cape and revealed live-action images.

One was of Gwen inside the weakened red beam en route to Idlebury.

Outside Idlebury Castle, Thane and Blabberdish practiced spells.

Inside Seedonia Castle, King Heroian begged his father-in-law, King Harvestor, for the many items needed for Idlebury's upcoming planting season.

In Hexidonia Castle, King Abracadabra studied the writing on his sword and mumbled a nonsensical chant.

In Deadonia, King Morrebidd consoled his weeping wife, Queen DeMysora, as they stood in front of a grave.

Dressed in rags, King Ovazealous of Imaginoria sat on a dilapidated throne and laughed to himself.

Deep in the Slothful Forest, Wilameena flashed in and out of existence as if she'd lost her powers.

The last image was of a man dressed as a wizard.

"Who is that?" Queen Filanthropi asked.

"That, Filanthropi, is the Great Wizard," the Soul Seeker said.

"But he does not exist," Queen Filanthropi said.

"Oh, but he does. Always has. Always will," the Soul Seeker replied.

Queen Matilda and Queen Filanthropi shared a knowing glance.

"Why are you showing us this?" Queen Matilda asked.

"Because these are the beings who have the power to irrevocably change the universe."

"Where is Mistofisee? Why haven't you shown my son?"

"Your son is of no consequence."

"I beg your pardon," the dragon queen said. "My son will

one day rule the kingdom of Beastonia—the most important kingdom in the universe."

"I did not say Mistofisee has no future or purpose, but at this moment in time, he is of no consequence. Unless…" The Soul Seeker paused.

"Unless what?" Queen Matilda asked.

"Unless he is called upon by the Great Wizard."

"Why would the Great Wizard need Mistofisee's help?"

The Soul Seeker folded his cape and disappeared. As the stars returned to view, an angered Queen Matilda yelled, "I asked why the Great Wizard would need Mistofisee's help?" When there was no reply, the dragon queen angrily spewed forth a stream of fire.

The voice of the Soul Seeker rang out from the distance. "Because the Great Wizard is not who you think he is—at least not for the time being."

"What? What did he say?" Queen Matilda asked.

"I believe he said the Great Wizard is not who we think he is—at least not for the time being," Queen Filanthropi replied.

"Dat's what he said, he did," Morgana said.

Queen Matilda stretched her long neck and looked eye to eye with Queen Filanthropi. "Well, that begs another question."

Queen Filanthropi stared back. "Okay. Go on. Ask."

"Who do you think is the Great Wizard?"

"I do not know." Queen Filanthropi looked down. "I did not get a good look at him."

"It seems we all saw the same person, and I know who he is. Don't you, Morgana?"

Morgana took a deep breath and scrunched her face as if contemplating her answer.

"Well? Who is it?" Queen Filanthropi demanded.

"I don't know," Morgana said.

"Neither do I." Queen Filanthropi smirked. "But it appears Matilda is acquainted with him."

"Come off it, Filanthropi. You and I both know who he is. And I'm suspicious as to why you refuse to admit it."

"I told you I do not know the man. End of discussion."

"You're so stubborn."

The dragon queen's remarks deeply hurt Queen Filanthropi's feelings. Of course she'd recognized the Great Wizard. But the Soul Seeker's departing words that the Great Wizard wasn't who she thought he was—at least not for the time being—nearly paralyzed her with fear.

The dragon queen waved a claw in Queen Filanthropi's face. "*Yo*. Snap out of it. We have business in Hedonia."

As Queen Filanthropi climbed on her dragon friend's back, the Soul Seeker's words echoed in her head. Her stomach churned. His words were a warning that the power of the Great Wizard had been unleashed. Meaning she could no longer deny the Great Wizard's existence. Worse, if the Great Wizard's powers had fallen into the wrong hands, the universe could be destroyed. And mother's intuition told her she might never see her children again. *"I must find my babies,"* she yelled.

CHAPTER TWENTY-NINE
THE RED BEAM'S PRECIOUS CARGO

Thane's body felt heavy. His movements were awkward and trying. He reached out for his desk chair, missed, and stumbled to the floor. He trembled. Something had changed. Something was horribly wrong. He looked at the mirror from which he was thrust back into his room and saw an image of a young man who had strikingly handsome features and flowing blond hair.

Thane examined the image. He looked around his room, but he didn't see the man anywhere. He grabbed his desk and pulled himself up. His muscles bulged and throbbed. With both hands flat on the desktop for support, he took a deep breath. Even that hurt. He looked up and gazed out his bedroom window at a full moon that cast a soft light over Idlebury. A few Idleburians walked about and chatted with each other, but the lighted homes were evidence most had retired for the evening. As Thane continued to look out over Idlebury, a sense of doom made him shiver. There was no doubt that although everything seemed all right, something was terribly wrong.

Upon seeing Thane peering out the window, a woman screamed, causing the other Idleburians to run for the safety of their homes. But one person remained still while everyone rushed around him. It was a young boy. Thane noticed the boy's beauty. But the child's engaging blue eyes, unbelievably visible from a distance as they sparkled under the light of the moon, captivated him.

The young boy waved at Thane. Thane tried to wave back, but he couldn't lift his hand. He noticed something about the child. "I don't believe it," he said. "That's me." He looked down at himself and said, "But this is me too." When he looked back, the boy was gone.

"Oh, come off it," Blabberdish said as he bounced on Thane's bed. "You've been looking out the window for hours. What's wrong with you?"

"That's what I'd like to know. What is wrong with me?"

Blabberdish chuckled and continued to jump up and down on the bed. "Well, there isn't enough time in the universe to answer that question."

"How can you kid around at a time like this?"

"Why is this time any different from any other?"

"Can't you see something is horribly wrong with me?"

Blabberdish hopped over to Thane and wriggled up on his shoe. "You look the same to me."

Thane picked up his friend. The boy and the worm stared at each other.

"Well?" Blabberdish asked, his eyes appearing unusually large through the thick lenses of his huge red glasses.

"Well, what?"

"What's ailing you?" Blabberdish jumped out of Thane's hand and onto the desk. "You look fine to me."

Thane looked at the mirror. To his relief, he was back to

normal. Yet he felt different. He was about to tell Blabberdish what had happened to him when something outside caught his attention. With his face pressed against the window, he said. "There's a red beam of light chasing someone."

Blabberdish gulped. "Did you say a red beam?"

"Yep, and it's chasing some crazy woman who's flailing her arms. I think she's screaming."

In seconds, Blabberdish was airborne. He smashed into the window and stuck on the glass like a blob of putty. At the sight of the red beam, he trembled. "That's not just a woman, that's— "

"Wilameena." Thane slammed his fist on the desk. "Will we ever be free of that woman?"

"Be careful what you wish for," Blabberdish said, still stuck on the window.

"What do you mean?"

"She serves a purpose." The worm wriggled and writhed in an attempt to spring himself from the window. "A purpose someone else will fulfill when she's gooone." Blabberdish finally freed himself and plopped on the desk.

"So?" Thane extended a finger to help his friend stand upright.

Blabberdish wrapped himself around Thane's finger and rose to his full height, all three inches of it. "So we might be better off with Wilameena than with—"

"Who?" Thane asked.

"I believe the correct question is with whom?"

"Just answer my question."

Blabberdish jumped off Thane's finger and landed on the desk. "I can't."

"Why not?" Thane watched Blabberdish pace frantically, seemingly unable to come up with a response.

"Because it would be pure conjecture on my part," Blabberdish exclaimed.

"So?"

"If I said the person's name, I could potentially be lying, and that would be wrong."

"Well, I can't think of anyone who is vile enough to take Wilameena's place."

"Don't worry. Prudence is a viable candidate. Or at least she will be. Oh boy. Open mouth, insert foot."

"Prudence?" Thane squinted at Blabberdish. "She's practically a baby."

"So she is," Blabberdish said. "My bad."

Thane leaned forward, his forehead touching the window. "Wilameena's screaming. What is she saying?"

Blabberdish jumped on the window again. "She's saying something about Oof."

Thane listened intently. The enchantress was now close enough for him to hear her screaming. "Oof, save me. Don't let her in. Save me. Please, Oof. If you love me, you'll listen to me."

"If you love me, you'll listen to me?" Thane laughed. "She can't possibly believe anyone, especially Oof, loves her."

Blabberdish jumped onto the desk and then nonchalantly leaned against a stack of books. "Truth is stranger than fiction."

But Thane didn't hear him because what he saw in the red beam fascinated him. It looked like a butterfly tucked in a cocoon. Something sparkled. *Are those diamonds? Gold? Silver? Water?* he wondered. He noticed what appeared to be beautiful clothing, possibly a cape. The beam stopped and pulsated as if trying to conserve energy. "What's up with the beam?"

Blabberdish casually ran his fingers across the spines of the books on Thane's desk. "It's tired."

"Why would it be tired?"

"Because it's carrying someone of great importance."

"Why did it stop?"

Blabberdish jumped on top of the books. "Because the person it carries has not accepted his, I mean her, fate."

"Why are you so calm about all this?"

"What do you mean?" Blabberdish jumped off the books and landed on Thane's arm.

"Well, let's see. Wilameena just ran into the castle, screaming for Oof to not let the beam or whomever the beam is carrying, into the castle. Then the beam appears weakened and stops. And you say it stopped because it's carrying someone of great importance who has not accepted her fate. It's weird this doesn't concern you. I would say you are—"

Pounding on the castle door stopped Thane in midsentence.

"Someone let me in," Wilameena yelled. "Please, before it's too late. Oof, I know who you are. Please open up. Let me in. I need to warn you. If you love me, you'll let me in."

The castle door creaked open. A bony hand reached out, grabbed Wilameena, and flung her skyward. As she disappeared into the far reaches of the universe, her screams echoed throughout the dimensions.

The beam pulsated faster and faster. Its color changed from red to orange as it gained strength.

Thane gasped.

Blabberdish took a flying leap onto the window. "It's happening," he yelled.

"What's happening?"

"She's accepted her fate." Blabberdish grinned. "The Great Wizard has returned."

Without warning, Thane snatched Blabberdish. "Let's follow her."

Thane squeezed Blabberdish so tight the worm could barely breathe, let alone talk or wiggle away. In other words, Thane had rendered Blabberdish powerless.

Chapter Thirty
The Hedonians Get Buzzed

The ruckus from Hedonia startled Queen Matilda. *Those people are having a little too much fun,* she thought. The dragon queen wanted to turn back, but she knew she had to speak to Queen Merry and ask her a question, the answer to which the queen of Hedonia had been entrusted to keep secret for hundreds of years. The queen of Beastonia was nearly paralyzed by angst, for once she asked the question, the one of whom it was asked was obligated to answer. Even more, to not answer the question would destroy the universe. And there was no guarantee the answer wouldn't do the same.

The dragon queen and her riders entered Hedonian airspace. When Queen Matilda made a low flyover, the Hedonians grabbed their children and ran for safety. The sudden silence of the Hedonians alerted King Funzy and Queen Merry that something of a serious nature required their attention. The royal couple rushed to the balcony and found their people huddling in fear, clutching their children, and shielding the youngsters' eyes.

The unmistakable figure of Queen Matilda appeared above them.

Queen Merry gasped. "She is alive. The queen of the

Innocents lives."

"My dear people," King Funzy said. "Queen Matilda of Beastonia wishes to pay us a visit. As you know, she is always welcome in our kingdom. We will receive her with the utmost respect and hospitality. Now return to your homes, shops, and restaurants. It is time to prepare for our honored guest."

The Hedonians refused their king's request.

The insolence of his people surprised King Funzy. So he clapped his hands loudly and in rhythm said, "Chop, chop, hop, hop, hurry up, and do not stop."

The Hedonians moaned their displeasure.

"This is blasphemous," a man yelled. "Do you mean to tell us we are to stop having fun?"

"This is Hedonia, where fun is serious business and serious business is no fun," a woman shouted.

"Who says receiving Queen Matilda of Beastonia will not be great fun?" King Funzy asked.

Queen Merry stepped forward, raised her gloved hand, and hushed the crowd. "My fellow Hedonians, you are correct. The presence of Queen Matilda of Beastonia is indeed a serious matter. A matter that needs to be addressed in order for Hedonia to continue its tradition of fun for all, at all times, in all ways."

"We will *not* let her land," another man yelled. "If serious business is no fun, then she has no business here."

The crowd jeered. Someone threw a pastry at the royal couple.

"Nothing like this has ever occurred," King Funzy said to Queen Merry. "There is no protocol for what actions are appropriate when the fun stops."

Queen Matilda buzzed the crowd. The force of wind created

by the flapping of her enormous wings blew a few Hedonians to the ground. Children cried. People screamed. The din of the Hedonians' fear drowned out Queen Merry's attempts to calm them.

The dragon queen buzzed the crowd again.

King Funzy made a move to run for the castle, but Queen Merry yanked him close to her, thwarting his escape. "Wait," she whispered. "If she does that one more time, we must hold still and find out what she wants."

"Why?"

"I will tell you later."

Queen Matilda buzzed the Hedonians a third time, this time blowing fire as she roared.

The Hedonians scattered.

"What does she think she's doing?" King Funzy asked. "She's terrifying our people."

"Not to worry. I know what she's doing. Besides, we have no choice but to receive the queen of the Innocents. After all, I'm half Innocent." Queen Merry glanced at her gloves, which covered her hoofed hands, and then glanced at her grossly unstylish, clunky, closed-toe shoes that concealed her hoofed feet. "That means Matilda, queen of Beastonia, is my queen too."

King Funzy nodded. "Understood, my dear."

Queen Matilda's triple flyover meant she was requesting entrance into the kingdom of Hedonia under the direst circumstances. Even more, she was requesting permission to ask the question that must be asked. Only Queen Merry could grant her that permission.

King Funzy raised his hand and miraculously silenced his people. In a tone that conveyed the utmost seriousness, he said,

"Please, step back. Make room for the queen of the Innocents to land."

The Hedonians groaned, but they did what their king requested and parted to allow the largest beast in the universe to land on their soil.

After Queen Matilda made a graceful landing in the land of fun and frolic, she swung her huge head, and with her massive yellow eyes, she scanned the crowd of terrified Hedonians. The dragon queen cleared her throat. "My dear Hedonians, it's obvious my unannounced arrival has interfered with your good time. I sincerely apologize, but my presence here is necessary in order to save the universe and hence, preserve your pleasure."

"Save the universe? From what or from whom?" a man asked.

"From he who is believed to not exist," the queen of Beastonia replied.

The crowd fell silent, for every Hedonian knew of whom Queen Matilda referred.

Queen Merry and King Funzy stepped forward and bowed before the dragon queen.

"No need for formalities," the queen of Beastonia said. "We must get on with the issue at hand."

"Ahem."

"Oh my, I completely forgot about my passengers." Queen Matilda unraveled her long tail, allowing Queen Filanthropi and Morgana to slide to the ground. King Funzy ran to the aid of the queen of Idlebury and her servant.

"Welcome, Queen Filanthropi." King Funzy kissed the queen's outstretched hand. "And who is the person with whom you travel?"

"Her name is Morgana. She is my most treasured servant, and in her heart, she carries a mother's love for my son, Thane, whom you probably know is in serious trouble."

"Yes." King Funzy smiled broadly. "I greatly admire Thane's spunk and sense of fun. He is a clever boy. I believe he will go far."

"As long as he does not become the victim of one of Queen Opunzayzme's wicked wands," Queen Filanthropi said.

"A wicked wand, you say? Your father King Harvestor would know something about that... wouldn't he?"

Queen Filanthropi furrowed her brow and stared at King Funzy, as if confused by his statement regarding her father, the king of Seedonia.

"Time is of the essence," Queen Matilda said impatiently. "There's something I must discuss with Queen Merry in private. I apologize if my departure is rude, but I must speak with her now."

"Go on then. I will just wait here." Queen Filanthropi dramatically plopped to the ground. "Do not worry about me or my children, who, by the way, are scattered throughout the universe and who could be in any number of harrowing situations, any of which at any moment could end their precious lives." She waved her hand dismissively at the queen of Beastonia. "No, no, do not make my situation any concern of yours, Matilda."

The dragon queen looked the sulking queen of Idlebury in the eye and said, "As you wish." With Queen Merry at her side, Queen Matilda lumbered toward Hedonia's castle.

Morgana rushed to Queen Filanthropi and made an attempt to console her. Of course the queen rejected her gestures. But when King Funzy offered his hand to the distraught queen, she allowed him to help her to her feet.

"My dear Filanthropi, I'm afraid I have offended you. I apologize for not being more sensitive in these sensitive times."

"Apology accepted. But I do expect you can show me a good time during what I hope will be a short stay."

"Why, of course." King Funzy turned to the Hedonians and waved his hand. "Let the good times roll."

Immediately the Hedonians resumed their day's festivities. As the music commenced, King Funzy held out his hand and asked Queen Filanthropi, "May I have this dance?"

Queen Filanthropi accepted King Funzy's offer, after which the two royals danced a traditional waltz. "For the first time in years, I feel like a princess." She giggled like a schoolgirl.

Chapter Thirty-One
The Curse of the Three Kings

J ust before midnight, the beam and its occupant glided down the drawbridge and stopped at the door of Idlebury Castle.

The beam hummed.

Its occupant moaned.

The door creaked open.

The beam slipped inside. Its soft glow lit the gray walls of the drab castle, casting eerie shadows. As it carried its occupant through the castle, it momentarily stopped at the grand staircase, under which large yellow eyes glimmered, revealing a not-so-secret hiding place.

As the beam and its occupant approached the great hall, the double doors sparkled, first softly, then gradually increasing in intensity, turning the old doors of wood into shimmering solid gold.

The beam hummed and pulsated as it waited outside the gilded doors. Soon the doors to the great hall opened. The beam entered the empty room and moved to an ancient symbol set in colored tiles on the floor. It continued to pulsate—slow and rhythmic, then faster and faster. The being it carried remained still as the beam swirled, gaining speed and intensity. It stopped abruptly before returning to a slow, rhythmic pulse. It buzzed, softly at first. Gradually it buzzed louder before it dissipated.

In its place was a person, huddled on the floor and covered by a red velvet cape adorned with diamonds, rubies, and pearls. The person was still, making it difficult to tell if he or she was alive or dead.

Several minutes passed. The caped person remained motionless. The Dimension Clock struck midnight, indicating it was time to begin.

A blast of light burst through the window and deposited a man next to the caped person. The man was old and skinny, yet impeccably dressed. He reached a bony hand toward the caped person. The person did not respond. He knelt next to the person, raised the hood of the cape, and whispered, "Gwendolyn the Great, Savior of Idlebury, Protector of the Universe, thank you for honoring my request. It is time."

"For what?" Gwen asked, refusing to look at the man.

"For your transformation." The man dropped the cape, once again covering the child.

Gwen pulled the velvet fabric tighter around her body. "But I'm scared. I don't think I can do it."

"Of course you can. Only you can save Thane."

"I'm not scared of that. I'm scared of you."

"Scared of me?" The man chuckled. "My, my, Gwendolyn. You know who I am."

"No, I don't. No one knows who the Great Wizard is."

The man stood, towering over the child who refused to leave the security of the cape. "Look at me, Gwendolyn. You will see that I, the Great Wizard, am no one to fear."

The cape moved as Gwen's arm emerged from its shelter.

She slowly lifted the red velvet fabric that covered her face and glanced up at the man. She bolted upright. "Oof? You? You're the Great Wizard?"

"Yes, I am."

"Then why don't you save Thane?"

"I cannot. There are reasons which I cannot explain. I am too weak. I need you to take on my powers. Temporarily, of course."

"Well, I don't—"

"Do not hesitate. You have agreed. That is why the beam brought you. And you are dressed in the cape of the Great Wizard. There is no turning back now."

Gwen tried to stand, but the weight of the jeweled robe made it difficult. She reached out to Oof for support.

Oof graciously helped Gwen up. "There, there. That wasn't so hard, now was it?"

Gwen felt light-headed and wobbly. Her knees shook. "I think I'm going to faint."

"No, you are not going to faint." Oof placed his hands on Gwen's shoulders. "You are merely experiencing what it feels like to be powerless. In a moment you will feel different. Are you ready?"

"Why am I powerless?"

"Your questions are wasting precious time."

"Please answer me."

Oof took a deep breath. "You have been stripped of all powers so you can take on the extraordinary powers of the Great Wizard, the most powerful being in the universe."

"Why have I been stripped of my powers?"

"Your powers will get in the way. You need to be empty, so

to speak, so you can absorb the powers of the Great Wizard."

Gwen shook her head. "I don't understand. I feel as if I've been stripped of my very being."

"Excellent observation. You *have* been stripped of your very being, leaving you vulnerable to evil forces—forces that, if they inhabit you, will consume you. Then you will no longer be Gwendolyn the Great, Savior of Idlebury, Protector of the Universe."

"What evil forces?" Gwen asked.

"For goodness' sake, girl. You are trying my patience. I am getting weaker by the moment. Soon I will be too weak to complete the transfer of my powers."

"*Answer me!* You ask me to take on the powers of the most powerful person in the universe, and you expect me to not question you?"

"There is no time. You have to trust me. The evil ones know you are helpless. They are on their way."

Gwen stepped closer to Oof and stared him down. "Don't try to scare me. Level with me."

A shadow caught Oof's eye. He glanced at it, then returned his attention to Gwen. "I cannot reveal the identities of the evil ones."

"Don't lie to me. It's unbecoming of the Great Wizard."

A shadow appeared before Gwen. A second later, another appeared. The two shadows closed in on the child. A third approached and floated next to Oof.

"It is too late. The evil ones are here." Oof stepped back from Gwen. "The transformation cannot take place."

A crack of thunder and a bolt of lightning startled Gwen. She checked herself for injury and noticed she was dressed in her own clothes, no longer wearing the Great Wizard's cape. She felt like herself again.

Oof was gone. In his place stood a handsome young man with long, wavy blond hair, clad in the elegant cape. He looked every bit like the Great Wizard.

The three shadows flew around and through the Great Wizard.

"Do something," one shadow said, its voice echoing throughout the room.

"Coward, show us what you've got," another shadow said devilishly.

"You were once one of us. Are you now too good for us, Oof?" the third shadow asked.

The first shadow took form and revealed itself to be King Morrebidd of Deadonia. The second shadow morphed into King Abracadabra of Hexidonia. The third shadow disappeared.

"I knew it," Gwen whispered.

"You know nothing, you idiotic child," King Morrebidd spat out.

"I would not be so sure of that," a discarnate voice said.

"Why would you say that, Ovazealous?"

"She knows," the invisible king of Imaginoria said.

King Morrebidd moved in front of Gwen and locked his eyes on her. "She knows what?"

"She figured it out," King Ovazealous said.

"She—"

"I can speak for myself." Gwen interrupted him. "Don't pretend you don't know what I know."

"Don't play word games with me," King Morrebidd said through clenched teeth. "Do you think because King Heroian, your weakling of a father, gave you a fancy title that you have powers?"

Gwen pulled away from the king of Deadonia. "Of course not. We all know a title means nothing. It's the character of the person that means everything."

King Abracadabra moved between Gwen and King Morrebidd. He glared at the child and said, "I think you are bluffing."

Gwen glanced at the Great Wizard as if to ask for his help. She took another step backward and bumped into King Morrebidd, who had moved behind her. She was now sandwiched between two of the most dangerously powerful beings in the universe.

"Tell them what you told me," King Ovazealous said.

"Yes, do tell us what you told our dear friend," King Morrebidd said with a sinister smile.

"He's not your friend," Gwen said.

"What makes you say that?" King Abracadabra said. "He is undoubtedly one of my dearest friends."

"He's not your friend because you're not his friend."

King Morrebidd shoved Gwen. "Just tell us what you told King Ovazealous."

"No." Gwen looked at the Great Wizard and thought it odd he appeared to smile at her. With her attention diverted, King Morrebidd and King Abracadabra each took a step and closed in tighter on her, yet she managed to turn and face the king of Hexidonia.

Gwen felt a light gust of air circle the trio. King Ovazealous whispered in her ear. "Go ahead. Tell them. It is okay."

Gwen shoved King Abracadabra, hoping the old king would be easy to push away. She was wrong. He felt as sturdy as a marble statue. "Okay, I'll tell you. Just give me some space."

King Abracadabra and King Morrebidd backed off, allowing Gwen to slip out.

"Get on with it," King Morrebidd said.

"Well, I told him I'd figured out who's colluding to get their grubby hands on *A Magic Maniac's Many Ways to Make Mischief.*"

"Everyone has wanted to get their hands on that old book since it went missing hundreds of years ago," King Abracadabra said. "Except me, of course. I do not want it. Besides, I cannot imagine there is a trick or spell in the book I do not already know."

"I think there's a lot in the book you don't know," Gwen said.

"Don't tell me a child as pathetic as you knows what we do or do not know," King Morrebidd said.

"Don't pretend you're not afraid of what I'm about to say."

"Afraid?" King Morrebidd said. "Why would I be afraid?"

"Because I'm about to reveal your evil plan."

King Morrebidd leaned toward Gwen. The stench of his breath nearly made her turn away, but she held her ground. "Go ahead," the king of the dead spat out.

"Okay. Let's dissect the phrase you, King Abracadabra, and King Ovazealous made up and told all the creatures everywhere if they were to repeat it, disaster would strike them and the universe."

King Morrebidd and King Abracadabra shared a glance.

Gwen felt King Ovazealous's breath on her neck as he whispered, "Tell them."

Gwen looked at the Great Wizard for support. His smile was

replaced by a furrowed brow. His intense stare sent a confusing message. *Should I tell them or not?* She felt energetic yet anxious. A feeling of doom came over her. Gwen glanced at the Great Wizard again. She felt another burst of energy. *If he is sending me energy, what should I do with it? Run? Fight?* She decided to fight. "Okay, let's start with *last night at—*"

"*Stop!*" King Abracadabra yelled.

The fear in the old king's eyes almost made Gwen feel sorry for him. She glanced at King Morrebidd. He smirked at her and tilted his head as if to dare her to continue. She couldn't see King Ovazealous. She waited a moment for him to whisper in her ear, but he didn't.

"Go on," the Great Wizard said.

Gwen was frightened, but she obeyed the Great Wizard. "Last night at ten o'clock this morning, an empty wagon full of people ran over a dead horse and killed it."

King Morrebidd and King Abracadabra locked eyes. Gwen felt King Ovazealous swirl around her. "Now you've done it," he said for all to hear.

"Done what?" Gwen asked. "I haven't finished yet."

"Oh, but you have," the Great Wizard said.

King Abracadabra and King Morrebidd crumbled into two piles of ash. A third pile of ash appeared next to Gwen. She knew it was what remained of King Ovazealous. In death, he was no longer invisible.

The Great Wizard stood next to Gwen and examined the piles of ash. "How did you figure it out?"

Gwen took a step back, attempting to distance herself from the Great Wizard. "Figure what out?" She glanced at the door to determine the possibility of a rapid escape from the Great Wizard's wrath if need be.

"There is no need to be afraid of me. I merely want to know how you knew the phrase only had power in the presence of the three beings by whom it was written."

"Well, it's like I told King Ovazealous. If you look for logic in the nonsensical phrase, it's quite obvious. For example, *Last night at ten o'clock this morning* makes no sense unless one can shift time. Only King Abracadabra is known to do that. *An empty wagon full of people* makes no sense unless the people in the wagon are invisible. Only the people of Imaginoria are invisible, so that implicates King Ovazealous. Finally, *ran over a dead horse and killed it* only makes sense if the horse was among the living dead. So it doesn't take a genius to know King Morrebidd of Deadonia is involved."

The Great Wizard placed his hand on Gwen's shoulder. "Well done," he said with enthusiasm he would never have expressed as Oof. "But how did you know all three of them had to be in the room together in order for the destructive power of the phrase to be released?"

"I didn't. But I suppose you did."

The Great Wizard smiled. His eyes sparkled. "Right again."

Gwen sighed. "Now what?"

But the Great Wizard didn't answer her. He walked over to the three piles of dust and pointed at each. "Eenie, meenie, miney, moe, one evil soul will have to go. The other two become but one, then use their power to save their foe."

The Great Wizard stood before the pile of ash that had once been King Ovazealous. He raised his arms in the air, tilted back his head, and took a deep breath. His cheeks expanded to ten times their normal size, making him unrecognizable.

Awed by the Great Wizard's feat, Gwen watched in silence as he blew the ashes of King Ovazealous straight up until they disappeared through the ceiling. With a wave of his hand, the two piles of ash rose and swirled together. The Great Wizard raised his arms above his head again, forcing the ashes to float to the ceiling. When he lowered his arms, the mixed ashes of King Abracadabra and King Morrebidd fell to the floor in one pile.

The Great Wizard smirked as he eyed the pile of ash. He smiled at Gwen and said, "Now it begins."

From behind the door of King Heroian's childhood secret hiding place, Thane and Blabberdish watched the entire event.

After Gwen recited the cursed phrase that caused King Abracadabra, King Morrebidd, and King Ovazealous to crumble into three piles of dust, Thane collapsed to the floor. When the Great Wizard blew King Ovazealous's ashes into space, Thane disappeared. In his place, a pile of ash smoldered.

"Oh no," Blabberdish said as he stared at the ash that only a few moments ago had been his flesh and blood friend. "Thane is not ready. This could be a disaster." He quickly wiggled out from under the door into the blinding sunlight. "No. This *will* be a disaster."

CHAPTER THIRTY-TWO
A HUGE LEAP OF LOGIC

Q ueen Matilda nearly filled the small room in which she and Queen Merry had taken refuge. Hunched over, her head touching the ceiling, and barely able to balance on a human-sized chair, her discomfort was obvious.

While the queen of Beastonia squirmed as she tried to make herself comfortable, the queen of Hedonia rushed through the room and opened every drawer, obviously looking for something. "Where is it? I swear I've searched every possible hiding place."

"Maybe it's in another room. Possibly one much larger and more comfortable than this," the dragon queen said.

"Oh Matilda, I nearly forgot you were here."

Queen Matilda pursed her lips. "How could you not notice a dragon in the room?"

Queen Merry squinted at Queen Matilda. "That's it," she exclaimed. "Matilda, if you don't mind, would you move to the other side of the room? I believe what I'm looking for is in the drawer in the chest behind you."

"Oh, no problem. I'll just scooch over a tad."

The dragon queen grunted and groaned, making sure to

display her displeasure. She had barely moved when Queen Merry charged behind her, opened a drawer in the chest, and squealed with delight.

"Here it is," the queen of Hedonia said, clutching a yellowed, tattered envelope. "Why is it when you're looking for something, it's always in the last place you look?"

"I'm befuddled. Why is it?" But Queen Merry's pressured and less formal speech puzzled Queen Matilda.

Queen Merry stared at her dragon friend as if to attempt to answer her own question. "Never mind. What's important is I've found it."

"You've found what?"

"I've found the answer to the question you're going to ask me."

"You don't know the answer off the top of your head?"

"No. I was never told the answer, only the question. The answer has been safely stored away for a thousand years."

"The answer to the most important question in the universe has been safely stored in that chest for a thousand years?"

"Well, not exactly. It used to be in a more secure place, but the hiding place kept getting broken into. So I thought I'd put it where no one would find it. You know, someplace obvious."

Queen Matilda scratched her head, still suspicious as to why Queen Merry seemed different. "Let's just get on with it. This chair isn't going to hold me much longer."

The queen of Hedonia held the envelope up to the light that streamed through the window. She turned it over and continued to examine it. Her eyes sparkled with excitement when she said, "Well, ask me."

"I feel as if you want me to ask you to marry me."

"Don't be silly, Matilda. I'm already married to King Funzy. Just ask me the question."

Queen Matilda hesitated. Something was definitely wrong with her friend. Despite being the queen of Hedonia, Queen Merry was known to get to the point. She would never give silly answers to serious questions. And Queen Matilda knew Queen Merry would never trust the answer to the most important question in the universe to be written on paper and stored in an obvious place. Nonetheless, she decided to play along.

"Okay, here's the question," Queen Matilda said. "Name the author of *A Magic Maniac's Many Ways to Make Mischief.*"

"That's not in the form of a question," Queen Merry said.

"Just answer it."

Queen Merry clutched the envelope to her chest. And with a great display of drama, she said, "And the answer is..." She ripped open the envelope. "Feefifofum Fiddledeedee Fiddledeedum."

"Beep. Wrong answer." Queen Matilda leaned close to Queen Merry and examined her friend with one of her huge eyes. "I thought you were dead, Wilameena."

Queen Merry transformed into Wilameena. "I am. You killed me. More precisely, you incinerated me."

"I will do it again if you don't tell me why you're here."

"Well, if you must know, I'm here to stop you."

"Stop me from doing what?"

"From awakening the Great Wizard."

"I don't know what you're talking about." Queen Matilda looked away.

"Lying is so unbecoming of you, Matilda."

"You dare to call me a liar?"

"I don't dare, I just did."

"What is it you want, Wilameena?"

"I… I want you to protect Oof."

"Protect Oof? Why?"

"I think you know why."

"No. Enlighten me."

"Because he's the Great Wizard and…"

"And?"

"I love him." Wilameena broke down in tears.

Queen Matilda strummed her talons on the windowsill, not knowing what to make of Wilameena's declaration of love and emotional breakdown. "You're right. I know Oof's the Great Wizard, even though he has sacrificed his powers." The dragon queen scrutinized Wilameena's behavior, wondering why the enchantress's crying made her feel ill at ease. *Why do I feel this way? Oh my, I feel sorry for her. She must be telling the truth.* "Wilameena, for some reason I believe you."

"You do?" The enchantress wiped her tears and looked at the dragon queen like an innocent child.

"Yes, I do."

"So you'll protect him?"

"Protect him. He's the Great Wizard. From whom or what does he need protecting?"

"Thane."

"Thane? Prince Thane of Idlebury?"

Wilameena pulled a handkerchief from her dress pocket and blew her nose. "Yes, that's the one."

"I can't make any promises. I'm here with Queen Filanthropi to find her son. I would never betray her."

"So you haven't heard?"

"Heard what?"

Wilameena was about to answer when Queen Merry barged into the room.

"Gracious. There you are. Hurry. Come with me."

Queen Matilda grumbled as she tried to move her body toward the door.

"Not you, Matilda. Wilameena. Hurry. Time is of the essence."

Queen Matilda glared at Queen Merry. She was about to say something when the queen of Hedonia cut her off. "Not now, Matilda. I will explain later. Just stay put." With that, Queen Merry rushed Wilameena out of the room.

"Well, I've never been so insulted in my life," the queen of Beastonia said.

The air in the tiny room was stifling, so the dragon queen opened a window to get a little fresh air. What she witnessed sent shivers through her massive body. Queen Filanthropi, Morgana, King Funzy, and Queen Merry hugged Wilameena as if she were a long-lost friend. A few seconds later, Queen Filanthropi pulled something from inside her dress and handed it to the enchantress. Wilameena paused and looked at Queen Filanthropi. The queen of Idlebury nodded, indicating it was okay for Wilameena to accept whatever she had offered.

Wilameena accepted the item, gave Queen Filanthropi a quick hug, and evaporated like steam escaping from a boiling teakettle. Queen Filanthropi cried on King Funzy's shoulder as he patted her back to console her.

Are they plotting against me? the dragon queen wondered. *Am I in danger? I'm the most powerful creature in the universe. They can't harm me. Or can they?*

The door opened and Queen Merry entered the room, pretending nothing had taken place.

"What was that about?" Queen Matilda said.

"What was what about?"

"Don't play with me, Merry. I saw Filanthropi, Morgana, Funzy, and you hug Wilameena like you're the best of friends. And I saw Filanthropi hand the old hag something. What did Filanthropi give her?"

"A wand."

Queen Matilda eyes blazed with anger. "No. She didn't. She wouldn't. She couldn't. She promised her father she'd guard it with her life."

"She did. She has."

"But Filanthropi promised never to give it to anyone other than the Great Wizard. Why did she do it?"

"To save Thane," Queen Merry said.

"So you're saying Wilameena is going to save Prince Thane?"

"No. Wilameena is going to give the wand to Queen Opunzayzme."

"*What?*" the dragon queen yelled with such force a puff of smoke escaped her mouth. "It's believed to be one of the most powerful wands in the universe. In the right hands, it can do great things. But in the wrong hands... in the hands of Opunzayzme... Well, I shudder to think of what it could do."

"I would not worry about such a silly thing. It is nothing more than a mediocre wand."

"Alone that's true, but it completes the Wicked Wand Collection." Queen Matilda shook her massive head. "What were you and Filanthropi thinking?" The dragon queen snorted, triggering a burst of fire to escape from her nostrils.

The queen of Hedonia turned away from Queen Matilda. "Oh dear, what has Filanthropi done?"

The door to the room slammed. Queen Filanthropi stood in the doorway, hands on her hips, her nostrils flared, and her eyes squinted. "Are you questioning my judgment?"

"Matter of fact, I am," Queen Matilda said. "Why do you want to give the wand to Opunzayzme, and what possessed you to trust Wilameena with it?"

"To answer the first part of your question, Opunzayzme has threatened to kill Thane if I do not give her the wand that completes her collection. So to save my son, I agreed to give it to her."

"Yes, you've just completed the Wicked Wand Collection." Queen Matilda snorted fire and smoke again.

Queen Filanthropi raised her hand to silence the dragon queen. "Hold on, I am not done. I happened to overhear your conversation with Wilameena regarding her love for Oof, whom we now know is the Great Wizard."

"Okay?"

"Well it gave me an idea." The queen of Idlebury arched an eyebrow and smiled. "Knowing Wilameena cannot be trusted, I figured if I told her the history of the wand and asked her to give it to Queen Opunzayzme, she would not."

"And?" the queen of Beastonia asked.

"Instead, Wilameena would do what was in her best interest and give it to Oof as an offering of her love."

Queen Matilda scratched her head and moaned. "That's a huge leap of logic."

"Yes, but it just might work," Queen Merry said enthusiastically.

"But why would you take such a risk, Filanthropi?" Queen Matilda asked.

Queen Filanthropi looked up at Queen Matilda. Her lower lip quivered. "Ashes to ashes and dust to dust, a mother will do what a mother must."

Queen Matilda smiled and nodded in agreement. "Let's hope Wilameena *can't* be trusted. Otherwise, I'll have to kill her for good."

"Well, Matilda, are you going to ask me the question you came here to ask?" Queen Merry said.

"Hmm…" The dragon queen grimaced as she pondered her response. "I don't know. I think it would open a can of worms. If you know what I mean?"

"I believe you are right. The last thing we need right now is to let the worm out of the can, so to speak."

CHAPTER THIRTY-THREE
LOVE CONQUERS ALL

From his hiding place in the hallway, King Heroian watched Gwen leave the great hall. *Why is she in such a hurry?* he wondered.

Once Gwen was out of sight, the king of Idlebury entered the great hall. For the first time, he noticed that despite the room's dilapidated appearance, there was an aura of grandeur. He felt kingly—a feeling he hadn't experienced in more than two hundred years. As he'd expected, Oof awaited his arrival. King Heroian smiled at the old man and then looked at the pile of ash on the floor in front of him. "So whom did you choose? Morrebidd? Abracadabra? Or Ovazealous?"

"Ovazealous is useless," Oof replied. So of course I chose Morrebidd and Abracadabra."

King Heroian stared at the remains of Oof's childhood friends. "All is falling into place. Where is Thane?"

Oof pointed to the invisible door King Heroian had discovered when he was just a boy. "He is in there."

"Is he...?" King Heroian wrung his hands and nervously shifted his footing.

"Ashes?" Oof asked. "Yes, he is ashes."

"But he is too young," the king of Idlebury lamented. "He is merely a boy."

"Thane's readiness is insignificant. You shall soon find out why. We must hurry. Things are happening in the universe that could thwart our success."

King Heroian nodded. He walked to where he knew the invisible door to be, then glanced back at Oof before he stepped through the wall into the secret chamber.

The room was dark. King Heroian moved with caution, careful not to step on Thane's ashes. He pulled a wand out of his coat sleeve and said, "Illuminousity Respecto."

The top of his wand glowed. When the king saw Thane's ashes dangerously close to the tips of his shoes, he stepped back. He carefully knelt before the pile that was once his son. In a hushed voice, emphasizing the three segments of the saying that had reduced King Morrebidd, King Ovazealous, and King Abracadabra to ashes, he said, "Last night at ten o'clock this morning... an empty wagon full of people... ran over a dead horse and killed it."

Thane's ashes stirred, then stopped. King Heroian watched in worried anticipation. Beads of sweat formed on his forehead. He waved his lighted wand over the pile of ash and waited for any sign of movement. *Why did it not work? What have I done? Have I killed my son?*

King Heroian walked around the edge of the pile of ash. Desperate to save his son, he raised his voice. "Last night at ten o'clock this morning... an empty wagon full of people... ran over a dead horse and killed it."

Again the pile of ash stirred but failed to take form.

King Heroian's hands shook. "This cannot be happening. This is not supposed to happen," he whispered.

"So do not let it happen, Heroian," the Wall of Passages said.

King Heroian looked for who had spoken. In a whiny voice, he said, "But how? I do not have the power of magic. I never have."

"You are right, Heroian. You are a poor wizard. But this is not about wizardry. This is about belief."

"Belief? Belief in what?"

"In yourself," the wall said. "Think of what the Soul Seeker has given you."

"I do not understand."

"Do not be a fool. Stop living in fear. Do what you must." In a mockingly singsong voice, the wall said, "Ashes to ashes and dust to dust, a *father* will do what a *father* must."

"*Yes!*" King Heroian yelled, "*Last night at ten o'clock this morning, an empty wagon full of people ran over a dead horse and killed it.*"

Still, nothing happened.

"Come on, Heroian. Believe. You must believe."

King Heroian screamed at the top of his lungs. "*Last night at ten o'clock this morning, an empty wagon full of people ran over a dead horse and killed it.*" But it was to no avail. Thane remained a pile of ash.

"Screaming will get you nowhere. You must *believe* in *yourself*. Seems to me you hope there is such a thing as magic."

King Heroian fell to his knees. "I feel hopeless and helpless. I always have."

"You have been given a second chance. Remember what Thane did for you when he was captured by the Soul Seeker?"

"Yes, he saved my soul as well as those of many others."

"Like I said, you have been given a second chance. Use it

wisely."

King Heroian knelt before the pile of ash. He slowly reached out his hand and grabbed a fistful of his son's ashes. He held them to his heart and wept. "Thane, I am sorry for not being the father you deserve. Sometimes I think I do not deserve you. I cannot let you go. I *will not* let you go." The king wept a little longer, then in a tired, hoarse voice he said, "I love you, Thane."

The pile stirred. A tornado of ash rose. The room burst with light. The ashes swirled. King Heroian looked up and tossed his handful of ash into the swirling mass.

"I love you too, Father," Thane said in a monstrously eerie voice that shook the small chamber.

King Heroian put his arms up as if to take in the splendor of Thane's energy. Inside the spinning gray mass, something took form. When the mass stopped, a person dressed as a wizard emerged.

"Thane? Is that you, my son?"

"No, it's me." The person faced King Heroian.

"Gwendolyn? Where is Thane?"

"He's fine. You saved him. Your love saved him. One day he'll be great, but he's not ready. I've been chosen as the temporary Great Wizard."

"Why?"

"Because the Great Wizard has something he must do."

"So?"

"He has to do it as a mortal," Gwen said. "Therefore he has transferred his powers to me."

"Mortal? How is that possible?"

"I wish I knew. I guess I'll help him somehow."

"Gwendolyn, I know you do not think of me as your father,

but as your birth father, I must warn you to be careful. I love you too."

"I didn't know." Gwen looked away. "I don't know how I feel about that."

"No matter. I have said my piece. Now go and do what you must."

CHAPTER THIRTY-FOUR
THE POWER OF FRIENDSHIP

G wen exited through the wall of the great hall's secret
chamber. Oof sat cross-legged on the floor in front of a pile
of ash. His wrinkled, veined hands were folded in his lap. His
bald head was bowed. He chanted softly.

"Blabber, dabble, snabble, and snoo. Crittle, brittle, prittle,
and droo. Wally, winkle, stinkle, and croo. Mumbo, jumbo,
crumbo, and zoo."

"I've heard that before. But where?" Gwen whispered.

Oof repeated the words over and over.

"I remember. Lightening spoke the same words to gain
passage into Crabbina's secret quarters." Soon she heard the
thunder of horse's hooves. She glanced out the window and
saw a white horse racing toward Idlebury Castle.
"Lightening?" she muttered.

Lightening ran at lightning speed. As he raced down the
drawbridge, the sound of his hooves grew louder. When he
reached the castle door, he rose on his hind legs, pounded the
door open with his front legs, and then raced through the castle
and crashed through the door to the great hall. He skidded to a
halt, barely avoiding running over Oof. The queen's steed

snorted, blowing ashes out of place.

"What are you doing?" he said.

Oof appeared not to notice Lightening's presence.

Queen Filanthropi's steed snorted again. *"What are you doing?"* he yelled.

Oof looked at Lightening, but he didn't stop chanting.

Lightening pushed the old man with his snout.

Oof held his ground.

"Stop it this instant," Lightening demanded.

Oof did not heed the steed's command.

Lightening wheeled around, lining up to kick the old man.

"Stop!" a person yelled in a raspy yet powerful voice.

"Crabbina, I was only trying—"

"You needn't explain. I know what you're trying to do," Crabbina said as she hobbled toward the horse. "I understand your intentions, but I had to intervene because your intentions are misguided."

Lightening backed away from Oof. For a moment his white coat flashed red, revealing his embarrassment.

"Go on Lightening," Crabbina demanded. "This is between Oof and me."

Lightening bowed and trotted out of the great hall.

Gwen watched the entire event, apparently unnoticed by the others in the room.

Crabbina, supported by a cane made from a craggy birch limb, wobbled over to Oof, who continued to chant. "Oof, you can stop now. I'm here."

Oof looked up at the old Sullywobble, his eyelids red and swollen. "Crabbina, I hoped you would come."

"I'm here. What is it you want?"

Oof tried to stand up but fell back in place. "I attempted to transfer my powers to Gwendolyn, but I failed. I have been reduced to a mere mortal. I need your help."

Crabbina extended her withered hand toward Oof. "First let's get you standing."

A look of surrender crossed Oof's face, making him look like a lost, scared child. He reached out his gnarled hand and accepted Crabbina's help. The old Sullywobble tugged Oof's arm, but he didn't have the strength to stand. Nonetheless, Crabbina refused to give up. So she pulled on Oof's arm until he spun in a circle. The silliness of the situation made Oof laugh, which appeared to give him energy. As he continued to pull on Crabbina, attempting to gain the leverage and strength he needed to stand, he accidently pulled the old creature to the floor.

Crabbina squealed as she toppled on Oof. Her cane slid to the other side of the room and stopped at Gwen's feet. The old Sullywobble and Oof shared a hearty laugh.

Crabbina pulled herself into a sitting position, face-to-face and knee-to-knee with Oof. "Well, this will work too." She took his hands in hers and said, "My dear old friend. Tell me how I may help."

Oof choked back his emotions, for he knew the words he needed to say would change the universe forever and maybe not for better.

Crabbina noted the sorrow in her old friend's eyes. In a gesture of support, she put a hand on Oof's shoulder. The energy of Crabbina's love surged through the old man's rickety body. For the first time in his life, he felt vulnerable yet safe with another being. His emotional barriers were down. The feeling was foreign, yet comforting, giving him the courage to do something he'd never done with any being—he allowed Crabbina to take him in her arms where he wept.

Crabbina rocked Oof as if he were a baby. "Oof, my dear man, cry all you want. I know you have a thousand years of emotional pain to release. It's okay. I'm a patient soul."

A while later, Oof wiped his eyes with the sleeve of his coat and said, "It is time."

"Time for what?" Crabbina asked.

"It is time for…" Oof struggled as he rose to his knees. When he finally stood, he said, "It is time for Prince Thane to kill me."

Gwen gasped.

Oof and Crabbina looked at Gwen.

"Come, my dear child," Crabbina said. "You are part of this as well. And while you're at it, bring my cane."

The weight of the cane made it difficult for Gwen to carry it. She struggled to hand the cane to the old Sullywobble.

"The cane is yours, Gwendolyn the Great, Savior of Idlebury, Protector of the Universe."

"Mine?" Gwen lifted the cane and studied it. Its energy pulsated through her. "What am I to do with it?"

Crabbina chuckled. "Anything you want."

"Why did you give it to me?"

The old Sullywobble touched the cane and petted it like a favorite pet. "It needs protecting. And you are the perfect person for the job."

"Why does it need protecting?"

"Because, my dear, it's not a cane."

Oof cleared his throat.

"Yes, Oof. Do you have something to add?"

"I do believe she needs to know the true purpose of the, as

you call it, cane."

Crabbina looked out the window and contemplated Oof's comment. "I believe you're right."

"Well?" Gwen asked impatiently.

"It's not a cane. It's a wand—one of the most powerful wands in the universe."

"I thought the most powerful wand in the universe belonged to the Great Wizard," Gwen said.

"No, my dear. The Great Wizard doesn't need a wand. He has been bequeathed with inner power, of which no single wand can defy. And since no wand has been bestowed with unbridled power, no being in the universe can wield more influence than the Great Wizard—with one important exception." Crabbina squinted at Oof, who nodded for her to continue. "When King Abracadabra's sword, Blabberdish's wand, and my cane are used simultaneously, they combine to create the most powerful wand in the universe. Most think the most powerful wand is the one that completes Queen Opunzayzme's Wicked Wand Collection. Not true. The wand has no real power, just as Queen Opunzayzme has no real power. Right now it's in the possession of someone who will try to use it for personal gain. It's up to Oof as to whether or not *she* succeeds."

Gwen raised Crabbina's cane. Oof and the old Sullywobble jumped back as if to protect themselves from the cane's power. "Does anyone—"

"Do not indiscriminately wave that wand," Oof demanded.

"I'm sorry," Gwen said as she fought to gain control of the cane. "But I don't appear to have much control over it."

"You must learn to control it, much as a parent must learn to control a child," Crabbina said. "Now, what is it you wanted to ask, my dear?"

"Does anyone, other than the three of us, know this cane is one of the most powerful wands in the universe?"

Oof and Crabbina shared a concerned glance.

"Should we?" Oof asked.

"No," Crabbina said. "On second thought, yes," she replied. "There is one other who knows of the power of my cane, but I can't tell you who or *what* it is."

"Why?"

"Don't worry your pretty little head about it. It will be revealed in due time." Crabbina walked over to the pile of ash and rubbed her chin. "Right now we have to contend with this mess. Has the third person been added?"

Oof joined the old Sullywobble. "Yes, it is done."

"Well, let's hope..." Crabbina noticed a hole in the door to the great hall where the doorknob had been. Through it, she saw a large yellow eye. She smiled and said, "Well, let's hope the merger is complete."

<hr>

Mistofisee lumbered out from under the staircase. "Nothing's changed. Big surprise." He snorted. The Idleburians are still as lazy and unimaginative as ever."

Chanting coming from the great hall roused the young dragon's curiosity. So he dragged his nearly adult-sized body down the hall of Idlebury Castle. When he reached the great hall, he put his ear against the door. He recognized the chant. It was the secret chant that gave one access to the undisclosed hideout of Crabbina and her followers. He'd heard it once before when Lightening took him and Gwen, as well as two of Gwen's other selves, Aislinn and Kendall, to see Crabbina before Gwen's investiture in Idlebury. "That's disturbing. The person sounds upset," he mumbled. "I need a better look." So, using his enormous talon, Mistofisee grabbed the doorknob and gave it a yank. The knob broke off, leaving a hole where it had been. "Hmm. Not what I wanted, but I guess it'll work."

As quietly as possible, Mistofisee lowered his ever-growing body to the floor. He rolled on his side and propped his head on his claw so he could peer through the hole. "Not bad. Pretty comfy, actually," he muttered.

He saw an old man sitting in the middle of the floor, chanting. A pile of ash was before him. Soon Gwen emerged through a wall.

Lightening burst through the front door of the castle and raced directly at Mistofisee. The dragon tried to get out of the steed's way but failed. In the nick of time, Lightening jumped over Mistofisee and charged into the great hall. For a moment Mistofisee's presence was revealed. But the doors to the room slammed shut, hiding the young dragon once again.

When Crabbina appeared, the chanting stopped. Mistofisee saw the old man, Crabbina, Lightening, and Gwen talking, but he heard nothing. "I've gone deaf," he said as he slapped his ear. "Ouch." Realizing he could hear himself perfectly well, he listened intently. He turned his ear to the hole, but still he couldn't hear the conversation.

He moved away just in time for Lightening to bolt through the doors, leap over him, and race out of Idlebury Castle. "What's up with him?" Mistofisee whispered before he went back to peeping through the doorknob hole.

"Oh brother, it's Oof," Mistofisee said when he saw Crabbina cradle the weeping old man. Soon the whole scene involving Gwen and Crabbina's cane unfolded before him. "Gwen, I'm here," he whispered. "I'm still a friend you can count on." He struggled to rise, but a force held him in place. He was powerless as he watched the event that would change the universe.

Chapter Thirty-Five
She Who Hesitates is Lost

From the balcony of Hedonia Castle, Queen Matilda, Queen Filanthropi, and Morgana smiled and waved at the crowd of Hedonians gathered to see them off on their journey to wherever.

"It is time," Queen Filanthropi said.

"For what?" the dragon queen asked.

"It is time for us to return to Idlebury," Queen Filanthropi said as she blew kisses to the crowd. "Thane is there. I can feel it."

Queen Matilda glared at Queen Filanthropi. "So this is all about you and your son. What about mine?"

Queen Filanthropi continued to play to the crowd, obviously enjoying the attention. "Mistofisee is safe. So there is nothing for you to worry about. But do not forget, I have three children who could be in the shadow of death."

Queen Matilda took a deep breath. "I understand *your* children have gone missing, Filanthropi, but I'm a mother too."

"As am I," Morgana said.

"I understand," Queen Filanthropi said as she continued to wave and blow kisses at the Hedonians. "But I do believe we need to return to Idlebury at once. Something is happening; something we mothers need to see."

The beam appeared.

The Hedonians scurried.

Queen Filanthropi gave King Funzy and Queen Merry a hug before making her way down the long staircase. Midway down the stairs of Hedonia Castle, she stopped. "I feel as if I have forgotten something important," she said. "*Oh my God*, I forgot about Prudea."

"What's Prudea got to do with anything?" the dragon queen asked.

"Thane cannot be saved without Prudea."

"Why?"

"Because she is the only person in the entire universe who… who can…" Queen Filanthropi paused.

"Who what?" Queen Matilda said. "Spit it out, Filanthropi."

"I cannot tell you."

"Don't play games. It could cost you your son."

"Because Queen Prudea is da only person in da universe who can decipher da etchin's on King Abracadabra's sword."

Queen Filanthropi gasped as she shot a disapproving glance at her servant. "What? What did you say?"

"I said, because Queen Prudea—"

"I heard you the first time." Queen Filanthropi clenched her teeth and visibly shook as she raised her hand in what appeared to be an attempt to slap her servant. When the queen of Idlebury saw fear in Morgana's eyes, she lowered her hand. Still shaking with rage, she said, "How do you know such things?"

"I know a lot of thin's, Yer Majesty." Morgana stepped back, obviously putting distance between herself and the crazed queen. "I'm not just some uneducated servant. I'm a keen observer and listener."

"You are a spy," Queen Filanthropi said through gritted teeth. "And I am a fool for trusting you."

"I'm no spy," Morgana said. "But when a servant has been around fer a long time, people talk in front of 'em as if dey were deaf. And I'm not deaf or dumb, ma'am."

"So who told you about..." Queen Filanthropi raised her right arm to her forehead as if she felt faint. "...about King Abracadabra's sword?"

"You did, ma'am."

"*Me?*"

"Yes, ma'am. When you were talkin' ta dat worm. You know, Blabberdish."

Queen Matilda thrust her huge head toward Queen Filanthropi. The queen of Idlebury jumped back. "Did you hear what she said, Merry?" Queen Matilda yelled to the queen of Hedonia.

Queen Merry shrugged, then motioned for her guests to proceed.

"You've got some explaining to do, Filanthropi," the dragon queen said as she lumbered toward the beam.

Queen Filanthropi followed behind and mumbled, "What a stellar performance I gave when I pretended to be incensed at Oof's remark about a bookworm teaching Thane magic. I thought I had fooled him. But it appears I have been fooled. The secret Prudea and I have shared since childhood is no secret at all."

The two women and the dragon stepped into the beam, ready for the next part of their journey. But the beam remained in place. In an eerie, electronic voice, it said, "Come, Merry."

"I cannot," Queen Merry said. "A mixed-breed is not allowed to journey via the beam."

"Who told you such nonsense?" the beam asked.

"Well... I do not recall. I have just always believed it was forbidden."

"Well, you were wrong. Now come."

Queen Merry hesitated. "But I have a duty to my husband and my people," she said.

"Excuses, excuses," the beam replied.

With the enthusiasm of a child who's been given permission to go with friends on an exciting adventure, she screamed, "I am coming, I am coming."

A clap of thunder and a bolt of lightning signaled the departure of the beam. The Hedonians squealed with fear, some huddled for protection. But when the theatrics ended, Queen Merry watched in disbelief as the beam disappeared.

"She who hesitates is lost," the beam said as it whisked its occupants to their next adventure. Only it knew where they were going and why. For if they'd known what was about to transpire, they would never have entered the beam.

Chapter Thirty-Six
Wilameena Accidentally Helps

The last thing Gwen remembered was Crabbina raising her skinny arms high above her head and twirling like a ballerina. Her cane, with which Gwen had been entrusted, flew out of the child's hands and rose high in the air. It spun above Crabbina as she whispered a chant and continued to twirl in the most dizzying manner. Suddenly Gwen plopped on a hard surface that she recognized all too well.

"More tea, dear?"

"Mom?" Gwen said as she stood and noticed she was ten years old again.

"Well, look who's graced us with her presence this morning," Gwen's father, Arston, said.

"Dad, how long have I been here?"

Gwen's father lowered the newspaper and checked his watch. "Well, you've been here nearly ten seconds. I suggest you stop wasting time and attend to your duties. I'm sure someone somewhere needs saving."

"What?" Gwen said as she pulled out a chair from the kitchen table and sat down.

"I'm afraid it's true, dear." Gwen's mother handed Gwen the

morning edition of *Universal Scandals* magazine. "You appear to be shirking your duties."

Gwen unfolded the magazine, only to be screamed at.

"Prince Thane Rules!

"Prince Thane has taken control of the universe. How and why remain a mystery. But last night at exactly ten o'clock, the ten-year-old son of King Heroian and Queen Filanthropi of Idlebury in Dimension XIII broadcast his intentions of ruling all creatures throughout the universe. Within seconds of his announcement, calls flooded in to the Bureau of Annoying and Unbelievable Statements. Due to the nature of the young prince's remarks, all calls were immediately referred to the Department of Universal Control and then transferred directly to the Office of General Nonsensical and Illogical Remarks by a Minor.

"Later it was determined Prince Thane had indeed taken control of the universe, at which time all calls were transferred to the Universal Bureau of Bureaus which immediately turned over all investigations of allegations to the Department of Outlandish Yet True Claims.

"King Heroian and Queen Filanthropi were unavailable for comment, as their whereabouts are unknown. Therefore, the larger question is, where is Gwendolyn the Great, Savior of Idlebury, Protector of the Universe, when you need her?

"At the time of publication, a universal manhunt was underway for Gwendolyn the Great. All sightings and clues as to her location are to be reported to Detective Laz E. Bonz of the Department of Truth, a division of the Department of Outlandish Yet True Claims at www.dtdoytc.gov. No calls will be accepted. All sightings and clues will be investigated in the order they are received."

Gwen slammed the *Universal Scandals* magazine on the kitchen table, nearly knocking over her father's cup of tea. "That spoiled-rotten brat," she said as she walked over to the kitchen window where for years she'd sat and enjoyed her imaginary life as a princess. "This is unthinkable. He's done it again. And I think the Great Wizard is to blame." Gwen cried. Her father touched her arm. The warmth of his hand was comforting. "I trusted Oof. I trusted Crabbina. I've been tricked. It was all just a ploy to get me out of the way so Thane could take over the universe."

"Now, now, dear," Gwen's mother said as she rubbed Gwen's shoulders. "Things aren't always what they seem."

"Well, this seems pretty bad."

"You shouldn't believe everything you read in that magazine," Gwen's father said.

Gwen grabbed the magazine, rolled it up, and hit it against the table.

"Hey, don't blame the messenger," the *Universal Scandals* magazine said.

"Shut up, you stupid, lying excuse for news."

"Ouch," the magazine said. "That hurts."

"You deserve to be hurt after all the hurt you've caused."

"Well, I think I can redeem myself. If you'll give me a chance, that is."

"Show me," Gwen said.

"Okay." The magazine wiggled out of Gwen's hand. "What if I give you a sneak preview of the biggest news ever?"

"Go on then," Gwen said, sounding like Queen Filanthropi.

The *Universal Scandals* magazine shook and flipped three times and then shook some more. Light flashed from its pages. Images appeared as its pages fluttered back and forth. The sound of people screaming filled the air.

"*Stop*," Gwen yelled.

"I can't," the *Universal Scandals* magazine said. "I'm weeding through the sensational news to get to the real story. Hold your horses. The truth is in here somewhere."

The magazine continued its antics. Gwen and her parents could do nothing but watch. As quickly as it all started, it stopped. The magazine landed on the kitchen table, opened to page twenty-three.

In a faint voice, the magazine said, *"A Magic Maniac's Many Ways to Make Mischief Magically Appears."*

Gwen grabbed the magazine and then read the article.

The most coveted book in the universe has been located in the most unlikely place. And to the horror of all, the unlikely place is none other than Idlebury Castle, where it was hidden.

Gwen gasped and continued reading.

Since the book's discovery, its magic powers have been unleashed, leaving the universe at the mercy of any creature that wishes to use its chants and spells for good or for evil. It is apparent some have already engaged magic for their own benefit without regard as to the harm of others. There is no telling if and when the universe will recover from the unimaginable damage that has been done.

Gwen noticed the article was dated five days in the future. "I've got to go," she announced. "I only have a few days to keep the most powerful book in the universe from falling into the wrong hands."

Evaline and Arston Fanny watched their daughter pace as she muttered to herself. "I don't know how to get back. Someone else has always taken me back. I don't know what to do." She buried her head in her father's chest and said, "I'm only a child."

Gwen's mother pulled her toward her and gave her a hug. "You may only be ten, but you're smarter and wiser than most people three times your age. You'll figure it out, sweetheart."

Gwen took refuge at the kitchen window and stared out into

the backyard. She recalled Lightening's words: *Your thoughts are powerful. You get what you focus on.* She hoped it was true. "Mistofisee, you saved me once, now save me twice. I trust you with my very life," she said and then meditated.

A faint knock on the front door broke the silence. Gwen slowly walked to the door. The house was eerily quiet. She put her hand on the doorknob, but she couldn't make herself open it. She heard the faint knock again.

"Gwen, are you there? It's me, Mistofisee."

Gwen still didn't open the door. Her gut told her not to.

"Gwen, open the door. It's me, Mistofisee."

Gwen jumped on the couch, landing on her knees so she could see out the window. She pulled back the curtain and peered out. She couldn't believe her eyes. A huge creature that looked like a dragon was at the door.

"No, it can't be," Gwen said.

"Gwen, it's Mistofisee. Please let me in."

Gwen flung open the front door. The creature stepped back, allowing the girl to get a view of his massive body.

Gwen jumped on the dragon's foot and hugged his leg. "Mistofisee, it really is you."

"Well, you called."

"I can't believe you heard me. I'm so happy to see you."

"I'm here to take you to Idlebury, as you wished."

Gwen looked into the young dragon's huge yellow eyes. "What makes you think I want to go to Idlebury?"

"Umm, that's what you asked while you were sitting at the window."

"You're right. That's exactly where I want to go. Let me get my things." Before she crossed the threshold, she felt something sharp on her back. As she pulled away to see what it was, her shirt tore.

"Where do you think you're going?" Mistofisee said, not sounding at all like himself.

"I'm going to get my things."

"You can't fool me. You don't need things."

"And you can't fool me either, Wilameena."

The dragon transformed into the enchantress. "I'm only trying to help you," she whined.

"The only way you could be of help is if you were dead."

"Oh come on," Wilameena said. Suddenly her face contorted. She looked as if she were having a stroke. Her body shook as if she'd gotten the most terrible chill. She fell to the ground as her body disappeared, leaving only her dress as evidence of her presence. Soon the ground gobbled the enchantress's dress, leaving behind a pile of ash.

Gwen was mortified. She stared at the pile of ash, wondering who would emerge—King Morrebidd? King Abracadabra? Thane? Or something beyond her imagination? She studied the ashes, careful to hold her breath so as not to breathe in the gray dust. But something sparkling caught her eye. She smiled as she cautiously picked up what looked like a tiny gold needle. She wiped it on her blouse to clean off the ashes. "I don't believe it," Gwen said as she inspected the item. She carefully placed it in the palm of her hand and closed her fingers to protect it. "Get me out of here," she said.

Instantly she landed in Hexidonia in Dimension II, transformed into her fifteen-year-old self. In one hand, she held Crabbina's cane, in her other hand, she clutched the small gold needle. She knew exactly what she needed to do. She needed to get her hands on King Abracadabra's sword.

Chapter Thirty-Seven
What's Not for Dinner

Mistofisee heard Gwen's plea for help and rushed to Dimension X, Planet Earth. Soon he landed on the porch of Gwen's house in Idleburg, Pennsylvania. He rang the bell. Moments later, Gwen's mother opened the door.

"Hello, my name is Mistofisee. I'm Gwen's friend. Is she home?"

Evaline Fanny stared at the massive creature that stood before her. She shook and her voice quavered when she said, "I'm sorry, but Gwen has already left." A second later, she passed out.

Gwen's father appeared and rushed to his wife's side. As much as Mistofisee wanted to help, he decided there wasn't a moment to waste in his search for Gwen. So he took flight and embarked on a journey that started out pleasantly but would prove to be harrowing.

Nearly an hour into his uneventful flight, he saw a beam in the near distance. He sped toward it. When he got close enough to feel the warmth of the beam's rays, he got a good look at who it was carrying.

"Mother," Mistofisee yelled, but evidently his mother

couldn't hear him or see him. She just stared into space, as did Queen Filanthropi and Morgana. "Mother, it's me, Mistofisee. Mother, look at me."

The beam took a sudden turn in the opposite direction. Mistofisee struggled to follow it, but his massive growth spurt made his body cumbersome and his movements awkward. He put forth tremendous energy in order to keep up.

As the beam entered Dimension XIII on an approach to the kingdom of East Wisdomere, it slowed. Mistofisee had never been to East Wisdomere, but he'd heard his mother mention that its palace, which was home to Queen Prudea and King Karful, was elegant in its simplicity. Mistofisee wasn't quite sure what his mother meant, but he had a feeling he would soon find out. He kept watch as the beam landed on the palace grounds and deposited two women and the dragon queen of Beastonia. Mistofisee's heart fluttered when he saw his mother.

Moments later he gently landed in East Wisdomere, but he was too far away from his mother for her to see him. "Wow! That *is* a beautiful palace. Boy, I'd love to get a look inside. I think I'll give a hi-de-ho to Queen Prudea and King Karful, he muttered.

"Don't even think about it."

"What do you want, Wilameena?" he said.

"Don't be snide with me. You're putting your snout where it doesn't belong." The dumpy old woman stepped close to Mistofisee and motioned with her finger for him to lower his head to her level. When Mistofisee complied, she said, "I'm only here to help."

"Oh brother." Mistofisee pulled away from the enchantress. "Help? You're a hindrance."

"Lies, nothing but lies. Forget what you've heard about me.

Stick with me and I'll let you in on a little secret that could be of great benefit in your search for Gwen."

Mistofisee squinted. "Like what?"

"Come," the enchantress said as she took off.

Mistofisee begrudgingly followed the enchantress. A while later, they landed in Beastonia.

"Why are we here?" Mistofisee asked. "You're not welcome in Beastonia, Land of the Innocents."

"Just follow me. And walk lightly. You've grown into a huge clod."

The enchantress's comment hurt Mistofisee's feelings, but he didn't say anything because he knew he needed Wilameena's help if he was to find Gwen. So he put aside his feelings and tiptoed behind her.

Mistofisee's talons could hardly maintain his weight any longer when Wilameena whispered, "We're here."

"Now what?" The dragon wiggled his claws, letting the blood rush back to his numb feet.

"Shush." The enchantress pointed to a wall in front of them. "Focus on that little red dot."

"Okay. But why me?"

"Because only an Innocent can open the door behind those bricks. And the last I checked, you were an Innocent."

"And proud of it," the prince of the Innocents said as he focused on the little red dot.

Wilameena removed a wand from her skirt pocket—the wand Queen Filanthropi had given her. She pointed it at the red spot, shook it until its tip glowed, then said, "Open, open, I demand, for I am the prince of your clan."

Nothing happened.

"Let me try." Mistofisee stared at the red dot and recited the secret code of the Innocents. "Blabber, dabble, snabble, and snoo. Crittle, brittle, prittle, and droo. Wally, winkle, stinkle, and croo. Mumbo, jumbo, crumbo, and zoo."

The bricks rippled and blurred as they peeled back to reveal a dark, cavernous hallway.

Wilameena gave Mistofisee a shove. "Well, go on. Step inside."

After Mistofisee had stepped inside, he looked to see if Wilameena had followed. All he saw was a brick wall. A soft touch on the wall confirmed it was rock solid. "She tricked me," he whined. "Oh well, there's nowhere to go but forward."

Up ahead, he saw a flicker of light. He lumbered toward it. As he approached the light, it grew larger, making the air hotter. Sweat dripped off his snout. He wiped his brow with his paw and mumbled, "Nerves don't fail me now."

Mistofisee trudged on. Puddles of sweat marked his every step. The light flickered faster. A shadow of two hunched creatures appeared to the side of the light.

"What's for dinner, dear?" the larger of the two creatures asked in a gruff voice.

"Something special," the smaller creature said. "Something we haven't had for nearly three hundred years."

"Dragon? We're having dragon?" the larger creature asked, its voice tinged with excitement.

Mistofisee stopped. "Dragon?" he whispered.

The smaller creature snorted and chuckled. "Matilda's firstborn sure was tasty."

Matilda's firstborn? I'm Matilda's firstborn. Mistofisee's heart pounded from the implication of what the creature had said.

"Ah yes," the larger creature said. "And sooo tender. So

where are we getting tonight's dragon special? Takeout?"

"No. We're having drop-in." The shorter creature came out of the shadow and pointed at Mistofisee.

"Crabbina?"

The larger of the two creatures appeared. "He thinks you're Crabbina."

"Fool," the smaller creature said. "He *is* his father's son."

The two skinny, nearly hairless Sullywobbles, one male and the other female, looked at Mistofisee and roared with laughter. "Come, my dear dragon," the male Sullywobble said. "Your death will be our dining pleasure."

Mistofisee approached the two Sullywobbles.

"Look, dear, he wants to be dinner," the female said.

"Yummy, yummy, yummy in my tummy, tummy, tummy," the male said.

With each step Mistofisee took forward, the Sullywobbles took a step back until they were trapped in the corner, their backs against a cold stone wall.

"Hi, my name is Mistofisee." He extended his claw to shake hands with the male Sullywobble. "I'm the prince of Beastonia. I believe you know my mother, Queen Matilda."

The two old Sullywobbles shared a concerned glance. The male bravely extended his hand to Mistofisee. "Why yes, of course we know your mother."

Mistofisee released his grip. "And if I heard you correctly, you ate my brother or sister for dinner."

"Yes. I cooked *her* to perfection." The female Sullywobble smacked her lips. "And I plan to do the same to you, although you look a little tough to me."

"Oh, I'm tougher than you think." Mistofisee touched his

chin with a talon and paused as if thinking. "You know, you've stirred my curiosity. You already know how delicious dragon meat tastes, but I have no idea how Sullywobble tastes."

"Oh, no need to wonder about that," the female Sullywobble said nervously. "We taste like chicken."

"Great. I love chicken."

The female Sullywobble looked at her husband. "Maybe we should make other dinner plans tonight, dear."

"Yes, I think that might be wise. We've waited nearly three hundred years to eat lip-smacking-delicious dragon meat. I guess we can wait a little longer."

"I agree, dear." The female Sullywobble motioned for Mistofisee to leave. "So be on your way. What did you say your name was again?"

"I am Mistofisee, prince of Beastonia, son of Queen Matilda and King Anima."

"Ooh, okay. Well, be off with you then." The female waved her hand, dismissing him. "We've made other dinner plans."

"How nice of you to spare me, but you see, I'm really hungry. And when I get hungry, I get really, really cranky. And when I get cranky and I'm standing before two creatures who killed my sister and ate her, I get really, really mad. And when I get really, really mad... Well, I—" Mistofisee roared and spewed fire on the two old Sullywobbles. They burst into flames and squealed as their flesh burned. The scent that filled the air smelled nothing like chicken. Smoke rose from their charred remains.

"Hmm, well done. I would have preferred medium rare." Mistofisee chuckled. As he examined the blackened bones of the old creatures, he shook his head in disgust. "You were an embarrassment to Sullywobbles. In fact, you were an embarrassment to the entire animal kingdom. Good riddance," he said as he headed out.

"Wait just a minute, young man."

"Crabbina, I can explain."

"No need to explain. I saw the whole thing."

"I… I'm sorry."

"Don't be sorry. Those two were a disgrace to the name Sullywobble. I'm just sorry you had to find out about your sister this way."

"Mother never told me."

"No, she wouldn't have. It is too painful for her to discuss. So I think it's best to keep it our little secret."

"Okay."

"Now go. Gwendolyn needs you."

"But I don't know how to get out of here."

"Go back the way you came. I think you'll find the door is open. Hurry. There's no time to spare."

"Telling a megaton dragon to hurry is like telling a hummingbird to flap its wings slowly," Mistofisee whined as he started to leave.

"I think you can hurry if you want."

He looked down the long hallway. Light streamed through a gap in the wall. "Gwen, here I come," he yelled as he flew like a torpedo out the opening and into the bright blue sky.

Chapter Thirty-Eight
Secrets Among Old Friends

Q ueen Prudea scribbled on a pad of paper with an ancient quill handed down from queen to queen of East Wisdomere for millennia. There was no purpose to her scribbling other than making her chambermaid believe she, the ever-dutiful queen, was hard at work on important communications with important people. As she dipped her quill in the inkwell, a loud noise startled her. She slowly pushed back her chair and gracefully rose.

"Do tell, did you hear something outside?" she said to her chambermaid.

"No, Your Majesty. I believe the noise came from downstairs."

"Well, do not just stand there. Go find out what the ruckus is about," Queen Prudea said. "Probably some klutzy servant breaking something for which I will have to raise taxes to repair or replace."

"Yes, ma'am. Right away, ma'am." The chambermaid tossed a pile of freshly washed laundry on the floor and rushed out of the room.

"Goodness' sake," Queen Prudea said as she retrieved her

clean clothes. "For the life of me, I do not know why that woman is so afraid of me. I do not bite."

As Queen Prudea placed the pile of clothes on her bed, a louder noise alarmed her. Heavy footsteps followed by guards yelling for someone to stop or they'd be shot scared her. She scurried around her chambers in search of a safe place to hide. The guard screamed, followed by the sound of his footsteps as he raced down the hall, obviously not intending to protect his queen. There was no time. She would have to face the intruders.

"Prudea, open up."

"Prudea? Who would have the nerve to address me as a commoner?"

"Did you hear me, Prudea? Open up. This is no time for a silly game of hide-and-seek."

"Who do you think you are, speaking to me like that? Need I remind you that I am the queen of East Wisdomere?" When no one answered, Queen Prudea said, "Well, that shut her up."

"No, it didn't shut me up. Now open up, you smarty mouth."

"Smarty mouth? Well, I never... Matilda?" Queen Prudea rushed to the door and flung it open. "You are alive. My gracious, why did you not say it was you?"

"I am here too," Queen Filanthropi said.

"Filanthropi, what a pleasant surprise." Queen Prudea reached out to her old friend. "It has been years since I have seen you and Heroian. I hope you both have been well. Do come in."

Queen Matilda, Queen Filanthropi, and Morgana entered Queen Prudea's posh chambers. Morgana's eyes were wide with wonder as she wandered the room, handled a few of the queen's possessions, touched the satin curtains, and ran her hand over the fine silk bedcover.

"And you are?" Queen Prudea said.

"Me?" Morgana asked.

"Yes, you… the person who appears to have neither manners nor knowledge of proper protocol."

Morgana curtsied and said, "My name is Morgana, Yer Majesty."

"I am sorry, Prudea," Queen Filanthropi said. "I should have introduced my servant."

Queen Prudea pursed her lips, arched her eyebrows, and batted her eyes, making the normally sophisticated woman look as if she were deranged, or more kindly, like she'd gotten a whiff of something horribly rotten. "You are traveling with a servant as if she is a friend?" she said. "Have you lost your mind?"

Queen Filanthropi mimicked Queen Prudea's expression. "Yes, I am traveling with my servant. And no, I have not lost my mind."

"Pray tell, why?" the queen of East Wisdomere said. "Do you think her to be your equal?"

"She is traveling with me to help me save my son."

"Okay."

"I'm travelin' with Queen Filanthropi ta save *our* son," Morgana said. "I love Thane as a son too. After all, I raised him fer da first five years of his life, I did."

"You mean you stole him from his rightful mother and father and hid him right under their noses for five years."

"Stifle yourself, Prudea," the dragon queen said, her eyes blazing with anger. "We're not here to discuss the moral implications of Morgana's past behavior. We're here on a dire matter."

Queen Prudea gave Matilda a dismissive wave and said, "Go on then. What is of such *dire* importance?"

"Have you seen the latest issue of *Universal Scandals* magazine?" Queen Filanthropi asked.

"No. I do not partake of such rubbish." Queen Prudea sprawled on a comfy lounge as if to express her boredom with the conversation. "Do enlighten me."

The queen of Idlebury took a deep breath, locked eyes with Queen Prudea, and said, "Well… certainly you are aware that my son, Thane, is in serious trouble for hopping around the universe, reciting…" Queen Filanthropi averted her eyes, "…a silly chant and making mischief. Are you not?"

"I would have to be dead if I were not aware of Thane's misbehaviors."

"Stop it," the queen of Beastonia said. "I'm tired of beating around the bush."

"Matilda, wait," Queen Filanthropi pleaded.

"No, Filanthropi, I'm going to get to the point."

"As you wish." Queen Filanthropi plopped on Queen Prudea's bed like a spoiled child who hadn't gotten her way.

"We need you to come with us to Hexidonia, steal King Abracadabra's sword, and tell us what the etchings on his sword mean."

"Oh that," Queen Prudea said as she rose from her lounge. "You need not get yourselves all atwitter. I know what the etchings say."

"What?" Queen Filanthropi and Queen Matilda said in unison.

"Let's just say the last time King Karful and I visited King

Abracadabra and Queen Opunzayzme, I took a little peek at the sword…" With a sparkle in her eyes and a grin on her face, she continued, "But I also did something much more intriguing."

"What?" Queen Filanthropi asked.

Queen Prudea opened the ancient, ornately carved door to her bedchamber a crack. It creaked as she peeked out to make sure the coast was clear before she motioned for Queen Matilda, Queen Filanthropi, and Morgana to follow her. Morgana and the dragon queen shared a skeptical glance as Queen Filanthropi rushed to join Queen Prudea. Without further hesitation, the three women and the dragon hurried down the hall.

"Prudea, aren't you afraid someone might see us?" Queen Matilda asked.

"One would have to be blind to miss you," Queen Prudea said. "Not to worry. There is nothing suspicious about what I am going to show you." She stopped in front of a beautifully etched wooden frame with thick glass. It obviously protected something important.

"What is this?" Queen Filanthropi asked.

"It is a rubbing of the writings on King Abracadabra's sword."

Queen Filanthropi gently ran her hand over the glass. "What is it doing on display for all to see?"

Queen Prudea chuckled and said, "Well, my dear, the best place to hide something is right in the open." She sneered at Morgana and said, "Would you not agree?"

Morgana didn't respond.

The dragon queen pressed her snout against the glass and said, "What does it say?"

"Not much," Queen Prudea said. "The etchings are nothing

more than that silly saying Thane was heard chanting throughout the universe."

"So you did read *Universal Scandals* magazine," Queen Filanthropi said.

Queen Prudea smirked at Queen Filanthropi. "But there is one itsy-bitsy difference."

"What?" Queen Matilda said.

"Well, this is what I read. "'Last night at ten o'clock this morning, an empty wagon full of people ran over a dead horse and killed it.'"

"We already know dat," Morgana chimed in.

"My dear woman, although you appear to know more than your prayers, you do not know this…" Queen Prudea pushed her way around Queen Matilda, positioned herself in front of the rubbing, and pointed to the bottom of the paper. "…it was signed."

"Signed?" Queen Filanthropi said.

"By whom?" Queen Matilda asked.

"I would tell you, but I cannot do so in the presence of your servant," Queen Prudea said.

"It was signed by King Abracadabra, King Morrebidd, and King Ovazealous," Morgana blurted out.

"What? How do you know such things?" Queen Filanthropi asked.

"I told ya before, ma'am, people talk in front of servants when dey shouldn't."

"And who was stupid enough to speak of such things in front of you?" Queen Prudea asked.

"I can't say." Morgana glanced at Queen Filanthropi, but when she saw the angry look in the queen of Idlebury's eyes, she lowered her head in shame. "I promised I would never repeat what I heard."

"Promises are made to be broken, my dear. Otherwise, why would someone swear one to secrecy," Queen Prudea said. "What is the fun in that? Am I right, Filanthropi?" Queen Prudea waited for a response, but the queen of Idlebury was mum. "Anyway, there is something else you should know." The queen of East Wisdomere motioned for the others to huddle around her, then she whispered, "King Abracadabra's sword is not a sword."

"Then what is it?" Queen Matilda asked.

"It is a wand," Queen Prudea said.

"It's da Great Wizard's wand, it is," Morgana said proudly, obviously ignorant of the angry glare Queen Filanthropi shot her way.

"The Great Wizard's wand?" Queen Matilda said. "You mean to tell me Abracadabra, that shriveled-up old prune, is the Great Wizard?"

"Do not put words in my mouth, Matilda," Queen Prudea said. "You already know the identity of the Great Wizard, and it is not that pathetic Abracadabra. And his sword is not the Great Wizard's wand, for the all-powerful Great Wizard needs no wand. Correct, Filanthropi?"

Queen Filanthropi didn't honor Queen Prudea with a reply. Instead, she poked her head closer to the etching and examined the signatures. A second later, she broke from the huddle and raced back to Queen Prudea's chambers, making sure she slammed the door behind her.

"What's up with her?" Queen Matilda said.

"The usual, I am sure," Queen Prudea replied as she led the dragon queen and Morgana back to her chambers where they found Queen Filanthropi sprawled on Queen Prudea's bed with her head buried in pillows.

After a few minutes, Queen Filanthropi went to the window. She leaned on the sill and stuck her head outside. A moment later, she took a deep breath and twirled around, managing to rest against the sill. She stared at her two old friends and servant.

"Come on, Filanthropi," Queen Matilda said. "Prudea and I are well aware of your dramatics. What is it you want to say?"

"My dramatics?" the queen of Idlebury said as she approached her friends. "Well, here is a little drama for your entertainment." The queen of Idlebury turned beet red, her eyes bulged as she screamed, "Enough of your charades. We have known since we were children that Oof is the Great Wizard. And we have known that King Abracadabra, King Morrebidd, and King Ovazealous are pawns in the Great Wizard's game. So none of this is news."

"Then why are you so huffy, my dear old friend?" Queen Prudea asked.

"Well…" Queen Filanthropi wrung her hands. "…I have a secret I have kept my entire life." She dramatically plopped on the bed and cried. "Well, I do not know if I can tell you now."

Queen Prudea rushed to Queen Filanthropi and put her arm around her friend's shoulders.

The dragon queen picked at her claw, obviously not impressed with Queen Filanthropi's behavior. "Do you think this is a good time to spill the beans, Filanthropi?"

With tear-filled eyes, Queen Filanthropi looked at the dragon queen and said, "What beans?"

"Oh Filanthropi, I guess it takes a smart woman to play stupid so well," the queen of Beastonia said.

"Stupid, you think I play—"

"Stop. We are wasting precious time." Queen Prudea patted her friend on the back. "What is it you want to say, my dear?"

"I promised I would never reveal the author of *A Magic Maniac's Many Ways to Make Mischief*."

"Oh please. We know who wrote the book," the queen of Beastonia said. "It was Feefifofum Fiddledeedee Fiddledeedum."

"That is true. But do you know the identity of Feefifofum Fiddledeedee Fiddledeedum?"

"Go on. I'm all ears," Queen Matilda said sarcastically.

"I cannot. I promised."

"Well, I didn't promise no one nothing," Morgana said. "Feefifofum Fiddledeedee Fiddledeedum is here in dis room."

Queen Matilda and Queen Prudea stared at each other, and then both queens stared at Morgana.

"Not her!" Queen Filanthropi yelled. "I'm Feefifofum Fiddledeedee Fiddledeedum. I penned the book with the help of that silly bookworm, Blabberdish. I used one of the spells we had written to turn Wilameena into a chicken, regretfully resulting in her abduction to Butcherdonia. After that unfortunate event, I was forced to forfeit the book to my father, who gave it to the Great Wizard for safekeeping. For several years, the book was kept under lock and key in a protective case in the Great Wizard's library. Then I fell madly in love with Heroian, who, as you know, is miserable at magic. So late one night, I snuck into the Great Wizard's library and chanted one of the spells I had written to open the lock. I stole *A Magic Maniac's Many Ways to Make Mischief* and gave it to my love, hoping it would help him master magic. He hid it. I am heartbroken to say it has been missing ever since."

Queen Prudea gasped. Queen Matilda roared with laughter.

"Prudea, give it up," Queen Matilda said.

"Give what up?" Queen Filanthropi said as she pulled away from the comfort of her friend. "You already knew? How dare you let me believe I held such a powerful secret?"

"Well"—Queen Matilda chuckled and winked at Queen Prudea—"that was our little secret."

"Matilda, this is no time to poke fun," Queen Prudea said. She reached out to Queen Filanthropi. "Come, come, dear. There are no secrets among old friends."

"That is what I am afraid of," Queen Filanthropi replied.

"Meaning?" Queen Matilda asked.

"Meaning," Queen Filanthropi said, "I think we know too much about each other."

"Hmm. Does that mean you are harboring a secret, Filanthropi?" Queen Prudea asked.

"None in plain sight," Queen Filanthropi said as she glared at Morgana. "Now we must go back to Idlebury."

"I'm with her," Queen Matilda said as she pushed her way out of Queen Prudea's bedchamber. "Are you coming, Prudea?"

"Unfortunately, I cannot at this time."

"Fine," Queen Filanthropi said, clearly miffed. "Will you escort us out?"

"You found your way in, I think you can find your way out."

Queen Filanthropi waved for Morgana to leave the room with her. "Ta," she said as she, her servant, and Queen Matilda left.

Once the trio was out of sight, Queen Prudea ran to the rubbing of King Abracadabra's sword. King Ovazealous's signature was gone. In its place, Thane's noticeably childish signature appeared.

"I swear that wasn't there before." She touched the glass that protected the rubbing. "She knows. Filanthropi knows her son has been sacrificed to the Great Wizard."

⟶⊙⊙⊙⟵

The people of East Wisdomere ignored Queen Filanthropi, Queen Matilda, and Morgana as they walked across the courtyard.

"What a bunch of snobs," Queen Matilda said.

"Where's da beam?" Morgana asked.

"Looks like we've been left to our own devices," Queen Matilda said. "Jump on."

Before the trio took off, Morgana whispered to Queen Filanthropi. "You sar it too, didn't you?"

"Saw what?"

"Thane's signature on the rubbing."

"Yes, which means there is nothing I can do for him now. He is on his own. I only hope Gwendolyn saves him before it is too late."

"Me too," Morgana said as Queen Matilda took flight into the far reaches of the universe.

Chapter Thirty-Nine
The Power Struggle

Deep in the Slothful Forest, the creature inhabited by Thane, King Morrebidd, and King Abracadabra hunkered down at the base of a towering tree to contemplate its next move. It twitched uncontrollably as the three entities fought for dominance. When it spotted the spire of Idlebury Castle off in the distance, Thane managed to emerge. "All I want is to be ten years old again and practice magic with Blabberdish and pretend I'm the most powerful wizard who ever lived," he said. A second later, he twitched and momentarily changed into Abracadabra, king of Hexidonia who twitched and changed into Morrebidd, king of Deadonia, who immediately changed back into Thane.

As much as Thane hated the beast's uncontrollable spasms, its transformation into the two kings provided insight into their minds, motives, and fears. And Thane knew both kings feared he would gain control. So they fought constantly for power. And in doing so, they weakened the energy of the beast they'd all become. Even more, Thane was angry about reports of his antics to garner control of the universe because his actions were not his own. King Abracadabra had been in charge last night. King Morrebidd had tried to take over, but he couldn't. It had taken every ounce of Thane's energy to stop the decrepit old king from doing what he'd vowed.

Something moved at the forest's edge. Thane tried to make out what or who it was, but he changed into King Abracadabra, whose eyes, hazy from old age, couldn't focus.

Soon the old king transformed into Thane. Through the clarity of his youthful eyes, he saw a man approaching. Thane tried to stand up but fell back on the mucky ground and transformed into the beast.

Soon the one man became two. The men walked side by side, slowly with deliberate steps. The beast couldn't tell if they could see it or not, but they were headed straight for it. It twitched and changed into King Morrebidd. "Well, if it isn't the two men for whom I have no use or respect," he said. Another twitch and Thane was back.

As the men stepped into the Slothful Forest, it was clear one man was very old and one much younger, yet they paced as one. The men closed in on the beast. Twitch, it changed into King Abracadabra but only for a moment before it changed into King Morrebidd.

"Good evening, Morrebidd," the younger of the two men said.

"Good evening, Heroian," King Morrebidd said as he twitched but remained himself. "Oof. Where are you off to on this lovely, dull, evening? Off to die, I hope."

When Thane recognized his father and Oof, he fought with all his might to take control from King Morrebidd. But the king of Deadonia maintained enough energy to keep Thane at bay.

"Come, Thane," Oof said. "Stop struggling with the others. They are no match for you."

"Yes, come, son," King Heroian said as he and Oof walked

farther into the Slothful Forest.

King Morrebidd flashed in and out. One second he was himself; in the next moment, he was Thane.

Thane tried to run after his father and Oof. But trying to remain in control was exhausting. Nonetheless, he followed as swiftly as he could.

King Heroian and Oof approached the Field of Wisdom. A bright light lit the field as if it was waiting for the men's arrival. As King Heroian reached the edge of the field, he realized Oof was not at his side. When he saw the old man sitting on the ground, head in hands, silently weeping, he immediately went to Oof's aid.

"Leave him be, Heroian," the Field of Wisdom announced.

"I will do nothing of the sort," King Heroian said angrily.

"You will do as I say," the field demanded. "Thane is approaching. It is time for the transition of power."

"No. Thane is not ready," the king of Idlebury said. "Besides, Gwendolyn is not here."

"That does not matter," the field replied.

"But she holds the power of the Great Wizard."

"No, she does not," Oof said as he staggered toward King Heroian. He was nearly side by side with the king when he stumbled. Instinctively King Heroian grabbed the old man's hand. As their fingers met, an electrical charge raced through Oof into the king of Idlebury. For a few seconds a shimmering light shrouded King Heroian. Oof fell to the ground.

"What have you done?" King Heroian asked.

Oof wheezed and coughed. "I have transferred my powers to you."

"Why?"

"Because you are the only person I can trust with them."

King Heroian shook his head. "I do not understand."

"You will."

"What about Gwendolyn? She believes she has the power of the Great Wizard."

"Belief is all she needs to succeed. She has great power of her own."

"What will happen to Thane? Is he not to be the next Great Wizard?"

"Yes, he will be the next Great Wizard but not before he learns to be a responsible man and earns the right to wield such power. That is where you come in, Heroian."

"I do not deserve such power," King Heroian whined. "I do not know what to do with it."

"You do not have to do anything. Just hold it until the time is right."

"How will I know when the time is right?"

"You will. Now go, step into the Field of Wisdom."

King Heroian stepped toward the field. When he reached the edge, a strong wind blew him back. In an eerie voice like that of a demon, someone yelled, "*No.*"

King Heroian fought to remain upright. The source of the wind and the voice hovered over the Field of Wisdom. It was hideous to behold. The king of Idlebury stared in disbelief. "Damn you, Morrebidd and Abracadabra. How dare you take my son?"

"Give us the power of the Great Wizard, and we'll give Thane back to you," the grotesque beast said.

"Never," King Heroian said. He tried again to step into the Field of Wisdom, but the wind blew him back.

"It's futile, Heroian," the beast said. "Give up. It's what you do best."

King Heroian glared at the beast, and with all his might, he stepped into the Field of Wisdom. A warm, comforting light hugged him. He glowed. Images of his life—past, present, and future—flashed before him. He saw who he had been, who he was, and who he would become. He wanted to scream out with joy. He experienced every emotion at once—joy, sadness, happiness, love, hate, disappointment, inspiration, defeat and more. He wept. He laughed. "I have never felt so alive in my life," he screamed.

Thane appeared, elevated above the Field of Wisdom. King Heroian's body stiffened. "Why am I afraid?" he yelled. "Why am I afraid of my son?" He trembled. "Why, my son? Why do you want to kill me?"

Thane morphed into the hideous beast and laughed maniacally. In a voice that can only be described as pure evil, it said, "The power of the Great Wizard belongs to me, not you. And it can only be transferred to me if you're dead. So if I have to kill you for it, Father, then so be it."

The Field of Wisdom released its hold on King Heroian. He dropped to the ground, exhausted. He looked up at the beast and said, "You are not my son. My son would never harm me. You are not Thane."

"Oh but I am, Father."

"Do not call me father."

"Then don't call me son," the beast said.

"Get out," the Field of Wisdom bellowed. "Heroian, get out now. It is your only chance."

King Heroian fought to stand. The beast tried to hold the king of Idlebury in place, but he broke free and ran out of the

Field of Wisdom. The beast flew after him. King Heroian ran past Oof. When the king of Idlebury saw despair in the old man's eyes, he stopped to offer his help.

"Go on," Oof said. "Leave me be."

King Heroian didn't respond. Instead, he picked up the old man, cradled him like a baby, and ran through the Slothful Forest toward Idlebury Castle.

The beast charged after King Heroian. "I'll kill you, Father," it shouted.

"*Stop*," a woman yelled as she came out from behind a tree.

"I will do nothing of the sort, you old excuse for an enchantress," the beast roared.

"But I believe I have something you want, Abracadabra," Wilameena said. "Or at least something your precious wife, Opunzayzme, wants."

The beast stopped. It flashed in and out, clearly losing strength. "Like what?"

"Like something Opunzayzme wants, you know, for her Wicked Wand Collection."

The beast took on the likeness of King Morrebidd. "Show me."

From her skirt pocket, Wilameena removed the wand Queen Filanthropi had given her in Hedonia. The beast reached out with a wart-covered, bony hand and tried to snatch the wand from the enchantress.

Wilameena yanked the wand away from the beast. "Oh no you don't, Morrebidd. I need to give this to Abracadabra."

The beast flickered as King Abracadabra struggled to gain control. After a few seconds, the beast transformed into the old wizard. Wilameena clutched the wand to her chest. The king of Hexidonia grabbed Wilameena's arm and tried to pry the wand from her grasp. She wiggled and turned her back to him as she kept hold of the wand. He grabbed her from behind and turned her toward him. He tugged the wand, but the enchantress had a tight grip. The old king grunted as he pulled on the wand, drawing Wilameena toward him as she pushed away, making the duo appear to be engaged in a strange dance rather than a fight. The old king yanked one more time on the wand, this time pulling Wilameena to him. The king of Hexidonia and the enchantress were now so close only the wand was between them.

Wilameena gave the old king one last push. "For God's sake, take the stupid thing."

King Abracadabra snatched the wand from the enchantress. Its power allowed the old king to break free from the beast. He was his old self again. He roared with laughter.

"Thank you, Wilameena. Opunzayzme will love it." King Abracadabra waved the wand and said, "Home." The wand disappeared, leaving Abracadabra staring at the beast.

The beast was weak. It flickered in and out. "Did you think you could get out of this alive, Abracadabra?" it yelled.

The king of Hexidonia took off running, his robe billowing behind him.

The beast grabbed the old wizard and growled like a rabid wolf. "I'm not done with you."

Chapter Forty
Gwen's Rescue

G wen stood outside the gate that protected Hexidonia and its citizens from the real world. As she stared at the barrier, she wondered why she hadn't landed inside Cauldron Castle's gate. *Is someone aware of my arrival? Has my mission to get King Abracadabra's sword been leaked?* She scanned the area but didn't see or hear anyone.

Convinced her arrival had gone unnoticed, she took a few steps toward the gate and then stopped. She leaned on Crabbina's cane, desperately trying to calm her nerves while thinking about how she could gain possession of King Abracadabra's sword. She knew she'd have to rely on magic, and she hoped she knew how to use Crabbina's cane or Blabberdish's small gold wand. She didn't feel worthy of the power the cane and wand bestowed upon her, but she was confident the powers Oof had transferred to her would protect her from harm.

Gwen moved closer to the massive gate. "Hmm, it's rather plain."

The gate shook. A face appeared and yawned as if awakening from a deep sleep. "That's because the real magic lies inside," it said.

"I request your permission to enter," Gwen said with authority.

"You're kidding, right?" the gate said. "I can't let you or anyone inside without instructions from Queen Opunzayzme."

"Well, I've been granted permission from King Abracadabra to enter at will," Gwen lied.

The gate laughed so hard it had a coughing fit, rattling its doors just enough to give Gwen a glimpse of Hexidonia. "King Abracadabra, you say?" The gate laughed and coughed again. "That shriveled-up old prune doesn't have any power here."

"What do you mean he has no power?" Gwen asked, wondering if the gate knew of the king's incineration. "He's the king of Hexidonia and one of the greatest wizards in the universe."

"You obviously don't listen too well. I said I need instructions from Queen Opunzayzme to allow you in. And for your information, it is the queen who wields the power in Hexidonia. She just lets the king, and the rest of the universe for that matter, think the power lies with him. In reality, it's quite hilarious." Once again, the gate broke out in laughter.

"I am Gwendolyn the Great, Savior of Idlebury, Protector of the Universe. I am on an important mission. You must let me in."

"Well, why didn't you say so at the beginning? You could have saved a lot of time, but I must admit, I appreciate the good laugh."

Gwen smiled and stepped forward, ready to enter the kingdom of magic. But the gate yawned and went back to sleep. "Hey, what part of I'm Gwendolyn the Great, Savior of Idlebury, Protector of the Universe do *you* not understand?"

The gate yawned again. "And what part of I need instructions from Queen Opunzayzme do *you* not understand?"

Gwen was flabbergasted. The stupid gate wasn't going to let her in. She knew she could use the power of Crabbina's cane or Blabberdish's wand, but the truth was she didn't have a clue how. She slumped, angry with herself for not having thought through the possible roadblocks to getting inside Hexidonia's castle. She decided to leave and work out a plan.

Suddenly bright lights blinded her. She raised her hand to shield her eyes while balancing herself on Crabbina's cane. A man approached her. She didn't recognize him. Her heart raced. Her sweaty palms caused Crabbina's cane to slip out of her hand and crash to the ground. The man picked up the wooden cane and then held it out toward Gwen as if to give it back to her. As she reached for it, the man yanked it back and thrust a microphone in her face.

"Well, well, well, if it isn't Gwendolyn the Great, Savior of Idlebury, Protector of the Universe. Tell me, Gwennie... I can call you Gwennie, can't I?" Without waiting for Gwen's response, he said, "What brings you here to Hexidonia?"

When Gwen's eyes focused, she recognized the man. "Mr. Muckraker, I think a better question would be what brings *you* here to Hexidonia?"

"Well, I guess you haven't read today's *Universal Scandals* magazine."

"Can't say that I have. As you can see, I'm busy." Gwen reached for Crabbina's cane.

"I see you have an interest in this old cane." Mike Muckraker quickly examined the cane. "Why is that?"

"No reason. I just like it, that's all."

Mike Muckraker eyed the cane a little longer and then handed it back to Gwen. "Now, Gwennie, how about answering my question: What are you doing here in

Hexidonia?"

Gwen kept a firm grip on Crabbina's cane. "I'm here on a secret mission to save the universe."

"There you have it, ladies and gentlemen; Gwendolyn the Great, Savior of Idlebury, Protector of the Universe is here in Hexidonia on a *secret* mission to save the universe. If you believe that, I have a bridge I'd like to sell you." Mike Muckraker shoved the mic back at Gwen, then pulled it back to make another statement. "So what do you think about the death of Thane, prince of Idlebury? Isn't he your brother?"

Although Gwen knew Thane had turned to ashes and blended with the ashes of King Abracadabra and King Morrebidd, she pretended Thane's death was news to her. "What?" she said, faking sadness. "I'm horribly saddened. But what does Thane's death have to do with Hexidonia?"

Mike Muckraker looked straight into the camera. "Shall I update her on what the rest of the universe already knows?" He pulled Gwen in front of the camera, put his arm around her shoulder, and said, "It appears Thane, King Morrebidd, King Abracadabra, and King Ovazealous are all dead and by some act of magic have become a hideous monster."

"That shows you how much you know, Mr. Muckraker," Gwen said as she freed herself from the newsman's grasp. "I know for a fact that all the people you mentioned are very much alive."

"We'll be right back after this break." Mike Muckraker grabbed Gwen, pulled her toward him, and in a sinister voice said, "Tell me what you know, and I'll get you into Hexidonia."

Gwen twisted away from Mike Muckraker. "You have no power to get me beyond the gate. I suggest you leave before you find yourself in a dangerous situation."

"Trying to scare me, are you?" Mike Muckraker grinned.

"Let's help each other."

"How?"

"Well… I've got it from a reliable source that King Abracadabra has something that if it falls into the wrong hands could do irreparable harm to the universe. And by wrong hands, I mean Queen Opunzayzme."

"What could King Abracadabra have that his wife doesn't already know about?"

Mike Muckraker whispered in Gwen's ear. "He has possession of the most powerful…" He paused, then glanced around as if to ensure no one could hear what he was about to say. "He has possession of the most powerful book in the universe, you know, *A Magic Maniac's Many Ways to Make Mischief.*"

Gwen tried to mask her relief that Mike Muckraker didn't know about the king of Hexidonia's sword. "Are you sure?"

"Absolutely. And if you get me into Hexidonia Castle, we can share the most coveted book in the universe. You'll have power beyond your wildest dreams."

"Wow. That's an offer that's hard to refuse." Gwen paused. *How do I get rid of this nuisance of a man?* she wondered. "Tell you what. I'll climb over the gate, unlock it, and let you in. Then the two of us, just the two of us, can get our hands on the book. But we have to do it together. If not, there's no deal."

Mike Muckraker bit his lower lip and scrunched his face as he considered Gwen's offer. "Sounds like a plan."

"Good. Now step back. I don't want you to get caught if I get caught."

"Right." Mike Muckraker motioned for his crew to back up.

Gwen raised Crabbina's cane, aimed it at Mike Muckraker and his crew, and said, "Move back a little bit more."

Mike Muckraker signaled for his crew to obey Gwen's request.

When they were sufficiently far away, Gwen thrust the cane at them. To her surprise, Crabbina's cane screamed, "Instant eraser." Mike Muckraker and his crew disappeared as if they were wiped out with a sweep of an invisible giant eraser. Gwen was now alone, once again standing before the gates of Hexidonia's Cauldron Castle. "Now what?" she mumbled.

Crabbina's cane started to shake. It took every ounce of Gwen's strength to hold on to it.

"Grip relinquish," the cane said. Instantly it freed itself from Gwen's grasp and jumped over the gate into Cauldron Castle's courtyard.

"Oh no. I let one of the most power wands in the world escape my control."

"You control nothing," a voice from the other side of the gate said.

Gwen remained silent. She didn't know if the voice had come from a person or Crabbina's cane.

"Did you hear me, young lady?" the voice said.

"Um… yes… I heard you."

"Well, keep in mind that when you're in Hexidonia, you have no control over anyone or anything. Do you understand me?"

"I think so."

"Wrong answer. You think nothing," the voice said. "You will obey my commands. Do you understand me?"

"Certainly, but who are you?"

The gate slowly opened, making a horrible screeching noise.

Gwen stepped back to avoid being struck by the massive doors. She took a deep breath and said, "I am Gwendolyn the Great, Savior of Idlebury, Protector of the Universe. Nothing can harm me."

The gate slammed shut, blowing dirt on Gwen and keeping her outside the courtyard. Crabbina's wand jumped back over the gate and crashed at Gwen's feet. Gwen, frozen with fear the cane had been damaged, stared at it.

"For goodness' sake, pick me up," the cane said.

Gwen tried with all her might to pick up the cane, but for some reason it weighed much more than before. She struggled to lift it but failed. "How come you're so heavy?"

"I'm heavy with knowledge. Knowledge you'll need for a successful mission." The cane rose and said, "Grab me."

When Gwen wrapped her fingers around the cane's knobby wood, it lit up like a glow stick. Light from the cane completely engulfed Gwen as it gave up its knowledge to her. When its light and power ceased, Gwen fell to the ground, barely conscious.

"Oh brother," the cane said. "I had no idea she couldn't handle the truth." The cane sighed. "I guess I'll just have to wait for her to come to her senses."

Gwen sat up and held her head as if to soothe a terrible headache. "What did you do to me?" she said as she kicked the cane with her foot.

"I gave you the truth, the most powerful thing in the universe."

Gwen moaned. "I feel like you gave me a whack upside the head."

"Well, if that's what it takes to get you moving."

A shadow appeared in the sky above Gwen, but she didn't notice because she was still holding her aching head.

"Hurry, take hold of me," the cane begged. "We're about to—"

Gwen grabbed the cane just as something grabbed her. Instantly she and the cane were airborne. Gwen looked up and saw two huge wings and realized she was dangling from the talons of a dragon. As she and the dragon soared over Hexidonia, she noticed something odd. The dragon from which she hung was too small to be Queen Matilda and too large to be Mistofisee. So she whacked the dragon with Crabbina's cane and yelled, "Let me go."—whack—"Who do you think you are?"—whack—"Put me down."—whack—"What part of put me down do you not understand?" Whack.

"As you wish," the dragon said as it flew low and dropped Gwen inside the gate of Hexidonia's Cauldron Castle.

Gwen rolled on the ground. When she came to a stop, she sat up and checked herself for injury. As she brushed off her clothes and picked up Crabbina's cane, she mumbled, "Well, I never… I could have been hurt… Who would do such a thing? And for your information, I don't need your help."

"Yes, you do," someone said.

What sounded like a handsome young man was, in fact, a large dragon. Gwen squinted and examined the creature. "Mistofisee? Is that you?"

"Who do you think I am?"

Gwen tossed Crabbina's cane to the ground, ran to her old friend, jumped on his foot, and hugged his leg. "I can't believe you're here. I've missed you so much." Gwen grabbed the cane and aimed it at the dragon. "Wait just a minute. If you're Wilameena, I'll—"

"I'm not Wilameena. It's me, Mistofisee."

"Prove it," Gwen said as she used all her strength to wave Crabbina's cane at the dragon.

"Okay." The dragon stared at Gwen.

"Well?"

"Well, I'm not sure how to prove who I am."

"What did you say to me before I entered the Wall of Passages?"

"Say? I don't remember what I said, but I do remember I was so afraid of losing your friendship I started to cry. Then one of my tears landed on you, right over your heart, and zing, you were gone."

"*Yes!*" Gwen shrieked. "Oh, Mistofisee, I'm so happy to see you."

The two friends hugged. Gwen was the first to pull away. "Why are you here?"

"I'm here to help you. What is it you want to do?"

"I need to get inside the castle and get King Abracadabra's sword."

"Okay. How do we do that?"

"If I knew, I'd already be in there," Gwen said. "You got any ideas?"

Mistofisee thought for a few seconds and said, "Nope."

"Stop it," Crabbina's cane said as it hopped over to Gwen. "You've got the power of truth. Did you learn nothing from the knowledge I instilled in you?"

"Oh, I forgot." Gwen thought for a moment. "Follow me. I have a brilliant plan," she said as she headed toward the door to Cauldron Castle.

"Oh no," Mistofisee mumbled. "Not one of her brilliant plans."

Crabbina's cane watched Gwen and Mistofisee walk away. "Stupid, stupid, stupid."

Chapter Forty-One
Merger of the Most Powerful Wands in the Universe

Inside Cauldron Castle, all was calm. Queen Opunzayzme, busy in her boudoir, performing her newest age-defying magic spell, giggled with delight. "I look thirty years younger than ever," she said. "In a few more days, I will look like a teenager. I will be the envy of every woman in the universe."

The queen of Hexidonia examined herself in a mirror and laughed. "The universe is full of stupid people who do not understand power. They think it is about intelligence, accomplishment, or brawn, but they are wrong. Envy is power. And I am the queen of envy."

As she continued to admire her youthful beauty, the cabinet in which she stored her infamous Wicked Wand Collection shook. "Heavens. What is that racket about?" Queen Opunzayzme reached in her dress pocket and gasped. "Oh horrors. I left the key to the cabinet on the table in Idlebury Castle's great hall."

The cabinet's doors flung open. She peered at the only empty slot. "If only I could get my hands on the last wand, not only would I be the most envied woman in the universe, I would be the most feared woman in the universe. Oh, to dream."

The words had barely crossed her lips when the window behind her shattered. Queen Opunzayzme jumped out of the way as something soared past her and entered the cabinet. The doors slammed shut.

The queen of Hexidonia slowly reached for the solid-gold knobs. As she treasured the coolness of the metal, she felt a surge of power. A light glowed from the space between the cabinet and its doors.

"No, it cannot be," she said.

Her heart raced.

Her chest heaved from excitement.

A quick count of the cabinet's contents caused Queen Opunzayzme to smile, for sure enough, every slot held a wand. "It is complete. My Wicked Wand Collection is complete." She carefully removed the new wand and examined it. "Hmm, it is ordinary," she said. She gave it a mighty flick, but nothing happened.

With the wand in hand, she admired herself in her mirror and examined her backside. "A little nip and tuck would be nice." So she waved the wand and said, "Rumpus reductionus." To her horror, her buttocks swelled to nearly three times their normal size. *Rumpus reductionus,*" Queen Opunzayzme yelled. She nearly fainted when she saw her buttocks had grown even larger. "Derriere reduction," she yelled as she flicked the wand again. *Oh no.*" The queen of Hexidonia gulped. Her buttocks were completely gone. She started to sit down to contemplate her misfortune but realized she had no buttocks on which to rest her body. She tried to walk over to the cabinet, hoping another wand could magically restore her backside, but without buttocks, she couldn't walk. "Why are you doing this to me?" she yelled at the wand.

In disgust, she flung the wand across the room. It landed on the floor in front of the cabinet, rose in the air, and then snorted at the queen before easing its way back in its slot. After the doors to the cabinet that housed the Wicked Wand Collection closed, an eerie voice said, "You no longer control us, we control you."

"I beg to differ," Queen Opunzayzme said.

"Go back to your silly beauty spells. You have no power."

"What?"

"Beauty is only skin deep. And dare we say your skin is more than a thousand years old?"

"Your point would be?"

"You are transparent. You old fool."

Queen Opunzayzme gritted her teeth and said, "I do not need you. I have many tricks up my sleeve, so to speak."

"You have nothing of the sort. You are a weak, pathetic woman. You are nothing more than a mere mortal."

The queen of Hexidonia was about to respond when she remembered something that could return her powers or at least her buttocks. So she lowered herself to the ground and slithered like a snake out of her chambers and down the hall. When she arrived at King Abracadabra's chambers, she heard voices coming from inside the room. She managed to push the door open just a crack. From her position on the floor, she peered in and saw the legs of what appeared to be a human female and the giant feet of a creature that was undeniably a dragon. She slithered into the room and slid along the floor, remaining close to the wall to make herself as inconspicuous as possible.

"Well, where is it?" the female said.

"Beats me," the dragon said. "I thought you knew."

"It's got to be here somewhere."

"Why's that?"

When the female turned and faced the dragon, Queen Opunzayzme saw it was none other than Gwendolyn the Great. "What is she doing here? Something must be horribly wrong," she whispered.

"If you were the owner of one of the most powerful wands in the universe, would you let it out of your sight?" Gwen asked.

"Depends," Mistofisee said.

"On what?"

"You're assuming King Abracadabra knows it's one of the most powerful wands in the universe."

"Unlikely," Gwen said. "Go on."

"So who in Cauldron Castle would be the keeper of the sword?"

"Well, since it's the king's sword, even if no one knew it was powerful, it would still be of value and therefore, King Abracadabra would be protective of it."

Queen Opunzayzme watched Gwen and Mistofisee and mumbled, "I can't believe Abracadabra's sword is one of the most powerful wands in the universe. I have to get my hands on it before they do."

"Yeah, like he'd only take it out for—"

"Shh!" Gwen said.

"What?" Mistofisee asked.

"I thought I heard something." Gwen scanned the room. When a flash of color caught her eye, she quickly returned to her conversation with Mistofisee. "Anyway, we're wasting our time in this room." Gwen headed toward the door. "I bet King Abracadabra's sword is on display somewhere in this castle."

Queen Opunzayzme managed to slither out the door just before it shut. "Morons. I know exactly where Abracadabra's sword is. And I will get to it long before you do," she said as she headed in the opposite direction from Gwen and Mistofisee.

Gwen grabbed Mistofisee's leg. "Stop," she said. "We need to head in the other direction."

"Why?"

"Because in case you didn't notice, Queen Opunzayzme was in the room with us. She heard everything we said. And she headed that way."

"Wait," Mistofisee said. "If she heard everything we said, then she knows about King Abracadabra's sword."

"Well, duh."

"We need to be careful, that's all."

"Are you afraid of that miserable old woman?" Gwen asked.

"No. Why would I be afraid of her?"

"You tell me."

"I'm not afraid of her, I'm afraid of… I'm afraid of her Wicked Wand Collection."

"Well, who isn't? Now let's go get the sword."

Mistofisee shook his head. "Can you spell death wish," he muttered.

For a few minutes Gwen and Mistofisee wandered silently through Cauldron Castle.

"The castle is amazingly plain," Gwen said. "I would have expected to see magical things."

Mistofisee spotted rows of doors on both sides of the hall. "Keep your eyes open; you may see them yet. Let's see what's behind door number one?" he said as he opened a door. "Wow, look at that."

Gwendolyn peeked inside the room to see what Mistofisee had discovered. "Holy moly. That's the most amazing thing I've ever seen."

Huge cauldrons of bubbling liquid spewed shapes of people, animals, and things in the most amazing colors. Many popped after only a few seconds. Those that held their shape floated to boxes already labeled for shipment to far-off lands neither Gwen nor Mistofisee had heard of. Gwen stepped inside the room to get a better look at the boxes and their contents.

Gwen spotted a box labeled for shipment to Idlebury. She carefully opened it. When she peered inside, she saw twelve sections, each containing a bubble. Each bubble encased the miniature likeness of one person—Queen Filanthropi, King Heroian, Thane, Prudence, Blabberdish, Oof, Matilda, Crabbina, King Morrebidd, King Abracadabra, and her. But one bubble appeared to be empty. She smiled, knowing full well it was the likeness of King Ovazealous. "King Abracadabra and Queen Opunzayzme are trying to interfere with Idlebury," she said to Mistofisee who had joined her. "They're trying to get control of the book."

"Well, duh," Mistofisee said. "They didn't go to the trouble to make these bubble people for nothing. Hey, where's me?"

Gwen spotted another box addressed for shipment to Idlebury. The label read USE IN CASE OF EMERGENCY ONLY. She raised the lid and looked inside. *I don't believe it. They're all Wilameena.* Gwen laughed mischievously as she poked the Wilameena bubbles. When she saw she'd destroyed them, she slammed the lid. "Let's go."

Fluid dripped from the box.

"Whom did you pop?" Mistofisee asked.

"No one of any importance." Gwen walked back into the hall of Cauldron Castle. "Let's go get the sword."

A short way down the hall, the twosome heard voices and saw light flashing from inside a room. They tiptoed closer.

"I beg your pardon," someone behind them said.

Gwen whipped around. She was face-to-face with a guard.

"I beg your pardon," the guard said again.

The guard appeared to be in a trance. Mistofisee reached out and tapped him with one of his talons. Instantly the guard popped, leaving a glistening puddle of water.

"A bubble person," Mistofisee said. "Most definitely a bubble person."

Gwen ignored Mistofisee's comment and focused her attention on the door. She put her ear against it and listened. "It's Queen Opunzayzme," she whispered. "Oh no, we need to get out of here… fast." She took off running.

"Hey, wait for me," Mistofisee said as he ran down the hall as fast as his huge body would allow him. For a moment he lost sight of Gwen. When he saw her again, she was standing before a long, ornately carved case hung on the wall.

Gwen looked at Mistofisee and mouthed, "Hurry up."

Mistofisee reached Gwen just as she opened the case and revealed its contents. There was no mistaking it. It was King Abracadabra's sword.

Gwen nearly touched it but withdrew her hand. "You do it."

"Me? It was your idea to steal it in the first place," Mistofisee whined.

"You're nothing but a big scaredy-cat."

Mistofisee snorted a puff of smoke. "I'm not stealing King Abracadabra's sword. It was your idea. You steal it."

"All right, I will." Gwen grabbed the sword. It wouldn't budge. She yanked it with all her might. Still it wouldn't budge. Something in her pocket started to shake. She reached in and pulled out Blabberdish's tiny gold wand. It glowed and vibrated in her closed hand. "Where's Crabbina's cane?" she screamed.

"Last I saw it, it was yelling at you outside the castle."

"Oh no, I left Crabbina's cane outside."

"No, you didn't. You silly girl," a female said.

Crabbina's cane hopped toward Gwen and Mistofisee. When it stopped next to Gwen, light from Blabberdish's wand seeped between her fingers. "Blabberdish's wand is raring to go," the cane said. It knelt before the sword, and said, "Last night at ten o'clock this morning…"

Blabberdish's glowing wand jumped out of Gwen's hand, floated in midair, and in a powerful voice, it said, "…an empty wagon full of people…"

In a booming voice, the sword said, "…ran over a dead horse and killed it."

King Abracadabra's sword shone with the brightness of the sun. The doors to the case burst open. The sword jumped out, and the three most powerful wands in the universe swirled around each other. Bolts of light bounced off the walls. Squeals, grunts, and groans echoed through the hall. As quickly as it started, it stopped.

A wand made of gold and adorned with twinkling jewels drifted toward Gwen.

She grabbed it and noticed it bore the writing etched on King Abracadabra's sword. "It's beautiful."

"Thanks," the wand responded. "Now take me to Idlebury Castle before I lose my power."

"Let's go," Gwen said.

"Okeydokey," Mistofisee said as he followed his friend.

When Gwen and Mistofisee were out of sight, a door creaked open. Queen Opunzayzme, still buttless and creeping on the floor, stuck out her head and saw the case that had held King Abracadabra's sword was empty. "Uh-oh," she muttered. "Too late. The wrath of the most powerful wand in the universe has been unleashed."

CHAPTER FORTY-TWO
QUEEN MATILDA'S
GOLDEN OPPORTUNITY

Dimension XIII was gone. Queen Matilda and her companions had just left East Wisdomere on their return to Idlebury when the entire dimension disappeared. She was baffled, concerned, and torn as to whether or not she should keep her mouth shut or share her finding with Queen Filanthropi and Morgana. She decided to keep quiet.

"Where are we going?" Queen Filanthropi said as the dragon queen soared past what should have been the kingdom of Idlebury.

"Um... well..."

"Do not stall, Matilda. I can see with my own eyes that something is amiss."

"Me too," Morgana chimed in.

"Well, I don't think it's anything to worry about," Queen Matilda said. "We'll just take another whirl around."

The dragon queen headed back, passing into Dimension XII. "Let's go to Hedonia and pay another visit to Merry and Funzy. Won't that be fun? And by the time we get back, I'm sure everything will have returned to normal."

The three women soared past Anhedonia. The whining of its inhabitants echoed across the dimension. Shortly, they passed Personadonia. A few minutes later, Hedonia came into view. As the queen of Beastonia homed in on the kingdom, she felt a tug. She looked around but didn't see anyone or anything. A second tug was so strong it momentarily stopped her, nearly tossing Queen Filanthropi and Morgana into space. Nonetheless, the dragon queen continued toward Hedonia. A stronger third tug nearly flung her off course. She looked behind her and saw Queen Filanthropi and Morgana hanging on for dear life. Queen Filanthropi shook with fear. Morgana clung to the queen with her head buried in her employer's back.

Up ahead, Queen Matilda saw the kingdom she'd sworn she'd never visit. "No," she said. "I will not... I will not go to that godforsaken place."

"Matilda, is that Egotonia up ahead?" Queen Filanthropi asked.

"I believe it is."

"Why are we headed there?"

"I'm not sure. It's out of my control."

Soon the trio was sucked into the kingdom of the self-absorbed. A large building made of solid gold glistened.

Queen Matilda gently landed and unloaded her passengers.

"You would think there would be a greeting party," Queen Filanthropi said as she brushed off her gown, smoothed her hair, and straightened her crown.

"What are the names of the king and queen?" Queen Matilda asked.

"King Van Haughty," Morgana said. "He has no queen."

"I believe that question was meant for me, Morgana." Queen

Filanthropi glared at her servant. "Your arrogance never ceases to amaze me."

Morgana shrugged.

"I believe I've met him before." The dragon queen scratched her head, lost in thought. "Yes. It was before I killed Anima."

Queen Filanthropi stomped her feet and screamed, "Okay, so you two have met. But why are we here when my babies are out there in danger or maybe even dead?"

The queen of Beastonia turned away, deliberately ignoring Queen Filanthropi's outburst, but as she did, she noticed Morgana smirking at the queen of Idlebury. She thought the servant woman's behavior was disrespectful, but worse, she thought it was odd, making her wonder if once again, Morgana knew something about Queen Filanthropi that she shouldn't.

"Let's find out why we're here, Filanthropi," Queen Matilda said as she plodded toward the gilded palace.

The two queens and the servant approached the palace, silenced by its overwhelming extravagance.

Queen Matilda was the first to reach the palace's circular drive. The dragon queen pointed to her left and said, "You go that way, Filanthropi." She pointed to her right. "I'll go this way. You know what they say: when you come to a fork in the road, take it." Queen Matilda grinned.

Queen Filanthropi scowled at her dragon friend.

Heralds' horns announced their arrival. The palace doors opened, revealing a tiny man with an unusually large head accompanied by an entourage of twenty servants, all of whom were stick thin and dressed in tight-fitting gold couture uniforms.

"Yes, that is him. Small body, big head," Queen Filanthropi declared as she stifled a laugh at seeing a tiny crown perched upon King Van Haughty's enormous head.

"You're kidding me," Queen Matilda said.

"Nope. Dat's definitely him," Morgana said.

King Van Haughty, with his right hand buried in his lapel, approached his guests. "What a pleasant surprise. Do come in," he said, then abruptly reentered his palace. His entourage scurried after him, leaving Queen Matilda, Queen Filanthropi, and Morgana to fend for themselves.

"Well, I never—"

"Put a sock in it, Filanthropi," Queen Matilda barked. "I think we've been brought here for a reason. So shut up."

Queen Filanthropi's face flushed from anger at Queen Matilda's rude remark. Nonetheless, she followed the queen of Beastonia into Egotonia's grand palace.

But Morgana quietly slipped away.

The dragon queen and the queen of Idlebury slowly walked down a massive mirrored hallway. On each side of the hall, gold statues kept watch. Many represented people frozen in action.

Queen Filanthropi's eyes darted back and forth as she tried to take in the opulence of the hall. One statue of a woman caught her attention. When she stopped for a closer look, she felt something drip on her shoulder. "Matilda, this place is literally dripping gold."

Queen Matilda looked behind her and noticed that Queen Filanthropi lagged behind. "What?" she said.

"I said, this place is literally dripping gold," the queen of Idlebury replied as she scooped the liquid gold off her shoulder.

"Filanthropi, no!"

Queen Matilda's warning was too late. As soon as Queen Filanthropi touched the gold, she turned into a gilded statue. At her feet, etched on a gold plaque, were the words: QUEEN FILANTHROPI, KINGDOM OF IDLEBURY. HER PEOPLE ARE POOR, BUT SHE IS WORTH MORE THAN HER WEIGHT IN GOLD.

Gold dripped on the carpet, barely missing Queen Matilda. When she saw drops of gold collecting on the ceiling, she knew she had to get out of the hallway or she would suffer the same fate as her friend. Worse, without clothing to prevent the gold droplets from touching her skin, she was in danger of becoming the largest gold statue in the universe.

"Hurry, Morgana," the dragon queen said. "We need to get out now." She scanned the long hallway, no Morgana. *"Morgana,"* she yelled. No answer. "No, she couldn't have. On second thought, I bet she did. She knows too much for a servant. She's on her own now."

Queen Matilda rushed down the hall. Moments later, she charged through forty-foot-high gilded doors and emerged in the courtyard where King Van Haughty and his staff waited.

In the distance, the queen of Beastonia saw a magnificent garden—luscious fruit hung off trees, bushes cut in shapes of animals and famous landmarks dotted the landscape, flowers adorned ornate pots, and the whiff of roses clung in the air. Egotonia's garden rivaled any garden, anywhere.

"Well… well… look who survived," King Van Haughty said as his staff applauded the arrival of Queen Matilda. "I so wanted you to be turned into gold." He smirked at his staff and said, "Can you imagine how much more I would be worth?"

His staff roared with laughter.

"You, King Van Haughty, are—"

"The most incredibly clever and, I must say, the best-looking person in the universe." The egotistical king interrupted her.

"I was going to say—"

"Do not waste your breath, Queen Matilda. You are going to need it."

Queen Matilda watched as the beautifully designed gardens rippled and then rose, proving to be nothing more than a curtain so meticulously painted it was indistinguishable from the image it portrayed. Beyond the curtain lay a large barren field.

King Van Haughty motioned for his servants to follow him. As they paraded onto the field, music filled the air. Dogs and horses ran with abandon. Matilda followed behind. The king of Egotonia held up his hand and signaled for everyone to stop.

An intricately carved wooden table made a graceful landing. It was so massive that at least one hundred guests could dine in comfort. Vases of flowers, finely etched crystal glasses, pitchers of wine and water, and gold trays piled high with meats, cheeses, pastries, fruits, and more took their place on the table.

At each end of the table, a chair appeared. One was enormous, clearly meant for Queen Matilda. The other was a tiny throne with stilt-like legs, obviously meant for King Van Haughty. Two male servants lifted the king of Egotonia and placed him on his chair. Queen Matilda took her place on the huge chair.

Plates were passed.

Drinks were poured.

Food was served.

King Van Haughty raised his glass and toasted Queen Matilda. "To you, Matilda, queen of Beastonia, the land of the Innocents. May your innocence serve you well."

Queen Matilda clutched a tiny glass of wine and returned the toast with a smile and a wink. She poured the contents of the glass in her mouth and muttered to herself, "May your big head snap your tiny neck."

King Van Haughty and Queen Matilda ate quietly, occasionally smiling and raising their glasses to each other. Just when the dragon queen thought she couldn't stand one more second of pretending to enjoy the king of Egotonia's company, horns blared, breaking the unbearable silence.

King Van Haughty stood on his throne, waved his hand, and said, "Let the games begin."

Seven gold statues slowly glided over the field. One by one, they settled on the ground. Matilda froze when she saw the statue of Queen Filanthropi among them.

"Queen Matilda," King Van Haughty said, bringing the dragon's attention back to him. "What do you think is the goal of my ingenious game?"

"I don't have a clue," the dragon queen responded. When she glanced back at the statue of Queen Filanthropi, a queasy feeling rose in her belly. "But I don't think it's for anyone's pleasure but yours."

"Right you are. In fact, it is for my pleasure and my financial gain."

"How could it be for your financial gain?"

"Well, let me explain. The purpose of this game is for the statues to fight to the death. And by death, I mean melting, which will result in a pool of pure gold that will harden into a priceless lump of gold, making me immensely richer."

"So if a statue melts, does it mean the person inside is freed?"

"You are too naïve, even for the queen of the Innocents," King Van Haughty replied as he squelched a laugh. "How can

326

they be freed when they are already dead?"

Queen Matilda glared at the king of Egotonia. The thought that Queen Filanthropi was dead was too much to bear. Nonetheless, she maintained her composure and said, "So how do they melt?"

"That is where you come in. You do not think you are here as an observer, now do you? You are nothing more than a pawn in my game."

"Why would I want to play your silly little game?" Queen Matilda asked, knowing full well the king of Egotonia expected her to blow fire on the statues, thus melting them and providing him with more gold.

"Because your life depends on it." King Van Haughty waited a few moments for Queen Matilda to react. When she didn't he added, "And because your son's life depends on it."

The dragon queen didn't flinch. She refused to allow the arrogant peewee of a king to rattle her senses. She stifled a smile as visions of crushing King Van Haughty with one step of her gigantic foot rushed through her head. *I could crush your tiny little self with my gigantic foot and squash you like a bug, and no one would notice,* she thought. "Okay, so what are the rules?"

"The rules are simple. Each statue has one…"

The queen of Beastonia had no intention of playing King Van Haughty's game. She zoned out as she focused on two statues, the one of Queen Filanthropi and one other. The gilded woman looked familiar. *Who is that?* she wondered. She zoomed her vision until she could see a close-up of the statue's face. "No. It can't be," she whispered. She zoomed in closer. "Wilameena?" *Think, Matilda. I don't believe the people in the statues are dead. King Van Haughty would have to be insane or just plain stupid to kill off people, particularly royals who entered his kingdom.* "Did you say I can choose only one statue?" Queen Matilda asked, interrupting King Van Haughty as he rambled on about the game's instructions.

King Van Haughty sneered at Matilda. "Correct," he said, and then he continued, "And you have two minutes—"

"Okay… I've made my choice," Queen Matilda blurted out.

"I'm not finished explaining the rules."

"That's okay." Queen Matilda dismissed the king of Egotonia with a wave of her paw. "I get the gist of it."

King Van Haughty raised his eyebrows, grinned, and said, "As you wish."

Queen Matilda bowed to King Van Haughty. When she faced the statues, she noticed two of them separated Queen Filanthropi and Wilameena. She studied the situation, plotted her move, and then stepped into the middle of the game area. One of the statues moved toward her. She ignored it. She kept her eyes on her goal. With one sweep of her massive head, she spewed fire on each statue, releasing the person held captive by their gold shell. As she took flight, she grabbed Queen Filanthropi and Wilameena.

"*Stop her!*" King Van Haughty screamed. "She did not play by the rules."

King Van Haughty's staff ran after the dragon queen.

"Catch *them*, you morons," the king of Egotonia yelled as he pointed at those recently freed by Queen Matilda. "They are getting away."

<hr>

Morgana watched the entire event from her hiding place behind a bush at the edge of the game area. But the power of the dragon queen's fire found her. As she examined her charred clothes, the scent of burned hair surrounded her. She touched her head. To her horror, her hair was singed. She touched her face, only to discover her eyebrows and eyelashes were gone. When she saw Queen Matilda fly overhead, carrying two people in her mighty talons, Morgana tried to yell, but her throat was too parched to make a sound. So she waved her arms frantically and jumped up and down, but the dragon queen flew on. She buried her head in her hands and wept. "She's left me behind, she has."

Suddenly the wind picked up. A shadow appeared. A second later, something grabbed Morgana. She kicked and screamed as she dangled above the ground, ascending rapidly.

"You've got some explaining to do," Queen Matilda said.

Morgana gulped.

CHAPTER FORTY-THREE
THE KNIGHT IN SHINING ARMOR'S TRUTH

The merge was complete. The beast no longer flashed in and out, taking the form of Prince Thane, King Abracadabra, or King Morrebidd. The hideous creature had come into its own. It dragged its hunched body to the edge of the Slothful Forest. Slime dribbled from its mouth. The sunlight nearly blinded its red eyes. Soon a building took form. The beast snorted and laughed, for in the distance stood Idlebury Castle. When it got closer, it studied the activities of the Idleburians.

"Ha! They've perfected the art of looking busy," it declared.

It took to the sky, swooped in for a closer look, and then flew low over the Idleburians.

No one took cover.

No one screamed.

No one looked up.

King Heroian holed up in the great hall. He knelt in the middle of the ancient mosaic and rocked back and forth, chanting a prayer as tears dotted the front of his shirt. He begged for the salvation of Thane's soul. He'd prayed for hours, refusing to stop until he received a message as to his son's well-being.

In a corner, Oof slumped in a chair, his body so frail and weak a gentle breeze would send him crashing to the floor. The edges of his eyelids were red and swollen from crying. His head bobbed as if he were agreeing with King Heroian's plea to save Thane's soul. Now a mere mortal, there was no doubt the former Great Wizard was nothing more than a defeated old man.

The Dimension Clock chimed, indicating something of importance was about to occur. King Heroian silently noted the clock's warning, but he didn't stop praying.

The beast landed outside the castle and peered through the window of the great hall. It saw King Heroian kneeling, his lips moving. It homed in on the old man sitting in the corner. "Ah, Oof. Alive or dead?" the beast said and then laughed. Drool poured from its mouth as it scanned the room. "No threat here," it said.

The sound of shattering glass preceded the beast's entrance into the great hall. Idlebury Castle shook with every step the beast took. It stood next to King Heroian and stared at him.

King Heroian stopped praying. He rose and motioned for the beast to follow him.

As the king of Idlebury and the beast walked through Idlebury Castle, none of the servants or staff paid attention to them. The king led the beast up the stairs to the third floor. Great gobs of drool dripped from the beast's mouth, leaving a path of warm, slippery saliva.

At the top of the stairs, king and beast began their trek down a long hallway. Up ahead, they saw a figure glittering as if it were made of diamonds. A few seconds later, they stopped in front of the Knight in Shining Armor.

"You have no right," the beast said.

"I have every right," King Heroian replied. "And I have every intention of discovering the truth as to who you are."

"You're not planning on using one of your pathetic spells, now are you?"

King Heroian glared at the beast.

"Your Majesty, how may I be of service?" the Knight in Shining Armor asked.

"As you are a man who can detect the true thoughts and feelings of someone, I ask that you tell me the true nature and intentions of the beast that stands before you."

"I mean no disrespect, sire, but I see no beast," the Knight in Shining Armor said.

"You do not see the great beast that stands before you?"

"No, sire."

"What or whom do you see?"

"I see King Abracadabra, King Morrebidd, and Thane, sire."

"Tell me the intentions of each."

"Yes, sire. My pleasure." The knight cleared his throat. "King Abracadabra's and King Morrebidd's intentions are the same. They both plan to destroy Idlebury, gain possession of *A Magic Maniac's Many Ways to Make Mischief,* and then kill the other and rule the universe."

"They have no intentions to harm Prince Thane?"

"No, sire, they do not."

"Why?"

The Knight in Shining Armor nervously shuffled his feet. "They deem him insignificant because he is merely a child."

"And?"

"They intend to deal with him later after they take over the universe."

"And what are Prince Thane's intentions?"

"Prince Thane just wants to come home. He is ever so sorry for all the chaos he has bestowed upon his family, Idlebury, and the universe."

"And what about his heart and soul?"

"His heart and soul are still pure and innocent. He intends no harm to anyone or anything."

"Thank you. I trust your observations are true."

"Yes, sire. I am incapable of telling a lie," the knight said.

King Heroian scratched his chin. "Why, my dear man, do I see a dreadful beast?"

The knight leaned closer to the king of Idlebury to ensure King Abracadabra and King Morrebidd couldn't hear what he was about to say. "Because they are *your* demons with which *you* must reckon," he whispered.

King Heroian knew the time had come for him to prove himself and save his son. "Come Abracadabra, Morrebidd, and Thane. I believe it is time for your reckoning."

Chapter Forty-Four
Mistofisee Smells Humans

"No, no, no," Gwen yelled. "Don't land us there."

Plop.

"Too late," Mistofisee said.

"Look what you've done. You've dropped us smack in the middle of the Field of Wisdom."

"And your point would be?"

"My point would be—"

"Quiet!" the field screamed.

Gwen glared at Mistofisee. The look in her eyes said *see what I mean?*

Mistofisee looked for the person who'd spoken. When he saw no one, he said, "Hark, who goes there?"

Gwen rolled her eyes at the silliness of Mistofisee's question.

"I said, *Quiet.*"

"If you insist," Mistofisee replied.

Gwen and Mistofisee waited. Nothing happened. Suddenly a bright light engulfed them.

The young dragon basked in the warmth of the light. Calmness swept through him. For the first time in his life, he felt blissful. He wanted to stay in the light forever. But the light had other plans. It pushed Mistofisee into the dark field, leaving Gwen captured in its rays. Mistofisee was confused, angry, and scared. He wanted to protest. He wanted to save his friend. But he decided to trust that Gwen could handle herself. After all, she was in possession of the most powerful wand in the universe.

Gwen dropped to her knees. The wand rose into the light. Voices screamed, "Last night at ten o'clock this morning, an empty wagon full of people ran over a dead horse and killed it." The voices screamed the phrase over and over until the loudness became deafening. Mistofisee cupped his ears with his paws, but Gwen appeared unaffected. The sword glowed. Chimes rang in the distance, muffling the voices.

"It's the Dimension Clock," Gwen yelled. "It's time."

"For what?" Mistofisee mouthed. He turned away from the Field of Wisdom. In the distance, a full moon cast a warm light on Idlebury Castle. He saw a large dark shadow swoop over the castle and land on the side where the great hall was located. He wanted to warn Gwen, but he knew she couldn't see or hear him. So he waited.

Fear.

Anxiety.

Anger.

Mistofisee found the emotions that flooded him to be unbearable. Yet he tolerated them and waited for his friend.

The light surrounding Gwen dissipated, yet she remained on her knees. The sword plopped next to her and broke into its three original forms—Crabbina's cane, King Abracadabra's sword, and Blabberdish's wand. Gwen gathered the three most powerful wands in the universe and slowly rose. She pointed

King Abracadabra's sword at Idlebury Castle. A second later, Gwen stood next to Mistofisee.

"Well, that was fascinating," she said. Gwen thrust the cane at the dragon and said, "Please do me the honor of carrying Crabbina's cane."

"I don't feel worthy," Mistofisee said as he accepted the cane from Gwen.

"Let's go," Gwen said. "The fun is about to begin."

"All righty then. Wouldn't want to miss the fun."

Gwen and Mistofisee trekked toward Idlebury Castle in silence.

When they reached the castle's drawbridge, Mistofisee said, "What are we doing here?"

"Shh," Gwen said. "Wait and see."

"I hate surprises. Give me a hint."

"No," Gwen replied.

The door to Idlebury Castle was ajar as if to invite Gwen and Mistofisee inside. Gwen pushed the door open just enough to allow her to look in.

The castle was still.

Not a servant in sight.

Not Oof.

Not even Syvil Gossep.

Gwen opened the door wide enough for her and Mistofisee to enter.

"Don't you find the emptiness of Idlebury Castle just a little disconcerting?" Mistofisee asked.

Gwen didn't respond. Instead, she rose on her tiptoes, hunched her shoulders, raised King Abracadabra's sword above her head, and started toward the great hall.

"Oh brother," Mistofisee mumbled. "She looks ridiculous hunched over, slinking through the castle."

As Gwen and Mistofisee continued toward the great hall, Mistofisee spotted something under the staircase and poked it with Crabbina's cane. "Why would someone hide a baby carriage under there?" he said and then continued to follow Gwen.

Soon Mistofisee smelled something odd. Whiff. "Smells like humans," he whispered. Whiff, whiff. "A lot of humans."

"Psst, psst." Mistofisee tried to get Gwen's attention, but she was obviously intent on getting to the great hall. "Ahem," he said loudly.

"What?" Gwen snapped. "What is it you want?"

"Shh! I don't think we're alone," Mistofisee whispered.

"So?"

"I smell a lot of humans, and one of them smells like it's up to no good."

"Good for you," Gwen said, then continued her trek toward the great hall.

"I think we're in danger," Mistofisee said louder.

"Come off it." Gwen lowered the sword and glared at Mistofisee. "You smell a lot of humans because a lot of humans work in this castle. Okay?"

"Oh, I hadn't thought of that." Mistofisee rolled his eyes. "Thanks for solving that little mystery."

With King Abracadabra's sword raised over her head like a guide leading a group of tourists, Gwen continued toward the great hall.

Whiff. Whiff. "I don't care what she says; I smell a lot of humans."

The Dimension Clock struck ten times, followed by the sound of wagon wheels squeaking as if they bounced over a cobblestone street. Gwen glanced at Mistofisee. Neither said a word.

When Gwen and Mistofisee reached the door to the great hall, Gwen lowered the sword and turned the doorknob. The door was stuck as if something blocked it.

Mistofisee gasped. "Gwen, look."

"At what?" Gwen said as she yanked the door as if she had the power and strength to open it.

"It's Lightening."

"Where?" Gwen looked down the hall. "I don't see him."

"He's lying in front of the door."

"Don't be ridiculous."

"I'm not. I think he's… dead."

The door blasted open, nearly knocking Gwen to the floor.

"Enter Gwendolyn the Great, Savior of Idlebury, Protector of the Universe," an unknown man said.

Gwen entered the room. Mistofisee looked down to avoid stepping on Lightening, but the steed had disappeared. While he was distracted, Crabbina's cane escaped his grasp, fell to the floor, and slithered toward the door. "Uh-oh," he said as he leaned forward, hoping to grab the cane. But he was too late. The door slammed in his face. And to his horror, he heard the unmistakable sound of Crabbina's cane rolling across the floor.

Mistofisee suddenly swung his head to the right. "Yikes." Sniff. Sniff. "I smell more humans." He swung his head to the left. No humans. He scanned the area. Nothing. No one. He put his ear to the door of the great hall. All was quiet. "I guess Gwen doesn't need me," he muttered. "I'll check out the carriage under the staircase."

Mistofisee had barely taken one step when bam, he was blinded by bright lights. A cold metal object was thrust in his face. He batted it away. The cold metal object reappeared. Mistofisee saw it was attached to a human hand. When his eyes adjusted to the light, he saw a crowd of people. "I did smell humans."

"Well, well. What have we here," a man said. "I believe it's a dragon. But it's smaller than Matilda, queen of Beastonia. Dare I say this must be her son, Mistofisee?"

"Who goes there?" Mistofisee said.

"How cute," the man said. "He thinks some antiquated phrase has the power to stop me. Well, he doesn't know who he's dealing with."

"Who are you?" Mistofisee asked.

"Mike Muckraker from *Universal Scandals Tonight*, reporting live from Idlebury Castle where word has it the most important event of the millennium is about to take place."

"And what might that be?"

"Oh, don't be coy. I believe you know every detail. After all, aren't you friends with Gwennie?"

"Gwennie? Never heard of her." Mistofisee pushed past Mike Muckraker. "I must be going."

The crowd of media people parted and let Mistofisee pass. Some ducked for cover as if afraid the dragon would step on them or blow fire at them.

"Momma, where are you when I need you?" Mistofisee whispered as he headed down the hall.

He stopped at the staircase, looked back, and saw Mike Muckraker and his crew hurrying toward the great hall. "Whew. That was close." He looked around and noticed he was alone, so he took a quick peek under the stairwell. The carriage he'd seen earlier was still there. And a worm wearing a pair of red glasses stared back at him.

Mistofisee shook his head and took a deep breath. "A worm with glasses. Now I've seen it all!"

CHAPTER FORTY-FIVE
THE FUTURE IS FORETOLD

K ing Heroian entered the great hall alone. He looked around, lost in memories of his pathetic attempts to master magic tricks in this very room. He recalled the day when at the age of twenty-four, he was crowned king of the lazy, demanding Idleburians. His parents celebrated as if he had accomplished a major success, but truth be told, it was nothing more than a title for a job he didn't want. Nonetheless, he took his new role as king seriously and did his level best for his ungrateful people.

Despite his recent successes in many kingdoms throughout the dimensions as well as some of his people's willingness to discard idleness for productivity, his past haunted him, and he reverted to his youthful feeling of failure. But today that feeling was magnified because he knew his youthful inadequacies paled in comparison to his failure as a father. He couldn't forgive himself for what had happened to Thane, and he knew Thane's insolence was partly due to an absentee father. Worse, he was clueless as to the whereabouts of his baby, Prudence.

King Heroian slowly walked to the middle of the room and stood in the center of the ancient mosaic that still depicted Idlebury's original royal seal — a man and a woman working in a field with an X over the image. "Why has no one updated the seal? It has been more than five years since I granted the Idleburians their freedom. Yet many of my people are still lazy and—"

"Well? Where are they?" the Soul Seeker asked as he emerged from a dark corner.

"Outside."

"You left them alone?"

"Yes."

"You are a fool, Heroian. Morrebidd and Abracadabra are not to be trusted."

"Yes, but Thane is. He will keep them in line."

"Let's get started."

"With what?"

"The great reveal of ABC."

"ABC?"

"Do not play dumb with me, Heroian. You know perfectly well ABC stands for Abracadabra, Blabberdish, and Crabbina, the keepers of the most powerful wands in the universe. Now let us get on with it."

"Why are you here? Where's Oof?"

"I am here in my brother's stead."

"It is not like Oof to allow you to do his dirty work."

"Do not mock my brother. He is, or was, a powerful man. He is not the person you knew. Without his powers, he is useless."

King Heroian looked at the Soul Seeker. Dread and doom coursed through him.

"Come, come, Heroian. It is not that bad," the Soul Seeker said.

"It is not your children's lives that are at stake."

"Forget them. It is the book that needs to be saved."

"*I beg your pardon,*" King Heroian yelled. "You think a book of silly chants is more important than my children?"

"Silly chants? That is what you think is in the book?"

"Yes."

"You *are* pathetic."

King Heroian laughed. "You do not seem yourself today, Oliphant."

"No one has called me by that name for hundreds of years." The Soul Seeker turned away from King Heroian. In a nearly inaudible voice, he said, "It is comforting to hear my human name."

"Despite what you have become, your name means great strength."

With his black-hooded face to King Heroian's, the Soul Seeker said, "I live up to my name every minute of every day. It requires great strength to handle the souls with which I am burdened."

"Whose soul are you harboring now?"

The Soul Seeker opened his cape, revealing the faces of the many souls under his care.

"Prudence? You have my Prudence?"

"I have had her ever since she pricked her finger on—"

"On what?"

"Blabberdish's wand."

"*What?*" King Heroian screamed. "Please tell me she did not."

"She did. And she will pay the price."

King Heroian dropped to his knees. "She is doomed to a life of evilness. Can you not help her?"

"I can only contain her soul until she is no longer at the age of innocence. After that, I have no control."

"We must start the reckoning now," King Heroian said as he rose. "We do not have a moment to spare."

"Agreed," the Soul Seeker said. "But not everyone has arrived."

"What do you mean?"

"For Thane to complete the transition, all those who love him most must be present."

"Who?"

"You, Filanthropi, Gwendolyn, Mistofisee, Matilda, Morgana, Crabbina, Oof, Blabberdish, Lightening, and—"

"And?"

"And the three most powerful wands in the universe."

"Abracadabra's sword, Blabberdish's wand, and Crabbina's cane?"

"Exactly."

"And how do you propose to gain possession of them?" King Heroian asked.

"Gwendolyn."

"Gwendolyn? Why would she have them?"

"They have already been presented to her. Now she must save Thane. By doing so, she will save the universe."

A ray of light swept across the room, revealing Gwen hunched in a corner, clutching Abracadabra's sword and Crabbina's cane.

"I see she's already here," the Soul Seeker said. "Come forth, my child, and bring the great and powerful wands with you."

The sword and the cane were too heavy for Gwen to handle, and as she took a step forward, they fell to the floor, producing a clanging noise so intense King Heroian covered his ears. But the noise didn't seem to bother the Soul Seeker. Gwen picked up the sword and cane. As she dragged them across the room, the sword sparked and made a screeching noise. The weight of the sword and cane made it difficult for her to move smoothly. Nonetheless, she wobbled over to King Heroian and the Soul Seeker.

The Soul Seeker pointed to the mosaic in the center of the great hall and then shoved Gwen forward. "Put the wands there."

Gwen struggled to lay Crabbina's cane on the ancient symbol of Idlebury.

"*Now,*" the Soul Seeker screamed.

"I will take my time," Gwen replied. "This is the most serious undertaking of my life. Much is at stake. To rush me could spell disaster."

"Just do it. Time is of the essence."

Gwen looked at King Heroian for support. He nodded, so she carefully laid the cane and the sword on the floor before removing Blabberdish's wand from her pocket and placing it with the others.

The doors of the great hall opened. One by one, Queen Filanthropi, Queen Matilda, Mistofisee, Crabbina, and Morgana, whose hair and eyebrows were still singed from the incident in Egotonia, silently entered.

"Where is Blabberdish," the Soul Seeker asked.

"If you would stop being so uppity and look down, you'd see I'm right here."

The Soul Seeker noticed Blabberdish standing on the tip of his shoe. "Well then, all we need is the book."

"Lightening and Oof are not here," King Heroian said.

345

"In due time," the Soul Seeker said. "Let us proceed. As I said, we need the book."

"Clarify which book?" Queen Filanthropi said.

The Soul Seeker wrapped his cloak tightly around himself and said, "*A Magic Maniac's Many Ways to Make Mischief.*"

"Oh, but you've left out something, my dear Oliphant, or may I call you Oli like old times?" Crabbina said.

"You will call me nothing of the sort. Now, who has the book?" The Soul Seeker glared at each member of the reckoning committee.

No one stirred.

Mistofisee stepped forward. "I have it."

Queen Matilda gasped and coughed smoke. "Where did you get it?"

Mistofisee looked at Blabberdish, who was still standing on the Soul Seeker's shoe. "It was in a doll carriage that was *conspicuously* parked under the stairwell. So you could say it was for the taking."

King Heroian, Queen Filanthropi, and Morgana glanced at each other.

"Give it to me," the Soul Seeker said.

"Just a minute, Oliphant," Crabbina said. "I believe Mistofisee is the perfect creature to say what you left out."

"What?" Mistofisee asked. "What am I supposed to say?"

"Just read the front cover of the book," Queen Matilda said. "Every word of it."

"Every word?"

"That's what I said. Now read it."

"Yes, Mother." Mistofisee slowly unfurled his massive claw to reveal the book. He lifted it to his eye, then pulled it back, then drew it closer again and withdrew it once more. "The type is too small. I can't read it."

"*A Magic Maniac's Many Ways to Make Mischief* by Feefifofum Fiddledeedee Fiddledeedum," Queen Filanthropi said.

No one moved. No one dared, because the book's title in conjunction with the author's name hadn't been voiced in the presence of Crabbina's cane, Blabberdish's wand, and King Abracadabra's sword in more than a thousand years.

Mistofisee was the first to break the silence. "Well, that didn't work."

King Heroian stepped into the middle of the great seal of Idlebury. He put out his hand and said, "Come, Filanthropi. Join me."

Queen Filanthropi moved next to her husband.

King Heroian extended a hand to Gwen. "You too, Gwendolyn."

Gwen stepped forward.

"You next, Morgana."

"I'd be honored, I would," Morgana said as she practically leaped to join the royal family.

"We are ready," King Heroian said to the Soul Seeker.

"What about us?" Mistofisee whined.

"You all have important parts to play." King Heroian said. "Now let us proceed."

"Yes," the Soul Seeker said. "Form two circles and join hands."

Queen Matilda, Crabbina, Mistofisee, and Blabberdish formed a circle. Crabbina and Mistofisee gripped Blabberdish's tiny hands, dangling him several feet above the floor.

When everyone was ready, the Soul Seeker gently laid the

magic book in the middle of those in the great seal and said, "Do proceed, Heroian. Or should I say, Great Wizard?"

King Heroian lowered his head and said, "Last night at ten o'clock this morning, an empty wagon full of people ran over a dead horse and killed it."

The Dimension Clock rang. The small hand slowly moved to the X and the big hand moved on XIII. When they stopped, the ground shook as the deafening sound of horse's hooves, clattering wagon wheels, and wailing people shattered the silence. Lightening appeared, lying on his side, motionless.

"Is he dead?" Gwen said. She looked at Queen Filanthropi, but the queen didn't notice, for three men approaching from the far end of the room captivated her.

"Welcome. Abracadabra. Morrebidd," the Soul Seeker said. "Nice to see you dressed for the occasion, Ovazealous."

"Just get on with it," King Morrebidd said.

"Of course. Will you three please join those in the middle of the great seal of Idlebury?" the Soul Seeker said.

"I don't know." King Morrebidd looked at King Abracadabra and King Ovazealous. "Will we?"

"This is not a game, Morrebidd," King Abracadabra said as he entered the circle.

King Ovazealous followed, but King Morrebidd remained outside the circle.

"What is it you want?" the Soul Seeker asked.

"I want to know that I will return to my kingdom more powerful than ever."

"I cannot guarantee your survival, let alone your power," the Soul Seeker replied.

"*Get on with it,*" Crabbina yelled. "You're wasting precious time."

King Morrebidd inhaled and then exhaled air so cold it frosted the others' clothing, hair, and eyelashes. He smiled, stepped into the circle, and joined hands with King Abracadabra and King Ovazealous.

"Heroian, recite the curse followed by the author's name," the Soul Seeker requested.

"But—"

The Soul Seeker clenched his teeth. "Do as I say."

"Last night at ten o'clock this morning, an empty wagon full of people ran over a dead horse and killed it…" King Heroian hesitated. "…by Feefifofum Fiddledeedee Fiddledeedum."

The room shook, the clock chimes rang, and lightning flashed across the room. The pages of *A Magic Maniac's Many Ways to Make Mischief* fluttered as stars twinkled over it. A mighty gust of wind blew open the doors to the great hall, revealing a figure standing in the doorway. A thick haze obscured the person's identity.

"Do not look at him," the Soul Seeker screamed.

A boy emerged and slowly walked over to the Soul Seeker.

"Is it time?" the boy asked.

"Yes, Thane, it is time."

"Shall I join the others?"

"Yes. Stand in the middle and hold the book."

Thane entered the circle and picked up the book. He faced his father, noticing fear in his father's eyes. "There's nothing to fear, Father. It's time."

Gwen arched her brow and glanced at Mistofisee in the other circle. He shrugged.

"Do you have something you want to say, Gwendolyn?" the

349

Soul Seeker asked.

"No, sir," Gwen whispered.

"Good. Thane, do continue."

Thane held *A Magic Maniac's Many Ways to Make Mischief*, and then he raised his hand over the three great wands still in the center of the circle and said, "Wand of magic, wand of lore, wand of secrets and so much more. When the three become one, the magic book shall be done." Thane put the book down, picked up the three wands, closed his eyes, and lowered his head. He raised Abracadabra's sword and said, "Feefifofum." The sword remained in midair over the magic book as he raised Crabbina's cane and said, "Fiddledeedee." The cane joined the sword as both floated above the magic book. Finally, Thane held up Blabberdish's wand and said, "Fiddledeedum." The tiny wand rose and joined the other two. The three most powerful wands in the universe spun faster and faster until they morphed into a torch. Sparks fell on *A Magic Maniac's Many Ways to Make Mischief*.

It burst into flames.

"Nooo!" the Soul Seeker yelled.

"That's not supposed to happen," King Morrebidd screamed.

Everyone else remained in panicked silence.

"Everyone out. Now!" the Soul Seeker shrieked.

The shuffling of feet and the rustling of clothes accompanied everyone's rushed departure from the great hall.

Once outside, King Heroian grabbed Thane and said, "What have you done?"

"I didn't do anything, Father," Thane replied.

"I risked my life trying to save yours, and you reward me by pulling a stunt," Queen Filanthropi said. "And look what has happened to your baby sister, Prudence. She will become the epitome of pure evil."

"You disgust me," Gwen said.

"For shame, young man," Crabbina said. "You have brought much despair to the universe."

"I love ya like a son, me do," Morgana said. "But you've disgraced me and your family."

Queen Matilda, too angry to speak, blew a fireball down the hall of Idlebury Castle. As the smoke cleared, a figure appeared. The sound of a horse's hooves echoed throughout the castle.

"Mother? Father?" a boy yelled from atop Lightening as the queen's steed stopped abruptly. The boy dismounted and raced toward the small crowd. "Has it started yet?" he shouted.

All eyes turned to the boy who looked exactly like Thane. Immediately everyone looked at the boy they believed to be Thane. In unison, they yelled, *"Wilameena!"*

The boy believed to be Thane morphed into Wilameena. "I can explain."

King Heroian grabbed the enchantress and shook her. "You've been a thorn in my side all my life. I hate you, Wilameena."

"Stop!" the Soul Seeker yelled. He stood at the door of the great hall. A man stood next to him.

"Well, if it isn't Oof and Oli," Blabberdish said and then snorted with laughter.

Oof joined Wilameena, who was crying from the sting of King Heroian's comment. He put his arm around her shoulder, pulled his handkerchief from his pocket, and gently wiped her tears. "There, there, Wilameena. They know you not as I do."

"I wish they knew I was only trying to help."

"And help you did, in the most astounding way." Oof reached out and said, "Come, Thane." After Thane joined Oof and Wilameena, Oof addressed the others. "It is true Thane is destined to replace me as the Great Wizard, but not today. He is not ready. He has not earned the privilege. The transfer of my powers to Thane would have resulted in my death, leaving no one with the knowledge and experience to teach one so young how to handle the vast responsibilities that come with unlimited power. One small mistake or misuse of those powers would wreak havoc and devastation on every creature throughout the universe. Wilameena knew that. And because of her love for me... and Thane, she..." Oof paused. "Well, for lack of a better word, she interfered. And in doing so, she achieved something that I, the Great Wizard, in my weakened state, could not. Out of pure love, she saved us all."

"But I thought you transferred your powers to me," King Heroian said.

"No, Heroian, I could not transfer my powers to you knowing that if Thane succeeded, you as the Great Wizard would die. What I gave you was the belief that you had powers, therefore giving you the fortitude to do what you needed. Belief in one's own abilities is the most powerful magic in the universe."

Not a word was spoken.

When the silence became unbearable, Wilameena said, "And I was only trying to help."

Everyone laughed, but this time they all laughed with her, not at her.

Matilda stepped forward and said, "Sorry we tried to kill you, Wilameena."

"Can you ever forgive us?" Queen Filanthropi added.

"Well, as annoying as you are, I'd miss you if you were gone," Gwen said.

"Me too," Mistofisee said.

"Oh brother," Blabberdish interjected. "Let's end this meeting of the Mutual Admiration Society and get back to conspiring against each other."

"Grand idea," King Morrebidd said. "What do you say, Abracadabra and Ovazealous?"

In unison, they said, "Last night at ten o'clock this morning, an empty wagon full of people ran over a dead horse and killed it."

With that, everyone disappeared, except Oof, who, dressed in the Great Wizard's robe, looked handsome and a thousand years younger.

"Silly chant," the Great Wizard mumbled.

Back in Thane's room:

Wow! That was close. I almost became the Great Wizard," Thane said as he looked out the window and half watched Blabberdish slink back and forth on the windowsill. "I'm glad I didn't because I'm done with magic. It got me and the rest of the universe in serious trouble."

"I beg your pardon," Blabberdish said. "No one and nothing got you in trouble but yourself."

"With a little help from you."

"Not true. I probably shouldn't tell you this, but..." Blabberdish stared at Thane.

"Tell me what?"

"Remember when you said I'd agreed to go on your adventures and I told you I didn't have a choice?"

"Yeah. You said something about being on a special assignment, but Lightening shut you up."

"Well..." Blabberdish paced Thane's desk. "...you were my special assignment."

"What? Why?"

"You are destined to become the Great Wizard. It is the most important position in the universe."

"Okay."

"Well, who you are as a child plays a major role as to who you become as an adult. And your mischievous, insolent behaviors are unbecoming of someone slated for greatness. Therefore, I and a few others were assigned to test you."

"And?"

"You failed. But you also showed potential."

"Was Wilameena one of the people who tested me?"

"No. She was trying to stop you for her own selfish reasons." Blabberdish jumped on Thane's arm. "But your choice to give up magic shows a new level of maturity. One day when you're responsible enough to respect the power of magic, you'll use its force for good."

"How? *A Magic Maniac's Many Ways to Make Mischief* was destroyed."

"Well, maybe not." Blabberdish twisted his face, scrunched his nose, and jumped off Thane's arm.

"What?"

"It may have been a copy."

"A copy?"

"Yes. I couldn't find the original, so I put my copy in the carriage under the stairwell."

"You made a copy?"

"Yep, been working on it for years." Blabberdish waved his hands at Thane. "I have little hands, you know."

"Are you sure you didn't make any mistakes?"

"I don't think I did."

"Where's the original?"

Blabberdish was about to answer when the door opened and Prudence and her doll carriage burst into the room.

"*Prudence,*" Thane exclaimed.

"Play with me and my dollies," she said.

"I don't want to play with dolls."

Prudence's eyes turned an evil yellow. Blabberdish ran behind Thane for protection. Angered by her brother's rejection, she yanked her doll carriage and stormed out of Thane's quarters.

As she scurried to her room, she said, "I'll play with my new book."

When Prudence opened the door to her room, she let out a maniacal laugh that shook Idlebury and resounded throughout the entire universe.

At once, a sense of foreboding coursed through every being in every kingdom in every dimension, leaving no doubt the myth that pure evil would one day rule the universe was about to come true.

About the Author

JM Hughson grew up in the Washington, D.C. area where her lifelong love of reading and writing began early. She wrote her first story, *The Whimsical Lion,* at the age of eight. As a child, her favorite book was *Jane Eyre* by Charlotte Bronte. She credits her mother's passion for reading and weekly trips to the library as a child for her love of books. She had a successful career as an advertising copywriter/creative director followed by a career as a mental health therapist. She won three awards for *Be Careful What You Wish For*, the first book in the Idlebury Series. She hopes her readers have as much fun reading her books as she had writing them.

www.ingramcontent.com/pod-product-compliance
Lightning Source LLC
Chambersburg PA
CBHW020241200626
46816CB00001BA/71